The Invisible Enemy:
Black Fox

Anthony R. Howard

www.anthonyRhoward.com

I dedicate this book to the woman who touched my life and the lives of so many others in a way words can not describe:

Jenetta E. Howard

ISBN: 978-099663-970-5

This book is printed on acid-free paper.

Printed in the United States of America

During the Cold War era, the KGB (the former Soviet Union's equivalent of the CIA) ruled using cutthroat rings of highly trained intelligence operatives. During this period, the Soviet arms count was estimated at over 40,000 nuclear weapons. Due to a variety of serious political and economic issues, the leaders of the Russian, Ukrainian, and Belarusian republics met on December 8, 1991, in Belavezhskaya, Pushcha, to issue a declaration that the Soviet Union was dissolved and replaced by the Commonwealth of Independent States (sometimes referred to as Russia or the Russian Federation). This political revolution exposed the 40,000-plus Soviet nuclear weapons to corrupted black markets, rampant theft, and widespread distribution to terrorist nations. Leading up to the 21st century, the solution to this critical issue was the Strategic Offensive Reduction Treaty (SORT) between the United States and Russia. The SORT treaty stated that Russia would dispose of most of its nuclear weapons to avoid further exploitation and export to terrorist nations, thus illustrating its commitment to world peace. In addition to this arms crisis, the collapse of the Soviet Union included dismantling the KGB, which ceased to exist after November 1991.

Because of the breakdown of the Soviet Union and its KGB, over 250,000 skilled Soviet spies—strategically planted around the world—suddenly found themselves out of work. However, for many of the displaced agents, it was still business as usual, as many of those unclaimed 250,000 spies were children . . . an enemy invisible to nearly any defense mechanism.

CHAPTER 1

"Get in and get out. What do you think this is, some kind of game?" Devin snarled.

"I just thought—"

"I do the thinking. All you do is what I say," Devin coldly replied.

Garret was silent. He looked into the boss's cold eyes and saw no understanding, no mercy, and no patience. There was no compassion between the two men.

"In and out," was Garret's meek reply, but it was just an act. There was no fear in Garret's heart.

"Take Teams A and F and complete the operation. You will signal Man 3 at 9:15 a.m., enter the facility at 9:18, expedite the operation exactly as planned, and exit at 9:21. Are there any questions, Mr. Garret?"

The boss's tone told him there had better not be.

"No, sir."

"Good. Team A will be waiting for you at the designated rendezvous point. The truck will be with them. Nightshade leads Team F at your signal. She already has the keys in her possession. Dismissed."

"Yes, sir." Garret turned to leave.

"Garret."

"Yes?"

"One more thing. Teams A and F are to be totally oblivious to each other. Is that understood?"

"Of course, sir."

"Sorry, everyone, the Pulitzer competition is now closed!" Dorian Valentine exclaimed on her way to work. Her exuberant

1

voice drowned out the excited morning DJ who was talking about critical peace talks between the U.S. and the Russian Federation.

Valentine felt better than she had ever felt in her life. She was immersed in an ultimate mental and spiritual euphoria that flowed through her body like blood. She had awakened at 5:00 that morning filled with anxiety. She felt absolutely on top of the world while eating her breakfast of waffles and eggs. Valentine had smiled the entire time she brushed her teeth. She marinated in her own joyful bliss and couldn't help but shiver as surges of her happiness tingled down her spine. Not even the sluggish traffic could break her mood. It was a beautiful morning. With the cumulus clouds scattered across the vast baby-blue sky, it looked to be a promising day.

She wove her giant navy-blue Expedition out of standstill lanes and into any lane she thought was moving an inch faster an hour. She cruised down Baltimore-Washington Parkway and passed the Fort Meade exit at about 30 mph in the congested traffic. The potholes and rough roads across the parkway and its exits did not bother her. She was far too excited. The only thing that was possibly missing from that morning was good sex. Valentine had no husband, no children, and had never been married. She enjoyed life as a single woman and had remained alone in her bed last night.

The soothing, relaxing rhythm from her favorite song, "Walked Outta Heaven" by Jagged Edge, placed her in a further state of enchantment. She sang out loud to the new hit song even though she didn't know the words. But it didn't matter, because Dorian Valentine had walked outta heaven. Not soon enough, it seemed, she was surrounded by the familiar city of Washington, D.C. She was still in a great mood, shouting and singing all the way to the *Washington Post*, where her status as a reporter had been "ordained," as she liked to say among close friends.

She didn't pay attention to the reports of the critical nuclear arms talks or the president's momentous upcoming trip to Moscow to discuss the treaty. The collapse of the Soviet Union back in December 1991 had left the Russian Federation with the bulk of the massive Soviet weapons of mass destruction. This Cold War legacy had allowed Russia to retain its nuclear power status even as its economy collapsed. The burden of supporting and validating more than forty thousand nuclear weapons strained the Russian political and economic system. Russia's nuclear and missile capabilities then started to leak outside its borders to treacherous organizations and insurgent governments. This eventually led to the formation of the Moscow-based Strategic Offensive Reductions Treaty (SORT). The SORT called for a severe reduction of all arms between the United States and the Russian Federation. Even to this day, in 2003, the remnants of chemical and biological weapons programs in Russia posed major environmental and proliferation threats worldwide. The SORT had been plastered all over television and radio like the OJ Simpson trial. Even when Valentine turned her television off, she still saw the nuclear arms reduction talks via osmosis. The world finally had a glimmer of hope for world peace from nuclear munitions. If the nuclear arms could be eradicated as outlined in the SORT, the arms would finally stop falling into the hands of terrorist nations and threatening the world's livelihood.

As an "ordained" reporter, Valentine considered it her responsibility to let the public know what was *really* going on—one side was cheating.

As Valentine pulled into her parking space and shifted the car into park, the reporter on her favorite radio station began to discuss the progress of arms control the Strategic Offensive Reductions Treaty had made.

The SORT Commission had turned into a powerful committee orchestrating the obliteration of all nuclear armaments worldwide. The Russian prime minister, Epifanii Yuklivitch, an ex-member of the former KGB, led this committee. The SORT Commission was notably the most politically influential organization ever in the way of eliminating nuclear threats worldwide. The majority of the members were from the two most nuclear-armed countries in the world, and if they couldn't get along, there would be no world peace. If they fought each other hard enough, war would be imminent.

Valentine checked her beautiful ebony complexion in the rearview mirror as she turned off the ignition. She then pulled up the emergency brake and turned the key back a quarter inch to hear the radio.

"...and a breakthrough yesterday by the *Washington Post* puts the Moscow-based Strategic Offensive Reductions Treaty Commission under serious scrutiny as the U.S. takes rapid steps to investigate the facts uncovered by *Washington Post* reporter Dorian Valentine."

Valentine smiled as her name spun off the newscaster's lips. She loved the sound of her name being called out for the public to hear. She wished she could somehow record this report and play it back for her own ears to savor again and again.

She remembered the time she spent the day shopping with her niece, Jamey. Valentine came out of the store's dressing room to find that Jamey was gone. A moment later, her name boomed loudly over the intercom.

"Dorian Valentine, please come to the front of the store. Dorian Valentine, to the front of the store." Jamey had opened the boxes of several toys and was playing with them in the aisle, blocking people from getting by.

" . . .Valentine has allegedly uncovered the plans for construction of a Russian stealth helicopter with post-nuclear capabilities. The chopper supposedly has the ability to launch a devastating advance strike system from considerable distances and at the speed of light. This new weapons system, having nearly nuclear impact and almost pinpoint accuracy, surely tops any war technology that is openly being constructed in today's critical defense market. In addition, Prime Minister Epifanii Yuklivitch, with his strong ties within the Russian government and his highly placed connections inside the Russian intelligence hierarchy, is assumed to have *known* about 'Operation Black Fox,' the secret production of this new Russian war machine. As the investigation begins, the free world holds its breath."

Why didn't they say my name again?

"She's here," a man inside a black Thunderbird with deeply tinted windows informed the others through his radio. Agent Steven Price watched as Valentine got out of her car.

"All right. Make sure she gets in safely," Albert Plack replied on the same channel inside the building.

"The roofs have been checked for snipers, and the perimeter has been sealed off to any newcomers," Price reported.

"After she is inside, seal off all exits. No one is to leave or enter until I give the word," Plack instructed.

"Roger that."

Valentine grabbed her purse and made her way inside the building, anticipating applause. She stepped on the elevator and received several congratulations from coworkers on the way to her floor. As she walked past the doors of the elevator, she received a standing ovation, and she welcomed it.

"Thank you, everyone," Valentine replied.

"Dorian, some people are here to see you in the boss's office," said Frederick Carson, one of her coworkers.

"Pulitzer here already?" she asked him, smiling.

"They're late," he shot back with a smile while pretending to check his watch.

"Good morning, Ms. Valentine," a stranger in a gray suit said, extending a hand. "Right this way, please."

As Valentine shook the stranger's hand, she noticed the grip was firm and that the smile suddenly faded from the man's face. He stepped in close and locked his arm in hers. He then started to walk quickly, leading her to the editor in chief's office and leaving her coworker with a confused grin. As Carson started after the man, a strong hand grabbed his arm tightly.

Carson looked back to see a decent-sized man in a suit similar to that of the man who had taken his coworker. A serious glance from the man told Carson, "Don't even think about it."

Inside the ambulance heading down Connecticut Avenue, there was no empathy. The vehicle was semi-crowded, but everyone inside was mentally focused and prepared for what the operation called for. No fear resided in the vehicle, and though the operatives inside looked like everyday citizens, this assumption could not have been further from the naked truth.

"All right!" Dennis Garret shouted with authority inside of the ambulance, looking his group—Team A, the superior of the elite— over. "We know the deal. Three minutes. I'll call the clock through the channel in twenty-second intervals, and A-2 will second it. On my mark, we move."

In a separate windowless van parked on a Washington side street, Kalisa Leonilla, known to her team as Nightshade, re-briefed Team F on the operation at hand.

"All right, take a good look at this picture," Nightshade instructed, handing a photo to the team's captain, Zlata Olimpan. Olimpan memorized the picture and passed it along to her teammates. "That is the man we want. Everyone and everything else is expendable."

"What's going on?" Valentine asked as she was hurriedly escorted into her boss's office.

Her escort did not answer.

She looked around the office and realized her boss was absent. Taking his place were two men with hard looks on their faces, plus the one wrapped around her arm.

"Leave us for a moment," one of the men spoke to the ruffian who had wrapped himself around her.

The escort quickly left, closing the door behind him, and stood sentry outside the office.

The usually cozy office now seemed like a dungeon—cold and unfriendly. Dorian Valentine stood erect, not intimidated by the situation at hand. She had been around men all her life, from her four brothers to her two boyfriends to the daily work environment at the *Washington Post.*

"What's the meaning of this?" she asked adamantly. "Who do you think you are, putting your hands on me? I ought to pick up the phone and call my lawyer right now. You'd better start explaining some things before you encounter some serious problems."

"Sit down, Dorian," one of the men said.

"I'm fine standing."

"Very well then," was the reply.

Valentine suspected the men already considered themselves greater than her because of her gender. The way they spoke and the way they looked betrayed their chauvinism. Their body language spoke louder than words. Then there was race to consider—two white males to one black female. If she sat down while they stood, they might feel like the president.

"Who are you?" Valentine asked.

"I think we'll ask the questions here, Ms. Valentine," one of the men replied.

"Really," Valentine asked, wide-eyed with a sarcastic twist. She was taken aback by the man's arrogance. She looked him up and down, and then she decided to give his self-confidence a small test. Anybody can talk down to a woman in front of his buddies. She looked down at his spotless shoes for several moments without speaking. Sure enough, the arrogant man looked down at his shoes. While trying to be discreet, he studied them intensely before looking up.

"Ms. Valentine, we are from the CIA," he continued.

Valentine made a freakish disgusted face while still looking down at the man's shoes.

The man then stopped talking and looked down at his shoes without trying to be incognito. He checked the left and right sides of both shoes while Valentine kept the same twisted look on her face.

Finally satisfied, she took her eyes off his shoes and looked up. "I'm sorry, what were you saying?" *You insecure prick. Gotcha.*

"I am the Deputy Director of Intelligence, and this is Franklin Turner from the Public and Agency Information Department." *You think you're funny don't you?*

"What is this all about?" *You still didn't tell me your name, Arro-gant.* Valentine looked the two men over carefully. Franklin hadn't said a word yet, but he looked like he hadn't come down here for chitchat. Franklin looked to be in his late forties. He had some gray hair he was not trying to hide and wore an ugly tie that attempted to complement his navy-blue suit. His skin had no wrinkles, and it looked like he hadn't really lived a hard life. Neither of the men's suits had wrinkles, but Valentine could tell both men had taken a trip to be there.

Mr. Arrogant looked to be in his late fifties. He had more gray hair than Franklin, and he had bags under his eyes even though he was wide awake. He had a saggy face like her varsity basketball coach in high school. His tie was better than Frankie's, but she didn't like either man. She looked at the small, funny-looking antenna on her boss's desk, then realized it was one of those electronic scramblers that made sure no one was listening in who wasn't supposed to…but she wasn't supposed to know that.

"This is about the article you wrote that is printed in this morning's paper," Arrogant stated. "I'm sure you know you've created absolute congressional pandemonium."

"Just doing my job—and what was your name?"

"Albert Plack, Deputy Director of Intelligence."

"You said your position already." *Was he restating his position to gain some psychological advantage over me?*

Valentine had already learned that a title meant nothing.

"Anyway, I'm sure you know the article written this morning is quite significant, considering the Strategic Offensive Reductions Treaty with our president and Russia's Prime Minister."

"I am aware of the talks, Mr. Plack, and that's all it is to me, just talk."

"Your personal opinions are irrelevant in this matter. You have absolutely no idea what you have done. For us to try and rectify this situation, we need some things from you. Number one, we want to know your source for this article."

"You know I don't have to do that. I know my rights as a reporter."

"Number two, we want the plans you supposedly have possession of for the helicopter."

"There is no 'supposedly' about it. The plans exist." *Damn, spoke too soon.*

"Three, we want your full cooperation in verifying the actual production of the chopper, if it has passed the planning stage."

"The helicopter has indeed passed the planning stage and is already being constructed," Valentine replied. "I wouldn't have broken the story if I didn't have evidence. Nor would the editor in chief permit the story to be printed if sufficient evidence had not been furnished. This is the *Washington Post*, not the *National Inquisitor*, Mr. Plack."

"Where, exactly, might Operation Black Fox be taking place, Ms. Valentine?" Plack asked.

"You're Deputy Director of Intelligence. You tell me," Valentine responded.

"Do you know who you're talking to?" Plack asked.

"Albert Plack, Deputy Director of Intelligence."

Franklin Turner wanted to laugh out loud but, out of respect, hardly flinched. Valentine noticed it.

———

Garret's synchronized watch read 9:15 a.m. "Man 3, move. Team F follows."

———

"Look, you two come in here looking like the Men in Black and make demands like—"

Turner cut in. "Hold on. Look, Dorian, I'd really appreciate your help in this matter. This is a serious issue, and the public is eating it up. Relations between the Russian Federation and the United States are shattered until we can get to the bottom of this Operation Black Fox issue. I need to know exactly what you know. I don't care where you got it. I need the plans and some kind of proof that the helicopter is actually being constructed. I need a picture, a witness, and a location, something concrete to go on. This is a matter of national security, and your safety might very well be in danger. If you help us, we can help you. Do we have a deal?"

Valentine liked Frankie. His tie looked a little better now. "I'll help you as much as I can without revealing my source."

"Excellent. First order, where are the helicopter plans?"

"The same place everything of value is kept in heavy news-breaking articles such as this one; in the—"

Valentine was cut off by the sounds of terrified screams coming from outside.

"Get down!" Turner yelled to Valentine. Plack drew his piece.

Automatic gunfire was heard over the screams, followed by shattering glass and chaos.

In the back of the *Washington Post* building, a university hospital ambulance backed into the service entrance. In four seconds, Team A was inside the building, suited in Washington, D.C. police uniforms. Every one of them had memorized the public record blueprints of the *Washington Post* building. This allowed them to maneuver toward their destinations without arousing suspicion. All four men sprinted rapidly around corners and through corridors with ease, as if they were in their own homes.

"Police business!" yelled Vladimir Yakof, otherwise known as A-2. He flashed a badge at any curious passersby.

Iake Tatomir, also called A-5, stopped as planned in one of the side corridors, to prevent service staff or any nosy reporters from following his team.

All members of the elite Team A were men—five of the world's best-kept secrets, groomed since youth in the most advanced training grounds available. Three of them did not stop sprinting for even a second. The fifth one, the leader, had been given a separate, solo agenda this round.

"Twenty," Garret muttered in the tiny microphone latched into his right sleeve. The transmitter on his left sleeve was channeled to a frequency that, other than Nightshade, only Team A would pick up.

A-2 heard the clock through his earpiece and, as briefed, repeated the count for the team, "Twenty!"

Upstairs in the main area, Nightshade squeezed off 22 rounds per second around the room with a new highly advanced, fully automatic rifle, the TH-7000.

"Everyone get your heads down!" Zlata Olimpan yelled.

Reporters scrambled to the floor like children playing hide-and-seek. All of Team F wore deep-black combat uniforms. Their head coverings consisted of protective plastic masks that matched their black combat boots. The masks resembled gas masks but served far more than one purpose, as they were equipped with several functions. They looked odd, like the heads of fierce, giant insects. Each team member moved quickly and with precision, all the while unceasingly scanning the environment.

Nightshade squeezed off more shots as smoking shells poured out of the weapon.

"Twenty!" Olimpan yelled. "If I see anyone move, they will die!" She raised two large, unique-looking, handheld, fully automatic pistols and shot around the room. Though Olimpan did not take her hands off either trigger, the bullets came out in loud bursts. "Ratatat-tat . . . ratatattat."

Oleg Lugor, or Man 3 for this mission, sprinted up the stairs to the roof with a long duffel bag. Like the rest of his team, he was dressed as a police officer. He hadn't expected to see anyone, but there was an agent on the roof. What the agent was doing, Lugor didn't know, nor did he care.

The agent yelled, "This is a restricted area, officer! You're going to have to go back down from here—now!"

Lugor yelled back, "Quick, come down here! There's some shooting downstairs in the main room!"

The agent began to run down the steps, and Lugor stepped aside to let him go through the door first. When the agent reached the third step from the bottom, Lugor leaped off the steps and curled himself into a ball in midair, feet facing forward. While still in the air, he quickly extended his legs and slammed both feet into the agent's back.

His mind flashed back for an instant to his defensive drill instructor, Sergeant Kiev. *"Make every blow count,"* Kiev had shouted at the nine-year-old Lugor as his young body wrestled a ferocious pit bull. Blood had been everywhere, and his adrenalin pumped so hard that he couldn't tell whether the blood was his or the animal's. He had become used to blood by that time. It was like seeing water.

The agent's back cracked from the blow as he crashed into the wall. Before he could put his hands out to stop the impact, his skull had cracked against the wall. The agent crumpled to the ground as crimson fluid rapidly oozed from his nose, mouth, and head.

Lugor stooped over him and, with both hands, snapped his neck. In three strides, Lugor was back up on the roof.

Lugor closed his eyes, opened his long sack, and pulled out a TH–7000. With his eyes still closed, he set up the weapon on its tripod. Continuing self-blinded, he screwed on the sights and slid in the magazine.

"Forty," Garret muttered to his wrist.

"Forty!" A-2 repeated to Team A.

"Forty!" Olimpan repeated for Team F.

"Man 3, report status," Garret said.

"Man 3 in position. Repeat, bird tower secure."

Impressive, Garret thought. *Forty seconds.*

Team A approached the vault and activated plastic explosives. After five seconds, the door was opened and all four men began tearing everything apart, searching.

Upstairs, Nightshade held several hostages and felt pity for those on Team F who were looking for the man in the photo shown during the briefing. The man in the photo was an American who had died over a decade ago.

"I know there are federal agents in this building!" Olimpan shouted. "If one of you even attempts to get a promotion this morning, you will die, as will three hostages for each attempt. Don't try us!"

Olimpan sprayed more shots out of her Rex-329 fully automatic pistols. Everyone hugged the floor and covered their heads.

"Sixty!" she yelled as the slide from both of her pistols remained positioned back, signaling both guns were empty.

As Olimpan attempted to slide another cartridge into her gun, a man tackled her. She went flying into a wooden desk, scattering papers everywhere. She grunted as the man attempted to wrestle the gun from her. Olimpan let the man roll on top of her and, with her legs, raised his body as far away from herself as she could.

Without a word, Nightshade pointed her automatic rifle at the hero and squeezed the trigger once. The TH-7000 automatic rifle emitted a loud, high-pitched squeal and a bright light as eleven rounds drove themselves into the man's body in half a second. The man contorted in pain as Olimpan quickly rolled him off of her and onto the floor.

"That was very stupid, hero," she said, watching him die.

Garret turned up his police radio frequency to hear how much time he had.

There had been several reports of shots fired, yet so far, only three or four units had been dispatched. With Lugor up there, that was cake.

"Team A, report," Garret instructed.

"Negative," was the reply.

"One hundred," Garret informed the operatives.

Dorian Valentine huddled behind the desk in her boss's office. Franklin Turner and Albert Plack crept to either side of the door with their pistols drawn and ready. Plack counted to three, opened the door, and started blasting. One of his bullets grazed Nightshade's bulletproof armor. The impact knocked her off balance and into a desk, then onto the floor. Team F stopped looking for the target and started firing at Plack. Nightshade recovered almost instantly and quickly executed three hostages as promised for Plack's interference.

"Okay, I surrender!" Plack shouted. "Stop killing innocent people!"

Nightshade silenced Plack with the TH-7000.

"One twenty!" Olimpan reported.

Outside, sirens were heard close by. From his position, Lugor could see all four units coming to save the day.

"Here comes the cavalry," he mumbled to himself as he got out his second tripod. Closing his eyes again for another challenge, he set up his newly developed dual-cannon missile launcher in twenty seconds.

"One forty," Garret informed both teams.

"Man 3 to Iceman," Lugor called to Garret through his wrist radio.

"I read, Man 3. Proceed."

"I see four approaching units," Lugor said, looking through his Hawk LX2, a pair of giant, high-tech binoculars. Lugor appreciated how advanced they were but did not like their dreary pine-green color, nor did he like that he was almost forced to hold them with both hands because of their irregular, gargantuan size. What he did like was that with these binoculars, he could record, save, alter, and play back what he saw, as well as upload the images to a computer. With his index finger, he pressed the T-sights button. As his finger pressed the button, the image zoomed in on the lead car. During the next second, with his middle finger, he depressed the Clean button, which clarified the image. Even though the vehicle was six blocks away, the view of the two drivers in the lead car was suddenly, right before Lugor's eyes, crystal clear.

"Lead car, two Caucasian males, about six blocks away. Estimated time of arrival: one minute."

"Proceed as planned. Operate in Code Blue," Garret instructed.

"Copy, Iceman."

In so many words, Code Blue meant to use the dual-cannon Eagle HSK-9500 anti-tank rocket launcher. Lugor already had it set up on the tripod. One of the most advanced armor-piercing weapons in existence around the world was at his fingertips.

"One sixty," Garret stated.

"One sixty!" Yakof informed Team A.

"One sixty!" Olimpan informed Team F.

"Team A, report status."

"Negative," Yakof replied.

What the hell is taking so long? Garret wondered from inside the van.

"Iceman to Nightshade, I need more time," Garret informed Nightshade. Things were taking longer than expected.

"Copy," Nightshade replied to Garret.

"Team F, Code Blue," Garret instructed Team F.

In response, Team F removed the gas bombs from their combat uniforms and activated them. The room was soon filled with thick green smoke.

"Dorian Valentine!" Nightshade called out as the smoke continued to spread. She had an electronic audio voice tuner in the mouthpiece of her mask, as did Olimpan. Her voice sounded raspy and inhuman, but nevertheless, untraceable indeed. Nightshade shifted her TH-7000 to her side by rotating her right arm and allowed the rifle strap to bear the weight of the high-powered automatic weapon. She then pulled out a small odd-looking pistol, a Vig-6.

Valentine heard her name called but remained still, cradling herself behind the office desk.

"Dorian Valentine!" Nightshade repeated while activating the smoke vision function on her mask. She could now see through the green smoke. She saw no movement.

"Dorian *Valentine*!"

Under normal circumstances, Valentine loved to hear her name called out to the public, but she now prayed not to hear it again.

Nightshade walked through the thick smoke, past the choking workers gasping for air, and stepped into the office, which was only partially infiltrated by the smoke. With her goggles on, Nightshade's peripheral vision was impaired as she entered the office. Before she saw him crouched beside the doorway, Franklin Turner tossed himself upon her.

Nightshade did not scream. Garret could not hear the struggle going on in the room, as the CIA's electronic scrambler was still activated. After a moment, Garret realized he no longer heard Nightshade calling out Valentine's name.

"F-4, check on Nightshade and neutralize any resistance she has encountered."

Hearing his code, Aleksander Straz made his way through the crowd toward the office and saw Nightshade standing over Frank Turner's dead body with the Vig-6 in hand. Though Turner had let out no scream and there was no blood, Nightshade did not bother to check his pulse. She knew he was no longer among the living.

"Counter neutralized," F-4 reported.

"One eighty," Garret announced.

"One eighty!" Yakof informed Team A.

"One eighty!" Olimpan informed Team F.

"Team A, report status."

"Negative, Iceman."

"Man 3, report," Garret said.

"Lead car approximately twenty seconds from perimeter," Lugor reported.

"Dorian Valentine!" Nightshade called out once again.

"The egg is captured," Yakof reported through his wrist. "Repeat. The operation is now positive."

"Team A, the operation is now positive. Man 3, stay in position," Garret directed.

"Dorian Valentine!" Nightshade repeated.

Valentine couldn't hold it any more. The gas had seared her lungs far beyond the point any human could tolerate. Although closed, her eyes burned as if they were on fire. She gasped loudly for air behind the desk, and when she opened her eyes, Nightshade was standing above her with the Vig-6.

"Dorian Valentine, please stand up."

Valentine slowly got to her feet. It was her final mistake. Nightshade looked Valentine in the eye and fired the Vig-6 without hesitation. Valentine suddenly felt a painful, electrifying sensation throughout her body. She died instantly, before her mind could fully process the agony.

"Two hundred," Garret reported.

"Two hundred!" Yakof informed Team A.

"Two hundred!" Olimpan informed Team F.

"Team A, report status."

"Coming home, Iceman," Yakof replied.

"Man 3, report."

"Lead car approaching perimeter with a tail. Other two units about 120 seconds from perimeter," Lugor reported.

"Neutralize the lead two cars and come home. You have 60 seconds."

Too much time, Lugor thought. *I need a challenge.*

"Nightshade, report."

"Target is eliminated. I'm coming home," she replied.

Lugor peered through the scope of his HSK-9500. He locked the rocket in the left cannon on the lead car and then locked the right rocket on its tail. In a moment, both sensors flashed green, indicating each heat source was locked on. He looked behind himself every ten seconds, while remembering the words of Sergeant Kiev: *Always remember to check six. What's behind you could change significantly in six seconds with no sound. Ears are clumsy. Eyes work better in open area daylight.*

Lugor pulled the extension back, pulled the left and right latches back, and then pressed the fire panel, simultaneously firing both rockets. They cruised through the air at over 800 mph, twisting and leaving a trail of white smoke as they raced toward their unsuspecting targets. While the rockets soared toward the vehicles, Lugor was busy taking the tripods down and putting his arsenal away.

Kaboom! The rocket launched from the left cannon hit the lead car. The first explosion covered up the second one moderately, creating a big cloud of orange and black. The two cars following behind the targets saw the explosion and screeched to a halt. After witnessing his handiwork, Lugor finished packing up and headed downstairs.

"Two twenty," Garret reported.

"Two twenty!" Yakof informed Team A.

"Two twenty!" Olimpan informed Team F.

Team A, with the exception of Man 3, jumped into the van and stripped off their uniforms. A moment later, Nightshade stepped inside and removed her mask and goggles. A-2 handed the helicopter plans to Garret, who promptly examined them.

"It can't be," Garret whispered to no one in particular, looking at the plans.

"What's the problem?" Nightshade asked.

"It's the AVLIS prototype," Garret mumbled. "God help us all."

"The what?" Nightshade asked. "And you know I don't believe in God."

"This is serious Doomsday business. Way beyond Hiroshima."

"Sounds major. Where is Oleg?" Nightshade asked.

"Man 3 is on his way," Garret answered, observing pieces of squad car raining down from the sky. "Are you sure you got the right person?"

"I said 'Dorian Valentine, stand up,' and she stood up. If she had only known that I had no idea what she looked like, she might still be around," Nightshade replied.

"What did she look like?" Garret inquired.

"Black woman, mid-thirties, not very tall. Some might call her pretty, others might not."

"We should have taken her," Garret muttered.

"Why didn't we?" Nightshade inquired.

"Devin wouldn't allow it."

"You know that we're behind schedule," she reminded him.

"It took an eon to find the plans," Garret responded, looking at his watch. "Two forty," he informed Olimpan.

Lugor hurried back to the truck. Though he didn't need assistance, Vladimir Yakof and Demitri Liutoboets pulled him inside.

"Move in 20 seconds," Garret instructed Olimpan while pulling off. He flicked the ambulance sirens on, maneuvered away from the two car skeletons, and pulled out and onto the city street. A moment later, he instructed Team F to exit.

In response, Team F activated another can of gas. This time, instead of green, the smoke was thick, black, and blinding. Under cover, Team F evacuated using the stairwell. The last one out, Aleksander Straz secured the escape by making sure there were no followers.

Garret sped down Massachusetts Avenue and merged off the New York Avenue ramp onto Interstate 395, heading toward the pick-up vehicle. Team A and Nightshade had changed clothes and were now looking like typical members of the American working class. Garret had picked the outfits himself and gone over them many times to make sure nothing was missing, like dress socks, ties, or anything that, if missing, would draw attention to them.

Rush hour was pretty much over. In the opposite direction toward D.C., it was still going on. They were covering pretty good distance. The speed limit was a meager 65 miles an hour, but Garret kept it steady at 75, keeping pace with the flow of traffic. Sixty-five miles an hour was like standing still. He knew a lot of the slower speed limits were set to affect gas consumption more than for safety reasons, but Garret did not break the flow of traffic. An ambulance already attracted enough attention.

Team F evacuated the building by going down into the receiving area, where they hopped into the back of a waiting garbage truck. The truck took off immediately and headed toward the rendezvous vehicle.

"All right." Garret spoke into his wrist. "Meet back at the nest at oh-eleven hundred. Iceman out." Satisfied, he disconnected the frequency.

C̲HAPTER 2

"**What do you** think?" Bryan Hughes, the Deputy Director of Science and Technology asked his colleague. His tone to the Executive Director of Intelligence was quiet and humble. The door was closed, and an electronic scrambler was already activated.

Walter Plack answered, already in mourning. "Very knowledgeable, with access to covert, advanced military weaponry. Extremely well trained, and very well funded. And between you and me, I know they had a lot of help with this one. Moscow continues to deny any connection to this event. The organization in question most definitely has ties to the underworld, or could be some elite terrorist organization, if such a thing truly exists."

Hughes looked around the room in awe. He had never seen anything like the scene before his eyes at that very moment. The building was in disarray, with blood and bullet holes everywhere. Dead bodies were being carried out of the room with bowels leaking from the body bags. It looked like a massacre. It *was* a massacre, and Hughes was in a state of controlled but horrified shock.

"Have we received any ransom demands for the plans?" Gregory Hunt, the Deputy Director of Operations, asked.

"No. We don't know if the plans ever existed. That's what my brother was here for. Who governed security? I was told the area would be secured while Valentine was being interviewed," Walter Plack said.

"All agents assigned to this operation have been lost, except one—Steven Price," Hunt answered.

"Were you in charge of this operation?" Plack asked.

"Well—"

"Were you in charge of this?"

17

"Yes, I was," Hunt lied. The truth was that Hunt had put the late Albert Plack in charge of the security operation; however, the timing for such a comment seemed slightly off. Hunt knew Plack would know the truth within the hour.

"Then what the hell happened? Why are all our agents dead? The one on the roof—dead! Jackson—dead! Roberts—dead! Steven Price—in the hospital, burned up. Dorian Valentine—dead! Franklin Turner—dead! My own brother—dead! Somebody tell me what the hell went on here! Who or what was behind this bloodbath? How did they know to go to the vault? Who the hell knew about the vault in this place, anyway? No one knows! And where is the editor in chief? Somebody get him in here! And I want a list of everyone who knew about the vault. They had to have help from the inside."

"They had to have a *lot* of help," Bryan Hughes whispered softly to his two colleagues. "These shells are from a TH-7000, the newest covert automatic rifle, and if what I think killed Frank and Valentine is really what killed them, we are in some trouble here."

"So what are you saying, Dr. Science?" Plack asked dryly.

"I'm saying there is no way these weapons could be available on the black market. There aren't even three dozen of them in existence worldwide."

Plack was silent for several moments. "What do you think took out Valentine and Frank?"

"I can't tell you here, guys. It's that serious. I've also seen some shells of the Rex-329. It's a fully automatic handgun." Hughes pointed to the wall. "Those small holes clumped together are from the Rex. Look at the shells. They are less than half the size of a Beretta or any other type of handgun. The advantage is that you really can't miss your target. The tiny bullets spread out upon explosion from the barrel. It's somewhat like a tiny, fully automatic shotgun but, of course, not nearly as powerful. I've practiced extensively with the Rex on the range. I would know its mark anywhere."

"I want a list of everyone who had access to either the Rex or the rifle, cross-referenced with the UB list. I want the list in my hands in one hour," Plack instructed.

The UB list was a list of all CIA agents having Unusual Behavior documented on their surveillance files. This included an unusually large amount of one-minute phone calls, local or long distance; unusual elevator use; uncommon exits or entrances into the building not coinciding with a person's work schedule; and unusual clothing or dress patterns revealed by the hidden surveillance cameras.

"There's a slight problem, sir," Hughes said to Plack.

"And what might that be?" Plack asked icily.

"I don't know who has had access to the TH-7000."

"You are the Deputy-fucking-Director of Science and Technology—and you don't know who in the hell has had access to our top-secret projects?"

"I know your brother has just passed—"

"Passed? He didn't pass. He was murdered, murdered in cold blood by our own top-secret weapons. How could you not know who has put their goddamned hands on the rifle!"

Hughes glanced at the scrambler to make sure it was functional before he answered. "It's not our rifle, Walter," Hughes replied.

"What?"

"The Rex-329 is ours, but the TH-7000 is a Russian project. We're just trying to copy it. We haven't even made one that works right yet."

"You mean to tell me this group comes in here with *our* covert weapons *and* theirs?"

"It looks that way, sir," Hughes replied. "And that's only the beginning."

"Cross the Rex people with the UB list and get back to me," Plack responded. "It looks as if we have an international organization on our hands. Hunt, get me an ID on any organization that could have in any way pulled this off. You have one hour for American suspects and another two for Russian contacts."

Dennis Garret, Kalisa Leonilla, and Devin sat in a moderate hotel room off the coast of the Atlantic, in Bethany Beach, Delaware, about 20 minutes from the Maryland state line. They were all ready for debriefing.

"Casualties in Team A?" Devin asked while looking over the helicopter plans.

"Zero," Garret replied.

"Casualties in Team F, Nightshade?"

"Zero," Kalisa replied.

"How much time?"

"Two forty for Team A," Garret replied.

Devin grimaced. "Why the extra minute? You were told to leave the facility at 09:18. What was the problem?"

"Team A reported that the vault was more cluttered than anticipated," Garret explained. "It took longer than we expected to locate the required documents. Not only that, but the cavalry was early."

Devin scowled at Garret. "It takes three minutes from when the dispatcher sends the call to when the car will arrive at the operation site. Considering Team F cut the phone lines upon entering the building, you should have been out of there sixty seconds before any law enforcement officer would have been in the vicinity."

"Nightshade and I pondered this matter during the trip here. We believe one of the reporters must have used a cellular phone. We could not put up a frequency scrambler and risk cutting off our own communication during the operation."

"I see."

There was an uneasy silence.

The boss turned to Kalisa. "Any problems?"

"Nothing I couldn't handle," she replied.

"How useful did the new equipment prove to be?"

"The TH–7000's were splendid," Kalisa answered. "They were able to neutralize any counter within one second, and that missile monster you gave us was also a success."

"And the Vig?" Devin inquired.

"I've never seen its equal. The weapon is totally efficient. Its convenience and effectiveness are unmatched."

"I'm glad they were worth the significant amount of money needed to acquire them," Devin stated.

"One thing you might want to be aware of," Kalisa offered.

"And what might this be, Nightshade?"

"The Rex-329s. Yes, they can hit anything you point at virtually without aiming, but they inconveniently need replenishing in a very short time."

"That is why I issued you two of them," Devin replied.

"I see, Devin. Ignorant of the disadvantage and to strengthen the fear element, one of the operatives felt the need to utilize both of them at the same time."

"Tell him or her that this is not the movies. How did the new vests and the audio tuner operate?"

"I felt like Darth Vader with that thing on," Kalisa replied.

"May the Force be with you," Devin remarked blandly. "And Valentine?"

"Eliminated. It was pitiful, Devin. Such a nonthreatening woman. She had crawled behind a desk."

"You're breaking my heart. She placed her neck where it did not belong—in my country."

"I still believe we should have acquired Valentine," Garret stated. He knew better than to inquire about the AVLIS technology and how it ended up creating the weapons system in a helicopter.

"I explained before; I do the thinking. How complicated can that concept be, Garret?"

"I'm in agreement with Garret," Kalisa added. "Valentine would have talked with the proper coercion. I'm positive of it."

"Kidnapping Valentine would have complicated things considerably. She would have jeopardized our entire operation by any struggle she would have exercised. I could not risk Team F's clean escape over a mere possibility that Valentine might reveal her source. The prime objective in this matter was to obtain the one and only copy of these post-nuclear helicopter plans. Team F was a decoy to get any and all roaming agents or security away from the authentic mission. The leak is not my problem. Do you understand this, Nightshade?"

"Yes, Devin, but I really don't think she would have had any more to do with Operation Black Fox after the episode today. She would have remained silent."

"What you think is irrelevant."

"I appreciate your candidness," Kalisa said.

"I wouldn't have it otherwise," Devin replied.

"I feel obligated to inform you that we had to neutralize some federal agents," Kalisa reported.

"This was inevitable. I appreciate your veracity," Devin muttered.

"I wouldn't have it otherwise," she replied.

Devin flashed a morbid smile. "Very well, dismissed," he said, finally. "The rest I can hear about on the six o'clock news."

Kalisa and Garret stood up, left Devin's room together, and walked around the corner to their room. Oleg Lugor lay sprawled out on the bed, watching TV. The rest of Team A were in another hotel.

"Brilliantly executed, comrade," Lugor complimented, getting up and hugging his childhood friend Dennis Garret.

They both sat down on the bed. They were both silent, but they had known each other too long not to know when the other was thinking about the Pit.

"You still think about it a lot, Oleg?" Garret asked.

"It was all I knew and *is* all I know," Lugor replied.

"It's still in my dreams, too," Kalisa put in. "It is part of us. We cannot shake what we have lived for an eternity, Dennis."

"Don't ever call me that when we're alone!" Reuban Zyablikov snapped. Throughout his life, Dennis Garret had owned almost no worldly possessions; but his real name was one, and it was sacred. It had been his since he created it, and yes, they could give him any name they wanted—switch it up along with his birthday at any time, and he'd better get it right if they asked him—but his name was his forever. It was a name he had given himself. It was the only link he had to some sort of identity, and he would cling to it as long as he was alive. The Pit was a place of unimaginable horror and punishment, where Zyablikov and his operatives had been trained from birth before being placed in America. A mere reflection on its events brought intense trepidation to the minds of the operatives.

"I'm sorry, Reuban," Kalisa apologized. "It must be out of habit."

"Please break the habit, sister."

"Broken, brother."

Kalisa Leonilla and Reuban Zyablikov were by no means maternal sister and brother, but in the Pit, one learned to grab family from only those who were worthy. Zyablikov remembered when he and Kalisa were thrown in the cold Russian wilderness for 48 hours without food, belongings, or water. Luckily, he found a small brook to camp by. In the frigid temperatures with no shelter, they engaged in sexual intercourse to keep from freezing. They were both fourteen.

He remembered groping around in the dark in the frigid air and among strange noises. He remembered Kalisa crying, and putting his arm around her.

Kalisa remembered the way he comforted her, the way he held her hand, and the way he would pick her up when she would stumble on the vast, icy whiteness. She remembered the things he said when she wanted to lay down and die and he would not let her. "Get up, sister!" he would yell. "Do you want to die like a dog?"

For the 48 hours they were in the snow, he was her salvation. They ate bark and leaves when they had to, and Kalisa always remembered the way Zyablikov braved the ice like a true champion, which is how everyone in the Pit had come to know him as the Iceman. The etymology for the name Zyablikov derived from the Russian term for iceman.

He remembered not only the physical stamina forced upon them from the Pit, but also the mental endurance. There were no clocks in the Pit, so time was only something to be wondered about. There were no calendars in the Pit during the early stages. Days and years were nothing. You knew a week had ended when you got to sleep until the sun was well in the sky. No birthdays were celebrated. Your birthday was when they told you it was, and they would switch it up every so often. Whatever the day, if one of the instructors asked you your birthday, it had better be off the tip of your tongue in one second or you would be taken away.

There were no outside telephone calls allowed, and no radio until you passed the third level. No real television until you passed the fifth level, and even then, you watched and listened to what you were told to watch and listen to. Zyablikov remembered his youth; everyone was stationed in front of a television to watch American cartoons such as *The Smurfs* and *Transformers*. He even remembered enjoying some of them. He guessed that the cartoons he was allowed to watch simulated his childhood.

At level seven or so, Vladimir Yakof, now known as A-2, secretly accessed the Internet to look at pornography. While on the Internet, he had the idea to search for a name for himself. He came across an etymology Web site. He printed some pages out, and from these pages, every member of the Pit chose a name for himself. The names were not *ever* to be repeated in public or around any instructor, but it helped hold their sanity, for a name provided some sort of identity and classification. Each name chosen was Russian, and even though none of the Pit students spoke Russian, they each knew it was their origin. The names were chosen according to each person's characteristics or talents. Their names were the only secret they could keep among themselves, away from every instructor. Though Yakof remembered to clean the cache files and browser history on the computer, the network monitoring equipment the instructors used had caught his actions. They saw the pornography pages but never could figure out what he used the etymology for.

The Pit students chose each person's last name. More specifically, each last name designated how the Pit students viewed that particular person. Each individual chose his or her own first name. The name-assigning process was entertaining, and several students became scarred with cruel or perhaps even hilarious names. The only rule was that once a name was voted on, it could not be changed. Zyablikov's name meant "to freeze," and was given to him mainly by Kalisa. Zyablikov nominated Kalisa's last name, Leonilla, meaning "lioness." It was given to her because of her aggressive and fearless nature. One instance in particular solidified this when she was thirteen. An academic instructor had ridiculed Kalisa in front of all the other students, and she became outraged. She rushed the instructor and tackled him on the spot. She clawed, punched, and kicked the man into unconsciousness while everyone rooted and cheered her on.

The instructor described the incident to the authorities before Kalisa was taken away. The instructor stated "she pounced upon me like a lioness," and the name stuck with Kalisa just as soon as Zyablikov nominated it. Kalisa had chosen her first name to mean "beautiful," pertaining to her physical attributes; however, her operational call sign, Nightshade, was granted for an aberrantly different reason. Three days a week, the individuals were tested on intelligence, and there was no cheating. Everyone had a different version of the tests. Zyablikov recalled one question he'd never forget: Test Number 2, Question 1: "Do you love your country?"

Zyablikov remembered looking up at his instructor. *Do I love my country?* he thought. *Where is it? I haven't seen it. All I see is this camp, this ice, and these cruel instructors. The only things I know about this world are those things I have been taught by your lying tongues and your biased textbooks. I can't know what I love.*

Though he didn't want to, he circled *yes*, knowing there would be severe consequences if he did otherwise. He guessed he was about four or five when the first test was given. The question appeared on every test from then on, sometimes four and five times. No one could really read proficiently at that age, so Mr. Jefferson initially gave the tests orally.

Even during the earlier levels, everyone figured out that no instructor's name was real; they just wanted everything American. Everyone spoke English, and anyone caught trying to learn Russian was taken away. Since birth, they were trained to be Americans. They learned American history, laws, traditions, culture, and religions. They knew twice as much about America as most Americans.

Not having much access to uncensored media in the Pit, neither Zyablikov nor his family had any knowledge of the political or economic deterioration existing outside of the Pit. Zyablikov first learned of the collapse of the Soviet Union when he was placed in America many years ago. To his team, everything had always been business as usual.

Zyablikov thought back to when his sister Kalisa was taken away during the third level, for getting fed up with that "Do you love your country?" question. On test number 243, the question appeared five times. On the fifth one, she bubbled in the letter B, as by this time, they had graduated from the oral tests to the written versions.

She was then taken away…to the Pound.

Apparently, she had been in total darkness for several days, for when she came back out, she couldn't open her eyes around any source of light. For the first day, during the early evening, she cupped a hand over one of her eyes and squinted with the other one if she wanted to take a peek at something. One of the instructors thought this was hilarious and nicknamed her for it: Nightshade. The name stuck forever, along with the nightmare.

Collectively, they had no childhood. They had experienced no period of adolescence, nor did they have any understanding of the concept of parenthood. They had no parents or guardians, just Sergeant Majors, Lieutenants, Captains, and teachers who wouldn't give them their real names if their lives depended on it. All students had American aliases, and by the twelfth level, they were all killing machines. None had ever had a Russian accent, nor could they even speak Russian. From the beginning to the present, they had been raised as Americans.

As far as intelligence, they were all among the 95th percentile or higher among American college graduates, but in matters of military strategic tactics and field combat, as a whole, they were absolutely unparalleled.

Devin leaned back and relaxed in his chair while he reviewed the Operation Black Fox plans. A splendid machine it was, indeed—not only capable of carrying, arming, and launching nuclear missiles, but also equipped to emit powerful nuclear energy pulses from incredible distances, pulses that were able to demolish small cities with one hit.

It also had stealth capabilities. Its unique design would allow radio waves to somehow pass over it. Devin estimated it would cost several hundred million dollars to build just a few, then several additional expenses for testing. Devin contemplated how a chopper could bounce through radio waves. He reflected on how horrifically dangerous an army of these choppers would be during an offensive assault. The battle could be won before the choppers got within eyesight. Devin reread Valentine's article and wondered what possible proof she could have possessed that the helicopter was actually being built. He truly doubted there was a photo somewhere that had been taken of the several workers building the chopper, and then smuggled out of their top secret base. And even if there was, Valentine couldn't possibly have afforded it. There could be no other source but an actual witness, and even that seemed unlikely. Why would a witness go to an American reporter? If the witness wanted money, he would either use blackmail or go to the CIA.

Either way, it was all in the past now. How the information got out of bounds was no longer his concern.

Devin closed his eyes and thought about Nightshade, the leader of Team F, the Special Forces team. She had black hair and beautiful brown eyes. She was athletic, intelligent, definitely sexy, and capable of killing on a moment's notice. To get to her, he knew he would have to go through Garret. He knew nothing about Dennis Garret except that he was a man who could get things done. Also with black hair, fairly handsome, and with a rough-looking face, Garret had to be the same age as Nightshade, about 24 or 25. At about 5'11" and weighing close to 180 pounds, he was skilled in hand-to-hand combat as well as with knives and any gun you could think of. He was the most superior of the elite.

Devin thought about the captain of Team A, who was called A-1, or Oleg Lugor, by those who knew him. His personality set him apart. Words could not describe the depth of his uncontrolled viciousness. In appearance and in combat, Lugor was truly an ugly man. Devin was fearful of Lugor. As he thought about him, Devin involuntarily flinched.

The etymology of the name Lugor derives from Likhar, meaning "evil." From childhood, many of the Pit's members were afraid of Lugor. Since any one of them could remember, Lugor had been a silent, demonic assassin. He had attacked several of them for the most trivial of provocations during his youth and had attempted to take their lives using anything near him: a pencil in the neck or maybe a fork in the heart. Zyablikov used to joke with him, saying he needed to take a bath in holy water. As a young adult, Lugor was the first to volunteer in sparring or anything else that involved hurting or killing. He would often pull the legs off of large insects or chase and catch small animals and see what creative way he could devise to kill them. There seemed not a chance he would develop a conscience or any sort of morality; Lugor was a pure product of the environment he had been placed in. The only thing separating him from the others was that during his term in the Pit, he did not try to cling to any source of sanity. He let it all go and became what they wanted him to become.

The man was about 6'2" and weighed in at about 215 pounds but was as fast and as tough as an alley cat. Devin had seen classified tapes of Lugor sparring against fellow "classmates" in the Pit, and it was nightmarish.

The highly covert operation was intended to produce the perfect "American" soldiers, though more highly advanced in all areas. They would be used for the ultimate trinity: intelligence, espionage, and warfare. How had the operation fared? The word "success" was an understatement.

Devin knew that the individuals graduating from this operation had never met their parents. Their parents were told that their beloved sons or daughters had died shortly after birth at the hospital. These were not just any children; they were actually bred through a eugenic process. Tests were issued to physically superior males with high intelligence and knowledge of military tactics. Healthy women who fit the same category were given the same tests. The women were then artificially inseminated with the top scorers' semen – sperm enhanced by a new form of biological technology and genetic engineering.

Devin also knew that any child who failed a level of the program more than once was terminated from the operation. He didn't know exactly what happened to many of the children who flunked out, but Devin was quite sure it was not something to be envied. Out of the 25 children that were bred, 16 of them lived through the project to satisfactorily meet its requirements.

He thought back to Lugor's aggressiveness and disregard for human life. Project Pit had created 16 highly intelligent human war machines—and under the right direction, he knew they were capable of absolutely anything. He pondered on the structure he led. Though all members were of absolute premium quality and trained in many areas of combat, each member was quite unique and had his or her own specialties. Devin had no clue of the names the Pit graduates had chosen for themselves, nor did he know the American aliases assigned to them. Only the Spymaster had the aliases and other key information. Only the Spymaster actually had the whole picture.

He knew Garret's job was to keep track of and communicate with the operatives. With the exception of Nightshade and Lugor, Devin was unaware of who the other Pit operatives were. He had seen Lugor before when he served as a backup to the debriefing in case something happened to Garret and Nightshade but had never spoken to him. He could pass by any of the Pit creations in a grocery store and not know them. Still, he did know they were a powerful group.

Team A, the elite five of the 16, was trained in every form of combat that existed, as well as in marine warfare and scuba diving. Garret was even trained to operate a submarine. All members were physically superior in too many ways to sit and discuss and had been given the American SAT in the 9th and 10th levels, scoring at the highest levels. Team A contained the most highly advanced soldiers the world would ever see, which was why Garret was chosen to lead them. There were no females on Team A, though Nightshade was worthy.

There was A-2, Vladimir Yakof, known inside the Pit for his exceptional ability to decipher or "break" encrypted codes, sometimes using a computer program of his own design. Yakof had a deep knowledge of computers and was a whiz kid when it came to anything having to do with them.

A-3, Demitri Liutoboets, was a blonde-haired man with unique silent military combat skills, mainly knives, but not knives exclusively. Liutoboets once had an erection during a sparring match with Kalisa. This event spawned his last name, Liutoboets, meaning "hard fighter." Liutoboets was also known in the Pit for standing strong in the field, with an uncanny ability to take down multiple enemies single-handedly.

A-4 was Gremis Nukludko, a master of explosives. Nukludko had always loved to create destructive combustible devices, hence the nickname Gremis, or Glorious Thunder. He created the explosive device that had opened the safe at the *Washington Post*. The name Nukludko was sprouted in the early stages of his Pit training, when he was assigned to the top bunk in the bedding hall. He would often roll off his bed, crashing onto the hard concrete floor. Despite his requests to switch to a bottom bunk, he was forced to sleep on the top bunk and teach himself to sleep like a log. Before this happened, however, Nukludko crashed to the floor during the night too many times to count. When he would fall, the guard would come in, snatch him up, and force him to stay awake the entire night, forever cursing him with the nickname "Restless."

A-5 was Iake Tatomir, whose superior agility and knowledge of the human body's weaknesses was unsurpassed within the team, except maybe by Garret, a true expert in all areas. A-5's desire to fight for no apparent reason led to his given name, Tatomir, meaning "thief of peace" and Iake, meaning "strong."

As Devin daydreamed of Nightshade and himself meeting in a different kind of life, Garret slipped back into his mind. He knew Garret was sent there to watch him, and that was why he would always know hardly anything about Garret. Everyone in Project Pit had authentic American names they were to use, complete with driver's licenses, Social Security cards, and other documents needed to successfully maneuver in society. But Dennis Garret was different. Devin was told nothing about him except he was to be given direct control of Teams A, B, D, and F while Devin was to head Teams C, E, and G and plan and present all missions.

Team C was composed of several genuine Americans and was therefore totally expendable. It bothered Devin that Garret was to lead the invaluable units while he himself was in charge of the errand boys. The Americans knew nothing of what they were involved in, nor had they seen any faces. No matter—they had sold their country out a long time ago for dollars. It was the American way. The Americans were charged with small-time assignments and hits and with retrieving small intelligence within the hour such as the blueprints for this morning's mission. Teams E and G did not physically exist but were created as a psychological tactic aimed at Garret. This tactic was supposed to keep absent any thoughts of Garret trying to run the operation by himself by preventing any speculation that he was running more than half the operation already, and it worked.

Devin didn't even know what Team B's function was. All he knew was that Garret was in charge of their operations, which frustrated Devin further. He imagined they might be pilots, or perhaps paratroopers, but he didn't waste thought on it. He realized he would never know if he was correct or not.

Though Devin hadn't been in combat for over twenty-six years, he was considered the top man in strategic planning for covert missions, and was compensated accordingly, but he had to make sure all teams remained ignorant of each other.

"Breaking news today with regards to the Strategic Offensive Reductions Treaty," the CNN reporter started. "Prime Minister Epifanii Yuklivitch is held under serious scrutiny after being accused of covering up the operation of a top-secret war machine. It seems the leader of the Strategic Offensive Reductions Treaty Commission has been the head of an intense hypocritical charade. He has strived to bring an end to all nuclear weapons in the United States while still secretly manufacturing new and innovative war machines in Russia. From past unethical behavior by KGB operatives, many key United States officials do assume that an extremely sinister and underhanded plot has been uncovered. They believe at this time that it is indeed Yuklivitch's intention to have the U.S. dispose of its nuclear weapons before Russia attempts a series of offensive assaults on specific territories across the globe, possibly to control key world resources, including oil. Though this assumption has not yet been confirmed by military strategists, many do think it is more than likely."

The screen then switched to a military spokesperson. "It is assumed that Yuklivitch did, indeed, know about Operation Black Fox while at the same time pushing the SORT forward. Yes, I do think he should be punished severely for playing on the benevolence of our nation."

The screen switched back to the CNN reporter. "Most military powers share this opinion of the situation—"

Bryan Hughes turned off his handheld TV and continued to create his list of technological suspects.

"When did Valentine give you the story about Operation Black Fox?" Gregory Hunt asked the editor in chief of the *Washington Post*. The editor was still a little flabbergasted from the morning's incident.

"Last night...about twelve thirty or so. Maybe one o'clock. I was here finishing up some editing."

"What did she say, exactly?" Hunt asked.

"She explained to me that she had gotten hold of some evidence that Russia was constructing a top-secret helicopter. I asked to see the evidence, and she showed me the plans."

"You saw the plans?"

"Yes, I did. I couldn't print an article like that without seeing the evidence for myself. I saw three separate pictures of three different pieces of paper. They looked like helicopters I had never seen before. After I saw them, I told her to put them in the vault. She was escorted to the vault by night guards and me."

"Where are the guards?"

"They work the night shift. They are probably home sleeping right now. Neither of them knew what was being put in the vault. All they saw was a brown envelope and a roll of film."

"Has the vault ever been broken into before?"

"No."

"Who knows about the vault?"

"No one, until last night. I was worried that a document of that significance should be protected and taken out of her hands for her own safety. She wanted to keep it, but I insisted on locking it up."

"So until last night, no one knew about the evidence vault."

"No. Definitely not. I usually put everything in there myself."

"Did Valentine have any copies?"

"Definitely not. That is why she put up such a fuss to take the pictures home with her. She is very adamant when she wants—" There was a sudden, solemn pause from the editor, then he continued. "I mean, she was very adamant when she wanted her way. I finally convinced her to leave them in the vault...she didn't want to."

"And you say Valentine approached you with the story around midnight?"

"No, it was twelve thirty, one o'clock."

Hunt was just checking. He switched off the microcassette recorder.

"Thank you, sir. We will contact you if we need any more information. You are not to leak to anyone what Valentine gave you, do you understand?"

"What about freedom of speech?" the editor asked.

"If you utter one word about what you have told us, you won't see the inside of a courtroom, and I can promise you will end up like Valentine. Do you understand there are people looking to silence anyone who knows what they are not supposed to?"

The editor nodded.

Hunt turned back to Bryan Hughes, who was talking with some of the witnesses, getting a description of the weapons that had been used and the sounds they had made.

"Green smoke?" he asked the witness.

"Uh huh."

"Did it have a smell?"

"It smelled like smoke."

"Did it affect you? Did it make your eyes water, or make you want to regurgitate? Did it make you sleepy or put you in a state of euphoria?"

"It was horrible. I remember I couldn't breathe, but I don't remember much else."

"Are you sure?"

"Yes. The one thing I do know is that even though the smoke was spreading out, thinning, I still couldn't breathe."

"Thank you, sir. I might be talking to you later," Hughes replied, happy to get away from this intellectually challenged witness.

Walter Plack walked up to Hughes, who was now standing by Hunt. He jerked his head toward a private office. The frequency scrambler was already set up. Plack addressed the men. "We need to get all the witnesses to our nearest secured facility for in-depth interviews as soon as possible."

"I don't think that would do any good, Walter," Hughes replied.

"And why is that?"

"I believe the green smoke all the witnesses refer to is some sort of memory-altering chemical. With the help of the local detectives, Gregory and I have interviewed every witness in here who saw anything. They all really don't remember *anything.* I mean, nothing at all. I was asking around, trying to get a positive ID on the description of the Rex, and the TH–7000   "

"You asked civilians for descriptions of top-secret weapons?" Plack interrupted.

"I didn't give any specifics. Besides, it doesn't look as if they're so top secret to these witnesses after this morning, now, does it?"

Plack thought about his brother and remained silent. It would only be a matter of time before they tried to yank the case out from under his jurisdiction with some garbage about how it wasn't ethical to have someone with personal ties on the case. But for now, he was not answering his ComLink.

He remembered the inscription in the foyer of his headquarters: *Ye Shall Seek the Truth and the Truth Will Make You Free.*

And the truth he would seek, at all costs.

"Continue, Bryan," Plack uttered.

"Well, it looks as if the green gas was definitely not lethal but contained some kind of memory-altering, anti-recall substance. I wish I could get a sample, but it's already evaporated. I rounded up all of the gas canisters, hoping there might be a trace of chemicals lingering. Most of the witnesses, the ones who remember anything worth mentioning, indicated the gas erupted from several sources."

"Anything else?"

"Actually, yes. While the anti-recall chemical in the gas was taking effect, the green smoke also temporarily neutralized all potential heroes from coming to action. They say it blinded them *and* choked them. And now, when they recover, they can hardly remember anything significant. One witness said he thought they were robots."

"Do either of you have any *good* news?"

"Yes," Hunt answered, "one fact remains consistent. Ninety percent of the witnesses say there were five people, dressed in all black, with gas masks over their faces. That's about the only thing any of these witnesses say they can be sure of. I do not think polygraph tests will be effective in the least, because most of them barely remember anything. In-depth interviews will be a waste of time also, except one guy says he remembers everything. I brought him up on the civilian files, and turns out he's an ex-Marine, honorably discharged from a helicopter training accident in '99. He's also a swimmer."

"What was he doing here?"

"He had an interview."

"Who interviewed the editor in chief?" Plack asked.

"I did, Walter," Hunt replied.

"What time did he say that Valentine brought him the plans?"

"He said he saw them about twelve thirty, one o'clock."

"Twelve thirty, one o'clock? How the hell did someone plan this entire operation in less than nine hours?" Plack asked his colleagues and himself. "How can an organization like this infiltrate our country and we not know about it? I want records of every flight that took off and landed within the last 24 hours. They had to get here from somewhere, somehow! I want statements from anyone who was around the building. Does anyone even know how the hell they walked out of here? Jesus Christ! It's as if they vaporized into thin air! Hunt, what did they do, fly out of here in a jumbo jet? Somebody get me some answers, and include how in the hell anyone could plan and execute this in nine hours!"

"I was speculating maybe someone else knew before that. Maybe Valentine told someone she knew, or maybe her source leaked the information to multiple sources," Hunt said.

Suddenly, all three heads looked up from their hushed conversation.

"Here come Barnum and Bailey," Hughes informed his colleagues.

"Great, when do we get to be on *Hard Copy?*" Hunt put in, devoid of any enthusiasm.

"FBI: Fucking Bureau of Idiots," Plack mumbled grimly.

Entering the small office was the notorious Special Agent Bruce Wallace, from the Federal Bureau of Investigation. The word "covert" did not exist in his vocabulary. His name was always in the papers, detailing some big case he had solved. He still lived off his big terrorist bust of 1988, during which he brought down the Libyan terrorist ring that had sent bomb threats to JFK Airport, halting flights for over three days. In 1998, with the DEA's help, he also brought down the Colombian drug lord, Carlos Mendez, who happened to be a diplomat. Topping it off, he also claimed to have a significant part in the Al Qaeda investigations.

He thought his intelligence transcended that of the mere mortals around him, and he let everyone know it. With him were two other men.

"Hello, Agent Wallace," Plack uttered dryly.

"You might as well call me Bruce. All the reporters do," Wallace replied with a smile. Plack did not smile back.

Wallace offered a hand. Plack slowly extended his arm and gave a terse, unfriendly handshake, as if Wallace had leprosy.

"Sorry to hear about your brother. Are you sure you're up to working on this case?"

"I'll be fine," Plack replied.

"Well, the sooner we catch these bastards, the better. I have been asked by the mayor of this city to come here and assist your investigation in any way possible."

"Thank you, but we really are taking care of things," Hunt said.

"Well, the last time I checked, any matter pertaining to national security, terrorism, or organized crime warranted the involvement of the Federal Bureau of Investigation. By the way, is this your idea of Homeland Security?"

"Listen," Plack growled, "if you come waltzing in here with that cocky attitude, continue, and I will personally teach you the definition of humility. If you knew what kind of organization you are dealing with here, and what just happened, you would wipe that goddamn gorilla smile off your face! And who are these guys?"

"These fine agents with me are Special Agent Marcus Thorn and Special Agent Laurence Acclaim."

Plack looked the two young men over and inwardly groaned. *Oh Christ, it's amateur hour*, he thought.

"I'm Bryan Hughes, Deputy Director of Science and Technology," Hughes said, breaking the icy silence. "Very shortly, I will have some vitally important information for you on the weapons used this morning. They are not from your average arsenal. I urge you to review it carefully."

"Thank you, Bryan," Wallace said, offering a hand.

Bryan shook it to make peace, but he didn't care for Bruce Wallace any more than his colleagues did. Wallace had nearly ruined numerous operations by "assisting in any way possible."

"What happened, exactly?" Wallace asked.

Gregory Hunt gave the three agents a brief rundown of what had happened.

"Do we know yet what or who took out Frank Turner and Valentine?"

"Not yet," replied Hughes. The two younger men did not have high enough clearance for him to explain what had really killed Valentine and Turner.

"Do you think Russia is behind this?" Wallace asked.

"Yes," Plack answered.

"What about another country   or terrorist organization?"

"Do you think another country would even dream of coming into our borders illegally and executing a mission like this over *alleged* helicopter plans? Whoever performed this job knew for a *fact* that the plans would be here."

"Then why do you call them alleged?" Wallace asked.

"Because no one standing here has seen them, except for the editor in chief. One civilian is all we have at this point."

"Valentine wouldn't talk?" Wallace asked.

Plack responded dryly. "No."

"Why do you think she was taken out?" Wallace asked.

"I suspect it was to silence her."

"You suspect?"

"Yes."

"Central Intelligence, huh?" This was a mumble from Wallace.

Plack remained silent.

"I would ask how an organization like this would find its way into the capital of our nation without your knowing about it, but the fact is, I don't think they found their way anywhere," Wallace continued.

"Go on," Plack invited.

"Now that I have your attention, I will tell you that they didn't have to go far."

"Get to the point."

"I think they were already here."

Plack thought for a minute.

Wallace continued, "Branching off your theory that Russia is behind this, which may or may not be correct, the organization had nine hours to plan *and* execute this assignment. Given that the travel time from here to Russia is at least nine or ten hours, top speed, it would have been impossible for them to pull it off, even if they had planned the whole caper on the flight over and moved as soon as they got their intelligence. What do we know about the bomb that opened the vault?"

Hughes spoke up. "One word: professional. The item used to set it off was impacted inside the explosive so the arming device would vaporize. Brilliantly crafted. There is absolutely nothing to analyze or trace. Had to be an explosive specialist. The best."

"What are you, a fan of his?" Wallace asked with a conceited smirk.

"How do you know it is a he?" Hughes retorted. "Do you play poker with him?"

"I was under the impression I would have full cooperation from your agency," Wallace stated.

"Forgive us for not rolling out the red carpet like you're used to, Bruce, but my brother and our coworkers have just been murdered," Plack growled.

"All right," Wallace started, "I'm going to check the possibility of an inside connection. I'll gather the witnesses' testimonies, and my team will send you our profiles of any organization able to pull off a job like this. I'll also check relative accounts and search for significant financial increases. Is there any additional information I should know about?"

"Yes," Plack stepped in. "I heard about what happened with several of your cases where you didn't keep your mouth shut. This case is classified! If I hear a peep from those reporters about you, this case is mine. Since we both want the bad guys, we will work together. Any time you talk about this case to one of your men, take and activate the scrambler. Do you trust these two men with your life?"

"Yes, I do," Wallace said solemnly.

"Okay, then, information about this case is not to go beyond the six men you see standing here."

"That is understood. I assume the same code applies at your agency," Wallace replied.

"You definitely don't have to worry about us," Plack assured him.

With a conciliatory nod, Wallace turned and, with his men, left the room.

ORGANIZATIONAL CHART OF AMERUS

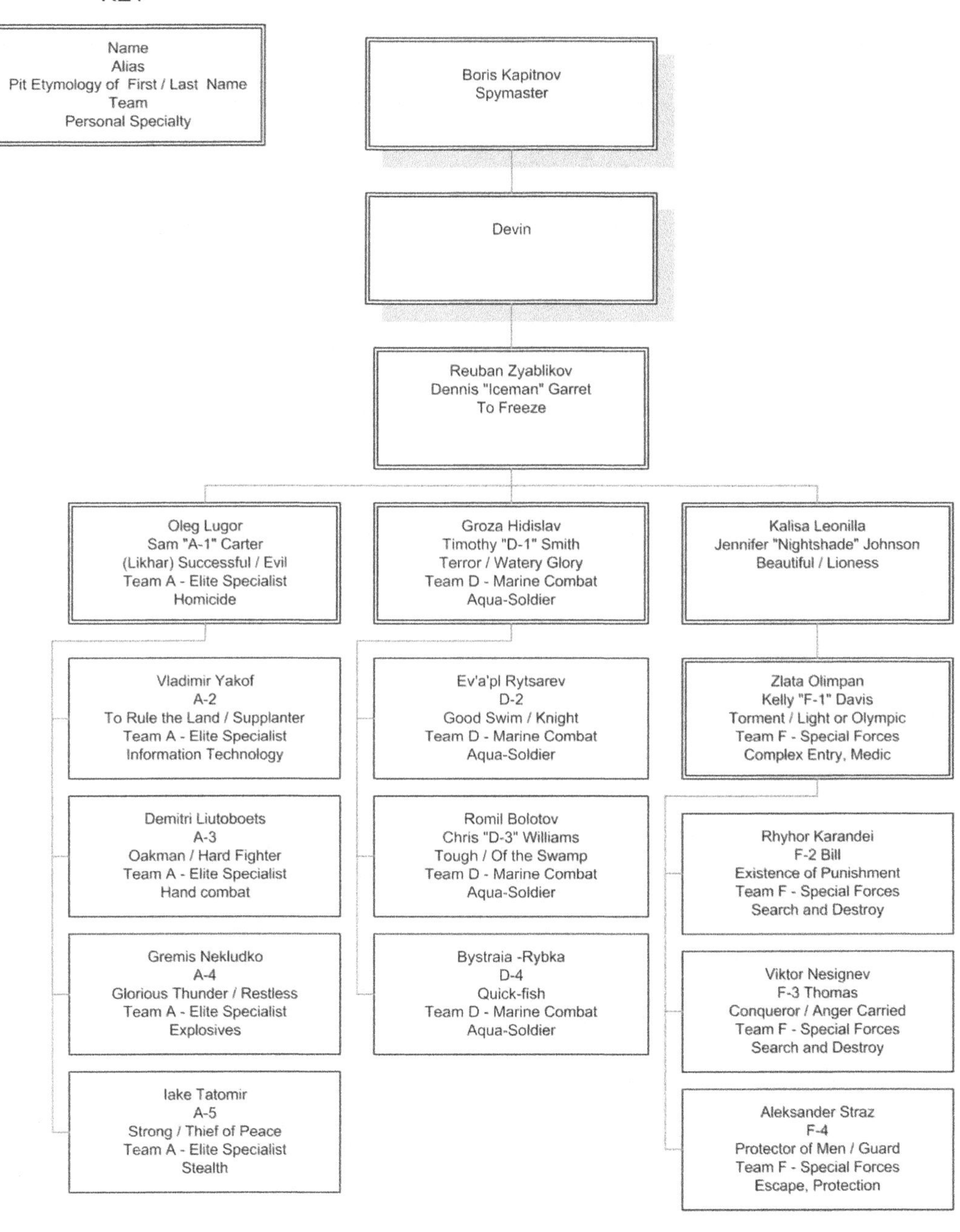

CHAPTER 3

Safe at home, in the darkness, Reuban Zyablikov turned on the television. He did not want to live like this for another day, and yet it was his reason for existing. It was why he had been created.

He knew more about the Pit project than he was supposed to, but they had to let him in on the juice, considering they wanted him to lead three of the seven teams. He knew that he was, in some ways, like a science project, but in other ways like the Million Dollar Man, running a billion-dollar operation. He never received a dime, but he knew it was in keeping with the philosophy of the Pit; rich people attracted attention. He closed his eyes and turned his thoughts back to the Pit, tuning out the noise of the small television.

"Faster, Dennis, harder!" Sergeant Brown would yell during sparring matches. "You want to knock someone down with that punch? You fight like a baby girl, you maggot!"

Zyablikov remembered Sergeant Brown pushing his sparring partner out of the way and stepping into the circle. "Come on, Garret. Knock me down!" Sergeant Brown was 6'5" and weighed 230 pounds, and his scary eyes bulged while he barked like a madman. Reuban didn't move. His class had stopped sparring and turned around to see the confrontation, remaining silent.

"Are you scared, little girl?"

Reuban threw his small fist into Brown's testicles and then pushed him onto the thin mat with as much force as his nine-year-old muscles could muster. He got ready for a battle. Brown lurched backwards but recovered and sent a foot to Zyablikov's face, causing him to stumble backwards—but Zyablikov refused to fall.

Blood flowed from Zyablikov's mouth onto his chin. He wiped it off with the back of his hand but continued moving, as he had been instructed to do since his first day of hand-to-hand training.

37

Brown threw a quick right and snapped it back with the speed of light. Zyablikov saw a flash of light when the punch impacted his face, and he stumbled backwards again. Before he could regain his stance on the mat, Zyablikov was in the air. Brown had quickly crept in and slid his forearm in between the little boy's legs, and scooped him up. To the audience, Brown looked like a tumbling acrobat. Still moving like lightning, Brown twisted himself while sliding to the ground, throwing the young Zyablikov to the mat on his back with a thud. Brown then smashed his fist into Zyablikov's chest with a loud and authoritative "Yah!"

Zyablikov lay on the mat, holding his chest, tears in his eyes. Brown arched his back and was on his feet. The audience was amazed at how quick their instructor was.

"Don't stop!" he yelled, pointing at the gasping Zyablikov. "Don't *ever* stop! When you stop to rest, your opponent gains strength. When you hit, hit hard! Every blow counts! Don't stop until your opponent stops breathing! Never stop! You think a kick in the balls will stop a man? You're lucky if you even get a clean hit! When your opponent is stumbling, hit the throat like I've taught you! Timothy, get in here!"

Groza Hidislav, presently D-1 and captain of the Marine Combat Team, stepped into the circle while Zyablikov slowly got to his feet.

"Timmy! Show this man how it's done."

Zyablikov knew Hidislav had once seriously injured a classmate in a sparring match and, even though only nine, didn't hesitate when it came to using kill spots.

Before Brown's command was completed, Hidislav was upon Zyablikov. Hidislav's arms swung wildly while he shouted "Arggh" with every swing. Zyablikov was quick and maneuvered around his punches, bobbing his head when he needed to. Hidislav swung with authority and became angrier every time he missed. Zyablikov dove at Hidislav, knocking him to the ground. Then, without thinking, Zyablikov formed his hand into a V and threw the V into his classmate's neck with aggressive force.

Hidislav gurgled noisily as Zyablikov repeatedly rammed his fist into his opponent's testicles. Hidislav squirmed and writhed but refused to scream. As Brown had told them, a scream told your opponent he was winning; it was inspiration. Scream only when *you* land a blow, he instructed. Screamers had been put in the Pound.

Brown saw Hidislav's pain but did not stop the fight. He watched the two nine-year-olds fight like savage dogs. Zyablikov shouted with every blow, like Brown always did, but his punches got harder with every strike. The nine-year-old audience did not cringe at the raw battle, nor were they shocked that Brown did not blow his whistle.

"All right, Garret. You fought your way out of the Pound."

Zyablikov nodded. He would have died in the Pound.

Still at the mind-boggling crime scene, Gregory Hunt opened his laptop and typed in his e-mail password. After the computer verified the password and an additional authorization code, then a retinal scan, Hunt was allowed to retrieve his messages after his application, "The Crypt" decrypted the coded information. There was a message from the National Security Council stating possible motives and organizations for such an operation as the one they were working to uncover. The data was in order of probability, as usual:

1) *The Rebellion*—Covert American terrorist organization. Led by Robert Lawton Baker. Highly dedicated members, advanced technology, deep underground connections. Suspected connection with the 1996 Olympic Airlines bombing in Atlanta, Georgia. Funding: random kidnappings, terrorist governments, several unknown sources, and robberies overseas. Estimated number of members: 40. Public enemy number: 2. Motive: Blackmail Russian Federation, form alliance, or possibly jeopardize the SORT conference. Founded: 1987. *Probability level: 32.713%.*

2) *Al Qaeda*, "The Base"—Hardcore international terrorist group. Led by Osama Bin Laden and Muhammad Atef. An international terrorist group, dedicated to opposing non-Islamic governments with force and violence. One of the principle goals of Al Qaeda is to drive the United States armed forces out of Saudi Arabia (and elsewhere on the Saudi-Arabian Peninsula) and Somalia by violence. Known for the 2001 September 11th terrorist activities, conspiracy to kill U.S. nationals, bombing of several U.S. embassies. Funding: private donations laundered through banks and charities. Estimated number of members: unknown (hundreds). Public enemy number: 1. Motives: Revenge, mercenary incomes, incite war against the United States. Founded: approximately 1989. Probability level: *21.304%.*

3) *Ironmen*—Mercenary terrorist group. Led by Ali Gobril Megran, former Director of Center for Strategic Studies, also head of security for Libyan Arab Airlines; and Karman Hasifa Ghiman, Libyan male intelligence officer operating under the cover of Libyan Arab Airlines. Both responsible for the Pan Am bombing which exploded over Lockerbie, Scotland, killing 259 passengers and crew

members in addition to 11 Lockerbie villagers. Both fugitives wanted by Interpol and for the killing of U.S. nationals. Ironmen are an infamous terrorist freelance organization available to pull jobs for the right fee. Ironmen are not known to have access to advanced technology. Funding: They receive full support and refuge from the Libyan government. Estimated number of members: 55. Public enemy number: 3. Motive: Under Russian hire to avoid international incident, and mercenary motive. Founded: 1980. Probability level: *16.304%*.

4) *Brotherhood of Longhorn*—Mercenary terrorist group. Led by Hans "Longhorn" Badenburg. Badenburg was born in Heidelberg, Germany and is a former German BND agent known to carry a sword cane. Longhorn is notorious for recruiting foreign agents and subsidizing foreign political campaigns and has been known to arrange for the assassination of problematic foreign leaders. Group members have knowledge of weapons and poisons. Known for shooting the kneecaps off victims and watching them bleed to death. Funding: Longhorns wanted in connection with the $7 million security corporation heist. Estimated number of members: 20. Public enemy number: 4. Motive: Political advantage or mercenary motive. Founded: 1979. Probability level: *11.622%*.

5) *Novus Ordo Mundi*—Covert society. Led by person or persons unknown. Formerly known as the Order of Perfectibilists or the Bavarian Illuminati. Novus Ordo Mundi is an extremely diabolical, secret society composed mostly of high upper-class citizens who occasionally refer to themselves as the Power Elite. Maintain an oath of secrecy. The organization aggressively plots a global conspiracy for world domination by way of an installation of a New World Sovereignty or a "Federal World Government." Group members also quietly fight for dynamic control of international banks for corrupt purposes, approaching the last steps to monopolize the monies of the world. Funding: not necessary; many known members are billionaires. Ability to purchase advanced technology. Estimated number of members: unknown. Public enemy number: 8. Motives: To sell plans to the highest bidder. Founded: Approximately 1960 by Adam Weishaupt. Probability Level: *9.361%*.

Due to base distance and the Central Intelligence reports recently received from all field agents, the National Security Council places all known Russian military forces remotely low in the probability of executing the *Washington Post* operation in Washington, D.C. Within the required time to execute the operation, no known flights had arrived in the airspace of any U.S. civilian or military airports inside the alert radius. All radar and satellite reports within the last 120 hours detected zero related Russian military or civilian-vessel movement within U.S. land, air, or sea territory. All covert agents have also reported no relevant aggressive movement or planning against the United States.

Hunt quickly reread the file, then wrote down the probability levels backwards along with his shorthand code chosen for each organization. Next, as he closed the file, it permanently deleted itself with its implanted security virus. He activated his frequency scrambler and called Plack through his ComLink, which was immune to the scrambler waves. The ComLink resembled a typical PDA, so it was easy enough to carry and use. Hunt also liked the biometric security features on the device, such as the handprint grid. However, since the ComLink was the major communications link between most field agents, the agency did not allow any customization of the ComLink. This didn't bother Hunt, though. He wasn't much for ringtones, pictures, and "brickbreaker" games.

He saw there was a message from the Public and Agency Information Department on the ComLink as he picked it up.

He pressed "Receive" and again checked the scrambler to make sure it was activated, as the message was deemed Classified.

The public will be informed that a terrorist organization attempted to kidnap Dorian Valentine in lieu of her recent article, and then eliminated her, as she would not submit without struggle. You and all agents are to act accordingly externally. Internally, proceed as needed.

Hunt then depressed the red button on his ComLink, and the message was erased. He dialed Plack's ComLink code and prepared to give him an update.

Oleg Lugor sat in the dark in his small apartment in New Jersey. It wasn't dark enough. He lay on his small weight bench and closed his eyes. He pushed the weight up and off the vertical safety bars and began lifting, not once opening his eyes. Eyes closed, Lugor was "looking" around his apartment. He "saw" the television and knew it was still on Channel 10, where he had left it before he was contacted. Eyes still closed, he imagined his American DVD player and its library of American movies he hardly watched. Even his old VHS tapes were still half rewound, to keep the act going. No other movies were allowed in his house, and he knew they checked on him. He knew Zyablikov was required to check on him and eliminate him if things were out of line.

Lugor continued pushing the weights off his chest rapidly. Without checking the amount before he got on, he knew he was lifting 225 pounds. "Twenty…twenty-one…" Lugor counted, not breaking pace or sweating. His mind drifted.

"Lift, Sam!" Coach Stephan shouted as Oleg struggled to lift the black handles on the high-tech bench press machine. "Lift! Your body doesn't want to lift it! Your mind does, Sam! Push with your mind; your body will follow! Your body is tired; your mind is strong! Push, Sam!"

Oleg pushed until the handles started to go up. His arms were on fire and his shoulders burned as the lactic acid built up and blood rushed much-needed oxygen back to his muscles. His face was red. His pectoral muscles were visibly shaking.

"Push! The mind is powerful!"

With a loud exhale, Oleg shoved the weight upward, and the red light on the machine turned green.

"Recover."

Hearing the word, Oleg let go of the handlebars and dropped his arms to his sides, panting.

There was no "Good job, Sam" or "I knew you could do it," just a small nod. But everyone was used to it. Never a "Congratulations" or any recognition whatsoever for anything. It was another way the Pit hardened their hearts.

Combat was all Lugor knew. Sometimes, he thought he was addicted to killing. He was not only taught to kill but also bred to kill. The only time he got to see his associates was when it was for the good of an operation. The only time he was allowed to leave his specified radius was when he was to track a target. He was conditioned to ignore his conscience to the point that he no longer had one. He had been taught to pull a gun at point-blank range and not aim for the head like in the movies, but at the neck, then the head. He used this double tap, since he had seen bullets enter the head, curve around the skull, and then exit out the other side to injure an innocent bystander while the target still lived. His whole life was centered on the missions. He was created to kill, and he had learned to live with it. At times his muscles would convulse and quiver if his need to attack was not fed. This drove him to the art of shadowboxing.

He practiced shadowboxing every night after his weightlifting, push-ups and sit-ups. He shadowboxed himself for hours with punches, kicks, and combinations. He remembered everything Brown had taught him and had added a few moves of his own.

———————————————

Walter Plack wiped his eyes and sniffled a few times before he had the strength to get up. He had cried for 45 minutes, grieving his brother, and someone was going to pay. He prayed the swimmer would have the information he needed to pinpoint the organization. He felt some comfort in knowing the witness was being interviewed at that moment. His wife was watching the news as he walked downstairs. He was glad she had left him alone to cry. He saw dinner was waiting for him on the table—his favorite: pork chops and mashed potatoes with country gravy and buttermilk rolls. They were store-bought, but he loved them just the same. And he loved her. He walked past her and into the kitchen. He wasn't hungry, but he had wanted some iced tea. As he passed the kitchen table, he noticed a sheet of yellow paper.

W, you have an urgent message on your link. I love you, the note read.

He started to cry again. His wife crept behind him, put her arms around him, and gave him a gentle kiss on the back of his neck while hugging him tightly.

In the background, he heard Prime Minister Epifanii Yuklivitch personally giving America his word that neither the Russian Federation nor the SORT Commission had any connection with the terrorist escapade that went down that morning. The prime minister went on to state that all plans were still a go on the SORT talks and that he and his country hoped the president was still coming to Moscow to sign the papers. He also denied any production of a post-nuclear helicopter and said if it would help make things run more smoothly, he would come to America.

An hour later, the President of the United States was addressing the nation, explaining that "even though Intelligence reports that Russia's direct role in the devastating episode is doubtful at this time, looking in this country's best interest, I am forced to postpone my trip to Moscow for three weeks, until a full investigation of today's tragic events has been brought to a close. As of yet, my intentions for signing the treaty have not changed, nor has my intention to travel to Moscow in the near future."

Plack saw Bruce Wallace standing by the President's Secret Service men. Then he saw Wallace step to the podium.

"I have taken on a great responsibility this morning," Wallace started. "I have assumed the leadership role in this investigation. An event like this on our country's sacred ground cannot and will not go unpunished. We have the most experienced—"

Sharon Plack flicked off the TV.

"Thank you, Sharon," her husband said softly.

In Washington D.C., Terrel Harris, a D.C. native, sat in a room with no windows. He had a tall glass of ice water. Gregory Hunt conducted the informal in-depth interview. What Harris did not know was that his beverage contained an odorless, tasteless, colorless, "truth powder" which dissolved instantly in liquid with no side effects. Though only a few individuals understood how the powder actually worked, it was known that the ingredients altered the electrochemical impulses of the brain, thus putting the victim in a heavily relaxed state. It also created the perception that external, nonphysical threats seemed nonexistent. Hunt had once overheard two scientists in the restroom joking with each other, comparing the chemical to LSD.

Hunt laid his microcassette recorder in the middle of the table and pretended to turn it on. All aspects of this case were classified and couldn't be recorded. The cassette recorder was merely a hoax. Though the recorder's lights were on and it turned the tape like a real device, it was just a prop for one of the many psychological aspects of this interview. Hunt uttered the time, date, location, and names of all individuals present: Bryan Hughes and Laurence Acclaim from the FBI, the interviewee, and himself. This was a classic stall tactic until Harris drank a sufficient amount of the water for the powder to take effect. There was also an audio wave analyzer attached to a monitor. This was relatively new technology, but was deemed dependable. By looking at the background color of the monitor screen, one could evaluate the statement.

"For the record, please state your whole name, along with any aliases." *Is Terrel Omar Harris your real name?*

"Terrel Omar Harris. My family calls me 'T' sometimes."

After a minute of irrelevant questions about Harris's past, such as where he presently worked, family members, and where he lived—purposely skipping his military background for the moment—Hunt watched Harris drink, and then started the actual interview after deciding the powder had by now taken effect.

"Mr. Harris, were you present this morning, the morning of April 6 in the *Washington Post's* headquarters?" *Are you the same man who was questioned at the scene of the crime?*

"Yes, I was." The audio wave analyzer came alive and flashed the waves of his voice on the screen. The background was green. Harris did not know that if the background had turned yellow, they were to regard his statement with suspicion, and if the background was red, the odds were that his statement was a lie.

"What were you doing there? State any and all motives for being at the *Washington Post* in Washington, D.C., this morning." *Were you only one there for an interview, Harris?*

"I had an interview for a helicopter pilot position for the new Intense Coverage Team they were creating." *I had no idea I would still be having an interview today*, Harris thought.

Hunt continued asking questions, and Harris passed the in-depth interview without suspicion. Though he could not provide helpful information, one witness was better than none. FBI Agent Acclaim escorted Harris out of the interrogation chamber.

"All right, now we need the audio guy," Hughes started after the witness and Acclaim were out of the room. "Are we going to let the FBI know what's really going on, or are they going to be a part of this kidnapping story?"

"We'll let Walter call it. For now, they stay with everyone else," Hunt replied.

"Did you see Bruce's show a little while ago?" Hughes asked.

"Golly, I missed it," Hunt said with a hint of sarcasm upon hearing Wallace's name.

"He said he was leading this investigation and had his best men on it. He promised victory. I hope Walter didn't see it, or Wallace has stirred up a hornet's nest he doesn't want to think about."

"The Council is smart," Hunt replied.

"How do you mean?"

"If they put one of us up there, it would scare the crap out of everyone in the nation. There would be pandemonium. They would be asking a million questions and spreading a million rumors if one of us was up there. The public sees the FBI as cops with brains. We're the agency everyone wants to be nosy about. You can thank the movies for that, my friend. The Council is trying to keep everything quiet. If Russia is building a team of these helicopters, there is a reason for it. First they hug us, and then they stick the knife in really deep. You don't build post-nuclear attack choppers because it's fun."

Hughes nodded. "What do you think about Harris? The screen changed when you asked him about helicopters."

"I think he's clean. I asked several incriminating questions, which he answered in full, and he dodged no issues. What did the polygraph indicate?"

"No hyperactivity."

"Well, now would be a damn good time to tell me about what killed Valentine and Frank. No blood, no wound, no bruising—like they just dropped dead. Talk to me, Bryan."

"I looked into it. My suspicions were correct. It was the Vig-6."

"The what?" Hunt asked.

"The Vig-6. We are now developing energy-pulsed lasers and particle-beam weapons systems that operate at the speed of light. Usually, satellites are equipped with this kind of technology, but this is the same thing, just on a lower, portable scale. Extremely deadly. There is no sound, no visible beam or light, no traceable point of impact, no wound, no nothing. From the outside, you can't tell the difference between a shot from the Vig and a heart attack. The only good news about this thing is that it can only be used at close range. Any more than 20 feet, and the energy pulse spreads. The Vig can't concentrate the beam like the satellites can. Within 20 feet, one shot is fatal, if the attacker wants it to be. There are basically two settings on the Vig: kill and knock-'em-down unconscious. You can guess what the Vig was set to on this go-round."

"Who makes the Vig?" Hunt asked.

"No one yet. It's still in the testing phases. Or is supposed to be. It has way too many flaws to be used in the field. You can't even tell when it is ready to fire again. After about two shots, it's empty, and right now it's far too expensive to be economically feasible. It looks like someone got a beta version and patched it up."

"Someone stole our weapon and then perfected it?"

Hughes nodded his head. "It looks that way. Greg, we've got our hands full here."

"Who has had access to the weapon?" Hunt asked.

"I couldn't tell you that, either. Russia stole the idea from Japan, and we stole it from Russia. We can't possibly trace the people who have had access to this weapon. Our best bet is the Rex. No one knows about it but our agency. Counterintelligence reports indicate that it has not leaked beyond our borders. That means it's still exclusively ours. We can trace it."

"I won't get my hopes up," Hunt said.

Hughes did not reply.

Hunt picked up his ComLink and pressed the blue button. "All right, get me the audio guy down here to go over the 911 tape, and make sure he's the best." He hung up.

"I did the research," Hunt continued. "Al Qaeda could not have done this. They do not have the technology, the military intelligence, or the resources to plan or pay someone to do it without us knowing about it."

"All the reports say you are right," Hughes agreed. "Anthrax, yes. This . . . no. I can't see Al Qaeda with this kind of surgical precision. And those bastards would have been on TV with this by now."

A moment later, a man in dirty jeans and a black sweatshirt walked into the room.

"All right," Hunt instructed without introductions, "tell me what you hear." Hunt pushed Play.

"911 emergency," he heard through shouts, screaming, and chaos.

"The people are petrified," the audio specialist stated.

"I know there are federal agents in this building," the mechanical voice started. "If one of you even attempts to get a promotion this morning, you will die, as well as three hostages per attempt! Don't try us!" The voice was mechanical, raspy, and inhuman.

Gunshots were heard.

"An automatic weapon," the specialist started, closing his eyes. "None—"

"That's definitely the Rex," Hughes cut in.

"Sixty!" A robotic voice.

"Hello?" The emergency operator.

"Rewind that part," the specialist requested.

Hunt stopped and rewound the tape, pressed Play again, then stopped it, ready for an analysis.

"He ran out of bullets," the specialist said, frowning.

"What?" Hunt asked.

"Whoever is shooting that Rex thing just ran out of bullets, like an asshole. I heard the slide lock back."

Hunt was halfway impressed.

"That's one of the problems with the Rex," Hughes remarked. "It's the most convenient and portable fully automatic weapon around, but it runs out after about six seconds of continuous firing."

Hunt pressed Play again.

"He hasn't got another clip in there yet," the specialist said after a second. "Someone is trying to take him down."

"Hello?" the 911 operator asked. "Is anyone there?"

"Will she shut up?" The specialist mumbled, as if to himself, "Somebody was pushed into something heavy, but movable, a table or something…papers flying." A high-pitched series of rapid bursts were heard.

"TH-7000," Hughes reported.

"Man fighting for his last breath," the specialist said, carefully concentrating.

Something in the background was mechanically uttered.

"What was that?" Hunt asked as he rewound and played it again.

"He called him 'stupid,'" the specialist answered.

"One hundred!" came across in a much clearer voice.

"Obviously, the phone call had been made near one of them. Someone was pretty brave," the specialist said. "Door opening, gunshots, a special ops, semi-auto."

"Albert's gun," Hunt realized.

"Someone falling hard onto the ground surface near the caller," the specialist continued.

"One of them was shot?" Hughes said out loud.

A loud barrage of shots was heard, but above all, they heard the dentist's drill.

"TH-7000 was fired," the specialist reported.

The connection suddenly got terrible as Albert started to shout something.

"What is he saying?" Hunt yelled.

"I can't make it out; the connection is too weak. I heard 'stop,'" the specialist answered.

Hunt stopped the tape. "Why have Albert's words been taken out? Who has had this tape?"

Hughes answered, "No one. The scrambler Albert had in the office scrambled the cellular frequency when he opened the door. Now that the scrambler has honed in on the cellular phone signal, it's jamming it. Nothing else will be audible. The cellular phone must have been several yards from the scrambler, with a closed door blocking any transmission. When the door opened, that freed the scrambler's search waves."

Hunt pushed Play, but all that was heard was static. He cursed. "Listen to the parts you can hear again until it makes you sick. Make sure you get everything."

The specialist reached over to rewind the tape and started to play it again.

In West Virginia, Kalisa Leonilla curled up in her bed with an American paperback novel. Her bookshelf was full of books she really couldn't care less about. It was for show, as was her job as an employee at the Fairfax County Recreation and Parks Department. Kalisa Leonilla lived an atypical life as Jennifer Johnson, the everyday American citizen.

She closed her eyes and thought about her office, and suddenly it changed.

She had to hurry. She had only a minute left. She was looking for the letter from Mr. Ward's concubine. She looked in the desk drawers, being careful not to move anything out of place. Next, she looked in the trash can. Where could it be? It had to be in here. She turned toward the bookshelf and scanned the titles on the higher shelves. *Principles of Our Economy*. It seemed boring enough. She pulled the book down from the shelf, leafed through it, and then tried another, being careful to put the books back in order. Finally, she found it. Kalisa unfolded it to be sure, shoved it down into her bra, put the book back on the shelf, and was out of the office.

She took the stairs to avoid meeting anyone. She had learned several years ago never to take the elevator if at all possible when on a covert job, as many government agencies—the CIA, for example—kept records of who got on the elevator, when they got on, at what floor they got off, and if they broke normal habits. The stairs were safer in most cases. She had long ago learned to study a camera's angle and could adjust her walk to casually hide her face. She exited the stairwell and returned to the lobby with a smile.

Mr. Tarner was waiting for her, and he was not smiling. He angrily snatched the paper from her and began to yell.

"You are the clumsiest girl I have ever met!" The trainer yanked her hair and led her back up the four flights of stairs, pulling her hair tightly. "Look at this mess!"

She looked around but could find nothing wrong.

"Look in the trash! What was on top of the trash, Jennifer?"

"An apple core," she replied, standing firm.

"What is there now?"

She looked in the trash. The apple core was nowhere to be found.

Mr. Tarner reached around inside the wastebasket and found the apple core.

"Now you will eat this!" he shouted. "That will teach you not to forget. And what is this? You want to put the books back in any order you want?"

"I didn't put each book back where I found it?"

There was a nasty grin as Mr. Tarner pointed to *Principles of Our Economy*. The book was in the right place, vertically, with the title facing out, but the title was now facing the left, not the right.

"You will die for certain if you do not learn this! Everyone else has! Try it again. Go back downstairs and try it again. It will be harder this time, and I will be watching you again. Now eat."

Kalisa's mind drifted to two members of her team, Team F, the Special Forces Team; the captain, Zlata Olimpan, was the only other female within the covert organization. Olimpan was assigned this name because of her acrobatic ability in combat. She could maneuver and twist her body in and out of many unnatural angles very quickly, like an Olympic gymnast.

F-4 was Aleksander Straz, the "tail" of Team F, which matched his name. He was responsible for covering the group during evacuations and escapes. He knew he was not to exit the operation site until all members were safe. Kalisa liked that Straz took pride in protecting the rest of the team.

The first ring of the phone brought her out of her reverie.

She reached over and picked it up. There was a dial tone. She snapped awake and anticipated the callback.

Like clockwork, the phone rang again.

"Hello?"

"It's me, sweetheart. I still love you." That was the code phrase. It was them.

"Hello, baby. I'm flattered, as usual." *What do you need?*

"Do you have panties on?" *Do you have company?*

"No, sweetheart."

"I need to see you. I miss you so much."

"Didn't I just see you two nights ago?"

"That night was so special. I need to see you again, please."

"I have to work."

"I need you, Jennifer; please don't do this to me. We still have a lot to talk about."

"We didn't do a lot of talking two nights ago."

"It'll be different this time, I promise. I need to see you."

Kalisa paused. "Okay, Johnny, when?"

"Tonight." *Two days from now.*

"Tonight?"

"Yes, Jennifer. Tonight. I miss you so much."

"I'm in bed."

"Get up and come over here."

"The things I put up with your ass. Do you have condoms?" *Do you have everything we need?*

"Yes."

"Then what time should I be there?"

"As soon as possible, sweetheart."

"Give me a time, please. You know how long it takes for me to get beautiful again."

There was a pause. "Just get here before 6 a.m., please. Don't have me waiting for you all night, woman." *Noon.*

"I wouldn't dream of it, baby. You better be ready."

"I'm waiting anxiously."

"You're at your apartment, right?" Kalisa confirmed.

"No, meet me at the same place we met last time."

"They probably know our faces by now."

"First name basis, baby, but I wouldn't have it any other way. Confusion is one thing we don't need in our relationship. Hurry up."

"I'm on my way." With that, Kalisa, aka Nightshade hung up and began to contact her team.

Another assignment had been issued, and she had been sent forth to serve in it. Two days from now, same place as last time, the Sheraton in Columbia, Maryland. It was less than two minutes from Interstate-95, which ran between Baltimore and Washington, D.C. It was the most convenient escape route ever. Columbia was a neutral, quiet spot, and even though the hotel was on MD Route 175, it was only a few miles from the state police barracks. They all liked this because the police in Columbia and its neighboring cities, Jessup and Laurel, were more concerned about harassing minorities than stopping any real crime.

In his Pennsylvania apartment, Reuban Zyablikov did "whippers," a drill he had learned in the Pit—ten push-ups, then as quick as his body would allow, he flipped over like a dying fish and did ten sit-ups, then repeat the process until he had done 200 of each.

The phone rang. He stood up and walked into the kitchen toward the phone. He didn't want to, but he had to. Hearing the phone stop after one ring, he knew the deal.

The phone rang again.

"Yeah," Zyablikov mumbled.

"We have to talk about our relationship."

"There is nothing to talk about. I'm finished with you."

"May I see you one last time before you put me out of your life?"

"Give me one reason."

"Because I love you." It was urgent, as all his assignments were.

"Really. How much?"

"I need you to come so I can show you. You're hard, aren't you?" *Company?*

"No."

"So I'll see you tonight? Same place."

"You know I just got home."

"Dennis, I need you."

"With you, I really don't have a choice, do I?"

"No, Dennis, you don't."

Zyablikov sighed. "I forgot the number of the apartment."

"Sixteen. Hurry, sweetheart." *Bring Teams A and F again. Hurry.*

"One last time, woman."

Zyablikov hung up the phone and began to contact his teams.

CHAPTER 4

"Greg," Hughes reported, "I crossed the people who have had access to the Rex with the UB list. There is one match—Janet Ford, one of our research scientists."

Hunt picked up the ComLink, pressed the blue button, and spoke: "Get someone on Janet Ford. I want to know what she has for breakfast, which way she combs her hair, the color of her vibrator, and how long she stays in the shower. Activate the phone taps on all of her addresses and any of her significant others' addresses."

"Yes, Mr. Hunt," came the reply from the other end of the ComLink.

Hunt looked at Laurence Acclaim. "Get all the info you can dig up on Ford."

Acclaim nodded.

Hughes picked up his ComLink and reminded Acclaim to dial with his thumb and activate the scrambler with his left hand. Hughes had to keep his right hand on the ComLink. If the hand didn't match the handprint-scanning grid on the grip of the ComLink, it would shut off and send an alarm to headquarters. Special CIA members were issued a ComLink, and due to the hand grid, no person could activate a grid that was not issued to them. Hughes was programming a ComLink for Acclaim. After Acclaim had been given a tutorial, Hughes issued one to him.

"Any intelligence on the Rebellion?" Hughes asked.

"They say the Rebellion hasn't made any moves, and the sources are reliable," Acclaim replied.

"What about the other groups?" Hunt asked.

"I really doubt Ali Baba and his men came from Libya and planned this whole thing in nine hours." Acclaim was referring to the Libyan terrorist group the Ironmen. "And the Longhorns would have

53

robbed everybody dry. They would have taken the printing presses with them. And as far as Al Qaeda, we all know this doesn't fit their method of operation. None of this does. Those organizations are good, but they're not that good. They can steal lots of money, blow up planes with innocent people on them, kill U.S. nationals, take hostages, and form alliances with terrorist governments, but they *could not* gain access to both Russian and U.S. top-secret weapons. The odds of any of those organizations acquiring sources within the highest ranks of the CIA *and* Russian intelligence are astronomical. I don't believe we have found our suspects yet. I know for a fact that none of the suspect organizations have combined forces. That would never happen without our knowledge."

"The Rebellion or Al Qaeda could have had our leak and then had Russia give them their weapons to help with the job. Remember, they could have been here in time because they were already here. They had the opportunity, the knowledge, the financing, the connections, the motive, and the ability to disappear afterwards," Hunt proposed.

"It still doesn't fit," Acclaim argued while turning the ComLink to its receiving mode as Hughes had taught him. "For every job that Al Qaeda or the Rebellion carries out, it's like they want to make some big point. We all know about September 11ᵗʰ, now let's examine the Rebellion, for instance. They're a very shrewd organization. Do you remember during the Olympics when their bomb went off? We fixed the story so the bomber was an amateur, and nobody got worried, and everybody stayed at Centennial Olympic Park for the games, bought millions of dollars' worth of memorabilia and paraphernalia, and the economy flourished. Great story. Most of the people went home happy, and sooner or later, the press forgot about it. So did those who were not there. No one even remembered that the real bomber wasn't caught. But some security guard was splashed all over the news as the prime suspect. If you had any idea how angry Baker got, you would know that he likes taking credit for his work. Not meaning he would admit to doing it, but in some way or another, he would let *us* know he did it. In the late 1980s, when the Rebellion was first surfacing, they were behind the Anita Hill and Clarence Thomas ordeal. They had gotten to her and exploited her to tell the White House that minorities don't belong in the Supreme Court, and he let us know he did it."

"How?" Hughes asked.

"He sent us a card," Acclaim replied.

"A greeting card?"

"Yes. It stated, 'Anita Hill Rebels against sexual harassment.' On the card, the word 'Rebels' was underlined twice. Since the organization was new, it took me some time to put it together. There was no return address and no fingerprints on the letter or the envelope. This is, of course, to remain classified," Acclaim reminded him. "Remember the Rodney King incident? One of Baker's guys was videotaping. Baker tried to blackmail us and threatened to mail the tape to the media if we didn't give in to his demands. Of course, you are aware of our country's policy not to negotiate with terrorist organizations, so he mailed the tape in, and there was hell to pay, but still, he let us know he did it. Do you remember Monica Lewinsky, the magical intern? She was on his payroll. Clinton wanted to pay him off, but he was asking too much, and Clinton thought he could cover it up. When he didn't pay, Monica opened her mouth, and Bill Clinton became one of the only presidents in our nation's history to be impeached. Heavy price to pay for a blowjob."

"I agree," Hunt said. "I hope it was decent. I don't see why Baker would want the plans, anyway. He sticks to domestic political terrorism. He only goes overseas for financing. You think he wants the plans to sell them? Or to blackmail the Russian Federation?"

"I don't think so," Acclaim answered. "He loves to blackmail, that's his specialty, but all this for a paycheck? He would have to risk Russia refusing his offer, then it would be all for nothing. His forty men couldn't be stupid enough to blackmail a country with nuclear capabilities comparable to ours. And he would have to know that with the Russian mafia so strong over there, they would be looking for his throat. On top of that, he would be on the run from Russian cutthroat intelligence agencies, in addition to powerful American agencies."

"Baker didn't do it, nor did Al Qaeda," an authoritative voice said from the doorway.

All three heads turned to face Walter Plack. He was in blue jeans and a navy-blue sweatshirt. He looked like vengeance in the flesh.

"Why do you say that?" Acclaim asked him.

"It's classified," Plack growled.

"I thought we were—"

"Where is your boss? Still on TV telling the nation how he will solve this case single-handedly when he should be checking the backgrounds of all the members of the crime scene. Chances are they had help from the inside."

"I didn't know he was going on TV, Walter. I don't like him very much, but I know he's passionate about protecting our country from any threat. He is also capable of getting the job done."

"He's got a big mouth. It is not his job to address the nation. It should have been one of the administrators, but I'm not worried about him right now. I'm worried about you. I checked you out, Acclaim. You're an outstanding agent, but a rookie in this area. Why did Wallace pick you for this case?"

"I requested it…with diligence. He agreed, along with my supervisor, that I had plenty of experience in the field as well as behind the desk. I am an expert in espionage and organized crime in addition to being highly experienced at collecting information in matters pertaining to national security."

"What about terrorism and counterintelligence?"

"I am not an expert in those areas, but I'm a quick learner. The fact is, I do not want to be where I'm not wanted. An operation cannot work successfully without total cohesion among all of its workers. An investigation like this is doomed to fail if everyone does not work as a unified team. Are we in agreement?"

"Yeah," Plack mumbled.

"So if my services are not needed, I will request to be off this case immediately."

"Why don't you do that," Plack growled. "Take Bruce and Sideshow Bob, and   "

"Wait a minute, Walter," Hunt interrupted. "Acclaim was with you from the beginning. He was saying that Baker was not responsible for the episode this morning. I believe having two agencies in this is better than one."

"I agree," Hughes put in. "I don't know about Bruce or the other guy, but Acclaim here is legit. You just said you checked him out yourself and found he was outstanding. I'm all for kicking Bruce to the curb, though."

Plack looked into the men's eyes, one by one. He turned to Acclaim. "I see you've made quite an impression on my colleagues, Laurence Raymond Acclaim. What do they call you?"

"Only the bad guys call me Laurence. You bad guys can call me Ray."

"You need to know our agency leads the operation. You will keep matters of national security between us four and no further, including Bruce." Plack gave him a stern look.

"Walter, this is not the first time I have been asked to hold information pertaining to national security from other agents. It will not be a problem."

Plack looked at Ray long and hard. "Can we trust you with our lives?"

"Most definitely, Walter. I have sworn an oath to protect my country."

"All right. He stays," Plack decided.

Hunt proceeded to tell Acclaim the real story and explained to Plack what he had missed.

The next morning, Plack woke up to his beeping ComLink. He threw his covers off, got up, and grabbed the ComLink off the dresser. The morning radio blasted the story of Valentine's blundered kidnapping but mentioned nothing about the alleged helicopter plans.

Before Plack could wonder where his wife was, he smelled fresh bacon in the air and heard eggs frying as the aroma of Belgian waffles floated to his nostrils, teasing them like a naughty schoolboy would a runt.

Plack returned his attention to the ComLink. He picked it up, and in less than two seconds, the handprint grid matched his hand to its program. The ComLink then rapidly flashed the green "okay" signal twice before returning dormant. The Link informed him that he had a message from Acclaim.

"Walter, I have the information on Ford. It's waiting for you on your desk. She looks pretty clean from the paperwork, but Hunt put two men on her, two on her husband, and one on her teenage son. I also checked her bank accounts and got her tax statements from the Internal Revenue Service. Copies are on your desk, along with my comments, but they don't show anything unusual. No outstanding purchases recently. All bills are normal. Utilities and phone bills have been paid via her account. I compared the checks she wrote with confiscated electric bills and phone bills from the respective agencies. It looks as if she assigned her checks the exact amounts she was billed. There were no unusual overpayments or refunds coming her way. I checked the husband out. Carl Ford. He takes care of the rent and both car notes, it seems, while she takes care of the utilities. Nothing suspicious in his accounts, either. I also looked for steady increases or a lack of withdrawals for a suspicious amount of time. As you probably know, when someone deposits an amount of money that is over our designated limit, the bank lets us know via phone or through the computer. We've never been notified about them before. Everything looked okay, but you can never tell in this game. I'll let you know about the son by this afternoon, but I've been up all night, and I've got to get some rest. See you in a few hours."

Three rapid red flashes indicated the message was over. Plack pressed the "repeat" button and listened to the message again. There was no need to store it. He pressed a red button and removed his hand from the grid, erasing the message.

He walked downstairs and greeted his wife with a good-morning kiss. She looked lovely in her pink pajamas.

She mixed the eggs with the whisk while sprinkling herb and garlic spice in the pan. She had fried only the whites, as usual, just as he liked them. The yolks were nothing but cholesterol, and he definitely didn't need more cholesterol.

"Good morning, honey," she greeted, giving him the long, tight hug he needed. He sat down at the kitchen table and saw she had laid the paper out for him. He looked at the first page. "Yuklivitch Coming to America," it read. Plack knew his wife had kindly removed and discarded the real front page that read "CIA Agents Slain in Washington Post Massacre, No Suspects."

He started to read the article. "Prime Minister Epifanii Yuklivitch, head of the Strategic Offensive Reductions Treaty Commission, has announced that he will come to America on April 8 to continue the SORT talks and to negotiate a mutual agreement, and further strengthen the argument that Russian military forces had no part in the botched attempted kidnapping of Dorian Valentine. Valentine was murdered when her struggles became too violent to be contained. Yuklivitch also plans to address the U.S. general public at an undisclosed location and time to explain the SORT Commission's full intentions and to assure every American that the alleged 'Operation Black Fox' was totally fabricated, and to deny any allegations of the existence of any secret project of the sort." Plack flipped past the article of Arnold Schwarzenegger being elected as the governor of California and read about the Environmental Protection Agency investigating Elite Nuclear Arms Production Corporation for improper disposal of nuclear waste.

He forgot about nuclear waste when the waffles were put in front of his face. Sharon put syrup and butter in the center of the table and then set her plate across from his. They prayed together before they ate.

"Walter, I will help you get through this any way I can," Sharon Plack promised, looking into her husband's eyes.

"I know, Sharon."

"Is there something I can do to help now?"

Walter shook his head. "I feel like there's a hole in me somewhere."

"My heart hurts to hear you say it. You'll catch the monsters. I know you will."

He pushed back his pain. "You bet."

"I went to see Lisa last night. She was hysterical. The kids aren't doing well, either. I'm going back over there in a little bit. I'll see if I can do anything useful at their house since I know you're going to the office. Please call me if you need anything, I mean anything at all. I'll be at Lisa's."

Plack nodded. "The waffles are delicious."

"Thank you."

"No, thank *you*. Thank you for everything."

Special Agent Bruce Wallace and his colleague Special Agent Marcus Thorn conducted a thorough research of the two night-shift security guards at the *Washington Post*. They examined bank accounts, property, and all other assets and purchases. They looked for periods when the guards' accounts remained dormant and cross-referenced everything with the Internal Revenue Service. They each checked into the accounts of immediate family, friends, parents, and former classmates. They found nothing suspicious, but Wallace decided on an interview anyway and sent for both of the guards.

Wallace had the tape of his little soliloquy last night with the president safe inside his desk. Every word he had uttered yesterday after the President spoke was archived on videocassette. He couldn't wait to watch it and see how he looked. *Professionally smooth,* he assured himself. *Or did I look like a serious, self-confident businessman?*

The media had plastered Yuklivitch's visit to America all over the newspapers and radio, but Wallace knew the SORT talks were now on hold. There was no way the president was going to sign anything until it was clear whether the choppers existed or not. And if they did, it would be another Cuban Missile Crisis, but on a higher scale. If the Russian Federation exploited the SORT in an attempt to disarm the U.S. before launching an attack, there would be serious repercussions. Wallace understood that post-nuclear weaponry was expensive to build. Engineers did not get together to construct post-nuclear helicopters because they had nothing better to do. If the helicopters did exist, there was a reason, and until the investigation was wrapped up, there would be anything but peace. Wallace was also smart enough to know that Russia did not create this technology without serious help.

The day after his brother's wake, Walter Plack sat on his bed and started to cry again. He felt the ComLink vibrate inside his suit pocket. Like clockwork, his wife left the room while he locked himself in the master bathroom and pulled the ComLink out. He pulled the scrambler out from the cabinet beneath the sink and activated it. It was Gregory Hunt with the results from the in-depth security guard interviews. Both guards were clean. Hunt also reported that the International Atomic Energy Agency refused to sanction a full investigation of any Russian facilities since no evidence of Operation Black Fox could be furnished and all Russian facilities had passed their last inspections.

"I do have some good news," Hunt added.

"I could use it."

"They're not trying to take you off this case. As a matter of fact, they want you on it."

"That is good news. It still doesn't change the fact that we can't tell the President that we're going to war because two civilians think they saw helicopter plans. The editor in chief told us himself that he had never seen helicopter plans before. Valentine could possibly have made them up to get a story. Personally, though, I don't think she did. We need something concrete. Any news on Valentine's source?"

"Nothing on her phone records or e-mail. She was discreet with this one. In her house, we found a passport, but there is no record of her having left the country recently."

"Stay on it. Any fingerprints at the *Post*?"

"Nothing. No fingerprints anywhere."

"Get on Valentine's family and whoever she called in the last two weeks. Valentine liked to talk. She had to tell someone something."

"I'm on it."

In the darkness, Oleg Lugor pumped iron like the madman he was. Another assignment this soon was not necessarily out of the ordinary, but then, nothing was ordinary in his life. He lifted faster, quickening his breaths. His arms started to burn, and he liked it. After ten more pumps, he sat up. Still in the dark, he maneuvered over to his chair, sat down, and then flicked on the TV with his remote. He flipped through the channels and adjusted the volume without looking down at the buttons. He didn't use the channel-up or channel-down buttons. He picked random numbers in his head and turned to that channel without looking down. He surfed faster. His thumb moved like lightning over the buttons, not missing one number. Going in order was too easy. He kept all the numbers random, and when he had hit every number from 01 to 99, he gave the remote a quick flip in the air. After it rotated in the air once, he caught it and pressed the power button.

The room was dark again, and he drifted.

The next morning it was announced that Prime Minister Epifanii Yuklivitch was going to speak outside at the White House, and Plack still didn't have a suspect he truly believed had plotted the operation and his brother's murder. His brother's funeral was scheduled a half hour before Yuklivitch's address, but he really didn't feel like hearing the lies construed for the public. The messages on his ComLink informed Plack that there were no solid leads yet. The security guards at the *Post* were clean. Acclaim had reported that Ford's son was clean, and he had even led the search two days ago on Valentine's premises, which turned up nothing. No valuable information yet on Valentine's family or coworkers. Valentine had developed the pictures herself and left neither negatives nor any recordings of any interviews with her source.

Where the hell could she have gotten those plans? Plack wondered. He couldn't exactly ask Moscow who had access to them, for they would deny their existence.

He thought about his own classified sources, who had informed him that the Rebellion was definitely not behind the *Post* incident. He kept his fingers crossed that he would hear from them again soon.

At the White House, the Secret Service was taking every precaution to ensure that Epifanii Yuklivitch remained safe throughout his address to the nation. There was a bulletproof cage constructed of impenetrable but transparent semi-glass. Men were on rooftops all over the block, positioned at designated angles that had been marked as primary sites for snipers, and at any angle where a bullet might ricochet into Yuklivitch. Pennsylvania Avenue and the surrounding streets had long been cleared of angles and areas where a sniper could get a decent shot, and vast open areas surrounded the White House for the Russian's protection. Undercover agents were abundant in the crowd, eyes keen for certain activities they had been trained to spot, along with uniformed officers who provided the usual crowd control. All streets and back roads had been blocked off, and all detours had guards posted. Men with binoculars scanned the crowd well, looking for anything out of the ordinary. Helicopters circled the crowd from above.

As news crews arrived, a man tested the microphones and made sure the sound worked adequately. After several moments, the chairman of the SORT Commission walked out onto the steps of the White House. He gave a friendly wave to the crowd, and the audience applauded. Secret Service agents were beside him, along with his own bodyguards. Underneath his black trenchcoat, just in case, Yuklivitch wore bulletproof body armor.

The big Russian stepped inside the large cage, which did not have a back, and greeted his audience with a warm smile.

"Good evening, my American friends," Yuklivitch began in his thick Russian accent. "It is a pleasure to speak to you this afternoon on behalf of my country, and on behalf of the Strategic Offensive Reductions Treaty Commission."

"A-1, report." Zyablikov spoke into his jumbo coffee mug, standing among the crowd. He wore a dark blue baseball cap with dark sunglasses. He had a long brown wig on top of his head that draped brown hair around his chin. He reminded himself of a '70s' hippie, but it gave him the harmless aura he needed. It was a decent disguise.

"In position," Lugor replied.

"It brings great sadness to our country to hear of the incident in this very city, at your renowned newspaper, the *Washington Post*. I have come to dispute the vicious misrepresentation of Russia's intentions."

"Nightshade, report."

"In position," Kalisa replied.

"I am here today to clear up all unauthenticated reports of Russian activity in constructing war machines...*any* variety of war machines."

"A-3, report."

"A-3 in position, Iceman," Demitri Liutoboets replied.

"Furthermore..."

"A-4, report."

"Ready," Gremis Nukludko replied.

"Go on my mark."

"The Strategic Offensive Reductions Treaty Commission rebukes any and all false accusations brought upon us. I have brought Bruce Wallace from the Federal Bureau of Investigation to testify that, indeed, no alleged plans have been seen by *any* eyes *ever,* at *any* point in time."

"Commence."

Suddenly, a thunderous explosion was heard a distance from the White House. The audience collectively flinched, and all heads turned away from Yuklivitch to face the source of the deafening eruption.

Nightshade pulled the trigger of her Z-M Knight Field Weapons CZ200 rifle. Because the target was so far away, she couldn't tell if she had hit it. Simultaneously, Liutoboets pulled his trigger. These two shots were not bullets and were not meant to kill, but to break through the cage.

"A-1."

Within a second, Lugor had pulled the trigger of his high-powered rifle and swiftly sent a bullet through Yuklivitch's throat, splattering blood all over the cage. Lugor packed up while men rushed into the cage. The crowd gasped as a staggering Yuklivitch fell to the ground with half of his neck no longer attached.

It took only three seconds from Zyablikov's command to assassinate Epifanii Yuklivitch. Zyablikov was the mastermind of the whole operation, standing four yards from a plainclothes police officer. His usual wrist microphone was inside his large coffee mug. When he wanted to send an order, he took a "sip." He heard every reply through his wireless receiver, hidden in his ear, and saw the assassination with his own eyes.

"Two," Zyablikov instructed a second before the second bomb went off, sending the police further away from Lugor's position. Lugor was the only one who had to worry about escaping. The others were already more than a mile away, mingling with the pandemonium. Olimpan was to pick up Nightshade; A-2 was to rendezvous with Lugor; and Iake Tatomir, A-5, was to pick up Liutoboets. Zyablikov himself was to pick up Gremis Nukludko, A-4. This inconvenience was to ensure that all members remained oblivious to all other teams. All rendezvous vehicles were yellow D.C. cabs, except for Zyablikov's. He rode in a Taurus, which was the perfect car to blend into the city.

Plack stared in disbelief at his television screen inside the limousine as he rode to his brother's burial site. Epifanii Yuklivitch had just been assassinated on the steps of the White House. There had been a shooting in front of the CIA headquarters quite a while ago, but comparatively, this miniaturized it. Plack remembered Mira Aangi Leigh, the Pakistani female who shot five people with an AK-47 assault rifle, leaving two dead and three wounded on the steps of the CIA headquarters. But an assassination on the White House porch? Absolutely unthinkable.

The priest said a solemn prayer over the coffin as they lowered Albert Plack's body into the six-foot hole. At the same time, a fragile woman suited in all black slowly made her way to Albert's mourning brother. She wore a large black hat that matched the black veil covering her face and complemented the long black gloves that came to her elbows. Walter Plack saw no signs of familiarity in the figure walking toward him. As the elderly woman approached, he saw she carried a card in her hand. Without speaking or looking up, she placed the card in his hand, then strolled off much more swiftly than she had approached. Briefly, even through the black gloves, Plack's keen senses had noticed the woman's hands were rather thick and healthy for an old woman. Just as suddenly as she had come, she was gone off in the distance. His wife opened her eyes from the prayer and looked at him with wide eyes that asked him gently, "Who was that?"

Plack shrugged and looked at the letter in his hands. It was a sealed, unmarked white envelope. After the priest finished the prayer, everyone opened their eyes and lifted their heads. Plack discreetly opened the envelope and pulled out a small, store-bought, blue card. On the outside, it read "Sorry For Your Loss." Plack opened the card, and on the inside, in typewritten black ink, it read, *"No Bakers, No Butchers."* There was no signature. Plack stared at the letter for several moments before finally understanding it. He quickly made a second scan of the area for the woman.

She had disappeared.

CHAPTER 5

After his brother was buried, Plack jumped on his ComLink, and as he guessed, even on the day of his brother's funeral, his Link overflowed with messages regarding the assassination. There was one from the man in charge, the Director of Central Intelligence, Arthur H. King, demanding an emergency meeting in one hour. Plack kissed his wife and was off. He brought the letter from the mysterious woman with him.

An hour later, he was in Langley, Virginia, at the CIA headquarters in the spacious office of the head of the Central Intelligence Agency. Also in the office was Clarence R. Bishop, the Deputy Director of Central intelligence, who was second in command of the CIA. Next to Plack were Gregory Hunt and his friend Bryan Hughes.

King was enraged. Plack had not seen King this infuriated since September 11th 2001, almost two years before.

"Listen. We have the nation going crazy here, and Russia is asking questions we can't answer! The chairperson of the Strategic Offensive Reductions Treaty Commission comes to discuss peace and gets his neck blown off on the steps of the White House! What kind of fucking operation are we running here? Two days ago, an unknown organization infiltrates our country and steals back Russia's helicopter plans while murdering several of our best agents, leaving one in the hospital with third-degree burns over his body! And all Intelligence can report is that it was the same organization! If we don't put an end to this, I will have to inform our president that he cannot go to Russia to sign the SORT, which will put us at DEFCON 3, if it doesn't start a goddamn cold war! Terrorism will not be tolerated. Tensions are already high with the alleged helicopter plans, and the assassination of Yuklivitch on our front porch multiplies them tenfold. Instead of having SORT talks in a week, we will be going to war. Russia does not forgive and forget when it comes to their diplomats. Now, all field intelligence reports the probability of Russian military behind these two incidents is minimal, so find the organization that is behind this and neutralize them immediately!"

"This case is highly unusual," Hughes started. "Intelligence is giving us nothing, nor is the council. The FBI is—"

"The FBI? The last time I checked, we were an independent agency. We don't need the Bruce Wallace Show aired over every channel with him singing about what goes on in our operations! What does this look like, Hollywood? Who authorized this joint operation?"

"I did," Plack answered. "The mayor called Bruce down, and he was at the crime scene before I was notified."

"The mayor? Does the mayor run this country now? I don't want Bruce *near* our operations. Let him feed the public by himself. You will find this terrorist organization without the Bureau's welfare, and then take care of them, ASAP! Your career with this organization depends on it. I don't care how you do it, find them! I authorize any means necessary."

"Sir, I have a request," Hughes said.

"What is it, Hughes?" King snapped without an ounce of patience in his voice.

"Agent Acclaim from the FBI has been of crucial assistance to us in our operations regarding the *Washington Post* incident. He has been briefed in full and has been an enormous asset to our investigation thus far. I request he be able to continue working with us. He has been thoroughly investigated and has experience in many useful areas such as espionage and organized crime."

"Whatever has to be done, do it and do it now!" There was a grave look on King's face. "I have assembled the best case officers we have, and they are all downstairs, waiting for a full briefing. You gentlemen are dismissed. Get back to me in two hours with an update. Clarence, stay here for a moment."

Bryan Hughes, Gregory Hunt, and Walter Plack exited while Bishop stayed behind in King's office. King gave Bishop a solemn stare.

"Yes, Arthur," Clarence said.

"Tell me this is not AVLIS," King pleaded.

"If this chopper exists, that would explain how its weaponry remained undetected for so long. However, it's still unknown at this time whether the Black Fox armaments were created by the laser isotope separation technology, Arthur. My concern is also who the real brain is behind this monster. Russia hasn't been a true threat in quite a while. In its current state, Russia couldn't have completed this without serious financial and technological assistance."

"Good point. And the Persian threat?"

"The news isn't great. They're gathering in strength. As long as we stand behind Israel, we'll be a major target."

"Bishop, I don't need to tell you what's at stake here. We need you to do what you do best. I've assembled the best agents we have in the briefing room. They are waiting for you."

Bishop nodded before walking out of King's office where Plack, Hughes, and Hunt were waiting. They all nodded to each of the security guards and headed toward the briefing room.

"Greg, this is nothing personal, but I am escalating this matter to a different kind of level," Bishop started. Bishop was notorious for his brusque disposition. He naturally intimidated many people very easily without any effort. Bishop also didn't care who he infuriated to get the results he needed to safeguard the integrity of Homeland Security. "All aspects of this case are now classified for the highest level of clearance. I have to remove you from this case immediately. If you are needed, you will be contacted."

Hunt was shocked. "Clarence, what are you talking about? I've been with the Agency for nine years. I have the highest clearance available."

"Gregory, this is honestly not the time for your crying. I have no choice. I understand your frustration, but now I have been forced to call in a higher power to resolve this bloodbath of carnage and political mayhem now upon us. I cannot expose you to what is going to happen next."

"With all due respect, Clarence, I know I can be an asset to the investigation. Bryan has only been with the agency for five years, yet you have decided to include him." Hunt turned to Hughes. "Nothing personal against you, Bryan. No offense intended."

"No offense taken," Hughes replied.

Bishop did not change his glare. "Greg, usually your hearing is pretty good. In case you've been in the Dark Ages for the past 48 hours, let me clue you in to this unholy mess that is now directly in my lap and bigger than my erection, Hunt. I have unknown terrorists within our national borders who are butchering their way through our beloved nation's capital with top-secret weapons, dusting off anyone who is not with their program. Their exhaustive list of public executions includes everyone from a *Washington Post* reporter to the distinguished prime minister of a nuclear power and anyone else they're moved to touch, including our own agents. This has nothing to do with your ability to do the job, Greg. It has to do with confidentiality. I am keeping Hughes because his knowledge of the secret weapons used is essential."

"What about my knowledge of this morning's incident?"

"Plack has the same knowledge. And I suspect he will be pursuing this matter with a certain motivation. The fact remains, I must remove you from this case. Effective immediately. I could have told you now or sent you an e-mail later. It's nothing personal, Greg. You're a capable agent. It's just that, with the assassination of Yuklivitch, things have gotten extremely heated. On the route I have chosen to take, I can only take the necessities with me. It's vitally important that what is about to happen be spread only amongst the absolute elemental personnel. King is not to be included, either."

"I'd like you to please reconsider, Clarence," Hunt protested.

"Greg, you see those funny-looking things on the side of your head? Those are ears. Yours are not working today, so maybe you can read lips. It. Can't. Happen. I have already said entirely too much."

"Let me know if you need my assistance," Hunt conceded.

"I will."

Hunt turned and walked off down the corridor toward the elevator. Bishop could tell he was not happy, but maintaining the interest of national security did not always satisfy people. Hunt was a good man, but the confidentiality factor that was about to be applied to the situation prevented Bishop from bringing anyone into the circle who wasn't absolutely required.

The three remaining agents walked inside the room and fell into an odd silence. The best case officers the agency had were assembled in the room to tackle the most momentous case in the nation's history. Every case officer was anticipating this briefing like a child did Christmas Eve.

Bishop spoke first. "All right, gentlemen. That will be all. Dismissed."

There were murmurs of confusion.

"Excuse me, sir?" one of them asked.

"I thank each and every one of you for your dedication, but this matter is going to be taken care of in a rather unorthodox matter. Your cooperation will not be needed."

All the officers stood up and walked out, not hiding their disappointment.

"What was that all about?" Plack asked Bishop as the last officer had shut the door behind him. "That was the best squad of officers that I have ever seen assembled in one place. They even pulled Harrison from France for this assignment."

"Gentlemen," Bishop started, "I have known each of you since you have been inside the Agency, and I am honored to say that I trust each of you with my life. So I will tell you this case is of more significance than you want to know; therefore I am calling AEGIS."

"AEGIS?" Hughes asked. "I've never heard of it. What is it?"

"Alpha Emergency Global Initiative Sector, also known as the Alpha Sector. They represent the last link between a post-nuclear holocaust and ourselves. This matter is definitely classified as an Alpha-level emergency. The agents you are about to meet do not exist, nor will they exist after this assignment. Any attempt to verify or research these agents will bring about the offender's demise. Is that clear?" Bishop asked with an icy grin on his face.

The men nodded.

"Does King know about this?" asked Hughes.

"Arthur King is a presidential appointee, not a company man. There are many things that he does not need to know and will never know. In and out of office in four years, the president himself sits his narrow ass down in the Oval Office and does what I say after I advise the Council. I have been in this position for 28 years, and this operation will go as I say. Disobedience will not be tolerated—that must be understood."

Two nods.

"Bruce stays away from the operation, along with Laurence Acclaim. No one outside of this circle will be exposed to any information regarding the Alpha Sector. Not under any circumstances whatsoever. Any outside leaks will be dealt with accordingly. The games are over, gentlemen. AEGIS has been called, and when they arrive, things will be like they've never been before."

Half an hour later, Plack, Hughes, and Bishop were still inside CIA headquarters, awaiting the arrival of Alpha Sector. They sat together, watching the news and discussing the mysterious card that had been given to Plack at his brother's funeral. There was outrage in Russia. The Russians across their Commonwealth of Independent States believed that Yuklivitch was assassinated by U.S. operatives in retaliation for the assumption that Yuklivitch was covering up Operation Black Fox. All over their newswires were old quotes from different top U.S. officials stating publicly that Yuklivitch should be punished for building a new war machine while at the same time pushing through the SORT. What nailed the coffin shut was an illegal tape recording of military personal discussing "the need to neutralize the situation immediately." There were announcements from Russian officials stating the SORT Commission was disbanding immediately. All American members were to be sent back to the United States third class, not to return "until a satisfactory conclusion could be reached." In short, Russia was heated.

"Russia is also very quietly mobilizing troops and positioning defense satellites," Bishop stated. "I got the report a half hour ago."

"Mobilizing troops for what?" Hughes asked.

"Just in case."

"In case?" Hughes responded.

"If we do go to war, their men will already be in place to take over specific regions and commandeer certain territory, crippling us. Considering how many troops they've moved and where they've stationed them, they are probably not going to strike unless prompted to. The fact that they're doing this quietly says something. The civilians don't know troops are being positioned, but if the media gets hold of this, they'll eat it up. What will tell us the story is what they do when they find out we know they've moved troops. If they keep moving them, that's not too good," Bishop explained. Hughes nodded as he looked back down at the puzzling card that had been handed to Plack at the funeral.

"'No Bakers, No Butchers'?" Hughes read, puzzled. He opened his laptop and rapidly punched keys, running the phrase through his decryption program. After a few minutes, he looked up. "It's a negative on the Alphamorphic and Polymorphic codes. The program also ran it through the more popular Beale code keys and came up with nothing."

"It's not a code," Plack replied. "It's a clue. It took me a while to figure it out, but when Greg gave me the suspect organization list from the National Security Council, I remembered the nickname from the Ironmen."

"What are you talking about?" Hughes inquired.

"Do you remember what George H. Bush called the Ironmen organization after the Pan Am bombing?"

"He called them butchers," Bishop recalled. "In front of the entire Council, he announced that he wanted 'these butchers caught and brought to justice.'"

"No Butchers, No Bakers. Robert Lawton Baker leads the Rebellion. The card is saying that neither the Rebellion nor the Ironmen had any part in this."

"You're going to eliminate our top two suspect organizations because some lady gave you this card?" Bishop asked. "I would rate this information D-minus, totally unreliable, and it should not be considered."

"No, Clarence. This information matches the intelligence from my class A-plus sources. Therefore, this source is rated B and is somewhat reliable."

Hughes's ComLink suddenly erupted. He picked it up, waited for the hand grid to authorize him, and began speaking. As he listened to the speaker, his eyes got wider, and his face dropped.

"I'll be right there," he muttered, hanging up. "That was the weapons specialist from the Yuklivitch crime scene. It looks like we've got a lot more trouble on our hands than we thought. They have requested me personally to go down to the crime scene. I think it's best that I depart for Washington immediately."

"Agreed," Bishop nodded. "AEGIS will be arriving any minute, but introductions can wait if necessary. Bryan and I will depart for Washington. Walter, get there as soon as you can." Picking up his ComLink, he informed Hughes, "A helicopter will be waiting for us in ten minutes."

Garret stared Devin in the eye.

"How did the operation go?" Devin asked.

"Clockwork, as always. Do you doubt me after all this time?"

"Casualties in Team A?"

"Zero."

"Casualties in Team F?"

"Zero," Nightshade reported, "and all teams remained unaware of any other teams in the vicinity."

"Excellent. Dismissed."

Nightshade and Zyablikov exited the room one at a time and returned to their separate but identical lives. They wanted to hug each other, but they did not even glance in each other's directions once they were out of the room.

Clarence Bishop rose to his feet as Alpha Sector entered the room. There were no smiles, for each of the highly covert agents knew for a fact that, if they had been called, things were far from a laughing matter, and even further from under control.

The Alpha Emergency Global Initiative Sector consisted of six personnel: five exceptionally trained first-rate men and one woman trained to the same superior degree.

"AEGIS, meet the Executive Director, Walter Plack. And this is Bryan Hughes, Director of Science and Technology, also the head of our research development lab. Bryan and I have been called to D.C. regarding the assassination of Yuklivitch, so you will forgive us if we skip formal introductions."

AEGIS was silent.

"As I explained before, Walter, the Alpha Sector does not exist. Get back to me in one hour with your progress, and every hour after that. Gentlemen, I have a chopper to catch." With that, Bryan Hughes and Clarence Bishop exited the room.

All looks on the faces of the AEGIS team were serious, and they did not look like a group to be careless or adverse with. As Plack briefed AEGIS on the situation, he looked the Alpha Sector over.

They all stood in a horizontal line, erect, healthy, and about business. They seemed to grin with contempt at Plack, as if they felt that, since they were called to the scene, someone couldn't do his job. They spoke no words but communicated to each other with discreet body language.

Plack scanned the group for the leader. Could it be the smaller one, with his neat beard and nice blue-and-silver tie? He looked like the aggressive, loud type, yet he listened intently to Plack as he spoke.

The tallest was a handsome man dressed in a gray power suit. He looked the true athlete and highly intelligent. Plack observed the subtle conceit in the smirk on his face, like that of a chemist sitting in on a high-school biology class.

"And as you all know," Plack finished, "Clarence and Bryan went to gather the intel on the White House incident. Now, forgive me for my ignorance of your group's capabilities. Please introduce yourselves and your specialties."

"We don't have specialties, director. We *are* a specialty," said the one he presumed to be the leader.

"And your name, sir."

"Jackal. Don't call me 'sir.' I work for a living. You sound like a dangerous amateur."

Plack looked Jackal over again. Average in size, and yes, he could see a contemptuous smirk on his face under the serious grin. Black hair, black eyes, and the skin on his face was smooth. He was about 5'9", but his ego made him a good nine feet. They shook hands, and then Plack moved to the next AEGIS member.

"Vadar," the 6'6" black man greeted in a deep voice as he shook hands with Plack. The grip was firm, though not necessarily friendly.

Vadar looked Plack in the eye and did not remove his hard grin until Plack looked away toward the next agent.

"Sparrow," the woman uttered without smiling. She had black hair like Jackal, and there was an air of masculinity about her. Sparrow's handshake was firm, and, like Vadar's, not necessarily receptive. She wore no make-up, no jewelry, and her nails were not dainty. Her navy-blue blouse gave her the attitude needed to exude that total I'm-as-bad-as-the-fellas-and-I-will-kill-you-just-as–quickly aura. She wore glasses, but they were probably fakes. Her eyes were beautiful, but he was careful not to stare at them too long, as she did not seem friendly. He could easily picture Sparrow killing on a moment's notice, and the atmosphere that hovered about her made him uneasy.

He moved to the next one.

"Hammer," the biggest of them said dryly while shaking hands. He had a larger build, seemed to be in shape, and was apparently not the type to be bumped into in a dark alley past midnight. His handshake was nearly bone-crunching. Plack flinched. Hammer had a serious mood about him, as if he had never laughed in his life.

"Jester," the next one announced. He was smaller than the rest of his team but did not seem in anyway a weak link. His grip was as firm as those of his team, and his tone was equally unfriendly.

"Felix," the last one muttered. He had on thick glasses but looked like he could handle himself as capably as the rest of them. His voice seemed slightly annoyed and definitely conceited. He was likely the type who had worn two pocket protectors in junior high school.

This was definitely not the most receptive group Plack had ever met. There were no smiles, no laughter, no talking, just hard stares from the Alpha Sector.

Back at his apartment, Zyablikov stretched out on his sofa, thinking about what possible rationale his country could have had for eliminating one of their own diplomats. He had been on stranger assignments, but they all made sense to him in one way or another. He knew Yuklivitch was a former KGB agent. In the underground world of espionage, "cleaning up" within your own boundaries was allowed, as long as it was done quietly. This operation was clearly not quiet. While he had acted upon direct orders, he somehow felt strange.

Kalisa Leonilla walked into her home and instantly knew something wasn't right. She backed up into the doorway and looked around the room without moving. There was no sound. She stealthily walked to her closet door, looking all around for movement of any kind. She reached under an old sweater on the coat-closet shelf and grabbed her Schuetzen Pistol Works Renegade, making sure her eight-shot magazine was loaded.

She crept into the kitchen. Everything was in place. She listened again—nothing. She crept back into the living room and noticed her remote on the coffee table beside the loveseat. She noticed the DVD player remote was on the right, and the television remote was on the left. She always put them the other way around. She turned on the television to find that the channel she had left it turned to when she departed had been changed. Without packing, she hurried out the door, looked back every three seconds, got in her car, and drove off.

Moments later, a man walked from out of the bathroom and became angry when he realized his target had just walked out of his zone. Frank Tortigla cursed as he zipped up his pants. He suddenly became worried, as the boss was highly unforgiving. In order to save his own life, he would have to tell the boss that Jennifer Johnson never came home.

An hour later, Zyablikov received a phone call.

"Hello."

"Dennis, this is your cousin James. Remember me? James, from Boston."

"Of course." *It was the Spymaster.*

A frightening sensation came over Zyablikov.

"I'm in town. I was going to come see you, but I forgot how to get there."

"It's good to hear from you," Zyablikov lied. He knew a call from the Spymaster only meant trouble. Heavyweight trouble. "Where are you now, James?"

"Where do you think?"

He looked out of his window, and, sure enough, there was a black sedan, waiting.

"I remember the place. I'll be right there." With that, he hung up and walked outside.

In Washington D.C., Bryan Hughes was about as shocked as he had ever been in his life. Instead of being mesmerized by the organization's ability and intelligence, he became frightened that such an organization could exist.

"Get everyone to Washington immediately," Hughes instructed Plack through the ComLink, "and on the way, pray that the Alpha Sector is something supernatural, because we're going to need a miracle."

Beyond the sirens, the yellow tape, and the news vans, a man watched Hughes from the distance. The man had no real identity, no past and no present, but he existed in hopes of a future.

He analyzed Bryan Hughes's every move. Every step Bryan took informed his observer more and more about him. The way he walked now told the man that Hughes was scared but trying to hide it. The observer blended in with the evening atmosphere in black, ragged jeans covered in dirt; a green jacket, filthy and unzipped to reveal a black T-shirt. His unkempt beard and bushy mustache matched those of the homeless individuals along the avenue, who clutched their precious wine bottles, their only way to escape their grim reality, before they came back down and faced their nightmares.

The night was mildly chilly, but he didn't feel it. He sat down on the bench and observed Hughes further. Some might call him skinny. Most would deem him average height. From his position, he looked about 5'8", give or take a little.

It was easy to spot Hughes because of the glasses, and the man already knew what Hughes looked like, so he didn't need to look through his tiny binoculars. He lay down under his newspapers while he watched Hughes talk with other people and become further frustrated. When the man was satisfied, he got up and left, leaving his newspapers on the bench for the next vagrant to savor before the beat officers came and pushed everyone along to wherever. As the stranger walked into the darkness, he decided that Hughes couldn't handle it.

CHAPTER **6**

Zyablikov sat in a sparsely lit room in an unknown location. The temperature was mild, but the atmosphere was grim and icy. There was silence throughout the room. He saw no carpet, no windows, and he heard no sounds that gave him a clue as to where he was. His left cheek was burning. He had just been hit across the face. His eyes adjusted. Standing in front of him, he saw, were Devin and a man he had seen only once before in his lifetime—a man he had hoped he would never have to see again. The man had appointed him to watch Devin. He was the powerful individual in charge of their whole operation: Spymaster Boris Kapitnov. Zyablikov was sitting in a chair, unrestrained, unarmed, and unaware of the situation in which he was now drowning in the nucleus of. The Spymaster and Devin both looked terribly furious. It was no secret at whom their anger was directed.

Zyablikov had no memory of how he had arrived at this current location or how long it had taken. As soon as he stepped into the sedan, he was sprayed in the face with an unknown substance. He had had more than three seconds to fight back, but he knew he would not be alive now if he had put up a struggle. No words had been spoken, yet he had a distinct feeling he was in trouble for something. For what, he did not know. He had, after all, executed both assignments exactly as planned.

He knew the men were not worried about the federal agents who had been killed in the Valentine mission, nor the extra minute it had taken to grab the helicopter plans. He thought further and realized that if he had been kept alive, there had to be some missing aspect of the case. Otherwise, these two heartless men would have already eliminated him. Because he was still alive, he knew he had a chance of leaving this room, but he also knew that if the Spymaster himself was there, something was horribly, severely wrong and the entire organization was compromised because of it.

Zyablikov was sitting, while the two men stood over him. As he looked in the shadows, he recognized Vladimir Yakof lurking menacingly in a dark corner. At any other time, he thought of Yakof as his friend A-2; but, at that moment, Zyablikov considered him the enemy.

"Strip," Devin coldly uttered.

A puzzled look came over Zyablikov's face as he hopelessly looked at the head man for a sign of humor. There was none. Slowly, Zyablikov removed his jacket and shirt, then unbuckled his pants and took them off. He stood before all three men in his boxer shorts and a white sleeveless T-shirt.

"All the way," Devin commanded.

Zyablikov again looked at Kapitnov for any sign. Kapitnov had a monstrously unfriendly glare on his face. This was no joke.

Zyablikov slowly removed his T-shirt and underwear and stood before his audience as naked as the day he was born. Vladimir emerged from the shadows, scooped up Zyablikov's clothes, and exited the room.

"Put these on," the boss said, tossing him some shorts and a T-shirt. Zyablikov put them on while Devin and Kapitnov watched carefully.

Outside, Vladimir Yakof threw Zyablikov's clothes into a huge canister of water and drenched them thoroughly before taking them out again and laying them on a white counter. He took out his enhanced magnifying utensil and his pocket metal detector, and started searching.

"What's going on?" Zyablikov asked.

No one responded. Zyablikov already felt uncomfortable with no underwear on. His testicles dangled freely in the lukewarm air that rushed up his shorts. The silent treatment furthered his discomfort, but he kept his face passive.

"What the hell have you done!" Kapitnov shouted in Russian. He stepped forward and smacked Zyablikov's face. Zyablikov pretended it hurt.

"What do you mean?" Zyablikov asked in English. Zyablikov had no knowledge of the Russian language through which to respond. He could scarcely understand what the Spymaster had yelled and had interpreted everything by the Spymaster's tone of voice.

Zyablikov continued. "I have done only what I was told! What is the meaning of this? Abducting me like I'm a traitor."

"A traitor you are!" Kapitnov shouted, this time in English. "Do you have any idea what you have done?"

"I have always followed orders. This has not changed since I was placed in America."

"No one told you to assassinate Epifanii Yuklivitch!" Devin shouted, slamming a fist into Zyablikov's gut. Zyablikov saw the attack coming and thwarted its impact, but not too aggressively, so that Kapitnov would see that Zyablikov was simply defending himself and had no intent to counterattack.

Outside, Yakof continued his search for any wires, microphones, microtransmitters, homing devices, or microreceivers hidden in the threading of Zyablikov's soaked clothing. The water had been to disable them. He had not found anything on the shirt and jacket. He quickly started on the pants, checking each button and each belt loop. With scissors, he cut open all the garments to check for internal devices, then ripped off all the buttons of his pants and put them in the pile with the rest of the buttons he had removed.

Zyablikov's tennis shoes remained soaked in the canister water, but Yakof saved the search of the shoes for last. He knew that anything could be hidden inside the rubber soles, including explosives.

Devin kept coming at him and screaming like a madman. Zyablikov dodged every punch Devin threw while Devin yelled on about Zyablikov's treachery.

"I am not a traitor!" Zyablikov shouted to Kapitnov. "I was given orders to assassinate Yuklivitch!"

"By whom?" Kapitnov shouted back.

"By the tactical officer you appointed to assign *all* missions—Devin!"

Devin came at Zyablikov once again, still shouting. "That's a lie, traitor! You will die for your treachery. Whom do you *really* work for?"

Devin stopped swinging and resumed his stance beside Kapitnov.

"I will ask once," Kapitnov stated with authority. "Whom do you work for?"

"I work for you, and no one else."

"Why did you assassinate Yuklivitch?"

"I was given direct orders."

"By Devin?"

"Yes."

"When was this?"

"The same night the Valentine assignment was executed. I received a call. Usual code phrases were used, and I communicated with the contact person through rehearsed methods. The contact responded to all phrases accordingly, and Devin personally gave the debriefing. The weapons we used were placed in Safe House Four, the same one from the Valentine assignment."

"You are a filthy liar, and you will die for your betrayal," Devin muttered nastily.

Zyablikov had to give it to Devin; he was a good actor.

"Do you have any evidence of these accusations?" the Spymaster asked.

Thoughts ran through Zyablikov's mind like lightning. The phone call had not been recorded, no one traveled with him, and there was no documentation for the assignment, as expected. All the weapons were already in his possession at the safe house in Annapolis, Maryland. The briefing and debriefing had both been oral, and Zyablikov himself had contacted the team members. He had but one hope…Kalisa.

"Yes."

"And where is this evidence, Garret?"

"It is a witness. Nightshade was present during the debriefing and had to be contacted also. She will tell you the assignment was taken on direct orders."

"Devin, where is Nightshade?" Kapitnov asked nonchalantly.

"She has disappeared. I tried to contact her to see if she had anything to do with the incident, but she is gone. I assume she is in Canada by now."

"Find her!" the Spymaster barked. "If she has breached the perimeter without our authorization, she will be punished as well!"

"We have already started looking for her, Boris, but who is to say that when we do retrieve her—and we will—that she will not lie for him?" Devin turned toward Zyablikov before finishing. "I know that you two have grown quite close."

"You have no honor and no code. It is you, not I, who will die," Zyablikov replied.

Devin turned toward Kapitnov. "She cannot run from us. As I stated before, a search is already underway. We are doing everything we can to locate Nightshade."

And indeed, they were.

"Garret, where is Nightshade?" Kapitnov asked Zyablikov.

"Director, I have not seen her since the last assignment. Contact with each other is forbidden."

"You do not have to remind me of the ordinances I established," Kapitnov sternly replied. "However, be aware that right this minute, agent A-2 is checking every millimeter of your clothing, and if he finds so much as a metal paper clip within the threads of your clothes, you will be executed in this room. I'm sure you know what modern technology has allowed one to do with wires, microtransmitters, and clothing."

Garret nodded. "Sir, if Devin is leading the search party, she will never be found. He will find her and kill her. She is the only one that can put Devin in his rightful place as a traitor."

"You have a quick mind, bastard," Devin retorted. "Do not try to claim innocence if the search comes up negative. She has been taught to disappear, but we shall find her anyway. If the search comes up negative, you alone shall be dealt with. Breach of the assigned perimeter is a much lesser crime than treason. You have already admitted it, you have spoken with your own words that you have killed Yuklivitch and started another Cold War."

"I made no actions without direct orders."

The Spymaster glared at Zyablikov with a terrifying scowl. "Your story is weak, and it is very convenient that you cannot find your only witness. Perhaps you gave her a reason to run, no?"

Garret wanted to rush Devin on the spot and snap his neck with his bare hands. It would take less than six seconds, but killing a senior officer carried a punishment worse than death.

"Let me lead the search. I will find Nightshade," Zyablikov pleaded.

"That's preposterous," Devin argued. "If we give him permission to leave his assigned radius, we will never see him again, and if he and Nightshade performed the assignment together, they will be overseas by sundown, Boris."

The Spymaster was silent as he thought. Devin had all but convinced him that Zyablikov was guilty. The Spymaster believed that if he gave Zyablikov permission to breach his perimeter, they might never see him again. Zyablikov was the best weapon on the planet. It didn't accomplish much to have him killed or incarcerated. If Devin was indeed a traitor, he needed to know. Either way, he needed all the facts. He couldn't have them both lead the investigation.

Zyablikov pleaded, "Director, how in the world would Devin find someone who was created to strike, then disappear? I have learned everything she has learned from the same instructors and have taught her a few tricks of my own. She would trust me to bring her back here alive. I would be more than happy to report directly to you. I have one request before you make your decision."

"What is that, Garret?"

"I myself am curious to learn why my colleague has departed so suddenly. When I find her, she may be anxious about coming back due to the consequences of breaching her domain. I ask that you grant her amnesty for this violation, deeming that her rationale for leaving is satisfactory."

"Agreed."

Devin was insistent. "Boris, I have already started the investigation. Team C is out searching as we speak."

"Team C?" Kapitnov asked. He knew that information regarding Team C—its activities or members—was to be held from Zyablikov. And he knew that Devin knew. The Spymaster leaned close to Devin and growled quietly in his ear, "You have the three Americans looking for our agents? No wonder she is gone! She probably spotted all of them while she was sleeping!"

The Spymaster now had potential reasons to doubt Devin. The man had exhibited a level of carelessness right before his eyes. While he awaited the results of the search of Garret's clothing, he would, even if only temporarily, offer Garret his support.

"Dennis, you are granted permission to lead the search. You are to get back to me with a full report every three hours stating your exact location and any and all information found regarding Night-shade's whereabouts."

"You're letting him go alone?" Devin protested. "At least wait until we finish checking his residence and clothes."

"Indeed. We will wait until the examination of his property is complete. As for the search, he will most certainly not go alone. He will take two members of his choice from Team A, and you will choose the second two men from whichever team you see fit. Commence the search immediately after the clothing inspection concludes if I see everything is satisfactory. Garret, you are responsible for all four agents. Make sure nothing happens to them."

"As always, Director."

"Devin, take Team C off the assignment. Now," the Spymaster instructed quietly.

"It will be done," Devin replied.

"Garret, you five are to expedite this assignment. The longer it takes, the more suspicious I get."

"Boris, do you think it wise to mix the teams?" Devin cut in. "You know, for security reasons, all teams need to remain unaware of each other."

"Garret, there will be no contact between the teams. After the initial arrival, each pair is to be separate. You will handle this, no?"

"Yes, Director."

"Two cars will be waiting for you. You must tell each pair that they are not to communicate with each other. Is that understood?"

"My men hold national-security issues inside their heads. I know they can forget about two strangers," Zyablikov replied.

"There is to be no contact between the teams," the Director reiterated. "And when you find Nightshade, she is to be brought back immediately. If I get any reports that you plan to do otherwise, I will come find you myself."

"That is crystal clear, Director."

"Garret, who was involved in the assassination of Yuklivitch?"

"Teams A and F were called."

Kapitnov nodded.

"In closing, I simply have this to say," Zyablikov stated. "Only two people know how to contact me. That is Devin and yourself, through Nightshade. Only two people can contact Nightshade, and that is, once again, Devin and yourself. There was no way to plan and execute the assassination, then escape clean with only one team. Are we in agreement, Director?"

"Yes, go on."

"To perform the assassination with Teams A *and* F without authorization, I would have had to contact Nightshade, and I have no clue how to do that. By your design, I don't know where she stays. I don't know what state, what number, what street, what zip code, what area code she lives in, nothing! So how could I have possibly established contact with Nightshade without authorization?"

"Do not try to silver tongue the Spymaster, traitor. You used one of your own teams for the assassination. Team B or D!" Devin yelled.

Zyablikov looked at Kapitnov. Devin had no idea that he had suggested that Zyablikov had performed the assassination with the Covert Intelligence Group or the Marine Combat Team.

Kapitnov paused but said not a word. Nor did he throw a knowing glance at Zyablikov.

"Garret, bring her to me alive, and soon."

Vladimir Yakof entered the room with a note, handed it to the Spymaster, and exited quickly. The Spymaster read the note. No devices were found in Zyablikov's clothing; and the men searching Zyablikov's residence had found nothing unusual.

The Spymaster spoke to Zyablikov again. "In two hours, Devin's two members of the search team will be at your house. The others you choose will meet at a location that I will give to you later. They will be in a second car. You are dismissed."

Without a word, Garret exited the room. He did not ask them to return his clothing.

Sooner than any civilian would think possible, AEGIS was in Washington D.C., along with Walter Plack. They were in a small room inside the White House, seated, facing Bryan Hughes. There were no smiles. Hughes was operating a large overhead projector. A huge screen covering the wall was behind him. He raised a laser pointer.

"Ready for class?" Jester mumbled to Jackal.

"I'm ready for anything," Jackal replied.

"All right," Hughes started, "I'm happy you all could arrive so fast, because time is of the essence. I have assembled you to examine the method of execution used in the Yuklivitch assassination. As you know, Yuklivitch was behind a cage constructed of bulletproof semi-glass, which had been thoroughly tested. No known bullets could have penetrated the shield. What we did not count on was this organization using a combination of bullets. First, they weakened the shield, and then they sent the kill shot. There were three different shots sent out. The first two shots were from this rifle."

Hughes activated the large overhead, and a large black rifle appeared on the wall-sized screen.

"This is the Knight CZ200, also known as the Cool Hand," Hughes explained.

AEGIS recognized it instantly, not needing the introduction.

"It is a liquid-projectile, high-powered sniper rifle. Its range is unsurpassed. The weapon can be fired with superior accuracy from over 1200 meters away, thus allowing the marksman to be sufficiently invisible from his target, making him difficult to locate, allowing the sniper to fire a shot, then escape quickly. The Cool Hand will be used in the future by several branches of the U.S. military such as the Army Rangers, Marine Corps Recon, and Navy Seals. Any questions so far, gentlemen?"

"There's a female here, too," Sparrow interjected, glaring at Hughes. Her grin was heavy and evil, unlike any glare he had received from anyone else.

"Sorry," Hughes said, apologizing. "Do you have any questions, Sparrow?"

"No," Sparrow replied. Her voice remained cold and unfriendly.

Jester felt like yawning out loud. Had his whole sector been dragged down here for a review? Each one of them had used the rifle at least eight times.

"Now the first two bullets that were used are known as the Ice Maiden, a liquid-filled small round." Hughes took the image of the rifle off the screen and replaced it with a labeled bullet. The dull gray bullet was shaped like half of a frankfurter. "The Ice Maiden is composed of frozen liquid nitrogen with advanced molecular breakdown kept at minus 196 degrees Celsius, which evaporates into its colorless, odorless, gaseous state shortly after discharge. As you can see from the screen—" Hughes activated his infrared pointer and continued, "The bullet has four main parts inside the casing." He pointed to every part with the laser as he discussed it. "The primer is in the rear, and the powder is in the back lower quadrant. The front bottom quadrant contains a bi-density polymer to keep the nitrogen intact until impact. The Cool Hand refers to the unique clip that can keep two rounds at the required minus 196 Celsius for up to six hours. Of course, the existence of the Cool Hand clip and the nitro rounds has never been officially confirmed. We have attempted to use the Kennedy Assassination Tool to line up the angles from where we think the shots were fired, but with only one point of impact, it is difficult to tell, considering the kill shot splattered everything."

Hammer signaled Hughes.

"Yes, Agent Hammer?"

"Not Agent Hammer. Just Hammer."

"Okay, what is your question, Hammer?"

"How is it that you can assume there were only two shots?"

"We can assume there was more than one shot because the space shattered on the shield was too large for only one round of the nitro bullets to handle. But, as you are stating, more than two shots, indeed, could have been fired, but I have a personal hunch that there were only two. This organization is the best I have ever seen, and I believe they would know that only two shots would be needed. Another sniper would be increasing the risk dramatically. The risk-to-benefit relationship would deter them from placing a third sniper on the grounds. It wouldn't make sense. As you six know, the Knight is a notoriously loud weapon. They set off the explosives to cover the sound while at the same time creating a spectacular diversion. The audience, the Secret Service, *and* the news cameras turned toward the explosion. No news crew even got the impact on tape for us to analyze. Again, a third shot is indeed possible, but highly unlikely. If I were a betting man, I would bet my house against it. Did I answer your question, Hammer?"

"Yes, you did."

Though no facial expressions had changed within the Alpha Sector, all six members sent discreet undetectable signals to each other approving of Hughes's answer. It was well thought out. He did not dodge the issue as most would if they didn't know, and his explanation proved his expertise in his field. He had scored points with AEGIS, which was not easily done. Vadar closed his eyes and, without moving his body, swiftly faced Hammer and turned his head back toward the front within a quarter second, telling Hammer, "Good job." The six had known the answer to Hammer's question before he asked it, but if they were going to be working with anyone outside of the Sector, they were going to test them thoroughly.

"About the kill shot," Hughes continued, switching the screen to a different rifle, also shown life-sized. "I believe it was the seven-millimeter Parabellum bolt-action rifle, nicknamed the China Doll. It is so nicknamed for its porcelain bullets, and it defies its delicate nickname with deadly force."

Hughes took down the image of the China Doll and replaced it with that of another deadly looking bullet that resembled a small rocket with a spiked tip. It hurt Plack to even *imagine* the bullet entering any part of him. The rocket was a goldish-bronze color and about the length of an ink pen.

"Its sleek and slippery design allows it to penetrate human flesh with brutal accuracy. However, upon impact with hard surfaces like brick, concrete, or steel, the bullet shatters, leaving no point of impact. As a result, bullet trajectories are extremely difficult to determine."

Jester signaled Hughes.

"Yes, Jester?"

"As I'm sure you know, the Germans invented the Doll during World War II as part of an effort to manufacture alternate munitions. After the war, the Germans established the Doll as a covert anti-persons rifle. As I'm sure you also know, Hans Badenburg is a former BND agent. Do you think the Longhorns were behind this assassination, or is this a feeble attempt to lead us astray?" Another test.

"Jester, I do not think it is either of those options. And you're right, during World War II, the Germans created the Doll, but ultimately, porcelain munitions were too expensive to make, and they were ineffective against hard targets. After the war, the Doll was reestablished by the BND. Even though our friends the Germans have been known to screw things up royally, they have no motive whatsoever for the assassination of Yuklivitch. Considering the condition of their political arena, performing any operation within our boundaries without our direct permission would be suicide. I can assure you our Public Enemy Number Four had no part of this—and you knew that before you asked me. Now, as for someone trying to give us a bounce in the wrong direction, it is not likely. If the Longhorns were behind this and wanted to stir things up, they would have used the nine-millimeter Parabellum, one of Russia's Sugar Daddies."

Hughes put the picture of the 7 mm Parabellum back on the screen. "The Doll can only be effectively shot—with accuracy—from no more than 500 meters away, even if you're the best. I would like to offer that the marksman was 400 meters away simply because he couldn't risk missing. This was a risky operation. If he was off by any more than two inches, the bullet would have shattered against the shield, and Yuklivitch would have been surrounded before the sniper could get another shot off."

AEGIS was impressed again but kept it among themselves. In half a second, without speaking, Vadar told Jester he could have picked a better question.

"As you can see, gentlemen and lady," Hughes started, being careful to eliminate the sexism in his address, "this organization is highly professional, well trained, well organized, and well funded. Keep in mind that the official location and time of the Yuklivitch address was not reported until six hours before Yuklivitch walked out onto the White House steps. Their intelligence sources must be deeply rooted, so we leave nothing to chance."

"I have a question for the executive director," Vadar stated.

Plack stood erect.

"What is the status on Terrel Harris, the former Marine soldier who was interviewed in Langley? What was found in his background and the interview?"

"Nothing terribly revolutionary was found in Terrel Harris's testimony. He is now in witness protection, as recommended. During his background check, we found his record to be quite distinguished, and he was also assigned to several covert military operations during his tenure in the Marines," Plack told them.

Hughes took back control of the show. "For now, we communicate only with each other through these." He put up a transparency of a faceless human head with a small pill in its right ear. "You all know what these are: intra-aural transmitters, IATs. They are your connection to Headquarters and to the rest of the world. Communication is facilitated with high-frequency and spread-spectrum technology. Communication is piggybacked onto signals sent by our global positioning satellite. The code word 'headlines' automatically opens an exclusive channel to your colleagues. I have added two little bonuses for you. There is a homing device inside the IAT that allows us to track you anywhere in the world except under water. If, for some reason, you want to talk amongst each other exclusively while you all are within a 500-mile radius, the code word is 'silence,' and your communication from Headquarters will be cut off. Just shove these babies deep inside your ears and test them out. You will still be able to hear out of each ear, I promise, and the IAT does not cause irritation in the least. You won't even know it's there. I've often used it myself."

Hammer signaled Hughes. "That will not be necessary, Hughes. I think we have everything we need already."

"You might believe so, but let me brief you on the *Washington Post* executions. During their operation, they used a device known as the Vig-6, which is an SOL, a speed-of-light weapon."

"We know what it is," Hammer interrupted. "We haven't been issued them. Get us half a dozen."

"I don't even know if there are that many in existence, but I will do my best to get you guys as many as I can. They are still in the testing phase."

"What information do you have about the gas used in the building?" Vadar asked.

"Also a new technology. I've never seen anything like it," Hughes answered.

"Are you done talking?" Jackal asked.

"Yes, I am," Hughes replied. "Feel free to get to work."

"I don't like to think of it as work," Jester offered. "I like to think of it as heroism."

CHAPTER 7

As the same stranger who had picked him up dropped him off at his apartment, Zyablikov was trying to decide which two men to take on the search. He knew the men would definitely have to be from Team A because Devin would likely choose men from his teams. If Devin found Kalisa before he did, she would never be seen again. Devin knew she was on the move, escaping farther and farther away with every second.

He knew that Vladimir Yakof was following orders by searching his clothes and didn't have a choice in the matter; but the question was, to whom was Yakof loyal? To Zyablikov, who had guided him through countless successful missions with never a casualty? He had saved Yakof's life on more than one occasion. Or was Yakof's loyalty to the Spymaster? It wasn't as if he could ask around, for a question like that would signal mutiny. If anyone were to report it, Zyablikov knew he would be on the run for the rest of his unnatural life.

He would take Oleg Lugor. His friend's loyalty had proven to be as solid as iron. Zyablikov decided Vladimir Yakof wouldn't be of much help. Yakof was a master of computers and electronics, as well as encryption and decryption, but that wouldn't solve much on this one. Gremis Nukludko, A-4, was the explosives expert who had proven his expertise too many times to be remembered, including during the last masterpiece. Yes, he would definitely be a man to trust. A-5, Iake Tatomir, was the hand-to-hand combat champion, but Zyablikov knew that of all the fighting that might come up, he and Lugor could handle it. He decided on Demitri Liutoboets over Nukludko. Liutoboets, the "hard fighter" had an uncanny knack for taking down multiple enemies solo and had fantastic ability in the silent-slaughter department, especially using knives.

Zyablikov's phone came alive. It rang once. After the long pause, it rang again. Zyablikov picked it up.

"Yes," Zyablikov answered matter-of-factly.

"What was the score of the game?"

"Eleven to fifteen, I think. I left early." *I will take A-1 and A-5.*

"I only wanted the winning score."

"I thought you said you wanted me to write down both," Zyablikov pleaded.

"No, just the winner. Nothing else matters."

"Well, even though they had only eleven, they played like dynamite. The other team was playing dirty. Give me the hard workers every time." *I choose A-1, then.*

"I'm hungry. Meet me at the corner market on Seventh and Madison in two hours. A brown van will be waiting for you."

The connection ended.

Zyablikov cursed out loud. Why the change? Why couldn't he bring two of his men?

Zyablikov drove to 7th and Madison two hours later, and, sure enough, as soon as he cruised by the brown van, it took off behind him. In the night blackness, he tried to see who was in the van. Who did Devin pick? Probably men from his teams that Zyablikov had never seen before.

When they were alone in the night, Zyablikov pulled into an unlighted area and waited to see who would get out of the car. Without a word, Lugor got out of the van and joined Zyablikov in his car.

"How many men are in the van?" Zyablikov asked Oleg.

"Two," he replied.

Zyablikov hit the dashboard hard as he cursed loudly. Why had Kapitnov changed his mind? It had surely been Kapitnov's electronically altered voice on the phone, not Devin's, but he knew there must be a reason for the change of heart.

"Who was in that car?" Zyablikov asked. Lugor described the men he had been riding with: Rhyhor Karandei, F-2, and Viktor Nesignev, F-3. Strictly bad news.

It didn't make sense. Why did Devin choose two members from Nightshade's team to search for her? Why didn't he send someone from his own teams to make sure Nightshade was found? Was that a tactic to try to show Kapitnov that he had no part in Kalisa's disappearance? Devin knew that if Nightshade was found, he would be executed for assigning the Yuklivitch assassination without authorization, so why was he screwing around? Zyablikov suddenly choked up as he slowly realized that Kalisa might have already been dead, and Devin could not therefore have cared less who performed the search.

Why was Kapitnov suddenly not so picky about merging the teams? All of them knew that the teams were to remain oblivious to each other's presence. That was an ironclad rule. Yet, here they were in concert for a search mission. It didn't feel right. Zyablikov had already searched his vehicle for bugs and knew he could talk freely, so he began to ask his friend a few questions.

"We have to find her, Oleg. Do you know where she is?"

"No," Oleg replied, "but I know she would have not left the perimeter unless she had to. Do you know what this is about?"

"We have been sold out, friend. The Yuklivitch assassination was not a real job. Devin has sold us out," Zyablikov explained.

"Devin. That is the man you talk to before we leave to return home from assignments?"

"Yes. You have not seen his face, but he has seen yours many times," Zyablikov answered.

"Why did Kalisa run?" Lugor asked.

"I don't know, but she is my only hope to prove to them that I'm innocent of treason. I did not execute the assassination without authorization. What do the other two think?"

"I was briefed alone before I met up with the other two in the van. I don't know what the other two were told. The information given to me was that Kalisa had run, we are to find her and bring her back. Reuban, where are we going? Do you know where she is?"

Reuban's answer was unexpected. "Yes and no."

CHAPTER 8

Sparrow walked 400 hundred yards away from the White House steps. She looked out on Pennsylvania Avenue, deep in thought. The satellites had given no leads, and the surveillance open-air taps had picked up no pertinent signals. If the organization was truly as skillful as they were alleged to be, they would have known agents would be at every decent angle, even the possible ricochets. They would know that an awkward spot would have to be selected. An awkward spot. Sparrow put herself in the position. The porcelain bullet was sent through Yuklivitch's throat, so the sniper had known Yuklivitch would be dead before he hit the ground. She climbed up a nearby tree and positioned herself as she would when assigned sniper operations. Her Hawk was clumsily strapped around her shoulder, but she easily maneuvered it in front of her face. She pressed the T-sights button, and the binoculars zoomed in to the White House porch.

It didn't feel right. This definitely was not the spot. She climbed down from the tree. It didn't matter if anyone saw her; she was well disguised. She looked like a white male in his late thirties. As she walked to another spot, she saw a vagrant quietly asleep on a bench. She had an idea. She walked back to the White House.

Felix thought hard. What motive would any organization have for killing Yuklivitch? The Russian mafia's arms black market would die if the SORT was signed, but the fact remained that they had no presence firmly rooted in this country. The world's leading nuclear-arms producer, Elite Nuclear Arms Production, would not be too happy with the treaty signed, either, but they could not have pulled that off without help. Felix suddenly remembered something—and snapped awake immediately.

"Walter, I have a question," Hughes said to Plack. They were alone inside an underground room in the White House. "How did you know that neither Baker, Al Qaeda, nor Ali and his men were involved in this? Back in the interrogation chamber, when you met Acclaim, you said it was classified. You knew even before you got the note."

Plack had known Hughes for twelve years, way back when Hughes was a lab rat. He knew Hughes could be trusted. Besides, he had clearance.

"NRO," Plack answered.

"NRO?"

"National Reconnaissance Office, one of the best-kept secrets in America. And it was *the* best-kept secret of Intelligence communications, until it was officially confirmed in 1992."

"They tell us about enemy territory and activity, too?"

"They supply intel through space and airborne recon. They use satellite technology to monitor global developments, like violations of arms-control agreements, and indications of military operations. The Air Force and our agency have a joint responsibility over the NRO. I know a member of the executive committee composed of both our agency *and* the Air Force. It's been around since about '81. Its annual budget for operations is over 250 billion dollars, a whole lot of money for something that didn't exist until '92."

"What did they tell you?"

"Apparently, Baker is getting ready for an assault overseas in Iraq. The NRO's satellites can see all of Baker's tanks over there in the desert, kicking up dust. There is no way he was over there *and* over here. One of the sats even got a close up of him pissing in the sand. Al Qaeda's moves are already heavily monitored by the NRO. They had nothing to do with this."

"How many satellites are up there? They have an agency just for the satellites?"

"Yup. There are countless satellites up there. We're running out of sky space. If you knew what was up there, you wouldn't walk out of your house."

"I've designed sats before. I know that many of them, especially the earlier models, have a limited lifetime. I know we don't go up there to get them. What happens when they malfunction or break?"

"They fall down, or float off into space. In fact, most of them float away."

"What about the ones that don't?"

"The small percentage that don't burn up in the atmosphere or fall into the ocean. Lucky for us, more than two-thirds of the world is covered with water."

"Well, how often does it rain satellites? Falling satellites sound like they might hurt."

Plack shrugged. "They fall often enough."

"So what happens to the ones that don't burn up and don't fall near water?"

"Oh, those? Those are your UFO sightings," Plack replied with a grin.

Hughes chuckled.

"Bryan, tell me some more about the speed-of-light weapons," Plack inquired.

"Well, what's not classified, I will gladly tell you. The Vig-6 is like a small handgun that—"

"No, not the Vig. I know all about the Vig already; it killed Valentine and Turner. I know the Vig is only the beginning. Tell me about the aerospace speed-of-light weapons, the ones the satellites are equipped with, and the ones in the Black Fox choppers."

Hughes took a deep breath. "We now have energy-pulsed lasers and particle-beam weapons systems that operate at the speed of light. At this very moment, we are spending billions to perfect what we have and discover and advance what we don't have. Are you sure you want to hear all this? It's something like a curse if you know too much. You lose sleep at night. At least I did. Then you get used to it. It's like you're living a nightmare."

"Go ahead and curse me. I'll call the witch doctor in the morning."

"Okay, sounds good to me. Compared to SOL weapons, the old ballistic nuclear missiles that travel at about 17,000 miles an hour are like slow-moving dinosaurs from a previous era. They are as inappropriate as the horse and chariot would be in a war today against tanks, and as easily eliminated. SOL weapons are best suited for space. The creator of the Vig must have realized this before risking the creation of a weapon that could get into the wrong hands. Besides the Vig, all SOL weaponry is present in the defense satellites. There are different kinds that operate in different ways, but all of them at the speed of light. Russia must have somehow found a way to get this technology into a goddamn helicopter. I honestly don't know exactly how they did it. I've helped to develop a global rapid-aiming and firing system that several hundred satellites are now equipped with. It locks onto multiple targets, firing up to fifty billion high-energy pulses in less than one second, each beam taking approximately a nanosecond—fifty billionths of a second—to get to its target. These are highly concentrated energy pulses. They are equal to a thousand missile knockdowns."

"Are you serious?" Plack asked.

"Deadly serious. And that's the old generation. The new, present generation drops the old into obsolescence, operating at the level of picoseconds."

Plack didn't quite know how fast a picosecond was, but he didn't interrupt Hughes to find out.

"Now comes the bad part," Hughes continued. "You have to realize the most serious consequence of the SOL weapons: They are entirely too fast for human comprehension, which is why we are hesitant to use them. We are accustomed to mechanized warfare and gun battles, but a war today would be a war of machines inconceivable to its participants. Machines would actually govern the moment-to-moment conflict that would last only minutes. With these weapons, a worldwide post-nuclear war, from start to finish, would be concluded in approximately three minutes."

"Three *minutes*?" Plack asked.

"Three minutes from start to finish," Hughes replied. "Several supercomputers would act and react at the speed of light, attacking, strategizing, counterattacking, analyzing, and exploiting the enemy's weaknesses. All at the speed of light. The computer tells the weapon to attack, and the SOL weapon strikes its target—all of this happens faster than we blink. Today's computers not only think for themselves but act for themselves, at the speed of light. Do you want to go further?" Hughes asked.

"I don't quite feel cursed yet," Plack responded.

"Such a war is only governable by machines," Hughes continued. "Human response times are ludicrously slow and would be preposterous to implement. Actually, they are too ridiculously slow to even be considered. World War III couldn't be a push-button war because it simply takes too long for a slow human to complete a keystroke. My statistics showed an average of 1.6 seconds for a human to press a button, an *eternity* in SOL warfare. One point six seconds? Walter, everyone in the state of Texas could be wiped out in 1.6 seconds. Cats, dogs, and coyote, too. We're just rocks."

"What do you mean 'we're just rocks'? Because we don't do anything?"

"No!" Hughes responded adamantly. "Because we *can't* do anything. It is not within our ability. In terms of war, humans are now officially stationary objects. We are absolute inanimate beings. A computer performs well over two million calculations in the time it takes man to blink. Therefore, knowing that computers and SOL weaponry will be fighting the next war, human beings will be totally stationary, unchanging objects … like rocks. Walter, just as no war in Earth's history has lasted long enough to be affected by any geological changes such as erosion, plate tectonics, or anything of that sort, presently, SOL wars would not *last* long enough to take into account the rate of human movement."

Plack was silent.

"Do you feel cursed yet?"

"Kind of, but this is interesting. A very riveting curse, indeed. Go on. And stop asking me if I want to go on. Tell me everything."

"Okay, where was I?"

"Humans are like rocks."

"Hey, thanks for listening. Well, this is only where the problem begins," Hughes explained. "Since humans are far too slow to react, it is now necessary to *totally* relinquish decision-making controls to the faster intelligence of computers. In short, computers of the future will not only govern every moment-to-moment decision of war but actually anticipate and initiate attack. Theoretically, if the computer believes its territory is about to be attacked after analyzing its opponent's moves, it may initiate a preemptive strike and, in the speed of light, obliterate millions of people. This would instantly start an SOL war because the other side will counterattack at the speed of light, given they are equipped with the technology. The war will last about three minutes, killing billions. Now, here's the quintillion-dollar question: What if the computer is mistaken? Billions will die before we even figure out what the hell went wrong, much less stop it. This is the speed-of-light dilemma we are talking about. Once we attack, the enemy attacks also, at the speed of light. And computers don't call truces, Walter. This is not tic-tac-toe. The computer will fight until the enemy is annihilated, or until itself is annihilated. The computer won't attack to 'teach the enemy a lesson.' Furthermore, if we decided to run the war at 'human speed' for our own protection, we would surely lose against any enemy with SOL technology. The only hope is to put *all* our trust in machines, making human values, judgment, morals, and thinking utterly obsolete." Hughes knew that World War III would be a war of technology—one that no one dared exert human influence over from fear of slowing the decision-making process. "This is why the SORT is so critically important. It's an agreement to end this."

Hughes was uncomfortable knowing that the fate of the world was placed in the lap of temperamental computers and satellites—which do indeed have a minimal probability of malfunctioning.

"Now tell me how anyone could manufacture the Black Fox choppers without us knowing about it," Plack said. "How can all the Russian facilities pass the scope of safeguards and inspections by the International Atomic Energy Agency and United Nations?"

"That's the scariest question I've heard, and it's the reason why the other side can so easily say that the Black Fox does not exist. I have my suspicions. However, I can only speculate like anyone else at this point."

Hughes turned his portable TV to the news. There, he saw a nightmare. The media had discovered that military troops across the Commonwealth of Independent States of the former Soviet Union had been mobilized, and they were broadcasting it all over the world. There were camera shots of grocery stores filled with people buying up canned goods and bottled water. The population was panic-stricken as the reporter embellished Russia's mobilization of troops.

Plack sighed.

Hughes tried to interpret the sigh but failed. "What's up, Walter?"

Plack answered, "Now we are going to have to respond to this by mobilizing our troops. Then they're going to have to respond by putting more troops on the line, and so on, back and forth. Sooner or later, there will be no more strategic placement. The next move will be war. This is a big mess. Yuklivitch was like the pope to them."

"Really?" Hughes asked.

"Really. Father Russia was assassinated on the White House steps, and they think we did it, that we lured him here to kill him. There will be hell to pay if we don't get to the bottom of this immediately. I hope AEGIS can walk on water. If not, there will be an army of post-nuclear helicopters put into motion, attacking us at the speed of light. We have to make a preemptive strike if we want to survive. We won't really stand a chance against those Black Fox choppers."

"Hey, sweetie," the vagrant said to the homeless woman who made a living room in the grass behind him.

"How goes it?" the woman said. "Sure was some action here today. Have a smoke." The man gratefully took a cigarette and pulled some matches out of his coat pocket.

"Yeah, it was some action, all right. It looked like Vietnam out here…boom!" the man shouted, intoxicated with cheap booze.

"You know what? I like you," the woman said.

"Well, see here. I like you, too, little lady," the man replied with one thing on his mind.

"What do you say we celebrate?" the woman asked, lifting booze from her torn jacket.

"Well, I'm all for celebrating, missy. What did you say your name was?"

"It's Martha, but call me Marty."

The man took a long swig of her booze and licked his lips. "Whew!" he shouted. "That's some great stuff you got there, Marty! I ain't seen you around these parts before. Where you from?" He took another long swig from her fifth.

"Here and there," the old woman replied, watching the liquid slide down the man's throat. When she had gauged that the truth agent had had a sufficient chance to become effective, Sparrow got down to business.

"Did you get a chance to see that man get shot up there?" the woman asked.

"Yuparoonee," he replied, smiling. "Me and all the fellas were watching everything from right there with the reporters. They didn't like it. But hey, it's free country," he chuckled.

"Where did you see the action, you lucky duck? You're going to be right there under the *headlines* tomorrow morning! Maybe you can show me while we celebrate some more." As soon as the code word "headlines" slid off of Sparrow's tongue, the IAT was activated.

Hughes walked into the White House restroom and saw Vadar, Jackal, Jester, and Hammer talking in hushed tones. Without looking at him, they let him know they acknowledged his presence. Jester chuckled lightly as if someone in the room had told a joke.

"I like jokes, too," Hughes said, looking at them calmly.

"I have a joke for you," Jester smiled. "A sniper was somewhere, 400 hundred yards away, watching the head of the Strategic Offensive Reductions Treaty Commission address the nation. He couldn't be anywhere in the vicinity, or Secret Service agents would have seen him. The intelligence on the two explosions indicated they were remote detonations that could have been set off from Siberia. He couldn't have had any natural angles to fire from because those were being covered. For the Häagen Dazs ice cream bar and the shiny toaster, where was the sniper?"

Hughes thought.

"Near the explosion. He would have to be near the explosion so the sound of the seven-millimeter Parabellum couldn't be heard. Since it is a bolt-action rifle, the sniper knew he had one shot, and one shot only, which was why he was a hundred yards closer than he could have been."

There was a sneering smirk on Jester's face as he continued with his game. "Near which explosion, Hughes? There were two. If the first was to cover the sound, why the second? For the trip to Jamaica, why was there a second explosion, and how in the world could a sniper get close enough to Yuklivitch to fire and not be noticed?"

Hughes thought again. Jester hummed the theme to Final Jeopardy.

Garret led the two-car team up Interstate 95, heading toward Washington, D.C. Lugor had remained awake. All of the graduates had learned to go many days with very little sleep, so staying awake for a few hours of riding was not a challenge.

"Are we going back?" Lugor asked.

"Yes, Oleg," Garret replied.

"You know where she is."

"Yes, I do. There is only one place she could go."

"Does Devin know?"

"No. No one else knows where she would go. But we have to get there before she does, so we can stop her."

"Stop her from what?"

"Oleg, I trust you with my life, but to leak this could bring about our entire family's demise."

"Not everyone is family."

"I know."

Zyablikov then shared what a stranger had told him long ago.

Oleg looked around as Zyablikov drove through Richmond, Virginia. He turned his head to look at the giant Marlboro cigarette towering above the interstate. It had its own lighting, so every color was accented, even at night. In less than two more hours, they were inside the capital of America.

Zyablikov drove into the city and did not slow down when he passed the Russian embassy. He remembered what an unknown man had told him and Kalisa before he was sent to America.

The voice had had a Russian accent, and the tone had been serious. "If something happens, I don't mean anything, I mean if something severe happens, you are to go to the embassy, speak to whoever is in charge, and tell him, "Zackiyus has died." He will refer you to someone, and you are to tell *that* person the situation in its entirety. Do not leave anything out!"

"If one of our group members die in a battle, should we go?" Kalisa had asked.

"No!" the voice screamed. "Or you will be sorry you were ever born! You go to the embassy under extreme circumstances. As long as everyone is accounted for, everything remains. If one of you turns to the Americans, then you are to go. Otherwise, do not ever set foot inside the embassy. Is that understood? You are to tell nothing to the secretary or to any guards. Speak only to whoever is in charge! And remember, this is not to be done unless there is grave danger to the operation and *all* of its members. Is that understood?"

Kalisa and Zyablikov had both nodded and never seen the man again.

All members knew that the penalty for breaching their assigned radii without authorization was death. Even though Kapitnov said he would consider a pardon, Zyablikov had been in the game for too long not to know it was a tactic. If Devin found her, there would be no thoughts of anything except silencing the only witness to his crime. He wondered again why Devin would send two of Kalisa's team to look for her and no operative from one of his own teams.

Devin had said a search was already underway. But Zyablikov became elated when he considered that if Nightshade had already been killed, Devin would have had to notify Kapitnov and would have pinned the murder on him. At that point, Kapitnov would have no choice but to perform an execution.

He had to find her now; there wasn't a moment to lose. Devin probably had his own search going, and with the homing device he was riding in, he was definitely letting Kapitnov and Devin know she was headed for Washington, D.C.

Where would Kalisa be at that very moment? Probably somewhere in disguise, hidden among American civilians, most likely in a small, unknown hotel.

The first thing she would have done was ditch the car. She knew their cars were armed with homing devices, implanted deep inside the engine blocks. Unlike with the microtransmitter, removing the homing device would have detonated the car. As soon as she ditched the car, she would have to find another mode of transportation. Not the bus; that was too slow, too unreliable, and too risky. Steal a car? No. Then she would have local and state police after her. They would only be arresting Jennifer Johnson, her civilian identity, but car theft would be the move of a truly desperate woman. Wasn't that what she was at that point? She didn't run for just any reason. Could she have taken a plane? Not a chance. Devin would be waiting for her at the airport when the plane touched ground.

Then it came to him.

"Oleg, let me see that laptop," Zyablikov instructed.

Lugor handed over the laptop computer, and Zyablikov pulled the car to the side of the road and turned off the headlights. The other car did the same. With the laptop in hand, Zyablikov got out of the car and walked over to the second vehicle. He signaled for Viktor Nesignev to get out of his car. Viktor Nesignev, F-3, was definitely bona fide crazy. He was savage enough to be on Team D, the Marine Combat Unit. Along with Team D, Nesignev had a severe temperamental disorder. He was given the name Nesignev because it meant "anger carried." Nesignev gave himself the first name of "conqueror."

Nesignev obeyed and stepped out of the passenger seat. Nesignev knew to cover the windows, so after Zyablikov was safely in the car in the seat he had just vacated, Nesignev leaned casually against the window and lit a cigarette.

Rhyhor Karandei looked at Zyablikov with suspicion as Zyablikov handed him the laptop. Zyablikov had thought it suspicious that the Spymaster and Devin had chosen the person who used to discipline the team in the Pit to look for Kalisa. Rhyhor Karandei served as F-2. Possibly because he was the oldest, during the earlier stages, the Pit instructors had used Karandei to discipline the others. Karandei was forced to beat and bruise his fellow classmates until he was ordered to stop. After several times, Karandei started to enjoy it and became the permanent enforcer. Though he would never admit it, the others knew he liked it. Garret knew if anyone were to step out of line here on American soil, Karandei would be the one sent to deal with him or her. Karandei meant "existence of punishment."

"Access Jennifer's bank records," Zyablikov instructed. "Liberty Bank, Fairfax, Virginia. I don't know the address."

Karandei slipped in a USB device, and the screen whirred to life. Zyablikov didn't know the exact process for computer hacking, but he knew Karandei had been into Liberty Bank's files so many times, he had his own password to bypass any additional security Liberty could have put on.

"What is her Social Security number?" Karandei asked.

Zyablikov gave him the nine-digit number and asked, "How much time do we have? They can't trace the signal, can they?"

"Their computer is tracing it right now," Karandei replied, punching keys rapidly.

Zyablikov knew their own signal was looped into several satellites, which would toss the probe back and forth between each satellite until the program could find its way out of the loop, but he didn't know how efficient Liberty's anti-probe tracking system was.

"How long?"

"About ten minutes. Their anti-theft system is pitiful."

Karandei entered the numbers, and Kalisa's financial records hit the screen.

"Print this out," Zyablikov instructed.

"The printer is not connected."

"Well, connect it."

"This is an American civilian operating system. I will have to restart the machine for the printer to be installed and the driver configured correctly. I can't print anything unless the printer is installed. Liberty has a failsafe system. When their defenses are breached, the computer system shuts down completely. This channel is still safe, but once we disconnect, we will be locked out."

"Go to today's date."

Karandei scrolled through Liberty's operating system like it was his own. He opened and closed application windows, entered passwords, overrode new security additions until he came to the right page.

"This is it."

Zyablikov looked at the date. Kalisa had withdrawn $499, and then it looked as if she had walked outside to the ATM and withdrawn $300 more.

She was very crafty, Zyablikov thought, and that was why he knew Devin had not caught her yet. Any withdrawal of $500 or above is reported to Devin immediately. By staying under the mark, she had an extra 24 hours' head start. Zyablikov knew ATM withdrawals or deposits usually did not clear until the next business day, so Nightshade could take as much as she wanted out of the machine, but as a security precaution, Liberty imposed a $300 daily withdrawal limit.

Kalisa had $800 dollars to last her, plus Zyablikov knew that she had a forbidden emergency stash, just as he did. He had no clue of the amount, but he knew it could be in the hundreds. It was difficult to save money. All assets they encountered had to be accounted for at all times. All members had direct deposit from their civilian jobs, and Team B, the covert intelligence team, personally investigated any suspicious activity. Even though he led the intelligence team, Zyablikov knew that Kapitnov knew how to reach any member of that group at any time.

He tapped the window, and Nesignev stepped away from the door.

"Are you finished?" Karandei asked.

Zyablikov looked back at the screen one last time and snapped a mental picture of it. He gave Karandei an affirmative nod as Karandei flipped off the computer. He got the unmistakable feeling that Karandei and Nesignev had not been summoned for a search assignment. This was a search-and-destroy mission if he had ever seen one. Zyablikov knew he was just needed for the search part.

Zyablikov walked to a pay phone while Lugor kept a watchful eye on him via the rearview mirror.

He unhooked the receiver, unscrewed the cover from the bottom of the handle, and slipped in his security device to make sure the line was clear. He then screwed the cover back on and waited until the tiny red light turned green. When it did, he started to dial.

"Hello?" a nebulous voice asked.

"Hey, buddy. You got that seven that you owe me?"

"Yeah, I got it." *He was alone.*

"That's good news. I know you're sleeping, but look, I need to know if you spoke to my cousin about your debt." This was not a standard code. Zyablikov was trying to ask B-2 if anyone had contacted him lately. He was hoping his colleague would pick up on it.

"Your cousin?"

"Yeah. No one called and asked about that seven?"

"Well, actually he called a couple hours ago."

"What did he want?"

"He wanted to know if he could borrow some of that money."

This was a totally unorthodox conversation. Zyablikov could not decrypt the reply.

"He wanted to borrow some of the money?"

"Yeah. He said part of it was his anyway."

Zyablikov could still not understand.

"Go on."

"He was acting all crazy. I think he knows his girlfriend is cheating on him."

Zyablikov picked it up. "Which girlfriend?"

"J." *Jennifer. Nightshade.*

"Why does he think that? She's as honest as they come."

"You know your cousin doesn't give specifics. He wanted to know if I knew anything."

"What did you tell him?"

"I told him she was faithful as far as I knew. You know I have to stay on top of everything."

"You haven't seen her, have you?"

"I haven't seen her in ages."

"OK. I need my money, though."

"I have it. Come get it when you need it."

"Will do. Good night."

Zyablikov hung up. Kapitnov had called B-2 earlier to find out where Jennifer was and thought she had turned to the Americans. This was terribly serious. Zyablikov now knew that if he found Kalisa, Rhyhor Karandei and Viktor Nesignev would kill her as they were assigned to do. This was a tricky game, but Zyablikov was used to it.

If he stalled, Kapitnov would kill him, thinking he and Nightshade had planned the Yuklivitch assassination together. If this new search team found her, she would die. If Devin found her, she would die.

Either way, he would have to wait until tomorrow when the embassy opened.

Hughes walked out to his car. It was in a secured garage, but he still walked swiftly. His hotel reservations had already been arranged, and he needed some rest. Jester had frustrated him with his game, and he didn't know the answer for the trip to Jamaica.

He got into his Infiniti and started the engine. He suddenly felt pressure against his temple. A gun was at his head.

"Don't look back, just drive," a deep voice said in a thick Russian accent.

"What do you want?" Hughes asked.

The gunman took the weapon away from his head. "I need you to be aware of what's going on around you, Bryan." The Russian accent was unmistakable and yet totally unfamiliar. "We are not in an amusement park." The accent had turned American.

Hughes looked back. It was Hammer, and he had no emotion on his face.

"You like games? Do you think we called you down here for games, son?" Bryan asked.

"First of all, you call me 'son' again, and I'll kill you. Second, you didn't call anyone. You don't run a damn thing here. Third, if this was a game," Hammer said as he cocked his fully automatic Rex-329 handgun purposefully, "you would have just lost. Now what I want to know about is the list. And if you stop driving, I will stop being patient."

"What list?"

"The Rex list. The list you crossed with the Unusual Behavior list."

"You mean all the people who had access to the project?"

"Yes, genius. Run the light."

Hughes slowed to see if anyone was coming, then sped through the red light as he was told.

"What about it?" Hughes asked.

"Why wasn't your name on the list? You had access to the project, didn't you?"

"Yes, I did. I have access to all projects that we work on."

"I didn't ask you that. Why wasn't your name on the list?"

Hughes was silent.

"Who made the list?"

"Walter asked me to construct the list."

"Did he tell you to leave your name off of it?"

"No. I simply forgot to include it. I don't consider myself a suspect."

"Well, we consider everyone a suspect. Stop at this light."

Hammer flicked a tiny light on and off behind Hughes's ear. As Hughes looked back, Hammer sprayed him with an unknown substance, temporarily blinding him. When Hughes recovered thirty seconds later, Hammer was gone.

AEGIS had already crossed Bryan Hughes with the UB list, and he had come up clean, which was why he was still alive. Hammer wanted Hughes to know he was being watched. AEGIS and Bishop knew Hughes was more important than anyone realized.

Fifteen minutes later, back at the White House, there was a small party.

"You slept with that homeless guy, didn't you?" Jester smirked at Sparrow.

"You've lost your mind," Sparrow snapped.

"You've lost your *clothes*," Jester replied. He humorously mimicked Sparrow in a high-pitched voice with his next sentence, "Maybe you can show me while we celebrate some more."

They laughed together, all except Vadar, who remained serious.

"That's *exactly* what you said," Jester chuckled. "He probably has every disease known to man." He made the sign of a crucifix. "Get away from me, O Unclean One," he said, laughing and scooting his chair away from her. He resumed watching the monitor they had set up.

"Jester, you *can't* be throwing stones. What about that German girl?" Sparrow retorted. On the monitor, the tape in the VCR played the assassination for the millionth time.

"I am the definition of a team player," Jester replied, unfazed. "That was one for the team, and it was strictly to get the information pertinent to matters of national security. I feel this country is in my debt."

"This country is in your debt because your tongue was between her legs?" Sparrow asked. "Those two events do not correlate. Please break down your rationale for us."

AEGIS broke into laughter again, except for Hammer, who remembered the incident but chose not to laugh. There was nothing funny about an assassination on the White House steps.

"There is absolutely no evidence for these ludicrous accusations." Jester grinned, folding his arms. "Hearsay has no place in this discussion. Anyone with documentation, please step forward. All others remain silent."

"Wasn't your tongue infected for three weeks?" Jackal laughed. He, too, was looking at the monitor. "It looked like you had yourself a cup of purple paint or something. She had all sorts of microbes and nasty critters lurking in that dungeon, and you just gobbled every last one of them up." He gave a loud "slurp" to accent his joke.

"Now the Whore of Babylon and the Royal Fools all need to remain silent," Vadar called out with his eyes still glued to the screen. "If there was—look!" he shouted. He was pointing at the screen.

The Alpha Sector looked at the screen.

"Rewind it," Vadar instructed. The jokes were over.

"Felix, you're closest," Jester said, lightening the situation.

Felix rewound the tape briefly and pressed the Play button.

"The SORT Commission rebukes any and all false accusations brought upon us," Yuklivitch said through the microphone. "I have brought Bruce Wallace from the Federal Bureau of Investigation to testify that, indeed, no alleged plans have been seen by *any* eyes *ever*, at *any* point in time."

They all knew the explosion was coming next.

"Look," Vadar pointed. "It's as clear as day. Look at the man with the coffee mug."

Felix rewound the tape again. They all looked for a coffee mug, and then it clicked. Felix rewound it a third time before he saw the man with the coffee cup who was standing next to a plainclothes officer. None of them could see the actual bullet hit Yuklivitch, for the camera had turned toward the explosion, but they sure enough spotted the man with the coffee mug.

"He wasn't on any of the other tapes," Felix commented.

"Because he's smart," Vadar replied very seriously. "He knew to stay away from the cameras. This camera was hidden. The satellites didn't get him, either. But what he didn't remember is that the camera not only catches your every action but your every *non*-action."

"He didn't even flinch from the explosion. He didn't spill his coffee, or even look toward the explosion," Hammer observed.

"Even if he's an experienced soldier, the sound wave records indicate that this blast was loud enough to make anyone flinch. Just look at the Secret Service men and the undercover agents," Vadar reported. "Study their actions. This man is drinking coffee without spilling a drop or batting an eyebrow."

Felix rewound the tape again. AEGIS saw everyone flinch, except for the man with the cup, who didn't even turn his head.

"There's Ryan." Vadar pointed out the undercover agent. "He is as experienced as they come, and look at him flinch." AEGIS looked at Ryan's involuntary bodily reaction as the explosion roared. The man with the mug ducked down quickly along with everyone else, but Vadar had already caught him. Act Two did not fool Vadar.

"We cannot rule out a hearing disorder," Sparrow reminded. "The man could be deaf."

"He could still feel the heat, plus the vibrations in the air," Vadar replied.

Felix rewound the tape again.

"Look at him wince when the man is testing the microphone." Felix paused so the other four members could hear the high-pitched screech as the audio technician tested the equipment. "Testing...testing," the tech was saying as Felix pressed Pause.

"That Starbucks gremlin is definitely not hard of hearing," Jackal announced. He was ready to go to war. "We need Plack to send this to Image Analysis and run a mix and match on our coffee bandit. Then we need to castrate Mr. Coffee with a rusty saw after I bash his head in with a cast-iron pot."

"Headlines," Hammer said into the air. "Walter, we have a tape for you to run through Image Analysis. Have someone pick it up immediately and run a mix and match."

Within a minute, the tape had been picked up.

"Silence," Hammer said into the air to shut anyone off their channel.

Pulling out a chair, Felix said, "I was thinking about motives, and I tossed things back and forth for an hour, and I finally figured that ENAP would have the most to lose by this treaty being signed. Their annual profit exceeds 75 billion dollars a year."

Jester gave a long, admiring whistle.

"If this treaty was signed, they would have to file Chapter 7," Felix continued. "Also, the black arms market would suffer."

"The EPA is all over them for pollution, anyway," Hammer put in. "Do you think they would have the balls to pull this off, already being under federal investigation? This is the President of the United States they're dealing with."

"I thought of that also, but then I remembered who the CEO of the Elite Nuclear Arms Production Corporation is."

"Gary Klingner," Hammer replied, "a member of the Novus Ordo Mundi."

Jester whistled again.

"My beloved brethren of the highest order," Felix grinned, referring to the Novus Ordo Mundi. Felix occasionally enjoyed mingling with the corrupted aristocrats. He fit in their cultivated circle nicely, which was why he made a masterfully exquisite undercover member in their brotherhood.

"Time to knuckle down," Jackal uttered.

Chapter 9

Early in the morning, Zyablikov rose from his bed in the beautiful St. Regis Hotel in Washington, D.C. Each member of the team had come in separately. Each had different rooms. They disguised themselves well enough not to be recognized if anyone saw them again. Though this was only a "search mission," normal precautions still had to be taken.

Without alerting anyone, Zyablikov headed down the stairwell and exited using the back door. He hailed a cab and rode to the embassy on Wisconsin Avenue. Exercising caution, he instructed the cab driver to drive a couple blocks past the embassy. He did not even glance at it as they rode past. Only after he got out of the cab, paid the driver, and had walked along Wisconsin Avenue toward Edmonson Avenue did he dare venture a glance toward the embassy. It was a gated complex of four buildings. Two were a fantastic marble-white color with vertical windows, while the other two were a dull brown. The complex was surrounded by a stone wall and brown ten-foot spears. The outer perimeter looked drearily uninviting. Amid the noise, Zyablikov turned to look around. Across the street, there were some rather nice single-family apartments, and they looked much more appealing than the embassy.

Zyablikov wore a gray business suit with a boring tie to fit in with all the American workers hustling for a paycheck. He sat down at a bus stop where he could see every frontal angle of the embassy and waited. Though it was still pretty early, the streets were crowded. He fit in perfectly. From the corner of his eye, he saw someone who could have been Kalisa, but she wasn't. The legs were too thin, and the walk was not sexy enough. While he waited, he wondered why in the world the Americans allowed the Russian embassy to be located on one of the highest points in the whole city. It gave a significant intelligence advantage to the Russians, considering radio waves and the other advanced technical equipment used to collect intelligence, and the Americans knew this. With the White House less than twenty miles away, the Russians had set up a premier intelligence factory.

After fifteen minutes, he saw her, disguised in perfect business attire, including fake glasses. Her hair was dyed brown, and it was tied in a conservative bun. She walked on the large, shiny, stone semi-circle driveway that allowed the cars with clearance to exit off the street and seek refuge while waiting for the ramp to open. The stone driveway stretched all the way across the path of entrance gate, a distance of about thirty yards.

Zyablikov quickly rose to his feet and approached the curb, as there was no crosswalk. There was no way across the busy street without a break in traffic. It was a full minute before he made his way across the street. Kalisa's walk was unmistakable, and her stride was quick. He watched her press the button on the intercom, but the clamor of cars rushing along Wisconsin Avenue drowned out her soft words.

Zyablikov broke into a brisk jog and crossed the street between a small gap in traffic as Kalisa entered the gate. Standing beside the Highview Towers Hotel, located next to the embassy, he observed his sister talking to the guard as she strolled further inside the complex. The guard looked younger than expected, about twenty-something. When Zyablikov reached the gate, Kalisa had already rounded the corner of the guard post and was out of sight.

She has to see the top man, Zyablikov thought. *She has to go directly to the top officer.*

Zyablikov quickly glanced up at the gate. It had to be fifteen feet tall. The tops were pointed like harpoons, and he had been given no instructions on how to get past the guards. He pressed the intercom button.

"Yes," the unfriendly voice declared. Zyablikov knew it was the young guard he had just seen. In front of the entrance gate, there was the small but formidable guardhouse with the entire glass wall facing him—a one-way mirror. He already knew what kind of equipment was inside it, observing him. There was a camera tracing his face outline and running the image through its large database. There was a voice-analysis system recording his every word, tracing its patterns and running his voice patterns through the database.

Zyablikov spoke in an urgent tone. "There is a problem. Who is in charge?"

"Who are you?" was the reply. Zyablikov knew that the guard was probably a $9-an-hour sentry. There was no way this guard had any clearance for anything. Zyablikov felt the cameras on him and knew he was wasting time standing outside. He spoke in a firmer tone. "I'm with the young woman you just let inside. This is a matter of national urgency."

"No, you are not with her. Do you have an appointment?"

Zyablikov stopped talking and started thinking. "Hello?" he said pressing the button over and over again. "Hello?"

The guard answered through the intercom, but Zyablikov kept acting.

"Is anyone there?" Zyablikov asked. "Sir, this is very urgent!...Hello?...This is not a joke, sir."

After a moment, the guard came from out of the guardhouse and spoke in irritated Russian. "What is the problem?" He nearly shouted at Zyablikov.

Three businessmen appeared on foot from around the corner, and the guard unlocked the gate for them to exit.

"Is there someone in charge I can talk to about an urgent matter?" Zyablikov persisted.

The guard had already opened the door for the visitors to exit, and he agreed to let Zyablikov inside the premises. The young guard led Zyablikov to a small, dimly lit room with a red telephone. Without dialing, he picked it up and spoke in hushed Russian. Zyablikov wondered why he was not frisked or checked for weapons. Were the X-ray sensors *that* reliable? He knew he was standing on a weight panel and that his image and weight were being run through agent files and cross-referenced with American agents.

A small portion of the wall he was looking at was a two-way mirror. Zyablikov looked through it to see a large man with a frizzy mop of black hair. Mop Head looked entirely unhappy with the young sentry for letting him inside the guard post.

They were passing signals back and forth. The trained Zyablikov caught every one of them. He could tell they were both rookies. While he caught their every signal, he could fully interpret none of them. Zyablikov read the large man's face and knew that unless he started with a plan, he would quickly be escorted back to Wisconsin Avenue.

The young guard handed him the red phone.

"Yes," Zyablikov answered, "to whom am I speaking?"

"This is the Director of Operations. What is your urgent message?"

Zyablikov knew whoever was at the end of the phone was not in charge. "I have strict instructions from my superior to give the orders directly to you, face to face. I am unarmed, and this is not a joke."

"Unfortunately, *we* have some restrictions—"

"There is a woman who is coming to see you. I am with her. I must speak with you also."

"We cannot let anyone past the outer gate without authorization or a valid appointment. Please cooperate with security as they escort you off the premises."

"May I help you, miss?" The secretary spoke cheerily while giving Kalisa a no-nonsense glare. Kalisa easily recognized the secretary as someone who wanted to be in charge, someone who enjoyed her job as the gatekeeper. Kalisa assumed that the secretary would not connect her with the head of affairs out of spite or because of a mere flaw in her personality.

"Yes, I have an urgent message for whomever is in charge of Russian domestic affairs. It is terribly urgent, and I have specific instructions to put this message in the direct hands of whomever runs your affairs," Kalisa replied with the air of one with important affairs.

"May I have your name, please?"

"Jennifer."

"Jennifer who?"

"Jennifer Zackiyus," Nightshade lied quickly. "He or she should know what I am talking about."

"I'm afraid he's in a meeting right now."

"I think he'll want to hear this. It's unimaginably urgent."

"I will make sure it gets in his hands."

"I have direct orders to put it into his hands and no others. This is directly related to national security. This is not a joke."

The woman paused and picked up the telephone. She spoke in hushed tones and then hung up the phone.

"He'll be with you in five minutes."

"Thank you," was the reply. Kalisa realized that perhaps her assumptions about the gatekeeper were wrong.

Zyablikov waited outside the embassy and pretended to read a newspaper. After a few minutes, he got up and started to walk the block around the embassy. He spotted a pay phone and walked toward it. Using a computer-generated calling card number, he began to dial. Less than twenty minutes later, Teams A and D had been instructed to take information from him only, unless otherwise notified. He also designated a code phrase for each team, to ensure the speaker's identity. This was the only way to lock Devin and Kapitnov out of the chain of command. It was too late to include covert intelligence Team B. They had already been contacted, and half of Team F was already in Washington.

Keeping the teams on his side was a risky move. If Kapitnov had somehow found out about it, which was actually a remote possibility, Zyablikov would surely have been seen as guilty. He would be executed along with Kalisa. Team D was the only combat team left that remained intact. The others had been combined, which only brought confusion to the operation. Confusion brought questions, and questions brought doubt. Confiscating Teams A and D brought another advantage to his side. If Devin ever decided to take out Kapitnov, Garret saw himself with the advantage. Kapitnov's disappearance was definitely a possibility, even though he was the head of the Russian Federation of Intelligence. A man killing his own national diplomat and then blaming his subordinate would probably have the audacity to create the Spymaster's mysterious disappearance.

Zyablikov reflected on the Spymaster's impressive system of checks and balances to keep everything under control and running smoothly. The only one who could ever control or understand the whole picture was the Spymaster himself. Devin could not make a move without Zyablikov, who knew how to get in contact with Team A, the Elite Forces Unit; Team B, the Covert Intelligence Unit; and Team D, the Marine Combat Team. But the key between them was Kalisa, captain of Team F, the Special Forces Team. Kalisa was the only operative who could contact Zyablikov, and only Kalisa herself knew how to give instructions to Team F before they were assembled for the briefing. Devin could not make a move without Zyablikov, and only Kalisa could contact Zyablikov. This scheme, Zyablikov assumed, was to give him an anchor if he even thought to compromise the organization. Devin was left in charge of Teams C, E, and G. Zyablikov did not know the operatives on Devin's teams, nor could he contact them, and the partial reverse was true for Devin. Devin did not know the aliases of the organization's operatives, nor could he contact them, but he did know some various abilities of each team. Zyablikov knew that all surviving members of the Pit were accounted for on his teams and wondered what Devin could possibly be doing with his operatives.

Only the Spymaster knew the entire system, knew the aliases of every operative, and could contact them at will. What he hadn't foreseen was Devin's ability to maneuver the entire organization by deceiving two of its members. It sickened Zyablikov to know that he was guilty until proven innocent and that if he wanted to stay alive, he would have to create his own rules and play by them—very carefully.

"The mix and match turned up nothing on the Coffee Bandit," Sparrow reported as she passed around a blown-up photo from Image Analysis.

The photo was crystal clear. It was as if they were looking at the suspect out of a window. The view of the suspect, however, was poor. It was a cramped side-angle view of a white male, long hair covering the side of his face, wearing a hat and sunglasses. The suspect also had a large coffee mug covering his lips and nose. Vadar, Jester, and Sparrow were the only ones present at the meeting. The other three members could hear every word via the intra-aural transmitters, as they had set out to check on Gary Klingner, Chief Executive Officer of Elite Nuclear Arms Production.

"The angle is too poor," Sparrow continued. "As we speak, they are running the photo through Interpol. Maybe this guy is wanted overseas."

Vadar yawned, "Let's not hold our breaths."

"They are still checking out Klingner. Perhaps we'll see some unusual activity in his accounts," Sparrow hoped.

"Don't get happy over that, either," Hammer commented from his remote location inside a minivan in Delaware as he examined the image of Gary Klingner's estates that a global positioning satellite was relaying back to him. "With the Novus Ordo Mundi on his team, he has more ways to launder money than we can count. I'm looking at his property now. He has an army in there—from canines to rooftop guards. We're not going to risk sneaking in. We're all cops today."

Gary Klingner stepped out of the shower. He smelled the aroma of breakfast in the air and couldn't resist coming downstairs with his towel wrapped around his waist to sample what was to come after he got dressed.

He entered the kitchen and saw Felix sitting down, eating from his good dishes and gourmet silverware and being served by Klingner's personal chef.

"Who are you?"

"Inspector Weishaupt," Felix replied. "*I am of the same, in the same, seek the same, and travel the same journey as one did before me.*"

Hammer, outside checking the perimeter, laughed. Felix had uttered one of the lines from a sacred Novus Ordo Mundi ritual. Felix had on gray slacks with a blue shirt and matching tie. He had a clipboard with yellow legal paper on it. His hair was red, and he spoke in a slightly higher-pitched voice than usual. Many items of his attire held significance to the organization.

"Why are you in my house? You are trespassing. You are to leave at once, or I will report your behavior to the precinct."

"I came to inquire about Yuklivitch."

"I don't know him. I thought he was assassinated on the White House steps. Why don't you go arrest the bastard who did it instead of eating my breakfast?"

"Yes, he was assassinated on the White House steps. You are indeed a veritable expert on current events. We just "

"What did you say your name was?" Klingner asked impatiently.

"Adam Weishaupt. Do I need to be more conspicuous?" Adam Weishaupt was the founder of the Novus Ordo Mundi.

"I'm calling security," Klingner answered. This was protocol for the brotherhood. The first and second signals of recognition were to be ignored to confuse or ward off imposters. The third direct signal was to be recognized. The first signal was derived from certain items of Felix's attire. The second cue was the phrase. On the third signal, Felix would be accepted as a brother. Any slip-ups, and Klingner would have him followed and then killed after interrogation.

"Such an uncongenial person. Your inhospitable temperament is quite disturbing. Do you treat all of us this way?"

"What the hell do you think this is? Do you have some identification?"

"Yes," Felix replied, "but it's very personal. I don't show it to just anyone. It's a divine part of me." Felix extended his hand, and Klingner embraced it. Casually, Felix slid his hand into the solemn grip of the Novus Ordo Mundi and made the grip noticeably forceful.

"Really," Klingner asked, widening his eyes, "why didn't you say so? What's with the inspector charade?"

"A little riddle. Thought you might pick it up. You may call me Oscar Nelson. I'm the rescue mission."

"Rescue from what?"

"Is this place secure? Perhaps we should talk somewhere else."

"Of course."

Felix followed Klingner into his study. After Klingner closed the doors, they gave each other the Novus Ordo Mundi greeting and a brotherly hug.

"What can I do for you?" Klingner asked.

"It is not I who need a favor, is it, Gary?"

"I don't understand."

"A few of us understand Yuklivitch's misfortune and want to know if you have any troubles. Whether it be with finances, or maybe even a path to smooth things out. Anything you need. We can also hold on to or pass through anything you wish, as well."

"We are on top of things, aren't we?" Klingner grinned.

"We have to be. How else can we run a nation?"

Klingner laughed. "Well, I don't seem to have any worries, Oscar."

"That's good to hear."

"Have we met?" Klingner asked.

"No, but I promise we will meet again. I am from the upper echelons. I am also a primary investor in Microsystems, the company that owns virtually all computers."

"I am familiar with your company. I would do some investing if it wasn't for your legal troubles. It seems we all have legal troubles these days. Do you have a card?"

"Yes." Felix opened his wallet and gave Klingner a business card.

Klingner pocketed the card before responding. "You may stay as long as you like. I've got to get to work. I have an important meeting this morning."

"All right, take care of business. You didn't obliterate all our topsoil or anything with your radioactive pollution, did you?"

Klingner laughed. "No, but I'll be sure to save you a flowerpot full of it for your garden."

Felix gave a hollow laugh.

"Can you get the EPA off my back?" Klingner asked.

"A hefty favor you ask, Brother Spartacus. Nonetheless, a hefty brotherhood we are immersed in. The EPA is the President of the United States, but you have my word I will do my best to rectify your situation. The EPA is underpaid. Throw a nickel in their direction, and you can buy a miracle."

"I would appreciate it."

"That's what we are here for. See you in three months," Felix said, referring to the Novus Ordo Mundi treasury meeting in New

York. "I've got to get back to New York. See you around, Gary. It was certainly a pleasure meeting you."

Oscar Nelson left the house and rode off in his Rolls Royce. He wasn't worried about the number on the business card. Everything would check out.

Walter Plack yawned and woke up, nearly forgetting he was in a hotel bed. He remembered he was in the Westin in Washington, D.C., and he wished Sharon was with him now. His heart still ached from the loss of his brother. He had slept deeply. It was the nature of grief. He sat up and breathed heavily, hoping no tears wanted to pour forth. The phone was ringing loudly, and it sounded to his ears like a foghorn.

"Hello?" Plack answered groggily.

"Mr. Plack?"

"Yes, who is this?"

"This is the front desk. You have an urgent message."

"Go ahead."

"The message is confidential and sealed. You'll have to come down and pick it up yourself at your earliest convenience."

"Thank you."

"Enjoy your day, Mr. Plack."

Plack knew that the message wasn't from the Alpha Sector or Hughes. They would have used the IAT, or at least the ComLink.

Plack got out of bed and immediately got dressed in jeans and a T-shirt. He took the elevator down to the lobby and walked to the front desk, still a bit sleepy.

"You have something for me?" he asked the woman at the front desk.

"Mr. Plack?" the attendant asked, much too cheerily for 7:00 in the morning. Though she was dressed as professionally as the other attendants, Plack knew instantly that the woman was new on the job.

"Yes," Plack said, showing identification.

The attendant reached under the desk and grabbed an envelope. She placed it on the counter and smiled.

"When did this come in?"

"About four o'clock this morning. Of course, we didn't want to wake you up. He said it wasn't necessary to do so but insisted it was urgent. The messenger also gave us explicit instructions that this message be put directly into your hands."

"It was urgent, but you weren't supposed to wake me up? That doesn't make any sense. Besides, you woke me up anyway. Who left this?"

"He flashed some kind of badge. He said he was one of your coworkers."

Plack knew instantly the messenger's story was a lie. This was not CIA procedure for contacting another agent. As a matter of fact, it violated roughly three rules of contact. Plack turned his back to the attendant and opened the letter. It was a store-bought "Thinking of You" card. On the inside of the card was a typewritten phrase: *"It is not what you see. It is what you do not see."*

"Who left this? Give me a description."

The woman thought for a moment. "Hispanic male, pretty nice suit, short, black hair."

"How tall?"

"Rather short, actually."

"Which way did he come in?"

"I'm not sure."

"Which way did he go out?"

"I'm not sure of that, either."

"Let me speak to your head of security."

"Is there a problem?"

"Just get me the head of security and there won't *be* a problem."

"Yes, sir."

The woman went into the back and came out with a well-dressed man who seemed full of energy.

"Yes, sir, I am Reginald Morgan, head of security. How may I help you this morning?"

Plack flashed his identification. "I need to see all of your surveillance camera's tapes from 3:30 to 4:30 this morning."

"If you would follow me, sir."

Morgan led Plack to the security office and informed the security guard stationed by the security monitors to give any needed assistance. Plack briefly explained that he was looking for a wanted man. He gave the description the woman had given him, and they both started watching the tapes carefully.

Kalisa had hidden her emotions. She had no idea what to expect, walking into the embassy, nor had she been given any clue how to proceed. She had been given no instructions on how to get past the young arrogant guard at the gate or on how to find who was in charge. Then she pondered for a moment. What if this was a test? A test to see if she would start talking if hard times fell upon the organization. Or perhaps it was a test to see if she could endure the weight of the organization on her shoulders. Then again, what if this *wasn't* a test? It was tough playing a game where there were no rules. She would pick the man's brain for angles; he was, after all, only a man. She would let him control the conversation until he revealed something she could use.

"Good day. Who are you?" the man who escorted Kalisa to the unfriendly room asked.

"Jennifer," she replied as they walked into a large office.

"Jennifer who?" the man behind the desk asked.

"Who I am is not important. The message I carry is of dire emergency to our country."

"What is this message? And from whom?"

"I have been strictly instructed to give this message to the head of Russian Affairs here in the United States."

"That is I, and I must inform you that my time is indeed precious."

"I have been instructed to give this message strictly to the head of Russian Affairs here in the United States," Kalisa repeated, knowing the person she was speaking to was definitely not in charge.

The man was silent for several moments. Kalisa wondered what the problem was until she realized the man in front of her was waiting until whoever else was listening to the conversation advised him what to do. As Kalisa stood silently, the man eyed her carefully.

"What is it, exactly, that you are looking for from me?" Kalisa asked.

"You must not understand, woman. It is I who am asking the questions, and it is I who am receiving information." The man's face was hard.

"My name is Jennifer, and I was sent with a message."

"Give me the message in its entirety."

"I was sent to tell you that Zackiyus has died."

"Is that the entire message?"

"I was given specific orders only to give the rest of the message to whoever is in charge of Russian Affairs."

"That is I."

Kalisa eyed the man with a hint of doubtfulness.

"Give me the message!" the man yelled, banging on the table.

Kalisa was not in the least intimidated. For an instant, she thought about faking a flinch, but the moment passed too quickly. The man noticed that Kalisa had not budged.

"Whom were you sent by, woman?"

This is going nowhere, Kalisa realized. This wasn't a test, and she knew she had to find her way out of the office immediately.

"I will ask you this question once again: What agency do you work for? You have made a grave mistake coming in here."

Kalisa was silent.

In an adjacent room, two men listened to the recording.

"What do you think?" the Head of Russian Affairs asked the Representative of Domestic Affairs as they rewound the tape to listen to it a second time. "Do you recognize the phrase?"

"I do not recognize the person or the phrase," the Representative of Domestic Affairs replied.

"Then send her to me immediately," the Head of Russian Affairs replied.

"Of course."

The man in front of Kalisa casually reached under his desk and pressed a red button. Kalisa noticed this. The man then stared into the air as if he was waiting. The phone on his desk rang. He picked it up and listened, then put the phone down and began to form an unnatural, sickening grin.

"Jennifer, I will tell you this: I don't have the slightest idea what you are talking about. No agency has ever heard of you, and if you want to leave this building unharmed, you will start talking. Follow me, if you will."

Kalisa stood erect and followed the man to another office. He then left her alone to face another man behind a desk.

Kalisa spoke first. "Good morning, sir. I was under the impression that the last gentleman I spoke with was the head officer in charge. I was told to give the message directly to whomever was in charge."

"Who are you exactly, Jennifer Zackiyus? I do not know you, nor do I have an understanding of what you speak of."

"The message I was sent to give you is 'Zackiyus has died.'"

The man pushed a button under his desk, signaling that she was to be followed on her way out. He was silent.

Kalisa noticed the action. She might not have noticed it if she wasn't looking for it, but she kept her senses acute. In a situation such as this, there were no rules, no expectations, and no boundaries. As with many situations within her lifestyle, outcomes were unpredictable, but there were very few situations that she had never encountered, and this was one. She knew the man in front of her had three options: One, have her followed and derive a solution for her actions once she left the building; two, have her followed from the room and killed before she left the building; or three, take her into custody.

The man grinned at her. His face had no mercy in it. "I have no idea who you are, and you'd better start talking."

Kalisa remained silent.

The man brought his fist down on the table with great force. As his fist hit the table, a thunderous "thud" was heard, along with a shout.

She couldn't run, and the truth was not an option. If she told her story, she would expose the entire network. She could kill the man sitting behind his desk in about seven seconds if she struck first and hard, as she was trained. If she killed him, she would never leave the building with life in her body. She noticed there were no windows in his office, and only one door, which was behind her. The man pressed another button under his desk, and two men came from the outside and walked toward Kalisa. She saw them coming but did not make a move. She was unarmed, and fighting now would bring death. One man placed her in handcuffs and pulled out a long rod. He activated the rod and touched Kalisa's heart with it. She collapsed to the floor, unconscious.

"How long have you been working here?" Plack asked the head of Westin Hotel security.

"Quite a while, actually. About five years now."

He can't be in on it, then, Plack thought.

"Is that who we're looking for?" Morgan asked, pointed a figure out. On the tape, there was a man standing in front of the desk, giving a card to the attendant.

"Rewind that," Plack instructed.

The tape was rewound, and Plack watched closely.

The man walked into the hotel as if he knew where all the cameras were. When at all possible, he kept himself immersed in the dark shadows, and his face was never seen until he was right up to the counter. There was a camera directly behind the counter, giving a decent view of the man's face, but toward an angle.

"Has he been here before?" Plack asked.

"No, sir. He's definitely not a guest here. I haven't seen him before."

"Print his face off the screen."

"We are not quite that advanced, sir."

"Is there a way I can get an image of his face without ripping the monitor down and bringing it with me?"

Morgan let out a small chuckle until he realized Plack was not laughing. The head of Security got serious.

"I can give you the tape, sir."
"I'll take what I can get."

Zyablikov looked up at the building for an instant. He wondered what was happening. He knew he should be getting back to the hotel before the others reported to Spymaster Kapitnov. He thought about why Devin would select members from outside of his own teams to locate a witness who could destroy him. Instead of choosing from his own teams, he had chosen two members from Kalisa's own team. He then realized with a smile that Devin either didn't have any teams, or they were incapable of handling this assignment. He became anxious as he realized he himself led and ran the network, not Devin. Devin simply handed down orders from Kapitnov.

The room had no lights and carried the odor of cooked flesh. A thick, foul, nasty stench invaded Kalisa's nostrils like a cold-blooded rapist. The bile in her stomach rose into her throat. Kalisa was strapped to a table-like apparatus. Her hands and feet were restrained tightly to the table, which was raised at a 45-degree angle, and the only part of her body she could move was her head.

The man switched on a lever. Kalisa's body jolted as unwanted electricity entered her. The tormentor quickly pulled the lever down.

"Now, this doesn't have to be painful. To stop the process, start talking," a voice said from the darkness around her.

Kalisa remained silent. The lever was jerked up and down again. Kalisa clenched her body against the shock and held in her screams.

"We'll start with your name."

Kalisa did not say a word.

"Well, let me introduce myself. My name is Death."

Kalisa still did not say a word. The man pulled the lever up for four eternal seconds. Kalisa squirmed and fought against the restraints, but she could not keep silent. She let out an angry scream.

Death smiled in the darkness. "Are you ready to talk?"

"I am ready to die before I dishonor my homeland and speak to you."

"Is that so?"

"You bastard. You have a woman locked up in the machine because you fear me. Let me loose, and I'll talk to you in a language you are very familiar with!"

"Such a bad attitude for a dead woman. I grow weary of this. I will give you one last chance. You will talk, or you will die."

Kalisa answered with an evil glare. She panted heavily and looked him straight in the eye with fury and vengeance. She grunted loudly and violently lurched forward at him, but the restraints held fast. She quickly thrust herself forward again. The machine restraints made noise but did not loosen an inch. More of a reaction than an action, the man threw the lever up and began to watch her die.

Kalisa could not fight against the unbearable pain. Her mere flesh became like raw meat as her cells began to fry. She contorted in the restraints, but there was no escape. Kalisa realized this man was going to continue until there was no life left in her body.

"Novasta!" she yelled.

Death pulled the lever down.

"What was that?"

"Novasta. My name is…Novasta."

"Tell me about your organization, Novasta."

"Our organization is in four levels. Political, civilian, technical, and military."

"Continue," encouraged Death's cold voice.

Kalisa started to slur her words and stutter purposely. "The political ring's goal is to infiltrate the highest levels of your legislative, executive, and judicial branches of government." Kalisa dropped her head heavily and pretended she couldn't lift it. She began to stutter terribly, and she dragged every word out. "Civilians are our spies, camouflaged as American citizens. They live the same life your citizens do." Kalisa forced tears as she continued. Technical level is into the level of microprocessing, and other numerous technologies that we consider valuable." She then collapsed into a coughing fit before she added, "And military is our defense intelligence."

"Which team are you a member of?"

"Civilian."

"How is communication achieved?"

"Many advanced techniques." She paused between words and took deep breaths. "Wire transfers. Deposits. When a certain amount is credited or debited to certain accounts, the certain amount that was sent, the receiving account, and the original account in addition to the actual amount transferred all carries a message down to the penny."

"What else?"

Kalisa slurred her speech, acted drowsy, closed her eyes, and chopped her sentences. The story she told had not one ounce of truth to it, but as long as the lever remained down, it was a plus.

Kalisa knew that Death had no intention of letting her out of his dungeon alive. But as long as she kept talking, she had a chance. She also knew that, even though his voice tried not to show it, Death believed every word. Now the trick was to convince him to let her out of the restraints, and then he would die. She pretended to think in slow motion.

"Well, there are many ways of communication. If I could have one glass of water, I will sit down and discuss what you want." She started to pant like a professional actor. "I don't feel too well. So tired...tired. Just a nap." She closed her eyes and started to mumble nonsense.

"No, you will talk!"

"Please, I hurt...so tired. . .please," Kalisa mumbled. She closed her eyes and remained still.

Instead of throwing electricity through her body, Death cursed and walked toward her. He smacked her. After receiving no response, he checked her pulse. Yes, she was still alive, but barely. He called in his men to take her to the interrogation chamber.

Death had stepped out of the room, and two muscular men quickly walked in. They unfastened Kalisa from the gigantic machine, and each grabbed an arm. Kalisa could not stand up on her own. They were not gentle with her, dragging her through the L-shaped exit corridor. She opened her eyes briefly a quarter of the way and searched for a weapon.

The man on her right had a pistol attached to his waist. As they approached the door with her, Kalisa felt the man on the left loosen his grip as he reached out to open the door. Kalisa instantly came alive and threw a quick jab to the right man's groin, and then ripped his pistol from the holster on his belt. The left man threw a thunderous fist at her head. The impact forced her to the ground, but she threw her left hand out to the floor, cradled the pistol against her breast, and used the momentum to perform a one-handed somersault, which she used to roll away from both men. When the somersault was through, with her amazing speed and agility, she dove into a corner and turned the safety off her new weapon. As expected, the second man had his pistol drawn as he came around the L-shaped corridor. The first man had a large knife.

Kalisa quickly let off three rounds into the gunman before he could see where they had come from. The silencer quieted the bullets into hushed tones instead of loud roars. The other man looked toward her.

"Do you want to live?"

The knifeman nodded.

"Then drop the knife and lead the way out of here."

The knifeman dropped the knife.

"Kick it over to me."

The man kicked the knife toward Kalisa. She picked it up and commanded, "Walk in front of me and do not say a word. Keep your hands by your waist at all times and do not stop walking. Before you open any door, tell me what is behind it. If I see anything different when it opens, you will die." Standing behind him, she placed the barrel of the gun between the man's legs and muttered, "Walk."

With the gun at the man's testicles, she led him out into a corridor. He walked toward an elevator.

"I don't think so," was the grim remark from Kalisa.

He continued down the corridor to the doorway of a stairwell. She shoved the barrel higher into her captive's crotch, and the man grunted.

"Behind the door are some stairs going up. The painting on the wall is white," the man informed Kalisa.

"Where is the camera?"

"There is no camera. This is a highly restricted area."

"Open the door and walk through it. Do not run, do not skip, and do not hop."

The man walked through the door. After a moment, Kalisa followed him. She shoved the gun back into the man's comfort zone. He winced again as Kalisa spoke. "Right now, as we walk, tell me how we're going to get out of here."

"We take the stairs up to the subbasement level. There's a door that—"

Kalisa's mind clicked. "How many people have gotten fried in that machine?"

"I don't know."

"How many bodies have you removed?"

"More than ten."

"I know damn well you don't drag ten dead bodies up three flights of steps in front of everyone every time someone doesn't share the news. Where do you take the bodies out of the building?"

The man was quiet. Kalisa pressed the gun deep into her hostage's critical spot.

"We have to turn around."

As Kalisa turned the man around, she wondered why the man had sealed his own death in exchange for a chance at a possible salary increase. The hostage led Kalisa back down the stairs, back down the same corridor, and into the same dark room where she had been tortured. The man reached behind one of the machines and pulled a lever. A door slid open to reveal a narrow corridor with nearly no light inside.

"Take off your clothes. You have thirty seconds." Kalisa took a step back to allow the man to follow her order.

The man quickly undressed, knowing that his captor was not interested in a striptease. Kalisa knew in that dark corridor that a man could pull a weapon in less than two seconds without any sudden movement if he was trained right.

"Move," came Kalisa's order.

The man walked through the corridor. With the barrel of the gun, Kalisa kindly reminded him he was forgetting something.

"Beyond this hall is an alley where we dispose of things."

They walked together. The man turned slowly and slid his hand along the wall. Eventually, a door slid open. Through the door was grim daylight. Kalisa stepped outside into the back alley with the naked man still in front of her.

"Lie down."

The man laid down among the garbage in the alley, and there Kalisa quickly executed him for his earlier tactics. A silent two to the head. Then, like the wind, she was gone.

"Boris Kapitnov is on our grounds. We got a satellite alarm some time ago," Jackal informed AEGIS through the IAT. "He was disguised better than usual, so it took the computers a while to find him. We have been tracking his every move for some hours now. Someone tell me I can go get the bastard for setting foot on my soil without permission."

"Ol' Spymaster Kapitnov, huh?" Jester replied. He opened his travel access application on his eight-gigahertz laptop a couple of miles away. "Wonder what he's doing around these parts. When did he get here?"

"Four o'clock this morning by plane," was the response from Jackal. "I'll get the guns. You bring the bats. I'm ready when you guys are."

"A little late-night flight for the Spymaster." Vadar thought for a minute. If he landed at four, he took off at about seven-ish. Hmm, less than an hour after Yuklivitch was decapitated. Coincidence? He didn't think so.

"Does he have flight arrangements out of here?" Sparrow asked.

"Nothing yet," Felix answered.

"Do we know his mood when he got off the plane?" Vadar asked from Columbia, Maryland.

"Sat angle couldn't get it," Jackal replied.

"Where is he staying now?" Jester asked.

"He has no reservations anywhere, and his aliases haven't shown up in any records anywhere, but we're sure he's here."

"If the Spymaster himself makes an unannounced visit at 4:00 a.m., we do have a situation," Hammer thought out loud in Hanover, Maryland, where he was searching Dorian Valentine's house. "Get on him. Put pressure on his office back home. Tell Plack to try to set as many urgent conferences as he can with him. Where is he now?"

"He was last seen in Latrobe, Pennsylvania. He landed in his unarmed private jet in a tiny, unheard-of local air yard. It's privately owned. No permission was granted for him to enter U.S. airspace."

"What else is new?" Jester yawned.

"Vadar, you're closest," Hammer informed.

"Hello? Hello?" Vadar called. "You're not coming in clear."

"Yeah, right. Get to Latrobe," Hammer instructed.

"Already on my way, coach," Vadar responded.

"Felix, how much was the price to take out Yuklivitch?" Jester asked.

"Possibly a billion, I imagine."

"Tell me how you launder a billion dollars. Tell me in what mattress does one hide a couple billion dollars. Maybe they'll help pay off the national debt," Jester replied.

"With the Novus Ordo Mundi and related organizations, yes, it can definitely be done. What they'll do is reroute a million pieces of it, and somehow, it'll end up in the hands of whoever it's supposed to. You know how that pyramid filtration process goes."

"I missed that class," Jester commented.

"Well, through several of Klingner's legitimate business operations, he'll route it in layers back and forth to each other, then to other businesses. Then these businesses distribute it to other businesses. By the time the money reaches the bottom of the pyramid, it'll be untraceable."

"To do this, they need accountants," Hammer responded. "Great accountants. Get a list of the ones who do the dirty work. Get the FBI and IRS cooperating. I know they didn't pull off a job like this on faith. They had to have some of the money up front. Find it. Remember, briefing at 3:00 a.m. All check."

"Check one," Sparrow replied from the White House steps, examining the crime scene.

"Check two," Vadar replied from a helicopter on the way to Latrobe.

"Check three," Jester remarked, still looking at the nation's travel arrangements in relation to Latrobe.

"Check four," Jackal replied, accessing a list of questionable accountants.

"Check five," Felix said from an underground facility, analyzing satellite images.

"Check six," Hammer called out from Valentine's basement.

"Felix, bring breakfast," Jester added.

Zyablikov continued walking along the block surrounding the embassy. It looked like an ugly fortress in the middle of the city. He saw a woman hailing a cab. As the cab slowed to a halt, he realized it was definitely Kalisa.

"Jennifer!" he called out. She looked up hurriedly. When she realized who it was, she stopped and signaled for him to get in. Zyablikov hustled over to the cab and got in beside her. They did not hug or speak.

"Where to?" the cab driver asked.

"Any parks around here?" Zyablikov asked. "Been a long morning. I need to relax."

"I got just the place for you," the cab driver replied.

After Vadar arrived on the premises of the small air yard, Felix picked up his ComLink, dialed Acclaim, and explained the situation to him. No one was to come on or off the premises, and anyone making an attempt at either was to be captured.

"Acclaim here," was his quick response.

"Hey, we have a Russian bigwig on our soil. We want to find out exactly what he's doing over here. He came unannounced. He's one of the chiefs of Russian intelligence. Director Boris Kapitnov, known to most as the Spymaster. Formerly KGB. We need a search for him. I'm transmitting to you now a photo of him along with some information from his files. This is all classified."

"Of course," was Acclaim's reply.

"I also need your cooperation in a containment operation and obtaining a search warrant for the Latrobe Airstrip."

"You got it."

"Get back to me with an update in one hour."

"Got it."

Felix turned his attention to Vadar's IAT transmissions. He had no visual, but support from audio relay was definitely better than nothing at all.

"Hey, who's in charge here?" Vadar was adamant as he stepped into the small air yard building.

"Is there a problem?" the clerk asked.

"I would say so." Vadar flashed his ID. "Special Agent Jackson, Federal Bureau of Investigation. Get whomever is in charge in front of me right now."

The clerk scooted out of her chair and went into another room.

A man came out and greeted him, arm extended for a handshake. "I'm Craig Benson. I'm in charge here."

"Is there a place we can talk, Craig?"

"Right through here, sir."

They both sat down. Vadar was disguised as a man slightly older than he actually was. He didn't have time to change his color, but Vadar knew the man wouldn't recognize him if he was seen again on different terms.

"Craig, let me get right to the point. An unauthorized flight landed on these premises about 4:00 a.m. I want to know where it came from, who was on it, and when it is leaving."

Craig checked his computer records. "No flight landed here at 4:00 a.m., sir."

"Craig, it would help if you were just honest. It would make things go a lot smoother and quicker. I'm really not asking much from you."

"I'm checking his financial information," Felix informed Vadar through the IAT. "There was a sizeable deposit this morning at First National when the bank opened. The amount was 5,000 dollars."

"Would you like to tell me where you got 5,000 dollars from?" Vadar asked.

"Excuse me?"

"No, excuse *me*, Craig. Excuse me for the madman I am about to become if you don't level with me. There was a deposit in your personal account at First National Bank this morning when the bank opened. Where did you get it, and where is the plane?"

"I have absolutely no idea what you are talking about."

Felix winced at what he knew was about to happen.

Vadar stood erect. "Where is the goddamn plane, Craig? There are only so many places you can hide an airplane on this thumbnail airport, and I will find it. Then I will shut you down. You have five seconds to show me where the plane is! Five, four, —one!" Vadar hit

Craig's wooden desk at full force with both hands, and it cracked in two. The papers on either side of the desk slid inward, causing a noisy paper avalanche.

"From the sat pictures, it looks like the biggest bunker has the plane in it. Walk out of the building so I can see you, then I will walk you to it from there," Felix instructed. He guided the satellite, controlling it from his 100-gigahertz laptop computer with a full 60 gigabytes of random access memory. "Acclaim already has the local police on their way with a warrant to search the premises."

Vadar stormed out of the small shack onto the runway.

"Where is it?" Vadar asked into the air.

"Turn to your right and walk forward."

Vadar did so.

"All the way down to the end, on your left," Felix said.

Craig came running out after Vadar. "Behind…"

"I hear him, Felix," Vadar replied.

"I want to see a warrant!" Craig screamed.

Vadar did not turn around. Craig ran up to Vadar from behind, still yelling. When the other man was three feet from him, Vadar spun around and aimed. He sprayed an anti-vision chemical into Craig's face. Craig grabbed his eyes as Vadar stepped out of the way of the bull charge. A few steps after Craig stumbled past Vadar, he fell onto the runway, still holding his eyes. Vadar stepped over him and continued toward the last bunker. He knew the spray put Craig's eyes on fire, but the pain was temporary and would leave no permanent damage.

As Vadar approached the bunker, he pulled out his Tracer 34X, a handgun like no other. The door was locked. Vadar put the Tracer back inside his jacket and pulled out the Rex. One shot from the Rex, and the door was unlocked. Vadar put the Rex away and pulled out the Tracer again. He opened the door. Beside the small jet was a guard reaching for his gun, which lay atop a large piece of machinery. The guard grabbed the gun and fired twice, but Vadar was out of the doorway by the time the bullets arrived.

The guard grabbed a machine gun from a metal counter and began running after Vadar. The guard quickly peered around the door to rule out an ambush before he left the safety of the bunker. Darting around the corner, he saw Vadar rounding the next corner and fired. The machine gun had a silencer, but the bullets that hit the side of the bunker were anything but silent.

"He's running toward the corner you just passed," Felix informed Vadar. "ETA five, four, three. . ."

Vadar removed the Tracer scope from the handgun as he rounded the third corner of the small rectangular bunker. He raced back toward the entrance side. Vadar then eased his wrist around the corner, with the Tracer scope held tightly in his hand. The machine gunner sprinted toward him. His body still hidden around the corner, Vadar checked the Tracer. The light on the barrel had turned green, meaning the scope had picked up and locked on to the primary heat source. Vadar walked inside the bunker and fired the Tracer out of the door. The Tracer missile turned the corner out of the doorway, turned the next corner, and struck the machine gunner before he could see what had hit him.

Still inside the bunker, Vadar heard the screaming. He fired another round from the Tracer. It followed the same path, faster this time and with more accuracy. The gunner fell silent mid-scream, at last relieved of his pain.

"He's finished," Felix remarked. "Splendid execution. No pun intended."

"Where is Craig?"

Felix zoomed out on the satellite image. "Still on the runway, yelping, and wailing like an obstreperous siren. He has also dispersed a maelstrom of outcries in relation to your affiliation with your mother." Felix zoomed out further until he could see the roofs of the surrounding buildings. "The local police will be arriving shortly."

"Guess I'd better clean up."

As Vadar left the bunker, he looked up in the sky toward the satellite and grinned at Felix. He rounded the corner and spotted the dead machine gunner. Slowly, he donned a pair of latex gloves. With sure fingers, he felt carefully around inside the man's chest and pulled out both of the Tracer bullets, then collected both of the shells. To the world, the weapon did not exist, nor did he. With the clean glove, he pulled off the bloody one and placed it in a plastic bag, then dropped the clean one in on top of the first. He sealed the bag and placed it in his jacket. Vadar stood, composed himself, and walked toward the helicopter.

"Felix, give Acclaim the clean version of what happened. Have him impound the plane and arrest Craig and his employees. I assume you've already snapped a picture of the bunker sentry over there in time-out."

"That's affirmative."

"Well, I'm out of here."

Acclaim looked at the records that his unknown accomplice had securely transmitted to him via datalink. There was a picture of Director Boris Kapitnov, and some information. He read the information and realized that there was indeed an urgent issue if this man had come to America unannounced. Politically, it was far too risky for him. He had been a leader in the former KGB while it ruled the Soviet Union with fear, terrorism, and oppression.

Following the breakup of the Soviet Union in 1991, the KGB First Directorate Chief, Boris Kapitnov became the head of Russia's brand-new Federal Counterintelligence Service, which replaced the KGB. As of mid-1995, reliable estimates placed the number of Federal Counterintelligence Service staff members at 237,900. The shrewd Kapitnov was instructed to report directly to the president; however it was known Kapitnov ran all operations without consulting anyone.

In January 1995, President Boris Yeltsin had received reports that Kapitnov's Federal Counterintelligence Service was growing too powerful, that it was continuing the reprehensible practices of the old KGB. President Yeltsin issued a decree merging the Federal Counterintelligence Service with the Ministry of Internal Affairs. The two agencies would coexist as the Ministry of Security and Internal Affairs. The Russian Constitutional Court, however, had reviewed the merger decree, declared it unconstitutional, and advised Yeltsin to annul it. Yeltsin had complied. Kapitnov was assumed to have been behind the decision of the Russian Constitutional Court.

In February 1995, the parliament undertook a study to recommend the manner in which political control over Kapitnov's Federal Counterintelligence Service could be ensured. The Federal Counterintelligence Service had originally been created to analyze threatening foreign situations, conduct counterintelligence, and collect intelligence in cooperation with the Foreign Intelligence Service. Suspiciously, the Federal Counterintelligence Service requested permission to monitor the political activity of Russian citizens. Despite Kapitnov's several attempts, this motion was denied.

Very soon, President Yeltsin became uncertain of the Federal Counterintelligence Service's loyalties during his struggle with Parliament, so the Federal Counterintelligence Service was disbanded in December 1995. It was soon replaced by the newly created Russian Federal Security Service (also known as the FSB, Federal'naya Sluzhba Bezopasnosti Rossiyskoi Federatsii). The council saw to it that Kapitnov did not head this organization, but it could not stop the new Minister of Defense from appointing Kapitnov as Director of the Foreign Intelligence Service

(SVR). The SVR was the fierce, external intelligence agency that was barely reformed from the KGB era. Under Kapitnov's command, the SVR successfully prepared and planted illegal agents, conducted terror operations, sabotage, and recruitment of foreign citizens. Kapitnov also used hundreds of private Russian companies and churches as "fronts" to fund and cover SVR operations. One newly hired, truly legitimate executive of a large unknown SVR front realized Kapitnov was transferring all of the company revenue to hundreds of banks the company had no real access to and that thousands of obscure employees on the company payroll were SVR operatives. The executive recovered some of the money that was being sent to the strange bank accounts and wrote a humble letter to Kapitnov politely requesting that the SVR pay the salaries of its own operatives. Kapitnov had the executive imprisoned for impeding government operations. Kapitnov's plethora of successful intelligence projects and his countless personally disciplined rings of well-trained spies before the collapse of the Soviet Union had nick-named him the Spymaster, for he was a man who had proven himself to be feared and respected.

Acclaim now realized the terrifying answer to a question that he and other agents often pondered: With the collapse of the Soviet Union and the KGB, what happened to the 250,000 skilled Soviet spies dispersed around the world? The former KGB had had astounding numbers of highly trained intelligence personnel before its collapse in 1991. An alarming percentage of them were still largely unaccounted for. Acclaim had heard speculation. He knew none of the disunited agents had 401K retirement plans; however, none of the theories were more disturbing than the cold truth he was now confronted with. Instead of working for a government or a particular country, the former Soviet espionage system now was run by a few astute individuals. Those 250,000 former KGB personnel operating worldwide were now run by men like the Spymaster—men who were still committed to the old ways. Worse yet, they were devoted to their own ideals and were governed by no one.

"The Spymaster is here," Zyablikov reported.
Kalisa almost gasped. "Why?"
"Kalisa, why did you run? Things are very bad now."
"I know, Reuban. I came home, and things weren't right."
"What do you mean 'not right'?"
"Things were out of place. Not like when you visit. Most of the times, I can't tell you were there. People had definitely been in my house. I didn't know what to think."

"I was sent to bring you back, but if I do, they will kill you. What happened in the embassy?"

Kalisa briefly described what had happened as Zyablikov checked his surroundings in the park. They were in an open area. It was about 9:45 in the morning. Zyablikov knew he had a long day ahead of him. Nesignev and Karandei surely must have reported his absence to Kapitnov, which now would imply that he had run off. If he returned with Kalisa to prove his innocence, Kalisa would die.

"Devin has sold us out. He has denied any connection to the last assignment. I've been put on trial for my loyalty. The only one who can clear my name is you, but I'm worried Kapitnov will neutralize you for breaching your perimeter. He told me otherwise...but you know how this works. Sis, do you have any of the $800 left?"

"Yes."

"Let's see if we can try something. First, I have to check in."

Zyablikov checked in with the others. He took the necessary steps to possibly get Kalisa and himself out of this situation with their lives. Zyablikov drove back to the team's hotel. There, he met Lugor, Karandei, and Nesignev, who were somewhat surprised at his return.

"Have you been contacted?" Zyablikov asked the three men. They each shook their heads.

Zyablikov briefly eyed F-2 and F-3. Though just 24 hours ago they had been under the direct order and supervision of Kalisa, they were now designated to be her assassins. They did not ask if he had found her, but Zyablikov knew they wanted to. Zyablikov opened his jacket and pulled out a handheld videocassette recorder, ejected the videotape from it, and waited to be contacted.

An hour later, the hotel phone rang. Zyablikov answered it.

"Hello."

"Hey, good morning to you, pal."

"And you as well, buddy," Zyablikov replied.

"Hey, did you ever come across that watch I lost?"

"Yup, found it this morning." Zyablikov did not recognize the voice. Even when Kapitnov's voice was electronically altered, he could kind of recognize the tone. This was definitely not Kapitnov.

"Where did you find it? That's amazing because I never find things I lose."

"It's a long story."

"Well, can I have it? You know what that thing means to me."

"Where can I meet you?"

A brief address was given. "Bring your friends with you. We can have a drink or something."

"All right. See you there."

The address was that of a restaurant. Zyablikov recognized instantly that it apparently was some sort of safe house. It had many of the signs he was taught to look for. The waiter led them to a private table that was near no windows. Exit doors were close by and easily accessible. The two men from Team F were led away, along with Lugor. Zyablikov was led to the Spymaster's table.

The Spymaster sat in the corner alone, but Zyablikov and his group knew there were several guns in the restaurant targeting them. Zyablikov casually looked around. Across the room, he saw a man with his jacket folded over his lap. Zyablikov instantly knew this was a gunman, but he wasn't worried. He knew the man was not necessarily there to kill without a reason. His objective was to protect. As long as his group made no sudden moves, whatever transpired would hopefully take a peaceful course.

The Spymaster looked the group over. When he noted that Kalisa was not among them, he scowled. "I will not hide my disappointment," the Spymaster started. He was disguised as an old man with a heavy, white beard and blue eyes instead of his regular black ones. "Someone had better start explaining why Ms. Johnson isn't here to join us for lunch, or my disappointment will turn into anger, which will not be healthy for anyone in my vicinity. You should know Epifanii Yuklivitch was a good friend of mine."

"Listen," Zyablikov started, "I have found Ms. Johnson, which was an extremely difficult task, considering the given constraints. She is afraid to come forward, for obvious reasons. I need something to convince her that her safety is not compromised."

"Where was she?" the Spymaster asked, ignoring Zyablikov's concerns.

Zyablikov knew he couldn't lie. The Spymaster would detect it. The greatest liar in the world stood no chance against the Spymaster. He would tell the truth, slanted in Nightshade's favor.

"She attempted to take refuge at the embassy until she could contact you safely."

"She went to the embassy?"

"Yes."

"What did she tell them?"

"She told them nothing, of course. She has not turned against us. She is willing to do whatever is necessary to prove it."

"Where is she now? I do not understand why she is not here. You have 45 seconds to explain."

"She is afraid to come forth. She understands that the commander of our operation is swift and unforgiving. Her caution is not unreasonable."

"I thought we agreed that she would not be punished if she was found."

"Yes, I did inform her that I vouched for her safety, but your word is stronger than mine."

"What does she want, documentation?" the Spymaster growled. "This is outrageous! She was to come here and explain why she breached her perimeter. Her absence is scandalous. Am I to think that you wanted your only witness to mysteriously come up missing? This does not look good for either of you."

"I contemplated this response, and as a token of our loyalty and our knowledge of the absolute necessity of a quick resolution of this situation, I bring forth this." Zyablikov reached inside his jacket pocket, making sure to move slowly and cautiously, as to not excite any of the gunmen strategically hidden around the restaurant.

"What is this?" the Spymaster asked, seemingly unimpressed.

"It's a statement from myself and Ms. Johnson. In it, you will see who the traitor is and why Ms. Johnson has breached her assigned perimeter."

The Spymaster signaled for the waiter, who was an obvious gunman. When the waiter was within range, he leaned forward, his ear about an inch from the Spymaster's mouth. The Spymaster spoke softly. Though Zyablikov was an above-average lip reader, he could not read the Spymaster's lips, because the waiter's head blocked his view to the Spymaster's mouth. Zyablikov could not even see Kapitnov's face.

Ten seconds later, the Spymaster stood up, and Zyablikov followed.

"Right this way," the waiter said, motioning both of them into the kitchen. They were then led into the freezer. Zyablikov noticed three human corpses lying in the freezer, two with the eyes still open. The waiter walked toward the end of the freezer, moved a stack of meat, and reached into the corner over a tall shelf. A door slid open. The waiter motioned for both of them to enter. They followed, and in the hidden room was video equipment. This room was significantly warmer than the freezer but eerily spooky. There were no windows, no air vents, and a lone bulb provided hardly any light.

The Spymaster motioned the waiter outside. The waiter quickly left, then stood guard outside the freezer. The Spymaster placed the tape that Zyablikov had given him inside the VCR.

After a brief static scene, Kalisa Leonilla came into clear focus in a dimly lit room and began speaking. "Spymaster, I come to you in need of your help," she spoke. "I fear our organization has been compromised by an operative codenamed 'Devin.'"

Kapitnov balled his fist and brought it backwards over Zyablikov's mouth. Zyablikov did not retaliate.

"Have you lost your mind, you imbecile?" From out of nowhere, the Spymaster pulled out a snub-nosed .38. "I should take your life now for this disgrace! What if this tape had been found by an American?"

Kapitnov pistol-whipped Zyablikov. "Where was this filmed? You don't know who could have been listening. Do you know the penalties for treason?"

Zyablikov scurried out of the way to avoid another pistol whipping. "Please, this tape was made less than a half hour ago! No one has viewed it, and there are no copies. It was made to prove our innocence. Devin sent men after Kalisa to kill her. She will tell you this!"

"Then why is she not here to tell me? Why is she hiding like a coward?"

"Listen to the tape! It tells the full story. She cannot risk her life coming out unless you are willing to protect her. Devin will try to kill her again!"

Kapitnov grunted again and turned toward the TV. Zyablikov passed off his chance to tackle the head of the organization. Not that he couldn't have taken the Spymaster down unarmed, but to do so in a situation such as this would have brought about his demise.

"This was your idea, no?" he growled.

Zyablikov nodded.

"How would I know you did not influence her speaking unless she is here to testify? Bring her to me now! You could have a shotgun behind the camera."

"For the sake of our country, please watch the tape."

"No! I will not watch the tape. Tell me where she is, and I will get her!"

Suddenly, like a giant mousetrap, the facts all snapped together. Zyablikov suppressed a gasp. Devin had gotten to Kapitnov already and convinced him that he had two traitors. If Kalisa had come, they would both be dead in this very back room. Zyablikov then realized that the only reason he was still alive was because he was the only one who knew Kalisa's whereabouts. His only leverage was Kalisa's location, and once the Spymaster had that, then Kalisa and Zyablikov would both die.

His only hope to fight the Spymaster's predetermined decision was to get him to look at the tape. The tape was the only hardcore evidence he had to prove his innocence if it wasn't already too late.

"The tape contains the whereabouts of Kalisa. We both were counting on your efforts to get to the truth. When the truth is revealed, we will retrieve Kalisa. She is not far." Before the Spymaster could respond, Zyablikov rewound the videocassette and pressed Play. Much to Zyablikov's surprise, the Spymaster watched. Zyablikov turned up the volume on the television.

"Spymaster, I come to you in need of help," a solemn Kalisa started. "I fear our organization has been compromised by an operative codenamed 'Devin.' Dennis tells me that he has been sent to retrieve me and that my breach looks terrible. I left for our current location as soon as I returned to my home after the events you are aware of. It was obvious men had been in my home, and they were definitely not our operatives. They left traces of their presence, and because I understand what kind of explosives and traps can be set in a household, I departed without contacting anyone. I am informing you now that Devin personally debriefed us. And I was contacted in the usual manner for the operation. The past events transpired because of a direct order from our superior officer, Devin."

Zyablikov then stepped in front of the camera with his pistol. The Spymaster looked with curiosity as Zyablikov gave the gun to Kalisa. Kalisa then pulled the magazine out of the gun, showed the top portion to the camera so the Spymaster could see it was full to the top. Next, she put the magazine back in the pistol and pointed the gun at Zyablikov's head. Zyablikov remained still.

"This is to prove there has been no coercion in this matter. If Dennis was a threat or had threatened my life or the organization, I could and would neutralize that threat right here and now. This statement is made of my own free will, and I will surrender as soon as the traitor is captured, as he had obviously sent men to kill me in hopes of framing Dennis. His men are most likely still looking for me, which is why I didn't come back with Dennis. When Devin is retrieved, Dennis knows where I can be found. Leader, you have my word I will surrender when the traitor is neutralized. Dennis knows my location, and I will remain at this location until you contact me. Dennis and I have spent our entire lives defending the organization and have gone to every extent to prove that we do not exist. We have sacrificed our lives for our country since our conception. Nothing has changed, and nothing ever will." Kalisa then walked behind the camera, and the movie was over.

The Spymaster was silent for a moment. There were four knocks at the door, then another three.

"Enter," the Spymaster shouted.

The waiter walked in with a small telephone in his hand. "Very urgent for you, sir. You need to take this," he said, handing the phone to Kapitnov.

Kapitnov put the phone to his ear. "Go ahead," he said.

"They have found the plane. We must evacuate you immediately or there will be a national incident," the caller said quickly. "We have 25 seconds."

Zyablikov noticed that as the Spymaster listened, his face became more solemn. It was as if someone had told him his brother had died.

Kapitnov spoke quickly. "Do they know I am here?"

"We do not know for sure. We need to evacuate you as soon as possible."

"I agree," Kapitnov replied. "Are you calling me with problems, or are you calling me with a plan? I am on the first flight out of here, no?"

"That's a negative," the caller replied. "The sky traffic is monitored too heavily. If they have captured the plane, then they will be looking for who was on the plane. They will also be looking for who is leaving the country, especially overseas. The skies are locked down. We cannot play that game."

The caller spoke extremely rapidly, but Kapitnov understood every word. "Suggestion?"

"There is one option."

"Boat," Kapitnov said.

"Yes."

"Is there a reasonable path?"

"We have to make one. They're putting too much pressure on us. You have several urgent messages that you have not responded to, and the liaison has done all she can do. We need to get you back on grounds. In the current political situation, it looks terrible. It looks like you're dodging them."

"Use Echo," the Spymaster demanded. Echo was a man the Russian government had used on several occasions to put people in places they were not. The Echo could change his voice to mock anyone at any time, male or female. He had fooled mothers, fathers, husbands, and wives. More importantly, he had, on countless occasions, fooled key political figures. He was used for special situations such as this, when key individuals were on covert travel and needed to keep it that way.

"Negative, they now use voice-wave analysis to verify identity. The Echo will not pass. We will get you out on a boat. No direct paths. I'll call back in one hour on relay six. Time up, sir."

There was an audible click as the caller hung up.

The Spymaster took a deep breath and remained silent for a moment.

Zyablikov clasped Kapitnov's shoulder. Kapitnov looked up. "Do you know who the traitor is now, comrade?"

"Where is she?" Kapitnov demanded.

"You're not sending Devin to retrieve her, are you? She is inno—"

"Where is she!" the Spymaster yelled. "Our agreement was for you to bring her to me! You headed for Washington hot on her trail immediately upon her departure. You knew where she was headed from the beginning. There is a reason for this, no?"

"I was not sure where she was headed. I came to Washington because it was where I would have gone. If we retrieve her—"

"Bring her to me now! You said out of your own mouth she is not far. F-2 and F-3 will go with you. If she is not back by the time relay six flashes green, she need not come back—or you, either. Hide well."

Zyablikov quickly walked out of the room and into the freezer, then past the waiter. He knew he was exempt from any gunfire until he returned with Kalisa. Then they would both die if Nesignev and Karandei did not kill her now, as they had probably been assigned to do from the beginning. This was why Kalisa's team had been chosen for this mission. They had seen her so many times, in so many disguises, that they couldn't help but recognize her even when she masked her identity. With her own team members looking for her, there would be no mistakes, no second-guessing. The same team members she had commanded in countless missions were now, on orders, hunting for her. What he didn't know was why Kapitnov had allowed A-1 to come along. Surely, he must have known the brotherhood between them. Surely, he must have been aware that there existed the possibility that Oleg Lugor would not carry out the order and, therefore, put the operation in jeopardy. Zyablikov believed this to be a weak pretense of cooperation, something, perhaps, to ease his nerves so he'd still trust the system. Not a chance.

Again, a click. Lugor would likely share the same sentence as Kalisa and himself. Knowing Lugor and Zyablikov were close, to prevent any avengement complications, Devin had probably cleverly interwove Lugor into the lie by portraying him as a party to their "unauthorized mission."

What possible story could Devin have come up with to convince the Spymaster that all three of us could have become mercenaries? Zyablikov knew that Devin's mind was the craftiest and most unpredictable he had ever encountered. Zyablikov contemplated this as he approached Viktor Nesignev, Rhyhor Karandei, and Oleg Lugor.

He realized that this scheme had probably been planned long ago. First, Devin had likely mentioned to Kapitnov that he suspected Garret as a possible mole. Kapitnov had asked why, and Devin had likely fabricated some spectacular answers. Zyablikov imagined Devin's well-rehearsed response: "Well, Director, he hasn't gone into his account in a while. I suspect he's been receiving financial support elsewhere." The Spymaster definitely would not have checked behind his number-one guy, and so once in a while, Devin probably sent to him false account information that showed he had not made any withdrawals. That was in fact not true, but it would have been easy enough to falsify.

Then again, Kapitnov was the only man who knew the whole picture. The only people Devin *could* set up were Kalisa, Oleg, and himself. Was Kapitnov on top of his game enough to realize this? He probably would be eventually, but only after it was too late.

Zyablikov walked out to where his teammates were. He signaled all three of them, including Oleg, and walked toward the door. Zyablikov eased beside Lugor and whispered, "Stay sharp." The phrase needed no additional words. Lugor nodded. Zyablikov then spoke in his normal voice. "He only wants Bill and Thomas," he said to Lugor, referring to F-2 and F-3. If Kapitnov came out and saw that any more than F-2 and F-3 were on the retrieval party, it would be a strike against Kalisa, Lugor, and himself. It would support the theory Zyablikov believed was already planted into the Spymaster's mind. Lugor obeyed the command and stayed behind.

All three men walked to the vehicle they had arrived in. Zyablikov made sure one of the members from Team F was in the front with him.

After pulling out onto the busy road, Zyablikov spoke. "We are retrieving Nightshade. My commander would like to speak with her. I do not expect resistance from her. When we get back, I am expected to walk in the door with her and lead her to the back of the restaurant. You two will sit at the same table you left." The message Zyablikov was sending was clear: The person who gave you the order to kill Kalisa and myself now wants to speak with Kalisa, so do not kill her. I am the one who is expected to bring her back, so do not kill me. I do not expect resistance from her, so do not be aggressive and pull the chainsaws out. Just relax.

He waited for F-2 and F-3 to somehow communicate   a signal, a look, any movement whatsoever. If they did, he would know his suspicions were correct, that the Spymaster had made his decision already and it was final. There was no such movement from Team F.

He drove back to the St. Regis Hotel they had just left and unlocked the door to and entered their room. Kalisa was sitting on the bed, watching television. She was dressed in Zyablikov's clothes. This was one of the few times Zyablikov had seen her out of disguise since they had been released in America. She was naturally beautiful. The curvature of her firm breasts beautifully accentuated her long, slender body. Her thighs were as firm and muscular as the rest of her body, and her shoulders, though indeed feminine, held a hint of masculinity. Zyablikov decided she looked sexy in his clothing, and though they hung only the slightest bit loosely, he wanted to jump inside his outfit along with her.

"Come, someone wants to see us," Zyablikov growled.

As she got up, he whispered in a quick mumble, "Stay sharp." Zyablikov gave Kalisa a seemingly thorough frisk for a weapon and then signaled her to go on outside. He grabbed the hotel key card he had given her from the opposite bed, and then the four walked toward the elevator. Zyablikov thought quickly.

"Two groups," he told them. "Nightshade and I will meet you out front in the car. You both have eight minutes. Do not use the stairs. There is a camera behind the front desk. Do not let it record your faces."

Nesignev and Karandei both gave affirmative nods. Zyablikov knew that he was giving his possible assassins eight minutes to communicate, but he needed these eight minutes even more—to talk alone with Kalisa.

The elevator opened, and no one was on it. Zyablikov and Kalisa got on together. When the doors closed, they spoke.

"What's going on, Reuban?"

"It's bad. He still believes I planned the last operation, and when you ran, you confirmed his suspicions. When I found you quickly, I further confirmed his assumptions."

"We can talk to him together."

"He will not listen. Devin has already gotten to him, and I believe we both are to be neutralized."

"No. . ."

"Yes. The Spymaster is beyond reasoning with. The tape evoked his fury, not our advantage."

"He *must* believe us!"

"I have tried. Maybe you can do better, for both our sakes. I felt a weapon on your inner thigh. What is it?"

"Whisper, a gift from the Embassy." A Whisper was a handgun notorious for its silent kills. It was constructed for government use only in Russia, but it was easily available on the black market.

"I suspect your team members may be the ones to carry out the order. That is why I separated us."

"You are on top of things, as always," Kalisa commented.

"I didn't know it was optional."

"Thanks for the outfit."

"You don't look too bad in it. I'm impressed by your team's devotion to you. One minute, they are your loyal subordinates without question. The next, loyal, unquestioning assassins after your blood."

"Not funny."

"Have you thought of what you're going to say to him?" Zyablikov asked.

"I'm thinking."

"Well, you need to go ahead and work something out. Immediately."

"I'm aware this is a crisis situation."

"I'll sleep a little better tonight knowing that you have personally acknowledged this as a crisis situation."

She was silent for a moment and then mouthed the words, "I love you, Reuban."

In that moment, Zyablikov wanted to take her in his arms and tell her that she was the only thing that truly meant anything to his heart. He wanted to embrace her and tell her how much he loved her. For a moment, he pictured a different kind of life for them. He wanted to open his mouth and tell Kalisa how he felt, but he did not respond to her. He suppressed his feelings instead, pushing them back down inside himself as he had been taught to do all his life.

"Keep the Whisper ready, and fire at the slightest hint of any slick movement. If they even exhale wrong, they will pay. I'll sit in the shotgun seat. You sit in the seat behind me. Keep your eye on who you're sitting next to."

Kalisa reached into her pants and pulled out the Whisper. She tucked it into her waistband and pulled her shirt over it.

The elevator doors opened. They walked outside to the car. Zyablikov sat in the front passenger seat, and Kalisa climbed in behind him in the back. She got the Whisper ready but kept it out of sight.

Zyablikov took his jacket off and handed it to her. "Hide it with this," he said.

"They'll spot the change. Do we want them to know?"

"At this point, it doesn't matter. They won't see him to report anything before he's made his final decision. If they are going to try for us, it'll be the one next to you. The driver will be busy. If you see him go for anything…no hesitation."

Five minutes later, Nesignev and Karandei were inside the car. Karandei was driving, with Nesignev in back next to Kalisa.

"Nightshade, are you all right?" Karandei asked, pulling onto the street.

"I've been better," she replied from behind him.

"There will be no talking." Zyablikov spoke without making eye contact with anyone. Nothing was certain. Any sentence could be a code. Any word could mean "shoot," and Zyablikov would not have any communication taking place that he was not a part of.

The trip back to the restaurant was silent. The four of them left the car and walked inside the restaurant. Zyablikov led Kalisa to the back of the kitchen, where the freezer was. The waiter was still guarding the door. When he saw Zyablikov, he opened the door and motioned to them to move inside.

All three of them walked into the freezer. Zyablikov looked for any out-of-the-ordinary movement from the guard. If there happened to be any, the guard would catch severe pain. The waiter opened the secret door and motioned to them to move inside. They did, and the door closed behind them. The waiter returned to his post outside of the freezer and stood sentry again.

"The prodigal daughter has returned home," the Spymaster spoke from his seat at a table.

"I have come to testify to our innocence once again," Zyablikov said to Kapitnov. "The operation was ordered by Devin, and both of us were debriefed by Devin personally. Never once have either of us joined forces without direct authorization."

"Tell me how is it that you two found time and money to make the video but not time to contact me. I do not think you stole the camera. I think you purchased it. Purchased it with unauthorized money that was hidden. You know stashing money is strictly forbidden."

The relay channel rang. The light square on the device was a bright red; the call was unsecured. It rang again, still red. On the third ring, the light turned green. The Spymaster turned his attention from Zyablikov and Kalisa and snatched the receiver.

"Yes," he said.

"We've found a channel from a cruise ship headed for Europe. From Europe, we have contacts that will transport you on grounds. You depart tonight. You must get to Florida at once. The ship departs at 8:00 tomorrow night. Your driver will know the place. You *must* leave immediately. The Americans are putting pressure on your office. You have several urgent messages that you have not responded to, and you have been absent from two teleconference meetings. If you are not back by tomorrow, they will have reason to suspect our role in recent events."

"I follow you. I'm on my way."

"We suspect they might be looking for you here as well, so you will need an escort. A bachelor on a European cruise, alone among many couples, will attract unwanted attention. We are looking for a female companion for you that is qualified. This is our only hold-up."

Kapitnov decided he needed Kalisa to ensure his clean escape. He would not kill her yet. The Spymaster replied, "I have one already, an American civilian. We'll leave immediately."

"Are you sure you want an American?"

"Yes. Come now."

"There is a car that will pick you up in about ten minutes. Clothes for you are already on board. Does your companion have clothes?"

"No."

"Give me some sizes for her."

The Spymaster turned toward Kalisa and looked her over for a moment, then turned back to his conversation. "She's about 5'10", 155, bra size is . . ." he turned toward Kalisa again.

"No time. We'll improvise. Make sure that the two of you board that ship with luggage. Those looking will notice the telltale signs of people who do not look like they are on a cruise. Blue BMW, tinted windows. Ask the driver for a two-dollar bill. You do not have time to stop. There will be food in the vehicle for you. From your description, your companion may be the same size as the one I had for you. Her belongings will be on site. Is your guest traveling on grounds with you?"

"Yes."

"Optimal. Blue BMW, ten minutes, outside. We have no time to waste. Time up." The caller hung up.

Kapitnov looked at Zyablikov angrily. Despite his actions, there was a small voice in his mind urging him to believe Garret—and he wanted to. All through the Pit training, Garret had never shown one symptom of treachery. Moreover, Garret's psychological profile showed him to be the least likely operative for betrayal.

Kapitnov remembered what the profile read: Highly intelligent, strategic, flexible, data intuitive, logistically inclined, data comprehension fully integrative with operative strategic planning. Driven to succeed at any given goals, capable and sustained through mental effort. Non-domineering. Not intellectually arrogant, inner desire for success, loyal to all colleagues.

Kapitnov also remembered Garret's weaknesses: Overly tenacious, emotional attachment to organizational members.

The last phrase the computer had given him stuck in his mind: 2.83445%, the chances that Garret would commit mutiny for mercenary motives. That was why Garret was still alive. Devin had convinced Kapitnov that Garret was guilty, but the impeccable computer program was the string that Garret's life dangled by. The psychological profiles had never been wrong. The tests were infallible. They had never been fooled. There were too many questions. Too many consistency measures, too many trip-ups. Devin was definitely the Spymaster's right-hand man, but in a way, the psychological profile system was his left-hand man.

Devin remembered Jennifer Johnson's profile: Confident in her abilities, constantly obedient if she respects the commanding officer. Will hold sacred what subject believes to be sacred. Confident in physical and mental appearance, diligent in pursuing goal, depressed. Looking for change in life, possibly new agenda, WARNING: **Possible flopover matrix.**

Though not widely discussed in the psychological field, the flopover matrix was a notion acknowledged in all government operatives. It was the possibility that, under extreme circumstances, the subject would convert and become the opposite of the presented diagnosis. Kapitnov remembered such an example in the horrific tragedy of his former colleague, Davyid.

Davyid's family was brutally murdered with chainsaws and axes. He was forced to watch. This act was a revenge sanctioned by the Germans. Davyid found out certain agencies had been aware of the oncoming assault before it happened but had chosen not to move on it because it was "insignificant toward primary objectives." When that happened, Davyid transformed to a flopover matrix state. He became the opposite of all previous psychological diagnoses. First, he became a mercenary for others...any others. He was paid with money, but he was after blood. Formerly passive, Davyid became intensely aggressive. Formerly cautious and covert, he was now the first to draw his gun. Formerly respectful of his fellow operatives, Davyid became concerned only with *his* objectives.

It was not a pleasant memory, and though Davyid's case was especially tragic, much subtler cases had been reported. The flopover matrix was especially applicable when an operative felt "tired of the life," which was how Kapitnov viewed Jennifer Johnson. She definitely wanted out of the organization, which was why she had been quick to run outside of her radius.

Time and time again, Kapitnov had been warned by the psychologists of the severe repercussions of exposing the members of his network to the intense mental, physical, emotional, and spiritual punishment of the Pit. The switching of identities every day was enough to drive a child crazy. The beatings and exposure to violence against loved ones was enough to push a small youth absolutely over the edge. Kapitnov had chosen to ignore the pleas of the doctors, but now he realized it did bring additional complications.

He thought back to Johnson's diagnosis. Candidate for flop over matrix: The subject might be open to methods to segregate herself from the organization—AWOL, hiding, or nonresponsive behavior, possibly compromising herself for the promise of a new life. Possibility of committing treason for mercenary motives: 10.75623%.

Even Devin had undergone a psychiatric evaluation. The output showed him to be the least likely to want to improve his standard of living, and he had pretty much been a "safe" character, as classified by the computer. What the master of the spy network didn't know was that Devin's associates had long ago hacked access to his psychiatric files and altered them before anyone had even laid eyes on the true results. Even Devin forgot what his results had stated, but he did remember one number: 82.83457%, his chances of compromising the organization. He had shifted the decimal point and wiped off the seven. The new number read 8.28345%, and he liked that number much better. He was one of the very few key individuals that knew the psychological files existed. Though he had once altered his, he couldn't find the means to alter Zyablikov's or Kalisa's, thus making his "mission" more difficult. Back when he had had access, an older system of security was integrated. Given enough time, one could have easily cracked into the system. Now, with the present random algorithmic-patterned passwords, all the time in the world wouldn't help an ounce. The same password at 3:00 p.m. would not work at 5:00 p.m. The password on the 16th of the month would not be effective on the 17th.

Devin had been insinuating for several months that he suspected Garret had been compromised. Though Kapitnov did not see what Devin had to gain by framing Zyablikov, Kapitnov could have easily executed Zyablikov but had decided against it. He would look into Zyablikov's counteraccusations. When he was safe in Moscow, he would decide how to clean up this situation.

"Garret, you are to remain inside your radius until you are contacted. Is this understood?"

"Yes, commander."

"You will direct Sam to do the same," the Spymaster finished, referring to Lugor. "Jennifer, we will depart immediately for home grounds. Come with me now."

Kalisa nodded. "Commander, I want to reiterate once again—"

"Enough!" Kapitnov yelled, cutting her off. "Come *now*!"

Kalisa nodded.

"Garret, head back to your home. Jennifer, tell Bill and Thomas to depart back to their radii as well. The search is over."

Zyablikov nodded and walked out of the door, troubled. He knew that once Kalisa was back on Russian grounds, she was a dead woman. Devin would make sure of it. He walked out of the restaurant with Lugor, and they both got into the car. Zyablikov took a deep breath.

"What's going on?" Lugor asked.

"I'm a dead man, and so is Kalisa. Devin has compromised the entire family, and Kalisa and I will pay the price for his treachery."

"Where is Kalisa?"

"He's taking her back, I believe. They know he's here."

"Really? Do you think Devin told them?"

Zyablikov had not considered that Devin's treachery would include the Spymaster. "I don't know. We have to get her back. I imagine Kapitnov has operatives watching us right now. They can't hear us. I took out the bugs in this car a long time ago. If I don't drop you off in your domain, they'll kill you, too. We both have to be back inside our radii by tonight."

"How do you think he's getting back? He can't fly."

"Boat, I imagine. He has no other alternative. He'll cruise out of American territory and connect with a flight somewhere else." Zyablikov started the engine and pulled out onto the busy Washington, D.C., street.

"Do we know where he's leaving from?" Lugor asked.

"He was leaving in a big hurry. I imagine it's very far; if it's close, he's leaving immediately."

"He can only leave by boat," Lugor reflected for a minute. "Over here, cruise ships leave from pretty much one area. That's a fact."

"Where is that?"

"Florida."

"Really?"

"Yes. The thing is, there are so many ports in Florida. A lot of the major cities have them."

"What's the closest to D.C.?"

"Well, it wouldn't be the closest port he would be worried about. It would be the port with a ship that he could get on immediately. He wants to get out of here as soon as possible," Lugor reminded him.

"I need to find out which boat he's leaving on. There can be only so many cruise ships leaving within a day or two that still allow you to make reservations today. And there are too many cruise lines to count. We don't even know the port, the destination, or the time—nothing. Our only hope is if my connections within the American agencies know something. We'll stop for gas along the highway, and I'll contact them."

Zyablikov pulled off the highway onto an exit ramp, and then drove to the closest gas station, knowing he was probably being followed. He walked to the nearest pay phone, placed the scrambler in the receiver, and dialed the number for B-3, his contact at the CIA. The contact was not at his desk. He next dialed B-2, his contact at the FBI.

Marcus Thorn picked up the phone.

"Thorn speaking."

"Hey, pal, this is Bill. Sorry to bother you at work. I was trying to see whether you were free for lunch tomorrow. I'm going to be in town, and I haven't seen you in a while. You still like a good filet, don't you, Ace?"

Thorn snapped awake. He had never before been contacted at work. "Let me check the calendar. Yeah, everything looks okay. Where do you want to meet?"

"There's a nice diner about fifteen minutes from here. I always eat there. What time do you want to meet?" *The usual place. When?*

"I'm starving as usual. Nothing late." *As soon as possible.*

"OK, see you there at noon." Zyablikov hung up the phone. There was no way he could tell Thorn the information he wanted while the call was being recorded, but there was no code to request complex information at the last minute. He hoped Thorn could figure out what he wanted.

Thorn knew he could not just get up from his desk, or it would be logged. He knew the Bureau logged all unusual behaviors of their employees, just as the CIA and all other American agencies did. The UB list was examined very carefully, and any movements he made were scrutinized. He knew the call had been recorded, but there was nothing that would come of the conversation. If he got up from his desk so soon after a phone call, it would be logged. He would have to wait an hour to be safe. He wondered what Zyablikov could have wanted. He decided to sniff around for hot information while he had to stay put. He thought for a moment, recalling the day's events. He had been with Acclaim before Acclaim had been instructed to leave for Latrobe to recover a Russian spymaster. Thorn assumed this was what Zyablikov's meeting would be about. A call at his job was absolutely absurd, so he knew it must be an emergency. He would have to carefully gather all the intelligence he could about the Spymaster and then depart for the meeting.

Chapter 10

"**Do you see** him?" Felix asked from his workstation in the bottom of the cruise ship.

"Nope, not yet. . . okay, there he goes," Jester replied.

"Paint him," Felix instructed.

Jester quickly caught up with the Spymaster and walked behind him for a few paces. He pulled out a small canister of breath spray, gave a long spray toward Kapitnov's head, and then, just as suddenly, melted into the crowd. Now, on the satellite image, there was a bright neon-green color covering the Spymaster's face, completely invisible to the naked eye. The shaded glasses Jester and Sparrow wore allowed them to see the bright green head amongst the crowd.

"Is he alone? Check," Sparrow said, boarding the ship.

"I don't see anyone else, but there could be someone watching from a distance. Whoa, it looks like he's got a hot date. There's a woman with him. What does he think this is, the Love Boat?" Jester replied. "Felix, tell me who the woman is."

Felix closed in on her with the sat.

"Sat image is no good," Felix replied. "All I get is the top of her head. I'm going to need a picture."

Coming right up, Sparrow thought. "Circumference," she said softly into the air.

Felix zoomed out on the satellite. "He's about twenty yards behind you with his friend. Move in east and you will meet them both. ETA fourteen, thirteen, twelve..."

Sparrow glanced around briefly to get a visual of her target and then twisted her diamond ring around on her finger until it was in perfect position. She reached behind her head, briefly pretending to scratch an irritating rash. She was taking pictures, one for each time the switch from the bottom of the ring brushed against the back of

150

her neck. After three pictures with the diamond lens, she discreetly removed the ring from her hand and headed on board and toward Felix.

After Felix received the ring, he removed the microdigital images from the ring ever so carefully with tweezers, loaded them into a special compartment in his laptop that analyzed the binary code, and immediately brought forth an image. He instructed the computer to do an "All" search, cross-referencing civilian, military, and top-secret agency photos with facial features.

"Height?" Felix asked Sparrow, who was walking back up onto the deck.

"5'10"," she replied, alone in the stairwell.

"Weight."

"I'll give her 155."

"Give me ten minutes," Felix replied. He watched as his laptop worked quickly to find a match.

"Are you sure you don't need another week?" Jester mumbled, continuing to watch his targets. "All aboard," he informed AEGIS as Kapitnov and his travel mate boarded the cruise ship. Jester followed them onto the ship. "No tails reported."

The Spymaster had no idea that, overnight, AEGIS had turned the cruise ship into a floating CIA headquarters.

Behind him, Felix's laptop beeped three times rapidly. He did not have to look up from the workstation; he knew the program had found a match.

"Bingo," he said. "Jennifer Johnson, born 1981, Fairfax, Virginia. Works for Fairfax Parks and Recreation. Single, decent credit, no priors, no affiliation with outside agencies. She's an American."

"I don't buy it," Hammer said.

"I'm absolutely sure the Spymaster did not crawl inside our boundaries to visit Miss All-American. The only reason he is even leaving this country is because we made him, and now he is taking an American with him."

"To help his disguise," Sparrow said, speculating. "A coupled man on a cruise ship full of couples is not likely to stick out."

"She's from Fairfax, Virginia. Why is she in Florida?" Hammer expressed his thought out loud. "Did she and Kapitnov meet in a bar?"

Hearing this on the way to the Environmental Protection Agency, Jackal opened his laptop and watched it whirl to life. Jackal punched in the woman's name and state and received her profile, including her work and home numbers. He picked up his cellular phone and dialed.

"Parks and Recs," a female voice answered.

"Jennifer, please. This is very urgent."

"I'm sorry, but Ms. Johnson hasn't been in today."

"Oh, she's sick? I'm sorry to hear that."

"Well, I don't actually know if she's sick. She's been missing all this week."

"That's not like her to miss work. She is usually at all the places she is supposed to be and practically always on time. I'm a good friend of hers. We had an appointment last night, and she never showed up. I'm very worried about her. Are you sure she didn't call in or *anything*? This is so unusual."

"Just a minute, let me check with her coworkers."

Jackal was placed on hold for a moment as he walked toward the EPA building. The secretary soon came back.

"Her coworkers say they have not heard a word from her all week, sir."

"Thank you for checking. If I hear from her, I'll let you know."

"Who should I say called for her?'

"K," Jackal replied. "Tell her K is thinking long and hard about her."

"I'll do that," the secretary replied with a brief laugh. Jackal hung up the phone.

"OK, grab the concubine," Jackal instructed his coworkers, using a bit of outdated humor. "No professional American goes on a weekday cruise without letting her job know. When I pull my dick out of her mouth, let's ask her why this cruise was so urgent."

"So you don't think he came over here for a little vacation, either?" Hammer remarked.

"He has mistresses in Russia. He wouldn't dare set foot on our ground, unannounced in this fragile and uncertain political climate to copulate with Lady Love," Felix said. With the Yuklivitch assassination, the last thing that would be on this man's mind is coming to America to see a woman, unless she is directly related to the incidents."

"He came by himself. That's incredibly risky—no tails, no nothing. It must be of dire importance or too top secret for anyone else to handle. AEGIS, our assignment has been upgraded," Hammer announced. "We are also to secure Johnson and bring her to Langley."

"Wait till we stop, or send a boat?" Sparrow asked.

"Use an unmarked boat and send Acclaim. We don't want to expose the operation. If the media finds out who is on that ship, there will be pandemonium. Sparrow and Jester, your equipment has already been placed in your rooms."

After two loud blows from the foghorn, the boat set sail with Hammer, Jester, Felix, and Sparrow on board.

"Come," the Spymaster ordered, leading Kalisa to their room. The room was exquisite, with a bed in the center and two circular windows with an ocean view. The dresser was expensive oak with a large mirror. The Spymaster strapped a portable enhanced polygraph device to Kalisa's head, neck, and arms, and then checked under the bed and in the closet before he spoke to her.

"You are not to leave this room for any reason," Kapitnov instructed.

AEGIS listened through microtransmitters threaded in the bed-sheets and placed in the light bulbs. The Spymaster opened his bag and pulled out food for himself and Kalisa. Sparrow watched through the mirror that hid the camera. Along with two thermoses, Kapitnov pulled out a Russian frequency scrambler. Static filled the transmitters for a moment until Felix adjusted the channel on his control panel.

"Why did you go to the embassy?" Kapitnov demanded with a rough growl.

"It was the only place I could go for safety after I saw that some-one had been in my house. I believed someone was trying to kill me. It was obvious someone had been in the house and was possibly still there."

"You say again someone had been in your house, no?"

"Yes, and it was sloppy. I knew I wasn't being checked on. It was something else."

"Something else like what?"

"Not a robbery. Someone had been looking around."

"Jester in place," Jester informed Hammer. He was dressed in a navy-blue room-service outfit. "Waiting for your mark."

"Wait," came the order. "This operation has now been altered again. We will wait until the conversation is over. Jester, fall back until Acclaim gets here."

"ETA?"

"Thirty-five minutes."

"Thirty-five minutes? What's he doing, walking over here?" Jester replied.

"What were 'they' looking for in your house?" the Spymaster inquired harshly. "What do you have?"

"I don't have anything, which is why I left. I feared for my life. At first, I thought it was the Americans. I didn't know what to expect, and I feared the operation had been exposed. Now I know it was Devin, or his men."

"What was at the embassy? Who did you see?"

"I asked to speak to whoever was in charge, and they tortured me. They wanted information, and they would have electrocuted me had I not escaped."

"What did you tell them?" Kapitnov barked.

At this point, Kalisa realized she was a dead woman. Kapitnov did not care that she had been tortured but was thinking only of whether she had spoken of the organization. There was but one consequence for any suspicion of such treason.

"I told them lies, all lies. I made up a name and a story to go along with it. I am loyal, Director. I have never gone against my country, even in training." She looked into the Spymaster's cold, unforgiving eyes. She suddenly realized she would have to seduce him and then kill him if she wanted to stay alive. She had to do it gently, or the Spymaster would see it coming. She forced tears as she spoke. "Director, I have been loyal from the beginning, and I am willing to do anything to convince you so."

"Right now, I want answers. Then, after the answers will come the convincing. The first question is, how were you contacted?"

"I was contacted by Devin."

"Who executed the mission?"

"Garret, as usual."

"Who planned the operation?"

"Devin debriefed Garret and me personally, and the tools used to complete the assignment were also placed in his safe house, as usual. Check, if you do not believe me."

The Spymaster was silent. "Say no more. We will continue this conversation later."

Zyablikov prepared his small boat for push-off. All the electronics had been tested, and his weapons stash had been placed in a box under the boat. Simply opening a hidden hatch in the floor would bring aboard the contents of the box. He was armed with a licensed 9mm handgun. He had fishing equipment all over the place to make his presence look official. He had direct communication with Team D through vibrating devices placed in their suits. The captain of Team

D, Groza Hidislav, communicated back to him with buttons on his suit that sent light patterns up to the deck's receiving devices. The colors were sent in patterns of red, yellow, green, and blue; each color carrying its own message. When Team D emerged from the water, Zyablikov would then be able to communicate with them through airwaves. He gave a quick, routine check by pressing the number three on his disguised cellular phone. This sent a quick pulse to the marine captain. Still underwater, the captain casually responded. The green light on the small boat's console lit up. It meant that everything was still as it was supposed to be. Communication was a difficult task with marine assignments, but Zyablikov had been executing assignments for far too many years not to know the tricks of the trade. He could go with the flow like no other individual. Even when his members made up signs out of desperation, he could figure them out and act on them.

Zyablikov didn't like the uneasiness he felt, but the power surge he savored while executing the mission was exhilarating. He had now broken all rules, and it would free him and the organization from the hand of Russia. There was now no turning back. This was the kind of excitement he lived for. There was no boss but himself. No one to answer to but himself. No one to report to but himself—and everything was at stake. Where the uneasiness came from was the incompleteness of his intelligence. He had no team for procurement of weapons and intelligence as Devin did. There was no one to tell him how many security guards were on the ship, how many floors were on the ship, how many people were on the ship, or how high the ship's balcony was from the water. Did the ship have radar that could spot Team D underwater? There was little intelligence to move on, and he knew there would be a lot of improvisation. That was what made a good spy a great spy. Zyablikov didn't like the level of improvisation in this case because there were far too many unknown factors.

The weapons on hand were traceable, albeit remotely, as there was no one to procure high-priced, untraceable weaponry. The boat had been his from an assignment three years ago. It had been kept simply because getting rid of it would have added complications to the mission. The boat wasn't traceable to the assignment it had been used in, and sinking it would have been a financial and tactical waste.

D-1, Groza Hidislav; D-2, Evapl Rytsarev; D-3, Romil Bolotov; and D-4, Bystraia Rybka, were each anchored under the cruise ship. Team D was equipped with extremely technically advanced marine-combat weapons that were quite accurate out of the water. They used suction cups to latch themselves to the belly of the ship. Under the ship, they were undetectable by any radar the ship might have. They had been lurking underwater since before sunset. Under the cover of semidarkness, all four had slipped into the water and submerged without a sound. It wasn't exactly air they were breathing out of the tanks, but it did the job. The nitrogen had been split from the air compound to make room for more oxygen. Then, using nanotechnology, an apparatus attached to their mouthpieces recycled the carbon dioxide they breathed out and turned a portion of it back into oxygen. The molecular structure of the oxygen was the same—two oxide molecules—but Zyablikov and Team D knew it wasn't the same. If exposed to this oxygen for several consecutive hours, the human body would have negative reactions: nausea, dizziness, and terribly bad breath. Team D had been trained for this breathing method for years, and Zyablikov was approaching violation of one of the few rules he had stood by since he could remember. He knew that any more than four hours of continuous exposure to the special oxygen would definitely have irrevocable consequences. He remembered when he himself was under the water and breathing through the mouthpiece. Everything had seemed fine until he had removed it, and his lungs, which had been exposed to one kind of oxygen for four hours, had been forced to switch on a moment's notice. He vividly remembered the chest pains, the choking, and the feeling that he would be sick or drown during the training. The physical complications of this tactic would certainly put any assignment in jeopardy.

All five of them had synchronized their maritime apparatuses to eliminate timing issues, and considering that Team D might need to use the tanks in the event something went wrong with the escape added yet another uncomfortable feeling. Zyablikov would not dare to endanger the marine team's lives or the operation's chances of success by letting them stay exposed to the recycled compound for longer than four hours. Besides, he cared about his comrades. Feelings aside, breaking this rule was completely asinine, and if Hidislav did it, Hidislav would die.

Though the four-hour limit was unquestionably a primary concern, as long as they were "up and at 'em" in four hours, there was no reason to worry. What Zyablikov was concerned about was Team D's uncanny knack for violence. Zyablikov was convinced that all four of them were mentally disturbed, as everyone in the organization was, in a way, but Team D was interminably addicted to killing. They were a team full of Oleg Lugors—but twice as wild. They were clearly certified psychopaths with heavy personal issues to deal with. They weren't exactly rambunctious or out of control. They always stayed on task during assignments. But when there was room for messy killings, they went into a frenzy that left blood splattered everywhere, with remorse nowhere to be found. Such behavior was partly due to the team captain, Hidislav.

Groza Hidislav was a born marine fighter and had been given the name Hidislav, meaning "watery glory." He could fight better in water than he could on land and could hold his breath for nearly as long as fish could. Zyablikov recalled the time he had been executing an assignment to commandeer a shipment of warheads being transported across the Atlantic Ocean to Iraq. Because the ship was literally in the middle of nowhere, once the radio communication was cut, noise and messiness were no longer of concern. There was no one around for hundreds of miles. After the slaughter of the deck guards, Hidislav and Zyablikov began tossing their bodies overboard. Hidislav plucked out one of the naval soldier's eyeballs and chewed it as if it was a grape. Zyablikov remembered how Hidislav had smacked loudly as he chewed the human eye and smiled as he licked the blood and optic fluids off of his lips. This behavior could be diagnosed as cannibalism or some other sickness of amorality. However, considering that every individual in the Pit had been created to be a killing machine, coupled with the intense violence they had been excessively exposed to, it could only be considered normal. Zyablikov had seen far worse than mere eyeball chewing, but he no longer wondered why Groza had chosen his first name, Terror.

"The conversation is over, Jester," Hammer realized. "Move *now*."

Jester quickly moved out into the corridor and approached the Spymaster's room.

Felix noticed a small blip on his radar screen. He turned to the satellite image of the surrounding area and focused on the coordinates where the radar told him the movement was. It seemed to be some type of local fishing boat. He quickly swiveled his chair around to the console and typed in the commands to bring up a profile of the shallow area of the Atlantic Ocean. The list was long. It even included turtles. The computer gave him a profile of what fish would be in the area and how edible they were: blues, tarpon, grouper, tuna, snooks, weakfish, sea bass, and tuna. *OK, maybe he does have a reason to be out here,* Felix thought, *but I don't want to take the chance.*

Felix grabbed the CIA-edition ComLink from his bag and pressed Acclaim's code.

"Acclaim here, go ahead," answered Acclaim.

"Listen, there's a local fishing boat. Send beach patrol to check him out. Looks like he's fishing, but he's following our ship. Get beach patrol down there on him immediately."

"It's done. Give me a visual description of the boat."

Felix glanced at his screen and then activated his image enhancer. The computer marked the gridlines. Otherwise, it was difficult to assess the size of objects with a bird's-eye view.

"White-and-blue boat. About 30 feet long, cruising east at 22 knots. Handle it, Acclaim. Then get over here. You are single-handedly holding up progress."

"ETA 15 minutes," Acclaim replied, "but the beach patrol should be at the spot in less than five."

"Get on it," Felix answered before disconnecting.

Acclaim had no idea who he had really spoken to, nor did he recognize the voice, but the directions came from the ComLink, and he would obey.

Zyablikov was now more relaxed. The sun had set, and the cover of darkness was upon him. This was the only thing he was waiting for. There was no need to wait until the cruise liner got out into the middle of the Atlantic. All that would mean was a higher risk in travel. His tiny boat sure couldn't walk over the rough waves of the ocean, and if there was a storm, the vessel would surely capsize. Under the cover of night, everything would work out.

He checked his fishing lines and his net. There was nothing, but it really didn't matter. Zyablikov was not an expert at fishing, yet he was not quite a novice. He had learned to fish in order to blend in with his surroundings. While performing certain marine assignments, fishing was necessary so as not to stand out. He knew some of the rules, had read a few books, and could talk a good game, but when it came to experience, he would rather stick to killing.

He reflected on his position and what failure would mean on this operation. The mission was twofold: assassinate Kapitnov and recover Kalisa. If Kalisa was not rescued, she would die, and if the Spymaster was not killed, Devin would make sure the manhunt for Zyablikov was successful and that his death was slow and painful. More important to Zyablikov than the death of the Spymaster was the rescue of his "sister." They had grown close, and though they did not speak to each other ever, except for assignments, there definitely was a bond. Kalisa was the only female Zyablikov had ever trusted or felt he had anything in common with. She was his only friend of the opposite sex. Others in the organization were more like schoolmates or coworkers than friends. The Pit instructors made sure that everyone competed against each other all of the time, alleviating true kinship and alliance. Members of all the teams followed his orders not because they liked him but because there was a chain of command. In the bowels of this game of high stakes, a swift and unforgiving chain of command was necessary to avoid disorder, chaos, and treason. The consequences were high for any deviation of orders, and the Pit gave captains the flexibility to exercise discipline among their respective teams.

He gave Hidislav a routine check again and received a green light. In a few moments, he would give the go-ahead.

There was a knock at the Spymaster's door.

"Yes?" he answered without opening the door.

"This is an emergency. Open up, please."

The Spymaster looked through the peephole, saw a uniformed officer, and opened the door.

"Sir, we have had a bomb threat on the deck. We need to evacuate all passengers on this floor to another level. We have a room waiting for you."

"Give us a second," the Spymaster replied.

"I can give you about 40 seconds. This is urgent."

The Spymaster threw some things into a bag, including the scrambler, motioned for Kalisa to follow, and then shadowed Jester into the corridor. The Spymaster looked around. "How come no one else is moving?" he growled at Jester.

Without breaking stride or looking back, Jester replied, "Sir, we are trying to do this quietly. We don't know if the threat is real or a practical joke, but we take these matters seriously. We don't want to ruin anyone's vacation by yelling 'bomb.' Everyone will be evacuated from this floor until the search is completed."

"You're not stopping the cruise?"

"By the time we would have gotten back to shore, the search would have been completed. Please, just follow me."

The Spymaster had no choice but to obey, or he would attract attention to himself. He followed Jester one floor below to a room at the end of a hallway and watched him open a door to let them both in. Sparrow quickly emerged from around the corner.

"Excuse me. Only men are allowed in that cabin. Please bear with us until we can get this crisis resolved quickly and quietly."

"She is with me," the Spymaster said adamantly.

"I'm sure she is with you. Hopefully, this will be no longer than 20 minutes. She will be right in the next room, just as safe as you will be. I am following regulations, sir. Federal law requires us to isolate males and females during emergency-level precautions. Children are the only exception. This is to prevent unnecessary conflicts by lowering the possibility of confusion or disturbance. The crew would be breaching federal law if we did not follow procedure in this circumstance. Miss, please follow me now. Sir, we have provided courtesy drinks for your convenience. Please help yourself." Her phase of the con was done. Sparrow walked out of the doorway.

Kalisa, not wanting to be near the Spymaster, followed Sparrow. She had never heard of the law Sparrow had fabricated but did not care. The Spymaster was a less attractive option than any type of bomb threat. Jester closed the door behind the Spymaster and walked the opposite way of Sparrow as she led Kalisa into the stairwell. Though this was strictly a plot to get the Spymaster alone, AEGIS had no idea of the irony of their hoax.

As he was about to signal Hidislav to move, Zyablikov heard a vessel approaching behind him. He looked and saw the Florida Coast Patrol emerging from the shadows. The boat flashed its blue and red lights but did not disrupt the night stillness with its siren. The lights temporarily blinded Zyablikov as the patrol boat drew closer. Zyablikov sat down, casually leaned back, and relaxed. The patrol-boat captain turned off the flashing lights and pulled alongside Zyablikov's boat.

The patrolman looked into the boat for a minute and then greeted the athletic-looking young man relaxing in his vessel.

"Howdy," the marine officer said.

"Hey, officer," Zyablikov replied. "I'm not breaking any laws tonight, am I?"

"Doesn't really look like it, but we've had some reports of illegal activities going on. Mind if I come aboard and look around?"

The Coast Patrol was definitely an obstruction to the mission. If they found the weapons, he wouldn't be able to signal Hidislav to move and the operation wouldn't even start. If he failed to allow the patrolman to board or asked for a warrant, he knew that his every move would be monitored from afar, and suspicions were sure to be aroused.

"What if you scare away the fish?" Zyablikov asked.

"I promise I won't scare away your dinner. I'm just going to come aboard, take a look around, and try to be back on shore in a half hour."

A half an hour, Zyablikov repeated inside his head. He could not wait that long. Once Nukludko cut the ship's lights off, the ship would radio for help, and help would arrive in ten minutes. He could not wait until the cop left to commence the operation. They would be too far out to sea, and the artificial air Team D was breathing would have disastrous effects within that half hour. He would have to execute the operation while talking to the patrolman.

"I guess a quick look wouldn't hurt anything," Zyablikov replied.

"Thanks for your cooperation," the officer said and started to climb into the boat.

Zyablikov looked into the patrol boat at the two other officers there. Zyablikov gave them a terse head nod. Each of the officers returned a dry wave.

Zyablikov could wait no longer. Team D was enough at risk. A minute longer, and he was eating into their sobriety. He looked at his synchronized watch and saw he had about 30 seconds to set the assignment off. Prolonged exposure to the recycled air affected judgment, and even seconds made a difference in this case. It was a known fact in training and past assignments that any longer than four hours was hazardous, possibly fatal. He wasn't too worried about the marine team drowning. With their training and exposure to the nanotechnology system, the possibility of fatal outcomes was extremely remote. He was more concerned about the dizziness and other side effects of the faux oxygen.

It seemed that darkness had taken forever to come. When it came, the patrol boat had come with it. The patrolman was fully in the boat now, and as he got his footing inside Zyablikov's small boat, Zyablikov reached into his pocket and felt for his transmitter. Orienting its layout by determining the direction of the antenna, he located the 9 button. He looked at the console; the yellow light flashed. The mission had started.

The patrolman saw the light from the corner of his eye. Zyablikov noticed it.

"What was that?" the patrolman asked, looking toward the front of the ship.

"What was what?" Zyablikov responded. "I didn't hear anything."

"There was a flashing light or something," the patrolman replied, "toward the front of the ship."

"Oh, that's flashing bait. It's supposed to attract dinner. Picked it up in this catalog. Couldn't resist."

"Does it work?"

"Nope. You see it's in this boat with us."

"Technology these days is something."

"You can say that again. At least I never lose the thing. It's about to change careers. It'll make a great keychain."

"Great idea," the patrolman responded. "I always lose my keys. Now, I hate to make you move all around while you're fishing, but I need to see some ID, your license, and registration."

"Not a problem," Zyablikov responded. He got up and went inside the small cabin. When he was out of the officer's sight, he quickly slid his earpiece into his ear and attached the Walkman to his belt. He could now hear Team D's every word to him. He pulled the microphone from up his sleeve to the front of his wrist, where it remained hidden by his sleeve. Now he would be able to talk to Team D and A-4 by placing his hand on his cheek and mumbling. He could listen through his "Walkman," which actually was an audio scrambler so anyone monitoring the open waves would hear distorted voice waves. Zyablikov opened the tiny drawer and retrieved Dennis Garret's paperwork. "A-4, move on the word 'officer,'" he whispered into his sleeve.

Team D stealthily emerged from the water. The four of them briefly looked around the water's surface and saw that though they were only so many miles from the shore, they were covered in darkness. They each slid off their marine-vision goggles and put on night-vision goggles. Hidislav did not understand how the lights would be out in the boat, but there were many things he did not understand about each mission. He understood the purpose of the clandestineness. He knew his next contact was to be when he was two-thirds of the way up the ship's wall, which would not be long.

Upon receiving the vibration, Gremis Nukludko, aka A-4, headed toward the breaker room, which he had found before the ship had left the port. He briefly wondered why the phrase to detonate the bomb had been changed and found it strange that there was no blueprint or map of the ship. No one even gave him a key to the electrical room as was usually done. Despite these minor issues, Nukludko had no problems constructing the bombs needed to complete his portion of the assignment. He walked toward the electrical room, eyeing the corridor for cameras. There were none. He removed a metal pen from his pocket and squirted a clear liquid between the doorknob and the doorframe. The clear liquid was an acid concocted by the Pit's lab scientists. It would eat through any regular metals and would practically liquefy anything weaker, like wood, clay, or skin. This was why the pen that carried the acid was made of a reinforced alloy of titanium. Though it was considered for use as a weapon, there was a problem of range. The acid would squirt only so many feet ahead of the shooter. Ideas to place the acid in pellets or capsules had been rendered infeasible. First, there was no viable material that could hold the acid long enough to do the necessary harm to stop someone in their tracks, or weak enough to explode and distribute the acid upon impact.

A-4 watched as the acid ate through the wood and lock without sound or smell. Then he opened the door and closed himself inside the room. Next, he pulled out his plastic explosives and placed them among the electrical circuits. Lastly, he activated them for instant remote detonation.

Though the Spymaster had ingested a small amount of the truth agent, Hammer thought it was time to start the interview. He knew to be gentle. The Spymaster was still a very important person to both sides. This meant no force and no roughhousing.

"Director Boris Kapitnov, welcome to America. It's too bad you're headed back home so soon. The Keys are very nice this time of year. And it's not every day we get to see the man himself." A cleverly disguised Hammer smiled at the Spymaster. He saw that the Spymaster had on a pretty masterful disguise himself, and thought that if any American had seen Kapitnov's face on the news, then had looked at this man, they would see no resemblance. "I was wondering what brought you to these parts."

"Who are you?"

"Agent Robinson, Special Forces, FBI. If we knew you were going to be on board, we would have hired some escorts. It's strange that you are without an entourage. This woman must be pretty special for you to go through these artful measures to spend time with her. Your lovely wife back home in Russia must be all broken up over your sudden unavoidable business trip. No worries. I won't get into your personal affairs. It's your business, of course. What I am here for is to make sure that your cruise is a safe one. The U.S. offers any service necessary to ensure you get back home safely."

The Spymaster's response was silence.

They both knew this was a farce, a game, but with the truth agent slowly taking effect, AEGIS could soon get answers to several questions.

Nukludko left the electrical room and headed to the stairwell, and there he waited.

Hidislav and his team scaled the wall of the ship, and when he estimated his crew was two-thirds of the way to the top, he signaled Zyablikov.

"D in position, Iceman."

On Zyablikov's boat, the Coast Patrol officer did not hear these words as he followed orders and searched the boat for illegal paraphernalia. All the patrolman heard was the small radio on board the boat playing soft music.

"Officer," Zyablikov said, signaling Nukludko. He then moved his wrist away from his mouth before continuing, "What kind of illegal activities have been surfacing in a nice town like this? I haven't noticed anything unusual."

Hearing the code, Nukludko set off the explosives, and with a muffled boom, the ship went dark.

Felix heard audio through his receiver again. It was static-covered, but this time, he definitely heard voices. As he reached for the audio devices, the ship's power went off, and Felix was sitting in the dark.

"Please tell me there is a *very* good reason for this," Felix snapped as all the lights faded from his electrical equipment. Only his laptop continued to function. Running on battery, it had been spared.

On the stairwell in the instantly spawned darkness, Kalisa quickly smashed Sparrow in the throat and started for the steps. If she made it up to the deck, she would jump overboard. Sparrow had never seen the blow coming but recovered quickly and leaped forward into the darkness at Kalisa, knocking her forward onto the steps. Sparrow reached for her pistol but was forced to shield herself as they both rolled back down the stairs, fighting.

Team D scurried over the top of the ledge and laid a large bag on the deck. In the total darkness, each man grabbed an automatic weapon from the bag. Each of the weapons was fitted with the most technologically advanced silencers available worldwide. They had already been screwed onto each barrel, along with infrared laser sights.

The team searched the deck for the stairwell.

"Iceman, I need a location for the stairwell," Hidislav requested.

"In the front of the ship," Zyablikov answered. The officer looked over as Zyablikov started speaking. "—are some chips and stuff. Feel free to help yourself." Zyablikov pointed for the officer's benefit and to keep the microphones away from his mouth. He wanted to avoid any confusion in his response to Team D.

"Don't mind if I do," replied the patrolman.

Team D hustled to the front of the ship and saw the stairwell. With their night-vision goggles, they had no problem maneuvering through the crowd. In the stairwell, they met Nukludko, who led them downstairs to the Spymaster's room. Hidislav kicked in the door with a violent yell, only to reveal that there was no one in sight inside the room. Team D quickly tore apart the room and rummaged any remote hiding place that a human body could possibly fit into. Rytsarev quickly searched the bathroom and signaled Hidislav that they were not found there. Hidislav cursed out loud when he realized the room was empty.

"The nest is empty." Hidislav spoke through the wire and then pressed the far right button on a pad attached to his wetsuit. Zyablikov saw the red light, the signal that there was an urgent situation and Team D needed immediate instructions on how to proceed.

Zyablikov was thinking. Neither the Spymaster nor Kalisa was in the room. Nukludko was supposed to have placed transmitters on both of them but had reported a tail following them, so Zyablikov had advised him to stay out of sight. If an agent was tailing the Spymaster, surely that agent would take note of whoever happened to bump into him. He thought the only place they could possibly be was on deck.

"Check up top," he instructed Team D and Nukludko and then finished the sentence, addressing the officer, "if you don't see the snacks on the right side of the cabinet." Team D quickly headed for the stairwell.

The two coast patrolmen signaled excitedly to their officer on Zyablikov's boat.

"There's a bomb on the cruise ship!" one of the officers exclaimed.

The officer on board Zyablikov's ship stopped what he was doing and mumbled, "Gotta go, buddy." He hurriedly climbed back into his patrol boat and was off, this time with sirens wailing.

Still recovering from Kalisa's precise and painful neck blow, Sparrow wrestled her way on top of Kalisa. Kalisa was irritated; she had no time to wrestle this woman. Should the lights come on before she was overboard, she would die by the Spymaster's hand for trying to escape. If she tried to run in this darkness, she knew a woman of this ferocity could catch her.

Sparrow knew how to block her opponent's hand from the proper spots in order stay alive but was awestruck by the strength of this woman. She recognized that this was not a regular American citizen but a trained assassin.

Kalisa was unarmed and needed a weapon to neutralize her fierce opponent. She looked around while punching but saw none available on the stairwell. Her punches were not landing where she wanted them to land. Sparrow would block them, knock them off target, or skillfully dodge them, all the while raining blows upon Kalisa with incredible precision. Kalisa bucked her torso like an acrobat and turned sideways, forcing Sparrow into the corner of the stairwell, and quickly followed the move with a powerful punch to Sparrow's face. The impact slammed Sparrow's head against the steel wall, rendering her senseless. There Sparrow lay while Kalisa pummeled her head with five more direct strikes, driving her head against the steel wall with each hit. When Sparrow stopped moving, Kalisa started up the stairs once again. Sprinting, she reached the second floor.

Rytsarev heard someone running up the stairs and looked behind him. He spotted Kalisa instantly with his night-vision goggles. She looked exactly as she had in the photo at the briefing.

"Jennifer Johnson, Iceman has asked that you follow us," Rytsarev stated.

Hearing her brother's codename, she quickly caught up with Team D.

"Where is the Director?" Hidislav asked.

"Downstairs, third room on the left," Kalisa replied.

Nukludko, Rybka, and Kalisa ran up the stairs toward the deck. Groza Hidislav, Evapl Rytsarev, and Romil Bolotov, now the assassination squad, headed downstairs.

Kalisa, Gremis Nukludko, and Bystraia Rybka sped across the deck in the darkness and went airborne at the end of the deck, diving into the vast waters. Nukludko knew he had only seconds. Still airborne, he yelled into his microphone, "The egg is captured."

Zyablikov wanted to shout in relief. "I'm coming, hold fast," he replied, placing red and blue police lights on the front of his boat. He activated them and sped off toward the cruise ship.

Rybka was the only one who had dove head-first off the cruise ship, but all three hit the water and felt the impact thoroughly. Nukludko and Kalisa were not equipped with scuba gear and saw that the shore was more than a few miles away. Rybka held out a neon glow stick so Zyablikov could locate them in the darkness. Though small, its glow was easy enough to spot in the pitch-black darkness. Bystraia

Rybka, 'Quick Fish,' had been named for his ability to operate efficiently and effectively underwater. Though the water was cold and dark, Rybka was able to keep everyone afloat until Zyablikov could make his way to their location.

Groza Hidislav, Romil Bolotov, and Evapl Rytsarev raced downstairs. Through their night-vision goggles, they saw Sparrow sitting up on the stairwell. Bolotov put his foot in Sparrow's chest and knocked her back to the floor. Once again, she was victimized in the thick darkness before she even saw it coming.

Rytsarev looked down at her. "Move and die," he said.

Sparrow lay on the steel floor until the men had exited the stairwell. Then she got up, pulled out her Rex, and started after them. "Floor three, armed gunmen coming your way, Hammer," Sparrow informed Hammer urgently through the IAT.

In response, Hammer quickly pulled the Spymaster to the ground and crawled to the bed. He pulled a large PAR-6800 pump-action rifle from under the bed and turned toward the door. "Get behind the bed!" Hammer yelled to Kapitnov. The Spymaster obeyed and dove behind the bed. Hammer quickly followed and poised the rifle atop the mattress. The luxury cotton bed was now a fortress.

The door that separated Hammer from the team of rigorous assassins soon fell inward, following a barrage of completely silent automatic gunfire from outside the door. Though he could barely see anything, Hammer returned fire. With a thunderous explosion, he blasted the doorway, but when the smoke cleared, he saw no one standing in the entrance. The window in this room provided dim lighting as the moonbeam gave a weak attempt to eat through the darkness, but he could see that no one had been hit. He knew the intense power of the PAR-6800, so he blasted again, tearing a large hole through the wall to the right of the doorframe. Through the large hole, he saw nothing. He cocked the PAR again and blasted to the left of the doorframe. Again, he saw nothing. It was as if his enemy were invisible. It was surely automatic gunfire that had caused the door to give in, and not a bomb, yet the shooter wasn't in the doorway, nor to the right of it, nor to its left.

Hammer was blind against three gunmen while he had a foreign officer to protect. He had been in worse situations and was not at all intimidated, but what worried him was that he did not know where his enemy was. Since he could not use his sight, he would have to double his other senses immediately. He remembered there was a Bible on the dresser beside him where the head of the bed and the wall met. He asked the Spymaster to reach over and grab it so no one would have to stand up, making themselves visible to the invisible enemy. Kapitnov found the Bible and blindly handed it to Hammer with a strange look on his face. Hammer said a quick prayer of apology, then began softly ripping wads of pages out of the Bible and scrunching them up.

Hidislav, Bolotov, and Rytsarev were lying on the carpet in the corridor. Hidislav and Rytsarev were to the left of the doorway, Bolotov to the right. Through the night-vision goggles, Bolotov saw Sparrow creeping in the darkness with her pistol drawn. Lying low, he sprayed his automatic weapon in her direction, being extremely careful not to harm his teammates lying across from him.

For the third time, before she knew what had hit her, Sparrow was knocked to the ground. She instinctively rolled back inside the stairwell before any more shots came. All she saw was the brief flash from the automatic weapon, and all she heard were the whispers of the silenced bullets coming after her. She saw that the flash came from an unnaturally low level, close to the ground, and softly alerted Hammer that his enemies were lying on the ground beside the doorway. Sparrow was shocked by the sudden attack and glad that her protective vest had kept her from any harm. She knew she was fortunate that the assailant was lying on the ground and had only fired a general spray in her direction. If he had been standing up, the heavy concentration of automatic fire would probably have penetrated the vest.

Hammer cursed the steel bureau drawers on either side of the doorway. If he shot at them with the PAR, the bullets would ricochet all over the room. Hammer pulled out his Rex and placed it on the floor to the left of him because though the PAR was the most powerful pump-action rifle in existence, it only had nine shots.

In the stairwell, Sparrow tried to come up with a plan to fight an enemy she couldn't see. Hammer's life depended on it. Her Tracer 34X was no good; it seemed that the scuba gear the enemy wore contained all body heat, leaving no way for her to lock on to her target. She cursed silently as she realized she also had brought no gas bombs with her. She laid belly-down on the ground and without a sound opened the stairwell door a crack. With the Rex, she blasted twice in the gunman's direction. Before the return fire, she had rolled back into the cover of the stairwell. Rytsarev's return shots hit the stairwell door as it closed.

Someone tapped Sparrow on the shoulder. Before she could lift the Rex in the tapper's direction, a hand forcefully grabbed her wrist, preventing her from lifting the gun.

"It's Jester," he whispered. "Put these on." He handed her a pair of high-reality night-vision goggles.

Rytsarev began to crawl toward the stairwell to finish off Sparrow. Hidislav motioned for him to stay put, then motioned them to move toward the primary target. Hidislav rolled through the doorway, letting loose a spray of bullets. This kept Hammer and the Spymaster ducked behind the bed while Bolotov and Rytsarev rushed into the Spymaster's room like lightning. They both crawled to either side of the large bed. When the quiet automatic spray stopped, Hammer poised the PAR again, blasted into the darkness, and hit no one.

"Will someone get these damn lights on," Hammer growled into the IAT.

Bolotov crawled belly-down toward the foot of the bed, and Hidislav threw a lamp behind the bed where Hammer was, hoping to force him around toward Bolotov. The lamp landed on Kapitnov.

"Director Kapitnov, please stand up, and you will not be harmed!" Hidislav shouted. "We have been sent to retrieve you."

Kapitnov did not stand up. The Spymaster was simply not fooled. Hidislav fell silent, watching Bolotov scoot to the foot of the bed adjacent to where Hammer was positioned. Hammer heard the Bible paper he had placed at the foot of the bed crunching underneath the weight of something. Without moving his body, he quietly grasped his Rex, reached around the corner of the bed to where he had placed the Bible pages, and blindly shot twice.

An ordinary pistol would have shot right over Bolotov, who was still belly-down on the floor, but the Rex was infamous for its spread shot and put tiny bullets in Bolotov's back. When Hammer heard the painful grunt, he quickly realized his enemy was lying flat on the ground. He aimed downward and fired two more times with the Rex. Both direct hits showered bullet pellets all over Bolotov's back. Hammer heard the Rex's slide lock back, signaling that the weapon was now empty.

Zyablikov saw the green glow in the water and picked up Nukludko, Kalisa, and Rybka. He enjoyed perfect camouflage with all the Coast Guard patrol boats speeding toward the cruise ship like vultures flocking to a fallen beast in the desert.

"D-1, report status," Zyablikov instructed.

"We've got him pinned down, Iceman," Hidislav reported.

Zyablikov saw two more patrol boats speed past him toward the scene. It was decision time. The police were surrounding the ship. Zyablikov knew with certainty that if Hidislav and his team stayed on the ship for 60 more seconds, they would be captured. If Team D could get overboard and under water before the boat was surrounded, then they would have a better than average chance of a safe return. But what of the Spymaster's return to Russia? Zyablikov would have hell to pay once Kapitnov and Devin got together. If he let Team D stay aboard to assassinate the Spymaster, it would be only himself against Devin, which pushed the odds highly in his favor. If Team D was captured, then the organization would be exposed and Zyablikov would be a dead man anyway. He decided to take his chances with the Spymaster based over in Russia, rather than be sought after by countless American agencies. Yet an unsuccessful attempt on the Spymaster's life put everyone in grave danger. He wanted to give Team D more time, but they had none. If all three of the team were captured, the risk of the Americans getting one of them to talk was three times as high, and the network could not be exposed to the Americans at *any* cost. He would take his chances with one man and would frame Devin for this charade: Devin had kidnapped Kalisa in order to stop her from testifying that Devin was behind the Yuklivitch assassination, and then tried to kill Kalisa and the Spymaster. It made perfect sense.

"Pull out," Zyablikov instructed.

"Iceman, we have the target pinned down. Give me 60 seconds," Hidislav replied.

Zyablikov looked at the patrol boats speeding toward the cruise ship like roaches toward a pile of wet sugar. He knew if they did not pull out now, they would be captured.

"Fall back, now."

"Fall back," Hidislav told his team while spraying bullets over the bed to keep Hammer at bay. Hidislav noticed Bolotov's sluggish movement, and as he looked longer with the night-vision goggles, he realized his comrade was bleeding. As Team D retreated to the corridor, Sparrow and Jester fired upon sight, both aiming for headshots. Bolotov turned toward them, and just before he took a body hit from Sparrow's Rex, he launched a spray of bullets toward both of them. The bullets embedded themselves into Sparrow and Jester's vests, knocking both of them onto the ground. From the ground, Sparrow blasted at the air tanks strapped to Team D's backs to prevent their escapes.

Upon impact with the second wave of Rex bullets, Bolotov's air tank exploded. He crashed into the wall of the corridor. Hidislav, blocked by an already wounded Bolotov, threw a smoke bomb, which released a cloud of thick white smoke upon impact with the ground. Sparrow and Jester blasted into the cloud with the Rexes but within moments started to choke from the thick smoke. Hidislav and Rytsarev rushed toward the stairwell through the smoke and past the choking Jester and Sparrow. As fast as lightning, they were up one flight of stairs. They both looked back for Bolotov; he was not behind them.

"D-3 down; please advise," Hidislav reported to Zyablikov.

"Pull out now. Do not stop," Zyablikov answered. As much as it hurt to do so, he had to leave Romil Bolotov behind. If he was dead, he couldn't do much talking, but if Hidislav and Rytsarev went back for him, they wouldn't make it off the ship.

Hidislav and Rytsarev continued up the steps toward the deck. A passenger was stumbling through the darkness, and Hidislav took his head off with his automatic weapon by shooting the man across the neck, not wanting to make the same mistake Bolotov had made with Sparrow. The man's head rolled down the stairwell like a lopsided soccer ball. Without missing a step after the murder, Hidislav and Rytsarev both emerged on deck. From the deck, they saw police boats on three sides of the ship. They ran to the far side of the deck and dove overboard. Wasting no time, they dropped their night-vision goggles into the ocean while airborne, replacing them with the marine-vision goggles hanging from their necks. They hit the black water with a splash, secured their mouthpieces, and submerged underwater, disappearing like ghosts.

Felix looked at his laptop radar and saw several vessels coming toward the cruise ship and one vessel speeding away. The satellite image was down, so Felix could not get an overhead view on the boat. He spoke to Jester. "I've spotted the getaway boat. It's heading northwest toward the docks." Felix groped in the darkness for his ComLink and dialed Acclaim.

"Acclaim here."

"The getaway vessel is heading northeast toward the docks. Do not let it get past you. I don't care if you have to sink it. Proceed with caution; suspects are armed and dangerous."

"On the way. Is there a visual on the boat?"

"That's a negative on the visual. There is only one boat heading away from the action. Get it!"

The tone was arrogant, but Acclaim knew this was a matter of extreme urgency. He ordered his boat to turn northeast and, with his binoculars, spotted the getaway boat. "Over there!" he shouted, pointing to the small speeding boat.

The unmarked FBI boat put on its sirens and turned on its high-wattage light, aiming it at the getaway vessel.

"Do not let them get away!" Acclaim shouted at his men. "Get the weapons ready; these aren't Boy Scouts we're dealing with," he ordered.

"Sparrow!" Hammer barked, rising from behind the bed. "Secure the director, then tell the ship's officers to take the injured suspect and hold him until we give further orders. I want six men transporting the director with you. Show your FBI badge for this one, and call Walter Plack down here. He'll handle this like it should be handled. Aquaman here doesn't exactly get his phone call. When the director is secure, go to wherever Walter is holding the suspect. We'll contact you later. Felix, get three wetsuits out here, and meet us up top on deck. You have 45 seconds!" AEGIS already knew they were going after the assassins. In less than a second, the hunted had become the hunters. Hammer, Jester, and Felix were on deck, and in less than five minutes, they had donned motor-propelled wetsuits and armed themselves with aquatic weaponry.

Zyablikov saw the light instantly, even though he wasn't facing it. He turned toward the wide illumination and spotted the large boat speeding toward them with lights flashing.

With nowhere to hide, he would have to outsmart them. He slowed down and looked at his comrade. He tossed D-4 what was needed and grunted, "Take care of them."

With a nod, Bystraia Rybka sat on the starboard-side railing of the vessel and then leaned backwards overboard and into the dark water. He silently crept through the water toward the larger boat, which was closing in fast on the small getaway vessel. His powerful strokes and thrusts allowed him to move along underwater at speeds not thought humanly possible. His spectacular marine vision goggles allowed him to easily see his target. He maneuvered himself upward toward the bottom of the ship and released a suction line from his belt, then attached the line to the ship. To an observer, his next action would have looked like Rybka had punched the boat. He had attached the suction device to the ship. It would keep him under the vessel and from having to keep up with it. He was now one with his target. With some work, he attached a brick-sized device to the ship's bottom. Though small, the device was highly dangerous, and Rybka felt no remorse about attaching the device to its target.

"I want your hands on top of your heads! All of you!" Special Agent Acclaim yelled through the bullhorn as he approached the smaller boat.

Everyone aboard the small getaway boat kept their eyes on Zyablikov. As he slowly raised his hands, his party mimicked him. "Do not move," he whispered without moving his lips.

Acclaim's unmarked boat kept the high-wattage lamp on all three suspects while Acclaim belted out his next orders. "Do not attempt to move the boat in any way!" Acclaim yelled. He removed the bullhorn from his mouth and instructed one of his associates to call for backup. If this was the same organization that had pulled off the *Washington Post* heist and the Yuklivitch assassination, there was no way this group was surrendering this easily. He had expected all three of them to dive into the water and disperse in different directions. He was suspicious.

Zyablikov's party remained still.

Acclaim pulled his ComLink out of his pocket and pushed the code he had been instructed to dial only in case of emergencies.

There was a high-pitched tone in the darkness on deck. Felix groped for his ComLink.

"Yes, go ahead," Felix said urgently while Jester assisted him with strapping his air tank on.

"Acclaim here. I have all three suspects aboard their getaway boat. One female, two males. Female and one male are soaking wet. Female is 5'10" or so, black hair. First male is 5'10", gray hair with a brown fishing cap on, about 190. He's the dry one. The other wet one is 6'1", black hair, about 175 or so. It looks like they have all surrendered, but I don't buy it. They're not moving, and it doesn't look like they are going to jump out of the boat."

"Do not put one nickel on the surrender game. Get two choppers out there now! Get all available local beach patrols out to the scene, and line the perimeter of the beach. Make sure all of the men are equipped and ready to go. Different rules here, kid. These guys are professional assassins, and dangerous, to say the least. If they get remotely slick with you, shoot first. Do not hesitate. If you happen to shoot one of them in the head, please do me a personal favor and not feel bad about it. I'll get a team there as soon as possible. Do not attempt to rescue any passengers from the boat. Get as much light as you can on the water beside your boat and the suspects. Make sure nothing unseen is lurking in the vicinity. If you see anything move in the water, shoot it. If it's a fish, we'll all eat it. Do not attempt to apprehend these individuals yourselves. This is not the time to be a hero. Let's play this smart. Wait until backup arrives, and keep them in the boat. Take pictures while you are waiting. When backup arrives, throw one of those gargantuan fishing nets under the water to surround the area, so I hope you guys didn't forget your wetsuits. I'll be there momentarily."

"How will I know it's you? What do you look like?"

"You won't know it's me, and you never will know what I look like. Just carry out the plan, Acclaim. Out."

Acclaim turned the ComLink off of transmit mode and stared at his trapped suspects. They looked a little too calm.

"Get some light on all the water. We might have a man under the surface! Anything that moves, shoot it," Acclaim instructed.

In less than two seconds, the area around both boats was illuminated. The water was still dark, but anything seen coming past the surface would be a target. Acclaim also radioed for choppers and requested that the local beach patrol get as many units as possible out to assist them.

Less than six feet under the dark ocean surface, Rybka saw the light above the surface. He swam deeper, down and away from the illumination. He swam toward Zyablikov's boat, and when he was sure he was under it, he ascended gracefully toward the bottom of the boat, away from the light. The only viable way to signal to Zyablikov that the device was placed was to use the only one of his five human senses he had left—sound. He rammed the bottom of the boat with his fist. Zyablikov heard the sound and interpreted it as a ready signal. The sound would have been somewhat audible to someone in the FBI boat who was listening carefully enough, but no one was, so it went unheard. The sound came again, louder. Zyablikov stood on his tiptoes and crashed down with as much force as possible as a signal to his teammate to quit banging. Rybka heard the noise and saw Zyablikov's boat bobble slightly. He correctly interpreted this as a signal to stop the racket.

Zyablikov had to figure a way to get to the detonator, which he had dropped when the federal guns came out. He scanned the floor for it. The Feds' illumination of the area helped immensely. He spotted the small device on the floor near Kalisa. There was no way to get to it. He looked over at Acclaim holding a shotgun on him from the opposite boat. Zyablikov pretended to stretch gently, and gracefully changed positions, toward the detonator.

Acclaim caught the movement. "Get your ass back there to the other side of the boat!" he yelled. "And if you move again one inch,

I *will* shoot you! If you think this is a game, roll the dice!" Acclaim now realized he had to keep his eyes on the suspects at *all* times. He quickly turned away from scanning the surface of the water and kept his eyes on the suspects. He studied them from head to toe and watched every move.

Zyablikov read the shotgun guard's eyes. Though some distance away, Zyablikov knew the guard wanted nothing better than to empty a 16-round burst into him. It was up to Kalisa to retrieve the device. Without moving his lips, he whispered her name.

With her hands still on top of her head, she twitched her elbow backward swiftly to tell Zyablikov that she could hear him and was ready for whatever he had to say.

Acclaim noticed the elbow but did not know what to make of it. Though the unknown man on the ComLink had told him to shoot first if anything funny happened, he couldn't quite bring himself to open fire on three individuals just because the woman fluttered an elbow. What if the unknown man denied he'd ever said that? There were many agents here that would say he ordered everyone to open fire on three suspects for no apparent reason. He was probably the only one that had seen the elbow budge a millimeter. He could not ignore it ,so he decided to hybrid the two options.

He angrily grabbed his shotgun off the deck's ledge, pumped it, and blasted a shot into the air. "If you maggots think you are about to communicate with me standing right here, you must be dumber than you look! There will be no stretching, whispering, itching, scratching, moving, or elbow twitching in my vicinity! Try anything again…" Acclaim pumped again and blasted the water near the boat for emphasis. "And I will shoot you!"

Acclaim's words struck no fear into the minds of anyone on the boat. They had been through far worse than a man on a boat yelling threats and insults and shooting the water.

Acclaim noticed that no one flinched to the sound of either gunshot. One of the men didn't even bother to look in his direction.

Without moving his lips, Zyablikov whispered to Kalisa, "Fake an asthma attack."

Kalisa heard this, and gradually began sucking in the air, softly at first, and then she quickened her pace and got a little louder. Everyone from the Pit remembered the one student who was known as Cory Collins. Cory had a severe case of asthma, and whenever there was thick smoke around, or the training got a little too heavy for him, he nearly went into convulsions. Everyone remembered how it looked, and everyone remembered how it sounded. The trainers knew he was not faking, because not one of the young students had yet learned what asthma was, nor did they know the symptoms at such a tender age. Though the Pit instructors knew it was truly a major health problem, they ignored it. One day, Cory had finally collapsed in an asthma attack. He was pleading for air and clutching his chest as his trainers watched him die. During his burial, the physical trainers ranted on about how "this is what happens to the weak," and so on. At that young age, no one had a medical concept of what asthma was. Only after they were released into America were they granted the freedom to analyze and investigate boundless knowledge and pursue self-enlightenment. Eventually, after they became exposed to different levels of medicine, they realized what little Cory had died from, and cursed their trainers for allowing him to die like an animal. Zyablikov briefly recalled how the group had thought Cory Collins was simply weak, that his body had not been strong enough to take the pain. Cory had often been picked on and frowned upon simply because none of the pupils had understood his health situation.

Zyablikov had witnessed Kalisa's professional acting skills many times before. He had chosen her for this act because she was a woman and everyone aboard the enemy boat was a man. A male will watch a male suffer, but few males will stand by and watch a female suffer. The act was fearfully realistic, and the guards' attention was directed at her immediately. Acclaim, however, kept his eyes on everyone.

Zyablikov waited for the guard to speak first.

"No one move! Now, what the hell is the matter with her?"

Zyablikov spoke. "She has severe asthma, sir! Please let me get her medicine. I will use one hand." Zyablikov started removing one hand off of his head, keeping the other one still. He dropped to his knees. "Her medicine is in the black bag." Zyablikov inched over to it.

"Do not move!" Acclaim yelled.

"Sir, she will die in five minutes if she does not get her medicine! *Please,* let me get to the bag!"

The detonator was near enough to the bag that if he could get to the bag, he could push the button that would blow the federal vessel sky high.

"Do not move, maggot!" Acclaim said. He directed the captain of the boat to steer closer to the surrendered vessel. Zyablikov became concerned. If the boat blew like it was supposed to, he and his teammates would go with it if it was too close. He had to think quickly, as usual.

"Hey," Zyablikov murmured without moving his lips. Kalisa skillfully eased her "asthma spell," continuing more quietly so she could hear her commander.

"Black thing on the floor, press the button." Talking without moving his lips was not difficult for him as long as he used one-syllable words. Zyablikov hoped Kalisa could understand him. The message sounded more like "Lack thing, on the lore, hress the hutton."

Like Cory Collins, Kalisa gasped for air and then collapsed to the floor of the boat, clutching her chest and breathing more sporadically. Kalisa continuously tried to take a deep breath. During her spasm, she looked for the "black thing," which had rolled away from her as the impact of her weight had shifted the boat.

"Hurry," Zyablikov murmured as the federal boat got closer. If it came another 20 feet closer, he would not detonate the C-4 placed under the ship. With the illumination that the FBI boat provided, Kalisa easily located the device, now about three feet from her toes, about six or seven feet from her hands. It was very tiny. She could not get to it without being obvious. She pretended to try to get up by dragging her knees under her body. Doing this, she gained about five feet toward the black thing. She reached over and grabbed the small black device and instantly knew what it was.

Acclaim saw the woman grab something. "Put it—"

The last words of his sentence were drowned out by a violent explosion in which the entire federal vessel became a fiery, orange cloud of debris raining from the sky.

Zyablikov's small boat was blown into the air and, mid-flight, flipped over. Everyone on Zyablikov's team was blown out of their vessel into the cold, dark, unfriendly water, but each remained conscious. From under the boat, Rybka felt the explosion and swam upward to the surface. The water became warmer all of a sudden, and Rybka was careful not to get hit by the falling metal and fiberglass debris. The escape vessel just happened to land right-side up, and for the most part looked fully operable. There was body damage, but it was a good thing the boat had blown away from the explosion, or the shower of metal and fiberglass surely would have caused severe damage to Zyablikov's boat and teammates.

Zyablikov looked around under water, trying to find which way was up. He saw the orange even from a distance, and that is how he spotted the surface. He put his head above water to breathe in oxygen and find his boat. It was about 50 feet away, floating quietly westward. He looked for his teammates, but the darkness covered everything. He didn't look toward the explosion for possible survivors. He knew there were none. He swam toward the lone vessel, and a hand grabbed him from above. It was Rybka, giving him a hand to climb aboard the ship. When Zyablikov was aboard, he saw that nearly everything had been dumped out of the boat. Luckily, the weapons that had been in the holding cabinet were all accounted for and looked untouched.

Zyablikov did not turn on any lights to look for his comrades, as this would signal their exact location to anyone bothering to look toward the explosion. He and Rybka carefully scanned the surface for Kalisa and Nukludko. There was no sign of them. Time was the one thing he did not have. He turned on the boat's engine, not to leave just yet, but to provide sound. Hopefully, they had survived and would hear the engine. Zyablikov determined he could wait 60 seconds before he started off toward the rendezvous point.

"They have a five-minute head start. We have motors and a job to do. Shoot first if in doubt," Hammer instructed before jumping over the ledge and hitting the cold, gloomy ocean. Jester and Felix followed. Felix carried an intense underwater lamp that made their sub-aquatic surroundings look like daylight. Even through his gloves, Felix could feel the warmth from the lamp. Underwater, they gave each other the thumbs-up to signify that their underwater equipment was functioning correctly. If anyone had signaled a thumbs-down, then all three would have resurfaced. Jester opened and closed his fist several times, indicating that he wanted their attention. He pointed toward the bottom of the boat. Felix pointed the lamp in that direction. There lay a small aquatic machine. The machine was shaped like the letter C and resembled no form of transportation they had ever seen. It was sleekly designed, with somewhat of a large cube and a windshield on the front of it. The contraption had several small device meters located on its front. The machine was attached to the boat by a suction apparatus and thin string that was invisible to the naked eye under water.

Hammer swam down toward the strange apparatus. Felix tried to signal Hammer to stay put until he could verify that the machine was not a bomb, but Hammer was already five feet from the device and realized it was an aquatic vehicle. With his hands, he ripped the wire that was keeping the vehicle underwater. Amazingly, it did not float to the top. Hammer put his hand an inch from the machine and felt its vibration in the water. The vehicle was running. He motioned to Felix to come closer with the lamp.

Felix brought the light closer, and Hammer saw two handgrips for a driver's hands. Hammer got between the legs of the C-shaped vehicle and put his hands on the driver's grips. The device did not move.

Felix saw a tiny switch on the corner of the cube that attracted his attention simply because it looked like it was hidden. He flipped the small switch, and the vessel came alive, moving rapidly out to sea. Felix quickly reached out and grabbed Hammer's leg and went along for the ride. Jester grabbed Felix's waist with both hands and rode along also. While steering, Hammer examined the squares on the steering cube. There were no numbers or letters anywhere, but on one square, he saw a directional compass. He also noticed a radar screen on the device as he searched for indicators that would speed up the aquamobile. It didn't make sense for the driver to have to take his hands off of the "handlebars" to control the device. As he felt around with his thumbs, he felt one button on each steering handle. He pressed the right button, and the vehicle slowed down immediately. He pressed the left button, and the vehicle spurted forward. The chase was on.

With one hand, Felix held the lamp above Hammer's shoulder, being careful not to burn him. Up ahead, Hammer saw only the open ocean. He looked at the radar on the vehicle and spotted the large cruise ship behind him, along with several scattered boats scurrying toward the cruise ship. He looked for anything heading away from the action. Off in the distance, he saw what must have been the intercepted escape vessel, hounded by the large federal ship. In five seconds, both ships disappeared off the radar, and in a short minute, the smaller ship reappeared and was not moving. Hammer was confused and thought the radar was malfunctioning. He still did not see the men who had come after the Spymaster. He realized that even if he were to push to this underwater vehicle's top speed, he would not catch his targets, not even with the addition of the motors attached to his shoulders. He was dragging two men and starting several minutes behind them. They were not even in sight. He checked the radar again and did not see his targets anywhere. He took his hand off of the acceleration button and pointed to the surface of the ocean. Both his colleagues understood that it was a lost cause; they would be chasing ghosts. When the vehicle broke the surface, Felix turned off his lamp and removed his mouthpiece.

"You're right. All three of us can't catch them, but one of us has a chance," Felix suggested. "Hammer, follow underwater in that buggy. I'll follow on top with a speedboat. In ten minutes, they could not have reached the shore yet. Let's grab that one." He was pointing to a police beach cruiser. "Stay about 20 feet ahead of us, and surface when you see them. I'll keep the lamp underwater for you."

Felix turned the lamp on to signal the beach cruiser. The officer slowed the beach cruiser to a stop.

"FBI!" Jester shouted. "We need your ship in order to pursue the bombing suspects."

The men on board quickly threw a rope into the water, and in a flash, Jester and Felix were aboard the boat.

"What about the other guy?" one of the officers asked.

"He'll lead us. Don't pull the rope up…and give me a long pole or something that I can hook this lamp onto. Is there a radar aboard this thing?"

"No, sir. There was another explosion a few minutes ago. We were heading towards it."

Jester looked to where the officer was pointing and grabbed the binoculars from another officer's hand. "Do you know what blew up?" he asked.

"A boat. Unmarked."

Jester signaled to Hammer before he submerged, and pointed to the explosion. "This way!" he shouted. The boat sped toward the explosion with Hammer in the lead about eight feet under the surface. Hammer was amazed at how fast the vehicle was allowing him to travel and how elegantly quietly the machine was able to propel itself. He looked at the radar on the cube. He was gradually pulling ahead of the police boat, and he assumed the police boat was traveling at top speed. He was out of range of Felix's lamp and now was speeding alone in the darkness. The only motion that took any effort on his part involved making a right-angle turn. To turn around, he merely forced the horseshoe up and flipped, traveled upside down for a second, and twisted his body—and he was going the other way. He tried not to admit it, but it was fun to ride this aquamobile. He pulled further away from the ship. He couldn't tell how fast he was going. There was nothing but the open ocean around him, and the gauges on the cubes only displayed colors and red lines in increments as a speedometer would. He looked at one meter that didn't seem to be moving. *This must be the fuel gauge,* he thought. If this device even ran on fuel. It was probably nuclear. Suddenly, the vessel jerked violently. Hammer could tell that something had hit his "windshield." He forcefully pushed down on the driver's handles, and the device swiftly turned upward toward the surface of the ocean. Hammer removed his mouthpiece and looked around. He was now 300 feet in front of the police boat and knew instantly that the assassins had definitely reached shore by now. He quickly observed that it was a boat that had exploded, based on the pieces of large metal, wood, and fiberglass he was surrounded by. He needed Felix's lamp to look below for survivors; there were definitely none on the surface. Hammer released the acceleration button. The machine slowed to a drift.

"Is there anyone here?" Hammer yelled. "If there is anyone out here, yell, make some kind of noise. I can barely see a thing out here!"

There was no response. Hammer suddenly saw a scary black sea animal floating menacingly beside him. With his left hand, he punched at it forcefully and gave a loud yell. He realized it was a jacket and grabbed it. It was charred, but on the back of the jacket, in giant yellow letters, was written "FBI."

Hammer cursed as he searched the radar on the aquamobile for a fleeing vessel. Suddenly, he saw it at the edge of the radar. He could not see how far away it was; there was no radius or scale marker on the radar. He checked to make sure his marine rifle had remained strapped to his back during the water ride. He attached his mouthpiece, pressed the accelerate button again, and sped off.

Three seconds later, and still in darkness, Hammer hit another piece of large metal and was stopped in his tracks. It was like trying to fly blind through an asteroid belt. Hammer looked toward the police boat and saw that it was almost upon him. He removed his mouthpiece. "Clemson," Hammer said to Felix, "I spot a vessel running southwest of here. I need the lamp to get out of this mess."

Felix pointed the lamp in the southwest direction. When Hammer submerged, he saw that it was impossible to maneuver through all of the debris. He would have to go around it. He looked at his radar and saw that the vessel was almost out of sight. As an FBI agent, Hammer could not order the ship to chase the suspects without looking for possible survivors in the explosion. It was standard protocol. He needed the lamp to chase the suspects, and they needed the lamp to look for survivors. The chase was no longer on. It was over.

"Get some more men out here," Hammer instructed. "There might be survivors! Clemson, stick that lamp a little deeper for me."

Chapter 11

Zyablikov reflected before he asked for a report. This was the first unsuccessful mission his teams had ever suffered. The most important segment of the mission had been accomplished; Kalisa had been retrieved, unharmed. But the Spymaster still lived, which meant Zyablikov was in grave danger. In addition to this, one man was unaccounted for. When the Spymaster reported the events to his contacts, he would have every agent looking for Dennis Garret and anyone who resembled him, Zyablikov knew.

He thought about Bolotov. This was totally unacceptable. A man left unaccounted for jeopardized the status of the entire organization. If somehow the FBI or CIA got him to talk, which was unlikely, the organization would be compromised. Zyablikov knew Bolotov wouldn't talk, but he still had to consider it as a possibility. One thing that the Pit had taught Zyablikov to do that he would always employ was to think clearly. To think about everything and anything that could come of a given situation. With the pressure that Bolotov would be receiving, who knew how they might extract information from him: torture, dehydration, or—the one that worried Zyablikov most—hypnosis. Who knew what the subconscious mind will spit out once it had a chance to? All those painful memories boxed inside a lonely man's head? If a small channel was opened into the subconscious mind of anyone who had experienced the Pit, the floodgates might open, and a capricious ocean of information could spill out. They were trained to resist hypnosis; however, nothing was completely infallible, especially after the mind has been weakened by extended periods of torture.

Romil Bolotov had chosen his first name, Tough. Zyablikov hoped he was tough enough to withstand the pressure the Americans would bring to bear. He thought back to when Bolotov would oversleep, and thus be denied a shower. After training exercises, he would emit a pungent body odor and had been given the last name "of the swamp" because he had smelled like one. It soon had been proven that not only did he smell like a swamp but could kill inside of one. He could slither through a muddy river like an iguana until he was right behind you. He was definitely mentally tough enough to be on the marine combat team, but with the tricky Americans, there was no telling what he would be exposed to. It comforted Zyablikov somewhat to know that Bolotov already had a way out of anything. The solution was taped to his body.

Zyablikov took a deep breath. He knew there was no second shot at the Spymaster, but he still recollected the call he had made to pull Team D out. Hidislav said he could have gotten the Spymaster over the wire, but surely all three of them would have been caught, which would have been a blueprint for the demise of the organization. The chances of getting one out of the three to talk would have increased significantly for the Americans. Zyablikov was well aware of the games played by professionals to turn one comrade against the other.

He remembered what Devin had suggested a few years ago be done to three Americans who would not spill the information he needed. Three undercover American spies were caught in Russia, transmitting messages through encrypted e-mail, transmissions they had thought were safe. Unfortunately, the Russian Federation of Intelligence had had the key to two or three of these messages, and therefore, all three of the messengers were caught. They were placed in small cells next to each other. For a couple hours a day, each agent was taken into a room and beaten for information. No one talked. After a while, this method proved to be ineffective and Devin was contacted for a suggestion. Devin came up with a sinister plan to play each agent against his own mind and his fellow agents. The same process of taking the agents out of their cells was repeated, only now, the agent who was thought to be the weakest was given what Devin called "the VIP treatment."

The VIP agent was not beaten at all but well fed, bathed, and allowed to consume alcohol at will. Women were brought in with whom he was allowed to conjugate. The other agents were being beaten during their hours out of their cells. This went on for weeks. Eventually, the other agents noticed the third agent was clean, was never hungry, smelled good, and never got sick. They began to show animosity toward the third agent, thinking he had given information to get these privileges. After another month, the other agents witnessed the third agent receiving sex in his cell. A plethora of other tactics were used that created thick animosity between the two agents against the third. The food he was being served was exposed to his fellow agents, who had not eaten or bathed in weeks. The very appearance of the third agent was enough to anger the other two, who were still being beaten. They were not beaten for information anymore, but simply to stoke their anger, and to create bruises that would show in the large wall-sized mirrors that Devin had placed in each of their cells. As Devin had predicted, it turned out that the VIP agent was the one that talked. It was explained to him that he would be locked in a cell with the other two agents for a night where he knew he would certainly be beaten to death. He had held fast for a while, but when night fell and the guard came to escort him to the cell to join the other two, he changed his mind and sang like a canary. Creative tactics such as these, Zyablikov could not risk being used upon himself and his organization.

"Nightshade, report," he requested.

"First, I would like to express my gratitude for—"

"Later," Zyablikov cut in.

"Of course, Garret," Kalisa replied. "I would like to state that it was definitely a trap, and they were expecting us."

"Why do you say that?"

"One, the director was taken out of our room as a bomb-threat precaution. I now believe this was false, because the director and I were separated once evacuated from the floor. Because of gender was the reason given. This is not likely, and during my escape, I encountered an agent."

"How do you know he was an agent?"

"It was a she. Her fighting agility and strength almost matched mine. She did not fight like a regular agent. She was swift, and her blows were hard. I would say she was a trained assassin."

"I would like to add to this," Hidislav reported. "Commander, I don't mean to speak out of turn, but I had never before seen the weapons used to protect the director. One that I saw was some sort of a projectile weapon that created explosions and damage similar to a stick of dynamite."

Zyablikov did not say a word. This changed the situation entirely. The Americans now had the Spymaster. He tried to decide if the situation was good or bad. He couldn't necessarily find a disadvantage in it, but it made things complicated. Complicated situations did not have foreseeable outcomes. This was a disadvantage. He knew the Spymaster would not utter a word to the Americans about the network. They couldn't exactly put him in a cell and beat him; the man was too powerful. How would the Spymaster explain his presence on the cruise ship? That would be an interesting tale. It would look bad to the Americans that the Spymaster had made a secret trip to American soil so soon after the assassination of Yuklivitch. It would look related. When the Spymaster got back to Russian soil, Devin would be waiting for him with a plan to take out the only people who could expose him. And now he had a perfect reason. Zyablikov realized that because getting to the Spymaster was no longer a possibility, the better option was to get the man who had put him in this position—Devin.

Where could Devin be found? Devin was probably safe in Russia by now, and probably had been there since the chilling interrogation of the Yuklivitch assassination and of Kalisa's whereabouts. If it meant a trip to Russia, then so be it. He remembered the one piece of leverage that he had and praised himself over and over for keeping in step with the rapid-paced life he led.

He could try to gather evidence on his own to convince the Spymaster of his innocence, but if the Spymaster was convinced of who was behind the assassination attempt, there would be no words. The agenda now was to get the word out to the Spymaster that Devin was behind the attempt. If this could be done, the situation could change.

Change to what? A life where he killed at the drop of a hat? A life of being on call 24 hours a day? A life ordering assassinations and removing people who were obstacles out of the way as if Earth was a chessboard? A life of silent killing and spying for reasons he often did not understand? A life in which a phone call could mean he had to kill again? Was it a life worth salvaging? Maybe not, but it was all he knew.

"Continue, Nightshade."

"That's about it. I was being taken to another floor, and the lights went out. I escaped from the woman whom I believe was an American assassin."

"How did you escape? Did you kill the American woman?"

"No. I was not able to. I knocked her away and threw several blows before running up the stairs along with two men. I jumped overboard."

Hidislav spoke next. "The woman she speaks of was obviously not a civilian. She was armed, and after we warned her not to move, she came after us with a hand weapon. The director also had some sort of bodyguards."

"Russian or American agents?"

"Sounded American. I never saw the one that stopped us from getting to him. He stayed behind the bed. He had the explosive rifle."

"One man?"

"I believe it was one man, Commander."

"One man stopped three of you from hitting the target."

"One was protecting him from behind the bed. Two were out in the corridor, including the woman. We were trying to get the target *and* neutralize the threat from the outside corridor. The target was cowering behind the bed. There was no direct angle we could use to hit him. We can't ricochet with the marine weapons."

"I am aware of this."

"We had him pinned. D-3 was adjacent to him, and I believe we could have gotten both the guard and the target."

"How did D-3 fall?"

"On the retreat, the American woman and the second guard opened fire. They were not cops. There was no warning and no opportunity for us to surrender or place our weapons down. They just opened fire. I threw the smoke grenade, radioed you, went overboard, retrieved the cycles, and escaped as planned. On the way up the stairs, there was another American, and I decapitated him. I did not want to make the same mistake we made with the American woman. He could have been an agent, too."

Zyablikov nodded. "What about the third cycle?"

"We left it behind," Hidislav replied.

"Did you cut it loose?"

Hidislav shook his head.

Zyablikov hit Hidislav across the mouth and dared him to react. "You cannot leave our technology behind! You were to cut it loose and send it out to sea. There, it would run out of fuel and sink. You left it attached to the cruise ship?"

Hidislav nodded.

Zyablikov banged the desk with both fists.

Hidislav defended himself. "How was I to know what to do? No man on my team has ever been left behind. D-3's cycle had drifted under the ship on the opposite side. I could not get to it without sacrificing the team's capture. There was no time to get to it. To swim under the boat would have cost us time we did not have."

Zyablikov recalled all of the boats racing to the scene and remembered why he had pulled Team D back from the beginning. Besides the safe return of Kalisa, Zyablikov considered this mission an absolute disaster, and it was not purely because of the American operatives, but due to the fact that had worried him before . . . lack of information. He needed a dynamic source of intelligence to replace Devin for the organization to operate as it should. Zyablikov decided he would have to use team B, the Covert Intelligence Team, to replace Devin's endless supply of flawless intelligence. This unusual assignment had cost him two of the organization's most precious attributes: one of his men and hard evidence of their confidential technology. There was now solid proof of the elite team's existence. There were no words, letters, or numbers on the submarine transport, so no one would be able to tell offhand who had created the vessel, but he didn't like the idea of their technology being outside of their own circles.

CHAPTER **12**

Plack stared at Romil Bolotov. A member of the organization that had killed his brother in cold blood now sat before him. Plack wore jeans and a sleeveless T-shirt, colored only burgundy-red by Bolotov's blood. Bolotov had no idea where he was, nor did he know why the man who stood before him was so irate, but he took an educated guess. Bolotov was only halfway out of his wetsuit, and Sparrow looked on from across the dark room as Plack beat him thoroughly. Bolotov had not made one attempt to talk, but his snide smirks angered Plack further. What Plack didn't understand is that Bolotov didn't actually feel the pain. He had learned to use his mind to block out external pain.

Bolotov listened as Plack's fist smashed against his flesh like a civilian would listen to a radio. Plack finally yelled something about his dead brother, and Bolotov finally figured out what the situation was. This man's brother had obviously been an obstacle to his team, and therefore had been removed. Bolotov felt no remorse about any killing he had ever done, from his preteen years through adulthood. He thought back through the different assignments and tried to remember anyone who resembled this guy. Could it have been the guard in the submarine that his team commandeered a few years ago? The guard that tried to play hero? Instead of receiving a Purple Heart, he received the full metal one. What about the Navy Seal team his crew took out before they could set foot into the missile silo in Trinidad? He gave up. There were simply too many bodies to count up in his memory.

His hands were handcuffed together around the back of an uncomfortable chair that was bolted down to the floor. His legs were chained tightly together to either front leg of the chair. He knew that if they found out what kind of organization they were dealing with, he would never leave this place alive. His back wounds had been patched up, and that's the only reason he suspected his wetsuit had been taken off halfway. Or perhaps they wanted to see his face before they killed him because he would not talk. He wouldn't construct a lie. He knew the Americans would kill him once they thought they had the truth, anyway.

He remembered being shot at several times and hit about four or five times. He remembered falling to the ground and smoke billowing all around him. He remembered taking another shot to the head, then losing consciousness. He recalled briefly being laid down on his stomach on a bed while someone probed at his wounds. He had lost consciousness again. He had awoke chained to this chair. If he could just get to his ankle, he would be out of this situation for good.

In an underground safe house in Florida, AEGIS minus one sat in a room together. It was 3:00 a.m. Eastern Standard Time, but no one felt tired. There was disbelief, frustration, and anger in the room. Though none of them would admit it out loud, there was also awe.

"Silence," Hammer said to seal the channel. "I can't believe they were on the goddamn boat. Jackal, are you with us?" Hammer asked into the air.

"Loud and clear," Jackal replied. He was in a chopper, heading toward Florida.

"They waltzed in here, killed a few people, and waltzed right out with a damn near clean escape," Hammer said. "Where the hell did they come from? One minute it's all clear; the next minute, they're on the boat."

Felix spoke up. "They were under the boat. The radar was on top of the boat, and they were positioned underneath the boat, Hammer. The radar can't see under the boat; the satellite can't see under the boat. The radar did several full sweeps of the area and picked up nothing. There were just fishing boats around doing some fishing. The only boat that was even remotely drifting after the cruise ship was a small fishing boat. I sent the beach patrol after it. The report was that everything was normal. There was one man aboard the vessel who looked like he was fishing. The officers even semi-searched the boat."

Hammer interjected, "Semi-searched it?"

"The explosion on the cruise liner went off as they were searching his boat, and they stopped the search to rush to the cruise ship."

"The explosion on the cruise liner went off as they were searching his boat?"

"Yes," Felix explained.

"Well, the enemy Seal team had to have someone guiding them. I could hear them responding to orders. They were told to pull out. Did we get anything on the air waves?"

"Yes and no. We can hear words under a plethora of static. It's going to take some time to cull the words out," Felix answered.

Sparrow offered her observations. "The Jennifer Johnson woman with the Spymaster was definitely not a civilian. When the lights went out, I was hit hard. Most men don't hit that hard. I then countered, but it was difficult in the new darkness. Before my eyes had adjusted, I was tackled down the stairs. The woman could block, attack, and dodge like a professional. She was clearly thoroughly trained in the arts of hand-to-hand combat, top level. If you ask me, she was an assassin. Someone or some agency had taught her exceptionally well how to kill with her hands."

"The Johnson character—did we ever figure out what happened to her?" Hammer asked.

Felix spoke up. "She was in the escape vessel."

"What makes you say that?"

"I called Acclaim through the link when I saw the getaway vessel."

"You saw the getaway vessel through the sat?"

"Well, when the power was off on the ship, all the satellite images were down. I had the radar streamlined through the laptop. The radar showed all devices within a certain radius. I set the radius at 20 miles, while we were still within 20 miles of the shore. After the bomb went off, the radar was flooded with vessels heading toward the scene. I saw one boat heading away rapidly. I put two and two together. I told Acclaim to get it. He called a few minutes later and said he had them. This was just before his boat blew. I told him not to apprehend them but to keep them pinned down until more backup arrived. I also told him to shoot if they so much as scratched suspiciously."

"How do you know she was on the boat? Did he say there was a female?"

"Yes, he said there were two males and a female. All in regular clothes, no scuba gear. He said two of them were soaking wet. One of the males and the female."

"The getaway driver was the dry one, the female was Johnson—"

"And the third one was the one that set off the bomb on the cruise ship. He couldn't exactly walk around the boat in scuba gear," Jester put in. "The bomb squad says they've never seen a device like it before. The door was melted through on the outside, which was why no alarms went off. The bomb that put the lights out was something out of the next century. Not only was it set to disable the lights, but also, there was a fail-safe computer inside of it. If any attempt was made to restore the lights or alter the device, another bomb would have gone off, blasting whoever was trying to restore the lights. The bomb was patched in to the circuit breaker. Whoever created it would not only have to be a professional bomber and a spectacular computer programmer but also an electrician. If he had crossed one wire incorrectly while planting the device, he would have blown up with his bomb, and he knew it."

"It doesn't make sense to me. If they wanted the Spymaster dead, why didn't they just blow up the cruise ship?" Jackal asked.

"It makes perfect sense," Hammer replied. "They had two missions that countered both of ours. Their first objective, of course, was to assassinate the Spymaster. The second one was to rescue Ms. Johnson."

"I mean after," Jackal replied. "After Johnson was on the getaway vehicle, why didn't they blow the ship, just like they did Acclaim's?"

"Maybe they didn't want to kill 1500 innocent people," Hammer replied.

"Are you saying that these individuals have a conscience?" Sparrow retorted to Hammer. "The same people that took off a guy's head because he was walking up the stairs at the same time they were. That guy had just gotten married less than a week ago and had a baby on the way. I don't buy the conscience story. I'm noticing a difference in the way this operation was carried out in comparison with the last two."

"You have our attention," Hammer said.

"The other assignments were lickety-split. Three seconds, to three minutes. Everything was planned. Every option seemed as if it had been gone over with a fine-toothed comb. No real witnesses, no evidence, no fingerprints; nothing. It seems as if they were operating a little less than top-notch here," Sparrow clarified.

A little less than top notch? Jester thought. *Didn't that lady beat you unconscious?*

"Take the *Washington Post* job," Sparrow continued. "They went in there; they knew where to go, what to get, how to get out, and who was who. That takes some high-quality intelligence. It seemed with this job, that same intelligence was missing. They didn't know where the Spymaster was. I do not believe they knew we were aboard the vessel, and two people had to jump off the ship into the freezing water with no scuba gear and wait for the pickup boat to scoop them up in the dark. Then they attempted a high-speed get-away in what I assume was a fishing boat. So that meant two individuals were soaking wet in their clothes, getting chilled by the wind on a speeding boat. They were probably shivering. This doesn't seem like the same strength of operation."

"Are you saying it was a different team?" Felix asked.

"No, definitely not. I know it was the same team by the technology alone, but just a different method of operation."

"Johnson wasn't worried about the damn windchill factor," Jackal commented. "She would have jumped off that boat at any chance she got. The Spymaster was about to ice her since she was part of the Yuklivitch assassination. The intelligence report indicates that the Spymaster and Epifanii Yuklivitch were good friends. Lady Johnson was about to get wasted like yesterday's newspaper."

"I agree," Hammer replied.

"From the conversation we recorded, it sounded like we can be reasonably sure that Russia was definitely behind the *Post* job. The controversy was over the Yuklivitch assassination. It seems that the Yuklivitch job was unauthorized," Felix said.

"Well, the order sure came from somewhere," Hammer stated.

"Devin. Whoever that is. We've searched databases far and wide. No one aliased Devin was found that could pull this off," Felix reported.

"Now we know why the Spymaster was visiting. If he came over to deal with the situation personally, then the Yuklivitch hit truly *was* unauthorized," Vadar added. "I imagine the Spymaster was not too delighted that his friend was showcased in a shameless, grandstand execution. Someone was sending a message."

Jackal spoke next. "So we know who was behind the assassination, but we don't know who. Elite Nuclear Arms Production was definitely behind the assassination, and Klingner hired these axemen to do it. So, if what Johnson was saying was true, Klingner contacted Devin, and Devin planned the Yuklivitch operation."

"How do we know that Johnson was telling the truth?" Sparrow asked. "She could have just been trying to save her neck."

"I used the Traffic Data Imagery System on the interstate and looked for Johnson's car. I grabbed Johnson's travel pattern. We knew where she left, and, fortunately, she drove the car that was registered in her name, so it wasn't that hard for the satellite database to find it. Sure enough, she took Route 66 East. She drove her 2000 gold

Camry. She didn't drive more than an hour. She left a day before the *Post* job and then came right back. Then, very early the next morning, she left again for Washington, for the Yuklivitch hit. Then she came back and left *again* for Washington," Vadar reported. "Why would she make three trips?"

"Well, keep in mind that no one knew when Yuklivitch's speech was. She probably didn't get the intel to move until then," Sparrow said.

"Felix, do we have the phone records?" Vadar asked.

"Yes," Felix said. "She was contacted the same night she got back. Pay phone. Call was about 35 seconds. The message is all static, undecipherable. The number that the call was traced to was listed as a pay phone in Delaware."

"Though Ms. Johnson will probably never set foot in Fairfax again, get some guys to wire her house. I want it turned into one big transmitter," Hammer instructed.

"I'm going to Russia tomorrow," Vadar announced. "I have a hunch on how this is all put together. I've been contemplating on Sparrow's observations. The Yuklivitch and Valentine missions were definitely not in sync with tonight's episode. If you think about it, the missions contradict each other. I don't know why we didn't pick this up before. We all agree that all three jobs were done by the same organization. The *Post* job was to take evidence that proved the existence of the Black Fox helicopter and then to kill the person who was running her mouth about it. This act would allow the SORT to go through. The next job took out Yuklivitch on the White House steps. This act did anything but slide the SORT together. It doesn't make sense. Two opposite motives by the same organization."

Hammer then put it together. "We know this is a Russian organization on the strength of Kapitnov's mere presence. We know it's an American-based group because Kapitnov came *here*, which was an extreme risk, and he suffered for it. Russia ordered the first job. They know damn well they're building war machines, but they still wanted the treaty to go through, and Klingner ordered the second job to stop the treaty from going through. There is obviously a liaison between Kapitnov and whoever is actually executing these missions, and that liaison would be Devin. We need to find Devin."

"We may already have him," Jackal cut in. "I've spoken with the Environmental Protection Agency. Things were moving a little too slow, so I went directly to the EAB, the Environmental Appeals Board. One of the Power Elite bastards that Felix knows grew up with one of the members of the board. Luckily, the board is only four people, and I was able get the EPA off Klingner's back. Now Klingner owes Felix a favor. For this favor, we will ask to be introduced to the same people he hired for the Yuklivitch deal, because we have another job for them. The contact will probably be Devin. Then we can bash his head in."

"Devin has probably been in contact with Klingner. Get the phone and travel records," Vadar suggested.

"I've already had the FBI on that for the past 48 hours. They turned up nothing. Absolutely nothing. No phone calls, no extraordinary travel, and the FBI still can't find where Klingner paid for the Yuklivitch job. It's like this guy Devin does not exist."

"Do you think Klingner will bite?" Hammer asked Felix.

"Oh, yes. It's the doctrine of the Novus Ordo Mundi. One good turn deserves another. They know nothing in life is free, and they live by it."

"Get on it first thing in the morning," Hammer instructed.

"Got it," Felix replied.

"Vadar, why are you going to Russia?" Jackal asked.

"That's where Black Fox is being built. I believe this is where the plans were leaked to Valentine. Quiet as it's kept, there is a major competitor of ENAP's over there. They have no stocks, no bonds, and no official employees. It's called the mafia. If the treaty was signed, the Russian mafia would lose billions in black-market arms deals, and I believe this is why the plans for the chopper were surrendered to Valentine. Then the Russian government found out about the leak. So to protect Russian interests, Kapitnov sent his men to the *Washington Post* to retrieve the helicopter plans and kill Valentine."

"You're going over there to visit the Russian mafia, huh?" Jester put in. "You *do* remember you're black, right? I'm sure you'll mix right in."

"Hey, wouldn't have it any other way, Smurfette," Vadar replied, referring to Jester's size. "Maybe you want to wake up with the fishes too?" he finished with a thick, heavy Russian accent.

"Hey that was pretty good," Sparrow said admiringly.

"I do other tricks too," Vadar joked before turning back to Hammer. "I have some contacts over there I met from some past assignments."

"Do you think they'll cooperate?" Felix asked.

"If I don't come back, then that would be a 'no,'" Vadar answered, smiling.

"When do you leave?" Hammer asked.

"As soon as this boring meeting is over."

"Are we keeping the Spymaster?" Sparrow asked.

"I considered it, but the timing for this is off," Hammer replied. "We don't want to start a war. We just want information. I don't think Russia would assassinate their own diplomat like that. They would have used poison or Polonium-210. I still believe Johnson. I think Klingner and Devin alone were behind the unauthorized Yuklivitch job, which makes the Spymaster's trip over here fit perfectly."

"If his organization has turned mercenary, maybe the Spymaster might help us catch them," Sparrow suggested.

"Despite the conversation with Johnson that we heard, the Spymaster still continues to deny that the organization exists. Some people from the CIA have him now. They're trying to get some more out of him. I doubt they'll have much luck. We can't touch him. We aren't having any luck with the truth agent, either. He won't talk. He is saying that American troops were behind his assassination attempt tonight, and he wants to be transported immediately back to Russia," Hammer replied.

"You can't be serious. The Spymaster thinks we were behind this?" Jester asked.

"We don't know what he thinks, but he sure is *saying* that American troops have made an attempt on his life."

"We now have an international incident on our hands. What if the press gets a hold of this? I'll be forced to thrash 50 investigation teams. Not that I mind," Jackal added.

"It is only a matter of time. One of the beach patrol saw the Spymaster when I brought him off the ship," Sparrow remembered. "I told him to keep his mouth shut, but he might decide to do otherwise. I'd say we have less than 24 hours before the media gets a grip of this. Since I imagine not too many people in the Russian parliament know the Spymaster is over here, it'll take a few hours before they realize that he's missing. This is going to get crazy. We have to give him back. We can't hold him. It's going to be a zoo if we don't. Russia's blood pressure is already up from the Yuklivitch assassination. They're going to say we're holding the Spymaster hostage."

"That's *exactly* what the Russian media will report, and our press will blow it out of proportion as well," Hammer replied.

"We don't have to give a damn thing back," Jackal stated. "Fuck 'em. He's out of bounds. He violated our airspace and border policy. Does he think he can come and go from our territory as he pleases? It's time we showed them what's real."

"We have to give him back," Vadar calmly said. "Tensions are already high. The Russians already believe we have assassinated Yuklivitch. If they believe we've taken the director, as well, they'll start fueling missiles. If they haven't already."

"He has to know we were not behind this," Jester added. "We were the ones that saved his life tonight. If we wanted him dead, he would already be dead!"

"The Spymaster knows what he is doing," Hammer concluded. "He not only knows that our side had nothing to do with his assassination attempt; he knows exactly who did it. He's making waves so he can get sent back to safe territory. If Russia finds out we are holding him against his will, they will strike. They would *have* to strike to save face. We are going to play a game of our own in response."

"If the group is now working as mercenaries, maybe someone paid some tall dollars to have the Spymaster taken care of," Sparrow put in.

"One thing wrong with that," Vadar started. "It seemed to me that the Johnson rescue took precedence. She got off the boat safely, but the Spymaster lived. They could have easily stayed an extra two minutes and finished the Spymaster. But they pulled out once they had Johnson."

"She and Devin are lovers," Sparrow contemplated.

"Oh, the true-love theory," Jester remarked. "Whose idea was it to have a woman on this team, again?"

Sparrow glared at Jester. "It's a known fact that one out of five men have homosexual tendencies. I'm pretty sure about the rest of the guys, Jester. Hmmm."

"Okay," Hammer interjected before there could be an outburst, "we know the motives behind the *Post* and Yuklivitch jobs, and we know the two motives from tonight. We know who ordered the first two operations, but who gave the order behind tonight's job? Why come on the boat for Johnson and Kapitnov?"

"Maybe Number Two wants to be Number One," Jackal answered, "and sent the hitmen after the head man. You don't ask for power. You take it."

"Gutsy move, taking out the Spymaster, but maybe you're right. Vadar, how are you getting to Russia?"

"The most efficient way I can get into Russia under current circumstances is if we return the Spymaster and I am on that vessel as a guard. Then I will be absolutely untraceable during my breach of borders."

"What is your alternative?" Hammer asked.

"I can fly into the Finland safeport and drive into the northwestern border."

"I'm not sure if I want to give up the Spymaster just yet," Hammer announced.

"Spoken like a true champion. That's right, fuck'em. Lock him under a septic tank or throw him in the alligator pit," Jackal replied.

"He is the only solid lead we have, and we need this intel immediately," Hammer explained. "Vadar, depart for Finland as soon as possible."

"I'll fly you," Jackal offered. "I had the easiest day today. I didn't even get shot at."

"Oh yeah," Jester cut in, "no hazard pay for you, by the way."

"I could use the company," Vadar said in response to Jackal. "We leave from Miami International in two hours. The plane is gassed up and waiting for us."

Hammer looked at Vadar.

Vadar grinned. "I knew you weren't giving up the Spymaster."

"And I have to go see Klingner and set up a meeting with Devin. This ought to be agreeably captivating," Felix commented.

"Report when you secure the meeting," Hammer instructed.

"It's only a matter of time before the other side knows the cruise ship never reached its destination," Vadar said. "It won't take them long to find out what happened to the ship. There were over 1500 people on that boat. I'm sure they're not all keeping tonight a secret."

"I know. Right now, we're going to see if the Spymaster can help us out with a few things," Hammer replied.

Chapter 13

Walter Plack sat up in his Four Points Hotel room in Miami after a rough night's sleep. The room was moderately luxurious, the bed was soft, and the temperature was comfortable. The loss of his brother still held him in emotional turmoil. He looked at the lamp on the stand by his bed. Filled with an unhealthy, furious rage, he threw the lamp against the wall, where it shattered with a thunderous crash. He took a slow, deep breath to calm himself. He knew his anger was not helping. However, he could not shake the seething fury or the unbearable pain. He grabbed the remote control from the lamp stand next to his bed and turned on the television. He changed the channel from the hotel's information channel to the news. He then reached over, picked up the phone, and then dialed the number to the only person that might heal his pain and fury. At least for the moment.

"Hello?" Sharon Plack answered.

"Hey, it's me."

"Good morning! You doing okay?"

"If breathing means I'm okay, I'm still breathing. But I can't sleep, I can't eat, and I can't really breathe right until I find them. I'll find these animals. It's just that no leads are coming through."

"Walter, I know you'll get them. I have so much faith in you, and I've just finished praying for you."

"Thank you. I sure could use it. How is Lisa?"

"Lisa was a mess the last time I saw her. There are a lot of people comforting her right now, but when they all leave and she is alone, she'll need the most consoling. The kids are destroyed. Walter, it's awful. When I walked into the house, it was like walking into sadness. It was horrible. I'll be back by there today after work. I miss you."

"I miss you, too," Plack replied. The images on the television suddenly diverted his attention from the phone conversation. Displayed on the television screen was another riot in Volgograd, Russia. This was another demonstration of the major outrage over Epifanii Yuklivitch's death. Many Russian organizations and Commonwealth governments again demanded retaliation. Plack saw the angry civilians brandish their picket signs, but because they were in Russian, he couldn't read them. Plack knew that Yuklivitch had been an exceptionally honored man in the Russian Federation, and the people considered him like a father or caretaker. Plack turned up the television and whispered to his wife, "Hold on, honey."

". . .and the restlessness continues as the citizens of Russia demand answers and retaliation for the assassination of Prime Minister Epifanii Yuklivitch, former head of the Strategic Offensive Reductions Treaty Commission. Yuklivitch's visit to the United States was to further discuss the Strategic Offensive Reductions Treaty and clear up any allegations prompted by the terrorist *Washington Post* incident in the United States capital, and the murder of *Washington Post* reporter, Dorian Valentine. Absolutely no evidence of the alleged Operation Black Fox has been found. With the Federal Bureau of Investigation coming up empty-handed in all efforts to secure *any* evidence of the project, its existence looks highly unlikely. Back to you, Ted."

Plack continued to listen as the screen flashed to the next reporter, standing outside the *Washington Post*. "Thank you, Cathy. Things seem a little quieter over here for now, but tensions are still skyrocketing. Most of us are still in utter disbelief about the terrorist incident that took place less than four days ago. The FBI claims no credible organization has stepped up and taken credit or responsibility for the murder of reporter Dorian Valentine, who had broken the story of the alleged Operation Black Fox, the construction of an assault helicopter with spectacular technological capabilities. Suspicions of Russian involvement are definitely extremely high at this point. The discovery of the construction of a post-nuclear helicopter while negotiating the SORT would not only insinuate bad faith and dishonesty but would be a mockery of our nation's Intelligence—in addition to a severe and treacherous breach of ethics."

The screen then switched to Bruce Wallace at a press conference.

"Hello?" Sharon asked her silent husband.

"I'm still here. There's some important stuff on the news. Hold on."

"Our best teams are attacking every issue with due diligence and the persistence that every American deserves," Wallace stated. "At this time, we have several leads we are following, and no physical evidence of Operation Black Fox has yet been brought to my attention. . ."

"OK, everything interesting is over. Wallace is just running his mouth."

"I miss you."

"I miss you, too. I'll find these guys."

"I know you will."

"I have to get going, Sharon."

"Have a great day, Walter."

"I'll try to," Plack replied before he hung up.

He switched the channel to another news station, which was talking about the Environmental Protection Agency's investigation of the Elite Nuclear Arms Production company. Plack stopped to listen for a minute as the screen switched to nightfall, and a burning cruise ship lit up the screen.

That's a hell of a cruise, Plack thought as the reporter explained how an electric fuse had caught fire and caused an explosion.

He switched to CNN. There was a report on how the U.S. had also mobilized troops on certain territorial ground, causing an angry standoff, both the U.S. and Russian sides waiting for the order to fire. Plack had already received an update stating that U.S. troops were to return fire upon any direct hostile action. Plack watched again on CNN as the angry Russian civilians demanded retaliation for the assassination of Yuklivitch. The country's population was convinced that the United States was behind the assassination. As Plack's Com-Link buzzed, he hoped the president of Russia would not go to war just to be reelected.

"Yeah, what is it?" Plack answered.

"This is Bryan. They got Acclaim," Hughes reported.

"What?" Plack gasped.

Hughes handed down the story as he had received it from AEGIS.

"So that exploding-fuse story I just saw on the news was garbage, right?"

"Pure cubic zirconia," Hughes replied.

"Did we get anything?" Plack asked.

"They wanted me to come in and look at something last night. AEGIS found one of their underwater escape vessels. It's something I've never seen before. I have no idea where they get this stuff. It cycles water through tubes for propulsion, along with a small motor. I did some poking, and it's definitely of Russian origin."

"How do you know?"

"Well, there were no numbers or letters on the vehicle, so there was no language to see, so I took it apart. Before I came to the agency, I was a micro-engineer for Microsystems. I designed microcircuitry. We were under a contract for a Russian project once, and I worked on it. They used a microchip that was of a completely different technology than any I—or any of our engineers—had ever seen. Everybody started calling it the Russian superchip. I can't tell you what the chip does, but I saw it in that contraption. No doubt."

"How long ago did they create the chip?"

"This was about 15 years ago. I had just gotten out of college."

"Yeah, right, so did I," Plack sarcastically replied.

"Thought I could fool you," Hughes replied.

"I'm smarter than you look."

Hughes chuckled. It was good to see a sense of humor in Plack. "Keep 'em coming. I don't have any feelings today."

"Seriously, if Acclaim is gone, we need another contact inside the FBI so Wallace doesn't screw things up."

"Actually, Wallace has managed to keep things under control with the press. They're not asking us too many questions yet, which is a darn good thing."

"You're right. Keep up the good work, Bryan."

"I'll be sure to do that," Hughes replied.

Vadar and Jackal crossed the Russian border by car at about noon. After showing identifying documents, they were on their way to St. Petersburg, which was actually less than a few hours' ride. The automobile they drove was courtesy of the Finnish safeport, already checked for bombs and microtransmitters. They were free to speak during the ride.

"Jackal, how did you get your name?" Vadar asked.

Jackal smiled at the inquiry. Jackal didn't smile often, so Vadar wondered what the story was.

"Bishop," was Jackal's terse reply.

"Give me the long version," Vadar replied, wondering what could make a hardened guy like Jackal grin from ear to ear. He knew Bishop was not known for his jovial personality.

"You know Bishop hand-picked all of us. I didn't know why, I didn't know how, but he called me one day. He called a private cell phone that I hadn't even given anyone the number to."

"This was back in your felonious days."

"Yeah," Jackal remembered, "back when I was known as *Il Spirito*."

Il Spirito's cell phone vibrated in his pocket. It was a blocked number, but since only certain people had this number, he decided to answer the call.

"Hello," was the cool greeting.

"Il Spirito, you're in some trouble and you don't know it yet. I'm going to help you."

"Who is this?"

"A very good friend of yours, if you're as smart as I know you to be."

"How did you get this number?"

"Because I'm the closest thing to God on this sad earth. And I can get anything."

"Well, I stopped believing in God when I buried my three brothers." Il Spirito hung up the phone.

Il Spirito soon pulled up to the rendezvous point in the Port of Miami. Today, he was overseeing the import of several tons of cocaine and chemicals used to process it. The delivery was coming from a containership that had already passed through customs.

Before the containers were even loaded onto the trucks, the port was overrun with local police and DEA agents. Without hesitation, Il Spirito's men pulled out their weapons, but on Il Spirito's signal, they placed their weapons down and surrendered. Il Spirito was placed alone in an interrogation chamber for hours. He wondered why no one was talking to him. After another hour, an older man walked through the door. Without a word, the man slowly unlatched Il Spirito's handcuffs, then sat down in front of him. The older man looked him in the eye and still did not say a word. This went on for minutes.

"Are you going to say something, old man?" Il Spirito asked.

The older man did not respond.

"I can tell you're not a cop, so what do you want?"

The mysterious man replied by continuing to look Il Spirito in the eye.

"Did you come in here to look at me all night, grandpa? What are you looking at?"

There was no reaction.

"Say your business or get from out my face!"

"So now you want to talk," the man whispered softly. His voice was barely audible.

"What?" Il Spirito asked, confused.

"You didn't want to do any talking this morning when I tried to save your stubborn ass from getting bagged up by these DEA boneheads."

"You're the one that called me this morning?" Il Spirito asked.

"Lower your voice!" the older man angrily whispered. "They are listening."

"Who are you?" Il Spirito asked in a low voice. "And if you are going to play good cop, aren't you supposed to bring a sandwich and some coffee in here?"

"No thank you. I'm not hungry," the old man responded.

Il Spirito almost smirked. "What's your name, old man?"

"You may call me Bishop."

"Like the chess piece?" Il Spirito asked.

"Yes," Bishop answered. "You know about chess, Marcello Ferretti. But do you know about strategy?"

"I know enough to survive in a game with no rules."

Bishop cracked a cynical smile. "I believe you do, Marcello. And that is precisely why I am here."

Vadar shook his head, smiling.

"What?" Jackal asked.

"Bishop knows how to set it up perfectly. He didn't call you to save you from the DEA. He called you because he knew you would hang up on him, then feel foolish about it later and listen to him when he walked in. Now he's your guardian angel, waiting in the wings to whisk you away in his arms. If he hadn't called you before the sting, you wouldn't have listened to him when he walked in. You would have thought he was some cop screwing with you."

"You sound like you're very familiar with these tactics, Vadar."

"You have no idea. I wasn't always in AEGIS, Il Spirito. I guarantee you Bishop was the one that tipped off the DEA to your operations in the Port of Miami. You never got curious as to how they knew exactly when and where to find you?"

"Just thought it was my time," Jackal answered, closing his eyes.

"You never answered my question. How did you get your name?"

"Bishop told me I would be released within the hour. He whispered an address for me to meet him that afternoon. I went to the restaurant, and there he was."

"Have a seat, Marcello," Bishop gestured.

"Tell me why I am here," Il Spirito demanded.

"Because I haven't eaten a damn thing all day. And you need me right now."

"Who do you think you are? You think I can't beat these trumped-up charges? I have $5000-an-hour lawyers waiting to crawl all over the whole setup. I'm good by myself."

"Sit down, Marcello."

"You think you're going to put me in your pocket because—"

"Cut the bullshit, Ferretti! Sit your eight-dollar candyass down in that chair before I chop your ass into gumdrop nickels. If you're so tough, walk out that door and spend the rest of your ruffian life in an eight-by-ten super-max cell. Let me explain to you how the conspiracy charges you are up against work, since you've haven't been to court before and you haven't talked to your $4973-an-hour law firm yet. You see, Mr. Ferretti, when the DA drags your hooligan ass before the grand jury, he doesn't need evidence against you. All the DA and his merry men need to do is tie you to the conspiracy. They can do that in 60 seconds by connecting you to the organization, which is tied to over a dozen bodies in the last six months. The murders are now on everyone's head, whether you were there or not, or whether you even knew what was going down. And Giorgio is rolling on your whole crew like a two-dollar whore. Salvatore will be next."

"Cut to the chase. What do you want?"

"I want you to work for me. I represent a small organization that protects this nation."

"Why do you want me? Do you want me to kill someone?"

Bishop smiled while eating his veal parmesan. "Look at that man in the southwest corner," Bishop directed without even looking up from his pasta. Il Spirito looked over to see a large man glaring at him. "Now look at the man in the northwest corner." Il Spirito did so and saw another gunman disguised as a patron having a beer. The second man looked back at him as if Il Spirito were a pedophile. "The waiter is on my team, too, so if I order anything else besides an iced tea, light ice, with two lemons, he will end you without hesitation. Need I continue?"

"Okay. You got muscle. So?"

"If I needed to annihilate, crucify, or otherwise slaughter someone, I'm well equipped. I don't need another hatchet man. What I need from you is your clever skill set and ingenuity. Marcello, I am recruiting you because at 22 years old, you have managed to run a multimillion-dollar illegal operation while the FBI and DEA had no clue who you were until today. You have no driver's license, no credit cards, no assets in your name, no known address or telephone number, and no criminal record. Almost supernatural. Like a ghost. Ergo, we get your name, Il Spirito, meaning "the spirit" in Italian. You achieved a leadership position in your organization by 18 years of age, working with the most dangerous men on earth, but somehow they respect you, including the Colombian cartels. This takes talent. It was mystifying at first how you got away with being undetected for so long. Not even a parking ticket or a library card. Then I figured it out. You alternate using the identities of your three dead brothers. It's harrowing that they all got gunned down right in front of you. Join my alliance, and we can make things right. Your Il Spirito game plan worked perfectly since you've never been arrested or fingerprinted. Being a brilliant, clandestine, multi-millionaire businessman and gangster takes vision, determination, and discipline. You're not flashy, you have no family or children to speak of, you've never been caught until today, and you are unknown to any narcotics database anywhere in the country. I have a use for someone who can remain invisible while getting things done despite any obstacles. You're not a desperado, a sociopath, or a butcher, either. When your crew was ready to light up the sky with automatic gunfire, you signaled them to stand down. Nice touch. You can join my team, or you can spend the next 75 years rotting in the underworld of a super-max penitentiary of federal choice. You're not invisible now, Il Spirito. It's decision time, son. What's it going to be?"

"Before I tell you my pay grade and have you make all these cooked-up charges disappear, tell me why you kept staring at me back in the interrogation room."

Bishop stopped eating and looked Il Spirito in the eye. "Because you have got to be the ugliest son of a bitch walking this solar system. You make me want to disappear. When I saw the surveillance photos from my men, I said, 'Jesus Christ, this half-pint Italian leprechaun can not be this grotesque.' But when I saw you for the first time with my own eyes, I saw that you were even more abominable in person. The frightful photo had actually done you a favor. Do you know who Anubis is?"

"Yeah. Anubis is the Egyptian god of the underworld."

"Well, aren't you a shiny penny. You might have even caught my earlier reference to the super-max underworld. Anubis is the Greek name for the ancient jackal-headed god of the dead. That's you. The head of a jackal and the body of some kind of troll."

"Bishop sure knows how to lay on the charm," Vadar said, chuckling. "And then he named you Jackal. Now that sounds just like Bishop."

"The man comes through when it counts, though."

"Indeed," Vadar replied.

"Now, tell me how the silent, borderline emotionless, world-class intellectual, sixth-degree blackbelt jiujitsu champion got into the game recruiting top talent for Bishop, Vadar. You recruited Sparrow, and you had to get close to her to do it. None of us went through the Process or visited the Campus or the Farm like the regular agents. So how did the old man pull you in? I know he showed up to your mother's funeral to recruit you."

"Another time, Anubis."

"Maybe we'll hear about the capers in your clandestine-services recruitment efforts later. 'Ey, coach, how close did you get to Sparrow?" Jackal winked.

"Here we are," Vadar announced, pulling into a St. Petersburg gas station. They both got out of the car and walked a few feet from it.

"Is he here?" Jackal asked Vadar in the chilled air.

"He'll be here shortly. He should be in a black vehicle. The vehicle will take us to meet Sergei Barayev. Barayev will tell us what we need to know. No sudden moves, no slick talking. Do not anger these men. When the vehicle arrives, I'll get in from the left side of the car. When I scoot over, you will get in beside me. Do *not* enter the vehicle from the right side, or they will shoot. This is a signal I have established. They are not expecting two people."

"I didn't know you and Sergei were tight buddies."

"There was a time when he was not on top, and he doesn't forget those who helped him out in such situations. Actually, and this is reaching for it, he really has nothing to lose by telling me how Valentine got the plans, who was sent to retrieve them, and why."

"Who are we?"

"He knows I work for the American government, and that is all he needs to know."

"You two met in the frozen-food section?"

"Nope. Prison. . . Carcer-Unda." Carcer-Unda, Latin for "water-prison" was a prison under the Atlantic Ocean for individuals in the great spy game who had gotten caught but refused to talk. They were held there—without trial, rights, or sunlight— until they agreed to speak. Vadar had spent less than a week down there undercover as an inmate but met Barayev during his two-month term as a guard. There had been an Iranian agent who held a vital encryption coding key title, and this information was needed during Desert Storm. Vadar had been sent to retrieve the information, and was successful.

Most individuals died in Carcer-Unda, but some lived to be 80 years old. There were no bank robbers or rapists in this prison. It was strictly for people who could not talk or people who committed serious crimes against the government. No sun, no mail, no windows, no rights or nourishment. Vadar had seen the eerie skin tone of the inmates who had been in Carcer-Unda for years. It was sickening, ugly, and pale, for their skin could never absorb the vital nutrients the sunlight provides. Varicose veins showed in their arms and legs, and when they drank, he could almost see the liquids flow down their throats.

He did not like the memory of the place, but he did make a worthwhile acquaintance. There was a man who had one wish in Carcer-Unda. Not a wish for freedom, food, sex, drugs, or money, but one wish to give his four-year-old daughter a letter. Barayev begged day and night to any guard who would listen. He offered money, sex, or any secular acquisition he thought would get the message to his daughter, but none of the hardened guards agreed. Vadar soon learned Barayev's story, and who he was: the son of a Russian mafia boss, kidnapped until his father turned over certain information. Barayev was not even part of the scenario, just a casualty of war. No prior record, no criminal history whatsoever, but there he was under the ocean. He was just snatched one day while traveling in America and woke up in Carcer-Unda. Vadar asked to see the letter one day and read it. It was full of heart-rending, father-to-daughter feelings, but Vadar still ran it through the National Security Agency anyway, to see if the letters letter held any codes, domestic or foreign. When the letter came up clean, Vadar rearranged some words and sentences, just to be sure there were no hidden messages. He then mailed the letter to Barayev's daughter in exchange for some minor intelligence needed about a group of mafia candidates running for office in Russia.

Eventually, Barayev was released from Carcer-Unda when his father finally gave up the information he had been withholding. Barayev was bound by the agreement that if he spoke one word about Carcer-Unda, he would be brought back for life. Soon after his son's release, Barayev's father died, and Barayev eventually stepped up in the ranks.

"He got out of Carcer-Unda?" Jackal asked.

"Stranger things have happened, friend."

"And this I know. Here comes our ride," Jackal replied, observing a black vehicle swiftly turning into the fuel station.

"Felix, are you with us?" Vadar mumbled into the air to Felix via the IAT.

Felix was safely in America, over 3000 miles away, preparing for his meeting with Gary Klingner to procure a meeting with Devin. Even so, Vadar's voice came in crystal clear through the IAT. "Check five," was Felix's response as the black vehicle pulled to a stop.

Vadar got in and scooted over. Jackal got in beside him on the same side and closed the door.

"Good afternoon, Officer Kale," the man in the front passenger seat greeted. He looked back with a grin as the vehicle pulled off onto the busy road. "I am Evstrat. The boss looks forward to seeing you. First, I need both of you to surrender your sidearms."

Vadar nodded at Jackal, and they both handed their pistols up front to Evstrat after removing the ammunition magazines.

"We appreciate you seeing us on such short notice. This is an absolute emergency, and we will not take up the boss's time." Vadar smiled.

"We had to reschedule an appointment, but from what I understand, he owes you a favor. I am here to see that your needs are taken care of. Champagne, gentlemen?" Evstrat offered.

Vadar politely held up his hand and shook his head. With a slight grin, he said, "That will be quite all right. Intoxication sounds tempting, but not right now."

"Vehicle's clean, gentlemen," Felix observed, checking the satellite image grid. "No bombs and no transmitters, but it looks like you have two tails on you, and I would like some of that champagne."

"I didn't expect a second guest," Evstrat mentioned to Vadar.

"This is Officer Walters," Vadar replied. "He's my American Express."

"Aha, a clever one indeed." Evstrat smiled.

After a brief drive with frigid conversation, the vehicle pulled up to the gate of a gargantuan mansion. The structure was extravagant, and the acres beyond it seemed to extend forever. It was beautifully designed, and as they approached, Vadar noticed the heavy amount of security around its perimeter. After a few moments, the gate opened. The car headed up a long, winding driveway, pulled up to the front door, and stopped. It had been six years since Vadar had last seen Barayev, and he wondered now if Barayev would recognize him. He had changed his facial disguise since leaving his position as a guard. Vadar and Jackal got out of the car and followed Evstrat into the house.

"Please, make yourselves comfortable while I will alert the boss of your arrival." On that note, Evstrat exited, leaving Jackal and Vadar alone. Jackal was astounded at the interior of the mansion. It was indeed magnificent, with marble floors, and beautiful oil paintings on the wall and crown molding along the ceiling. The furniture must have cost a fortune. The main lobby area was brilliantly lit. Vadar looked up to see a unique glass chandelier hoisted high above the main lobby, illuminating the entire area.

"Remarkable layout," Felix observed from above. "Infrared beams, armed guards, attack dogs, and hidden cameras. This gentleman's got a cozy little fortress here." Felix moved his mouse over a green upside-down arrow. The satellite image turned into gridlines. This was necessary if he wanted to see the inside of a building from miles above it. Walls became red lines, and blue lines indicated stairs. "Checking the basement. . .motion sensing. . .hazard scanning. . .radio waves. . .opcon one clean . . .stand by. . .all clear. Vadar, I need you to walk over to the small table."

Vadar walked to a small coffee table.

"OK, you were standing too close to Jackal. I couldn't see you, wanted to make sure there was no malfunction here. We're good to go. Every man you have walked near has a pistol. I can't see what type from here."

Felix switched on the heat sensor screen. The grid disappeared as Felix converted back to a regular satellite image. The solid image of snipers and attack dogs disappeared as well and turned into a mass of color clouds. Felix observed them for a moment and then spoke. "Atmosphere seems very relaxed," Felix remarked. "Attack dogs aren't on edge, snipers seem half ready to go to sleep. Looks as if all is well. Just another sunny day in the life of the Russian mafia."

Barayev walked down the large winding stairway. He was sharply dressed in light-brown linen pants, brown dress shoes and a pure white linen shirt. He had aged in six years but looked good. His beard was neatly trimmed, and his hair was still curly. He was not nearly as heavyset as his father. He was a taller, more athletically built man.

"Officer Kale. A pleasure to meet you again. I'm not quite sure what brings you overseas like this, but welcome to Russia."

"I have but one humble favor," Vadar started. "Is there a place we can talk privately?"

"Why, of course. Follow me."

Barayev led them into his study, where Vadar and Jackal were frisked again for weapons. Evstrat reappeared, whispered into the guard's ear, then left the room.

"Is there a problem?" Vadar asked the guard, but was he was actually addressing Felix. The guard made no indication that he had heard Vadar.

"Not that I can see, pal," Felix replied. "Everything's cool. No commotion by the interior guards, and…" Felix switched to the heat sensors again, and Evstrat became a small red dot in the living room. Evstrat was moving toward what Felix believed to be the kitchen from the amount of metal the sensors picked up and its position in the house. Evstrat looked cool as a red dot, but there was no way to get a solid visual. The heat sensors indicated everything was still normal. "I couldn't quite make out what he whispered. Too garbled, too fast, too soft, too Russian."

"Only one person is allowed in the study, sir," the guard said quietly to Vadar.

Vadar nodded to Jackal, who returned to the living room. Vadar was then allowed into the study with Barayev. Another guard closed the door and locked it.

"What can I do for you, sir?" Barayev smiled. He motioned, offering Vadar a seat.

"Information is all. Is this room secured?" Vadar asked. He sat in the nearest chair, a plush Victorian.

"Yes, it is. We are alone." He sat across from Vadar, in a matching chair.

"No one here but us satellites," Felix humorously reminded AEGIS.

"I understand your organization has a lot to lose from the SORT agreement being signed. I know it is not a coincidence the plans for the Russian Black Fox chopper ended up in an American reporter's hand. I need to know how they got there and why, and who was sent to retrieve them."

The smile on Barayev's face dropped instantly. "A steep favor you ask, Kale."

"A steep favor was given unto you. This matter is urgent. Please, I need this information."

"Leaking this could prove to be disastrous for many dangerous people."

"I promise you will never see or hear from me again after today without invitation, and this information will not be used against any member of your organization. The American reporter who broke the story was murdered the same day. She was a relative of mine." It was a lie, but a necessary one.

Barayev was silent. After a few moments, he stood up slowly. "I cannot ever hear your voice or see you again. And our conversation does not leave this library."

"Agreed," Vadar replied.

"Perhaps it was us who caused the leak of the plans. Perhaps it was the motive you stated earlier. An engineer who works for the Russian branch of ENAP but is connected to us as well could have given up the plans. He was working on the helicopter."

"So the helicopter is in the production stage, correct?"

Barayev nodded. "It remained undetected due to a new kind of technology used to create the weapons-grade uranium needed for the weapons system. This new technology circumvents any of the world's traditional methods and safeguards for detecting nuclear weapon production. The helicopter plans were given to your relative, Dorian Valentine, who was expected to break the story immediately, which she did."

Vadar knew the technology Barayev was referring to. It disturbed him to hear confirmed that the laser isotope separation technology was now completely uncontained, as they had feared. This meant anyone from insurgent nations to terrorist organizations could build nuclear weaponry with a minimal chance of being caught, even upon inspection. He could not inquire further on how ENAP had come to acquire the technology or it would arouse suspicion, which in this game meant he would be chopped into pieces and fed to Barayev's canines and Jackal would be their tasty dessert.

"Who was sent to get the helicopter plans back?" Vadar asked.

"I'm assuming the same organization that killed our connection with the helicopter within ENAP. His body was found disemboweled yesterday in the river. I suspect this is because someone was not happy he had taken pictures of the plans and had made contact with an American reporter."

"Who chose Dorian? Why her, out of all the newspapers reporters?" Vadar asked this question not because he cared about the answer, but to keep up the vengeful relative charade.

"The minor decisions were not mine to make. I assume it was because she was easy to contact and would surely break the story immediately, without hesitation. That is my best guess."

"How soon did they find out your contact had taken pictures of the plans?"

"About two hours, and somehow they knew Valentine was the contact. I suspect he was not too careful in his operations…or unable to withstand the torture."

"Any leads to his murderer?"

"I have men investigating as we speak, but no leads. I suspect it was a very powerful and dangerous organization, to kill a member of my bloodline and leave him in my river like that. I shall soon show these men how dangerous the force of Barayev can be. Now forgive me; I have some very urgent matters to attend to. Evstrat will take you anywhere you wish to go. Remember, with these revelations, I have compromised the secrecy of our organization by telling you what I have. You are never to return, Officer Kale."

"That is agreed." Vadar stood, and the men firmly shook hands. They walked out of the library and into the living room, where Evstrat was waiting for them.

"Evstrat," Barayev instructed, "please escort my two colleagues anywhere they wish to go. Then return promptly."

Evstrat nodded and led Vadar and Jackal outside toward the vehicle.

"It's good to see you again, friend," Klingner announced.

"Indeed," Felix replied.

"What brings you to the marvelous state of Delaware?" Klingner asked.

"I wanted to ask for a small favor."

"One good turn deserves another," Klingner replied. "Since the EPA issue has been resolved, I am more than happy to accommodate whatever you need."

"I'm elated you feel this way. What I need is for you to introduce me to someone."

"Is that all? You must enjoy traveling and spending your tax-deductible resources, to visit the home of tax-free shopping."

Felix chuckled. "Well, this isn't just anyone. I need to meet some friends of yours who were also in disagreement with Yuklivitch's stand on the SORT talks."

"I see," Klingner replied.

"Can this be arranged?"

"In ordinary circumstances, I would have to say no. But considering I am in debt for your granting a serious favor, I will oblige you."

"I knew you were a businessman," Felix replied.

"And you, as well, are very strategic in the manner you choose to operate," Klingner replied. "I am now very pleased you did not use open means of communication."

"When can the meeting be arranged? This matter is very urgent."

"You do know that they operate on a highly exclusive pay level," Klingner warned.

"I am aware of this. There is something that belongs to me, and I want it back. Money is no issue; I will pay up front. I have seen their capability, and I am impressed. The job will not be difficult for an organization of this caliber. Also, I can also provide additional intelligence if needed. When can the meeting be arranged?"

"How long will you be in town?"

"As long as you need me to be. This issue takes precedence over any of my day-to-day matters."

"Okay, give me a few hours, and I'll meet you here at my house. I'll have the information and the meeting place."

"Okay, Gary. I look forward to seeing you then."

"So now we're getting somewhere," Sparrow commented after hearing about Vadar's adventures in Russia and the report of Felix's meeting with Klingner.

"Indeed," Vadar agreed. "The puzzle comes together."

"Well, run it down for the cheap seats," Jester remarked. "Bishop has requested an update."

"Don't mind if I do," Sparrow smiled. She was putting on her headphones with a thin microphone attached. "I like this little thing. Wish I had one of these in high school."

Sparrow started to speak. As she spoke, her words and sentences, perfectly punctuated and correctly spelled, appeared on the screen of Felix's laptop.

"Update for Clarence Bishop," Sparrow announced. "The *Washington Post* operation was performed by covert Russian operatives based in the United States under assumed aliases. The operatives were under the direct order of Spymaster Boris Kapitnov. The first motive for the *Post* operation was to retrieve stolen post-nuclear helicopter plans in order for the Strategic Offensive Reductions Treaty to go through. These helicopter plans do, in fact, exist. The helicopter is, without doubt, past the planning stage and in the production stage. The helicopter project was kept hidden from the world via a new way of creating enriched uranium that eludes detection. An Elite Nuclear Arms Production engineer at the Russian site leaked the helicopter plans to Dorian Valentine by order of strong powers in the Russian mafia. The mafia's motive was to expose the Russian government's intention to breach the SORT Treaty from the beginning, therefore sabotaging the treaty and saving themselves from billions of dollars in losses in black-market arms deals. An A-minus–ranked informant confirmed this information. The ENAP engineer who leaked the plans was part of the construction team constructing the helicopter. Shortly after the plans were given to Valentine, the leak was discovered, and the engineer was found disemboweled in a St. Petersburg river. This information has also been verified accordingly. The second motive of the *Washington Post* operation was to neutralize Valentine, who was proved to be another leak.

"The Yuklivitch assassination was also performed by the same operatives, but this time under a different command. This operation was definitely not authorized by Director Kapitnov. It was possibly authorized by a liaison between the operatives and the Spymaster himself. This liaison is codenamed Devin. It seems that Gary Klingner has compromised Devin. The motive behind the assassination was to *prevent* the SORT. We are aggressively in pursuit of Devin.

"The third mission, which took place on the cruise ship, was twofold, like the first one. Objective number one was to rescue an operative of the organization whose alias is Jennifer Johnson. The second objective was to assassinate Kapitnov. It is unclear at this time who instigated this mission. We believe this organization has turned mercenary. We also believe apprehending Devin will provide the additional intelligence we need. Our current objective is clear at this time: *Fully neutralize all parties and affiliates of this dynamic organization, code named Amerus, by any means necessary—immediately.* We will exclude Spymaster Boris Kapitnov from this objective."

Sparrow removed her headphones. She added no signature or any sign of identification. AEGIS existed neither on paper nor in any database.

"Amerus?" Jackal spoke up after Sparrow had finished.

"They're an American-based organization that took orders and objectives directly from Russia," Sparrow answered.

"OK. I've seen more creativity in my life," Jackal replied.

"You have a better name?" Sparrow asked, challenging him.

"Yes, I do," Jackal said.

"And what might this innovative title be?"

"Whore Bastards," Jackal muttered.

Felix spoke next. He wasted no time sharing his update. "The meeting with Klingner to get the appointment time is tonight at his house, so I have to be back there tonight."

"We have to draw this organization out into the open," Hammer commented.

Vadar agreed. "We also have to give the impression that the man we captured is talking. Then Amerus will try to kill him. We have to bait the hook," he offered.

"Good idea. I'll arrange it with the media now. The *Post* will most definitely be interested," Hammer added.

Felix's ComLink suddenly came to life. He picked it up and spoke. "Yeah," was his greeting. There was a pause as Felix listened to the caller.

"How the hell did he get into his sock?" Felix yelled into the phone. Another pause. "Well, get him to a hospital!" He listened again. "No, we're not done with him! . . . I'm on my way!" Felix placed the ComLink on the table. With no hand on its hand grid, the ComLink shut down.

"The captured scuba man had a suicide pill taped to his ankle. He swallowed it," Felix spat out. His frustration was clear to his partners.

Hammer, a quick-thinking man of action, barked orders. "Felix, you meet Klingner at his house; Jester, on sat. Sparrow, you have truth duty. Vadar and I will head to the hospital to meet Aquaman. Jackal, see if you can get the static out of the transmission from the cruise operation."

AEGIS turned from refreshment to labor.

"Have you read this?" Plack said to Clarence Bishop, handing him a confidential memorandum. "I knew Wallace was nothing but trouble. There's information roaming around the FBI regarding this operation."

Bishop read the memo. In so many words, it informed him that inside the Federal Bureau of Investigation, Bruce Wallace was loosely spreading false information that ENAP in Russia was behind the Yuklivitch assassination. The motive of this leakage was presumed to be to bring credit to his name.

Bishop gasped. "This is outlandish! Doesn't he know the external repercussions for this? In the wrong hands, this is dangerous information. Damn. We'll neutralize him if we have to. This is absolutely unacceptable. If you have to parade down to 935 Pennsylvania Avenue to the deplorably hideous J. Edgar Hoover building and slap this chattering raccoon upside his head with a dolomite limestone brick, do so expeditiously. Quiet this noise. Right away. Wallace's quest for fame is going to be the downfall of all of us."

Plack offered a reminder. "The press has a way of finding things out, Clarence. I'm sure Wallace has his sources, just as we do. He's got the story mixed up, but Russia isn't indicated in his statements, strictly the ENAP branch in Russia. Bureaucracy is not tainted."

Bishop grinned. "There are organizations out there who this information angers. Very powerful organizations that will engage in an underground war if the press gets a hold of this. And the casualties will be quiet, but quite severe. We'll have a quiet bloodbath on our streets. There is no way to reverse this. We need to get this issue resolved instantly before we have a war of international secret societies in our backyard. How did Wallace get a hold of this flawed information? What about the contact I authorized at the FBI—Laurence Acclaim?"

"His boat went up in flames with about six federal officers," Plack explained. "It was blown up off the coast of Florida when the organization in question attempted to assassinate Kapitnov. Acclaim had the suspects surrounded, then Kaboom! We're still investigating the cause. We also had Acclaim working within the FBI to find where Klingner paid the fee for the services rendered. We made sure Wallace wasn't given the assignment, but with Acclaim gone, we do not have a direct inside link with the FBI who can keep things quiet and away from Wallace. Wallace probably snatched up the case. It was out of our control. We needed the FBI's assistance to reach all of ENAP's financial records to try and trace a payment for either of the events that took place. Wallace somehow got to it anyway. Let me make it clear that neither Acclaim nor Wallace know about the task force you put together, though."

Bishop gave an empty glance at Plack before he spoke. "Well, someone shut him up before he brings more chaos into this situation. And I don't mean an hour from now."

"Has the task force given you an update yet?" Plack asked.

Bishop put on a passive face. "What task force? You keep asking me about this phantom task force."

Plack quickly moved on. "What do you want us to do with Kapitnov? He's denying any connection to the past events. He demands to be taken back into his home country."

"Has he contacted Russia?"

"No, but it is only a matter of time before their media find out he is in our custody. When they do find out, it'll be yet another uncomfortable situation. I know we haven't had much time to watch the news, but I caught a glimpse. They are angry over there and demand retaliation. We are already at DEFCON 4. If they find out we have Kapitnov, it will look very bad. In their eyes, we have accused them of building post-nuclear assault helicopters that we can't even prove exist. The paper of our nation's capital has blatantly accused them of flagrant treachery and has slandered their name as well as degraded their worldwide image. We sat around and watched while an American-based organization killed their pope-like prime minister. On top of that, we have zero suspects to report to the press, which means to them that the likelihood that we were behind the assassination is increasing. Russia knows that the location of Yuklivitch's speech was not given out until the last minute. It looks like we set him up to have his head blown off. Now we have taken hostage the most powerful man in their federation. Countries have gone to war for less than this. I want these bastards, too, but I don't want a war. The Spymaster has demanded several times to be released. We are officially holding him against his will, and it will be public knowledge in a brief period of time. We've also denied him contact with anyone. We claim it's for his own safety, but that story won't ride for much longer."

"Hold off on Kapitnov's release for now. Put him in the Legion until further notice." Bishop wanted to let AEGIS call this one. "And grab a suspect from somewhere to flash around the TV screen. Make it look good and believable, Walter. Report back to me when Kapitnov is in the Legion."

The Legion was a fake five-star hotel that was actually a large undercover CIA minibase. Only a few of the floors resembled the inside of a hotel. The other floors looked like they belonged in an office building. To get off at any of the office floors required a keycard, hidden in the emergency phone panel. Though it looked like a five-star hotel, it was often used as a prison in cases such as these for the directors, where harm to powerful individuals could cause severe consequences. Ironically, the hotel did have authentic guests and authentic five-star rates in order to maintain its realistic facade. Though the hotel was listed in the District's phone book, the agency made sure it was not listed in any tour guidebook or any other massive advertisement venue such as the Internet.

So it all comes together, Zyablikov thought to himself after talking with B-2, his contact in the Federal Bureau of Investigation. A nuclear arms company was behind the Yuklivitch operation. Devin had sold out to the almighty dollar. Zyablikov had only one lead to find Devin, and that was Gary Klingner.

He needed two things right now: money and information. The fortunate thing was that one brought the other. Weapons were on the way from the safe house, and he knew Kapitnov had not revealed the location of the safe house to Devin. Team B had proven to be his greatest asset in this time of reengineering his organization. There was now no need to keep each team oblivious to each other. It had never made sense to Zyablikov, anyway; they had all been raised on the same block in hell. After Teams A and D were mixed to rescue Kalisa, it now held no purpose to keep the rest of the teams in the dark. Team B would be held separate; they were the only team that could provide the necessary intelligence to operate. He and Kalisa had already begun planning the operation to retrieve Gary Klingner. All that was missing were the blueprints of the Klingner mansion, and Team B would provide them shortly.

Zyablikov wondered if there was a way to know if Bolotov was dead or alive. That was something that even Team B could not tell him. As far as his contact at the FBI knew, no prisoners had been taken. Zyablikov had planned a way to get the information he needed from a multi-billionaire, and had contacted the necessary units needed to carry out this operation. He had instructed Kalisa to not set foot outside the doors of the safe house. She was presently a known affiliate of the organization, and her life as a civilian was now over.

Next Chapter from

The Invisible Enemy Book II: *Vendetta*
First they were operatives. Now it's Personal.

Available in stores now!

Zyablikov parked his truck on the curb about a mile away from Gary Klingner's house. He waited until 3:00 a.m.—when he knew Klingner would be sleeping soundly. This time Zyablikov was ready. He had the intelligence, and though he had only had two days to plan the entire operation, swift planning was his specialty, which made his organization remarkably more potent and eminently dangerous. He felt as well prepared as he had when operating with Devin's intelligence, and now this was the second official assignment under his own administration. He had faith in himself, and faith in his soldiers. The objective was clear: Get Klingner. He'll know how to find Devin.

"Team A, report," Garret spoke into his tactical microphone.

"A-1, looking sharp," Oleg Lugor reported from his position atop a large hill, a little inside of a mile away from the scene. He was equipped with his Barrett .50-caliber sniper rifle, which was already set up on its bi-pod with the long silencer tightly screwed on. The specially designed silencer would not only quiet the sound but also eliminate the muzzle flash. The flash shield not only protected Lugor's location but also prevented the sight disorientation that occurred when the Barrett's bright flash put blue spots in his eyes for a few seconds, preventing him from aiming quickly again.

"A-2, red light," Vladimir Yakof replied from near a tree just outside of the back of the estates. He had already put together his Heckler and Koch PSG-1 .30-caliber rifle but was not yet in position. Yakof climbed up the nearby tree and comfortably positioned himself among its branches. He cursed his position in the treetop but knew that if Zyablikov had placed him here, there was no other option. He knew Lugor was about a mile way, and he did not envy him.

"A-2, green light, Iceman," Yakof reported after he was in position.

221

"A-3 ready on signal," Demitri Liutoboets replied.

"A-4 in place," Gremis Nukludko responded.

"A-5 awaiting your mark," Iake Tatomir reported.

"Team F, report," Zyablikov instructed.

"F-1 standing by," Zlata Olimpan announced.

"F-2 ready," Rhyhor Karandei said.

"F-3, check," Viktor Nesignev answered.

"F-4, green light," Aleksander Straz reported.

"Team F, move."

Olimpan pulled a small vial of metal-eating acid out from her belt. It was the same acid Nukludko had used on the cruise ship; Zyablikov could not stop finding new uses for this creation. Olimpan quietly poured the acid onto the ten-foot metal gate that was built into the ten-foot-high brick wall. In less than a minute, they were inside the Klingner estate. The estate was well illuminated, and the teams had to cross more than 800 feet before they reached the mansion. All four entry soldiers crouched along in the shadows and away from the motion sensors, as Zyablikov had warned.

Lugor aimed for the guard on the roof whose binoculars were facing the front of the estate. In a few moments, the roof guard was in his crosshairs. He fired the shot from almost a mile way away, and the guard collapsed with no shout and almost no sound.

"One down," Lugor reported to Zyablikov.

The second guard was patrolling another area of the roof, but his position still classified him as a threat. He could still turn around and possibly spot Team F. Lugor studied the guard's paces for one full minute. He thought back to his training in the Pit: *One shot, one kill. No exceptions.* It was the motto for the range game, so he made sure to take the extra few moments for the shot. The second guard held his binoculars up to his eyes, looking out at the front of the estates, just as the first guard had. He suffered the same penalty. The rifle bullet went straight through the guard's back and then exited through his chest in several pieces. No shout, no noise. Lugor had blessed him with a swift and painless death.

"Two down," he reported.

Team F sprinted through the shadows, and before the second rooftop guard had shaken hands with death, the team was within 150 feet of the back patio of the Klingner mansion.

Through his sights, Yakof spotted two more sentries patrolling the backyard area. He picked the one who was closest to Team F and sent one silent shot after him. The guard's head exploded. He stumbled, headless, for two steps, before collapsing silently onto the grass.

The second sentry was walking through the open area with a large canine. Yakof was glad Zyablikov had put him at an angle to the mansion, or he would have had to shoot at a difficult sideward view of his target. With the PSG-1 being an automatic rifle, Yakof was able to quickly execute the human first with a swift shot through the heart, then quickly fire twice at the dog. The dog made a pitiful yelp before slouching over and collapsing near his master, whining. Yakof didn't know where a dog's heart was, so he fired once more into the dog's head, taking the life from him.

"Sixteen," Yakof mumbled to himself as a reminder of how many bullets he had left in his clip. "Area 1 secure," Yakof reported.

"A-4, move out," Zyablikov instructed. "A-3, A-5, follow."

Gremis Nukludko left the main group to catch up with Team F. Liutoboets and Tatomir crept along slowly, in the shadows of the wall.

Straz pulled out his pistol with the silencer screwed on and blasted the large-wattage motion light on the back corner of the mansion. Team F crept inside the new darkness toward the patio and its large sliding-glass door. Nukludko crept around the corner and located a large metal box attached to the wall of the mansion. He severed the phone line to the mansion and shorted the central junction box that supplied power to the east wing of the mansion. This would buy Zyablikov the amount of time he needed before any external forces came onto the premises. The far side of the mansion would still have power, but this was irrelevant. The only thing that worried him was the possibility that one of the guards could have a cellular phone and might have the brains to call for the authorities before attempting to investigate the situation. On the other hand, a lot of private security agencies and bodyguards liked to be the heroes. This could be to Zyablikov's favor tonight. He hoped all the guards were the cowboy types and that no one would call for outside assistance.

Olimpan gave the hand signal for Team F to stay put. She then crept onto the large patio without a sound and quickly approached the door. She held a baseball-sized semi-sphere, which she pressed against the patio glass near the door handle. She turned the semi-sphere counterclockwise, released it, and then turned it again to complete one rotation. When she removed the semi-sphere, attached to it was a circle of glass from the patio door. Olimpan reached inside and carefully curled her wrist around to unlock the patio door from the inside.

"Breach 1 complete," Olimpan reported.

"A-4, report status."

"Breach 2 complete. Ground lines cut. Power cut," Nukludko reported.

Zyablikov instructed Team F. "Move in. You have five minutes."

Olimpan signaled the team to move in, then Team F and Nukludko slipped onto the patio in the darkness. Olimpan eased open the patio door and heard the two rapid beeps as the alarm waited for someone to press the deactivation code. The assignment briefing had indicated these beeps were not supposed to occur. The security system was run through the phone lines, which had been cut.

"Security line still active," Olimpan reported. "Please advise."

"A-4, Breach 2 is incomplete," Zyablikov relayed to Nukludko.

Nukludko looked at the severed wire and did not understand how the phone line could still be active. He turned on his tiny flashlight and inspected the severed wire. He then saw the brand name of the security device: Kamodo. It was the most complicated and expensive security system ever created. Though the phone lines were severed, the system now relied on a gigantic battery backup. The silent alarm could still go off, but no call would be transmitted to the Kamodo station through the telephone line. The call would be transmitted via satellite, which would take minutes rather than seconds. The backup was buried underground and was totally inaccessible.

"Kamodo security system does not allow second breach," Nukludko replied. "Ground line is cut and power is out. Alert will be relayed by sat."

"ETA of sat relay?" Zyablikov asked.

"Two minutes, maximum," Nukludko replied.

Zyablikov understood that he actually had a little more time than this by way of logistics; the estate was quite a distance from the nearest police station. Zyablikov assumed Klingner wanted it this way, since he had his own private police.

"Move in," Zyablikov instructed Team F. "You have two minutes."

Team F moved inside the mansion to the living room. They had each worn night-vision goggles, which also were equipped to spot infrared beams. Each team member carried with them rapid-fire weapons with silencers attached. Olimpan toted a Benelli M1 Super 90 12-gauge shotgun. The 14-inch barrel allowed her to move in and out of the rooms without having to maneuver the weapon. It was a specialized entry gun; one blast was enough to kill any man. Its mere five-shot magazine concerned her at times. In the Pit, they had always convinced her that large amounts of ammunition were not needed. "If you need a lot of ammunition for a covert operation, you're doing something wrong," she remembered her assault instructor saying. Still, Olimpan would not have minded a few more rounds, just in case. There were no rules in her occupation. Anything could happen.

A-5, Tatomir, crept in the shadows along the back of the house until he was under Klingner's bedroom windows. Then, aiming precisely, he tossed a grapple hook over the roof of the mansion, where it landed with a muffled clang. He gave the rope a firm tug before he quietly shimmied his way upward.

"A-2, give me a reading," Liutoboets requested.

Yakof looked through his infrared scope into Klingner's bedroom, and through the heavy curtains, he saw two figures. Both were moving, but from the mass of colors that he saw through his scope, he could not tell what they were doing. They were standing very close together. "Two inside the room," was his report to Liutoboets.

In the bedroom of the Klingner mansion, Gary Klingner was dressed in a leather vest, leather boots, and nothing else. There was a naked teenage girl with a ball gag in her mouth tied to the bedpost. Whip marks and blood covered her stomach and chest from Klingner's cat-o'-nine-tails. Tears streamed down the girl's face, but her captor didn't seem to notice.

The night had begun with exhilaration for Kelly Bainbridge, but not now. Now she was receiving more than she had bargained for. The thought of sex with a multi-billionaire had at first intrigued her. But little by little, with her hands tied up and a ball gag stuffed in her mouth, the tide had begun to change from excitement to horror.

Until tonight, she had not believed a U.S. senator's daughter would ever have to worry about the deranged segment of society. She had always been protected from and had not suffered the treacherous and the uncertain. Tonight was different. She had stepped out on her own—and no one even knew where she was. Tonight, there was no one to protect her, and she could not even scream at this sick man to tell him who her father was or that her uncle was the head of the CIA. The young girl didn't realize that inside the Klingner estate, it didn't matter who her father was; Klingner was the Poppa.

The affair had begun as flirty chatting on the Internet over a month ago. Tonight it had descended into sadistic inhumanity. Kelly realized with growing terror that her captor did not even view her as a person, but as a mere object to entertain him. She was like a circus animal or a new toy to him. She knew the guards could hear her screaming before she had been gagged, and she did not understand why no one had come running to her rescue her.

Klingner was enjoying himself to the utmost. The whips and leather excited him, as did the control. An enthusiastic sadomasochist, Klingner was further turned on by the fear the young girl displayed. Her eyes were wide with terror, and deep behind the ball gag, she was screaming. He could tell she wondered what the newspaper on the bedroom floor was for, and when Klingner brought it over to her, she became puzzled—and more terrified, as well.

For Kelly, everything moved in slow motion. It was like a sick dream she could not wake up from. She pulled at her restraints violently as Klingner placed the newspaper by her feet and lit a match. Kelly shook her head frantically as the flames flitted about, trying to ignite. Klingner removed a green squirt gun from his dresser and aimed at Kelly's young body. He happily squirted several times at her, like a kid playing cops and robbers. Kelly soon caught a whiff of the gasoline on her body and screamed behind the gag once again. And again. And again.

Olimpan pointed to the infrared beams attempting to block the way to the staircase. It was a series of beams running from across the large lobby at a series of heights. There was a large diagonal one from the northwest corner to the southeast corner. Team F quickly looked around the room for guards or moving objects. There were none.

Straz gave Olimpan a thumbs-up signal. Olimpan placed her M1 Super 90 on the floor and then swiftly maneuvered her way through the infrared beams. She turned, bridged, and twisted her body in turn to avoid each beam, somersaulting into a sideward roll to get under the last beam. It was a fantastic display of gracefulness and athleticism. She came out on the other side of the beams in less than nine seconds and rolled into the bottom of the stairwell with a soft thunk. Her name, "Olympics," was well earned. She stood up and spotted the beam-control switch at the top of the stairwell. Suddenly, two shots were fired from Straz's gun. An unseen guard had emerged around the corner, a move for which he had paid the ultimate price. The guard took a bullet in the side and tumbled loudly down the steps. Olimpan quickly raced up the steps and stopped the guard's noisy descent. She pulled her large knife from the leg holster of her black combat suit and slit the guard's throat from ear to ear, silencing him quietly.

"One minute," Zyablikov reported.

Still beyond the estate, watching through the sights on their high-powered rifles, Lugor and Yakof saw commotion amongst the guards on the roof. The guards were rushing toward the east wing.

"Breach detected," Yakof reported to the teams.

Olimpan quickly ran up the staircase, with not quite the stealth of her previous movements. She turned the beam-control knob counterclockwise. The beams suddenly, almost eerily, disappeared.

Olimpan aggressively gave the "move" signal, and Team F quickly caught up to her. The four night soldiers sprinted up to the third floor of the mansion, and Straz handed Olimpan back her shotgun.

Before they turned into the corridor toward Klingner's bedroom, they knelt in a single-file line.

Olimpan reported.

"Level three," she informed Zyablikov. She pulled a thin device from her suit.

"One thirty," Zyablikov replied, checking his watch.

Olimpan extended the antenna-like pole. Fastened to it was a tiny square mirror. Without exposing her body, she extended the mirror around the corner at floor level and tilted the mirror up. She slowly raised the mirror and stopped when she saw four guards positioned strategically along the corridor. She could not take out one without the others seeing it. With two hand signals, she informed her team of the four armed guards around the corner.

Team F swiftly and silently slid around the corner, positioning themselves belly-down on the black marble floor. They immediately opened silent automatic gunfire. No silencer existed for the M1 shotgun, so Olimpan did not shoot.

The corridor was dimly lit, and while the guards returned fire immediately, one ran into Klingner's bedroom. Without night-vision goggles, Klingner's troops had poor aim. All of Team F sent Teflon-coated bullets through the air at their targets with nearly perfect aim. The loud return fire echoed throughout the mansion, and suddenly, the ceiling became alive with light. The lights were now on in the east wing, and through the giant windows of the mansion, Lugor and Yakof were able to spot the guards rushing to the commotion, like ants to a mound of sugar.

"Guards are on full alert!" Yakof reported from the tree.

"A-5, report," Zyablikov said.

"Breach 3 almost complete," Tatomir replied outside Klingner's window.

"ETC," Zyablikov requested.

"Fifteen seconds."

Klingner watched with eager eyes as the flames burned Kelly's body. Suddenly, the door burst open and the captain of his armed forces ran through the door.

"Mr. Klingner!" the captain exclaimed. "We have armed intruders!"